continued ...

Also by Ashley March

Seducing the Duchess

Romancing the Countess

ASHLEY MARCH

A SIGNET ECLIPSE BOOK

SIGNET ECLIPSE
Published by New American Library, a division of
Penguin Group (USA) Inc., 375 Hudson Street,
New York, New York 10014, USA
Penguin Group (Canada), 90 Eglinton Avenue East, Suite 700, Toronto,
Ontario M4P 2Y3, Canada (a division of Pearson Penguin Canada Inc.)
Penguin Books Ltd., 80 Strand, London WC2R 0RL, England
Penguin Ireland, 25 St. Stephen's Green, Dublin 2,
Ireland (a division of Penguin Books Ltd.)
Penguin Group (Australia), 250 Camberwell Road, Camberwell, Victoria 3124,
Australia (a division of Pearson Australia Group Pty. Ltd.)
Penguin Books India Pvt. Ltd., 11 Community Centre, Panchsheel Park,
New Delhi - 110 017, India
Penguin Group (NZ), 67 Apollo Drive, Rosedale, Auckland 0632,
New Zealand (a division of Pearson New Zealand Ltd.)
Penguin Books (South Africa) (Pty.) Ltd., 24 Sturdee Avenue,
Rosebank, Johannesburg 2196, South Africa

Penguin Books Ltd., Registered Offices:
80 Strand, London WC2R 0RL, England

First published by Signet Eclipse, an imprint of New American Library,
a division of Penguin Group (USA) Inc.

First Printing, September 2011
10 9 8 7 6 5 4 3 2 1

To Luke, because after deciding to make the sacrifice of actually reading a "romance" book, you've now become my #1 fan. Oh, and for all that "cleaning and cooking and taking care of the children" stuff, too. If you didn't know already, I'm your #1 fan. 143, always.

ACKNOWLEDGMENTS

Thank you to my editor, Jesse Feldman. You've quickly become my sanity in this writing journey. You transform good ideas into brilliant ones, talk me off of ledges, and somehow make sense of all of my rambling. Also, thank you for the laugh about a certain proposed carriage scene. I'm so glad that serendipity landed me on your desk, and so very grateful to have your support and guidance.

Thank you to my dream agent, Sara Megibow, who continually manages to exceed my expectations. Every day I'm thrilled to know that I have you on my side, and I'm so proud to be part of your team. In an effort to save the rain forests by not listing all the reasons why I adore you, I'll simply say: Thank you for everything.

As always, a humongous thank-you to Anna Randol and Kat Brauer, my two amazing critique partners and fellow authors, who are soon going to rock the world. No amount of words could ever be enough to express my gratitude and happiness to see us all achieve our dreams.

Thank you to my family and friends for encouraging my new role as a romance author. A special thank-you to the Henderson-Metzgers for buying copies of my debut for the entire world, and to Lynett, who showed me how to put the baby to good use in hand-selling my books.

And finally, thank you to all the authors, book bloggers, and readers who made my first year as a romance author absolutely wonderful. Especially to Rita, Danielle, Paige, Linda, Shane, Kris, Katharine, Jeanne, Buffie,

Aislynn, Kati, Ely, Alyssa, Donna, my fellow NLA agency mates, CRW authors, the RA Army, and everyone who participated in or joined the First Annual March Madness Blog Party. The romance community rocks because of you.

Chapter 1

London, April 1849

*A*s on most every other night, Leah lay in the center of the bed and watched the shadows cast from the firelight flicker across the canopy. The steady lash of rain and wind rattled the windows in their cases, a buffer against the usual silence.

Lightning flashed through the room, and her breath caught as she stared at the illumination of silver-threaded flowers overhead. Even if the bedchamber had been suffused in darkness, she still could have recited each detail of the bed's rococo-style construction. The fluted mahogany posts with their serpentine cornices. The shallow frieze of interwoven palmettes and draperies of lush, midnight velvet. The feet fashioned as lion heads below and the domed canopy above. When the lightning came again, Leah measured her breath, anticipating the accompanying growl of thunder.

She imagined the women who had come before her: her husband's mother, his grandmother. Had they, too, stared at the canopy so long that they began to dream of its embroidered ribbons and flower garlands, of shimmering, silvery threads and roses turned black by the shadows? Had hours and hours passed until they imagined they could see each impeccable stitch, counting them only to forget the number when a sound downstairs erupted from the silence, startling them into awareness?

With her heart pounding, Leah waited for the sound to transform into footsteps up the stairs, to distinguish itself into the pattern of Ian's steady, swaggering gait. How foolish she'd once been to admire the way he walked—to admire his easy grin, the golden shine of his sun-swept hair ... anything about him. And how even greater a fool she was now to dread his arrival into her bedchamber, when she knew he would easily accept her plea of a headache. He might even be glad for the reprieve.

Still, as the echo of footsteps climbed within her hearing, she remained in the center of the bed. Neither on the left nor the right, but rigidly in the middle, as if the few feet on either side could serve to sufficiently delay the moment when he leaned across her and began stroking her breasts in solicitous, husbandly regard. He could have spared her that, at least.

Leah's breath hitched at the sound of footsteps in the corridor. Then, slowly, she sighed with relief. It wasn't her husband. These footsteps were too hasty, the stride too short. Her gaze retreated from the door to the canopy overhead, her fingers released their stranglehold on the counterpane, and she began counting the stitches again.

One, two, three, four ...

"Madam?"

Leah's gaze stumbled over the width of the ribbon and flew toward the direction of the housekeeper's voice.

"Mrs. George? I apologize for disturbing you . . ."

"No, no. Not at all," Leah called. Tearing the covers aside, she hurried across the room. Anything to leave the bed. She had already opened the hallway door and raised her arm to invite Mrs. Kemble inside when she froze, arrested by the housekeeper's expression. Gone was the woman's usual implacable cheerfulness; in its place was a face worn with time, each wrinkle sagging with the weight of her age. Her brows were lowered, her teeth buried in her upper lip, and the hands clasped at the front of her waist trembled as she met Leah's eyes.

"I'm sorry, madam. There's . . . there's been an accident."

Leah blinked. The housekeeper's mouth seemed to be moving at an extraordinarily slow pace, as if each syllable struggled to escape. "An accident?" she repeated. And somehow, simply by saying the words, she knew that he was gone.

"Yes, Mr. George . . ."

They stared at each other for what seemed an impossibly long time, until Leah was certain she could have counted at least a hundred canopy stitches.

Finally, she forced the words out. Not as a question, but a blunt, sure statement. "He's dead."

Mrs. Kemble nodded, her chin quivering. "Oh, my dear, I'm so sorry. If there is anything—"

Gone. Ian, her husband, was dead. Never again would she lie awake at night, waiting for him to return from his lover's arms. Never again would she listen for his footsteps or count the stitching or bear his torturous, sensual lovemaking.

He was gone.

And Leah, who had vowed never to cry for him again, sank to her knees, her hands clutched in the housekeeper's skirt, and wept.

* * *

"Rook to queen. Check."

Sebastian nodded and considered the whimsical dance of the fire's shadows as they played across what little remained of his ivory army. He slid a lonely pawn forward.

His brother uttered a low oath and planted his bishop near Sebastian's king. "Checkmate. Damnation, Seb, that's four in a row. Do you even realize you're losing?"

Lifting his gaze from the chessboard, Sebastian raised an idle brow. "Yes. And I thought you'd be happy."

James swept aside the pieces and began arranging them anew. "I'd be happy if you found a new role. Something other than heartsick lover. At least condescend enough to pretend to notice my presence. It's only been half a day."

"Fourteen hours." Sebastian rolled the ivory queen between his thumb and forefinger.

Precisely fourteen hours had passed since Angela left for their country estate in Hampshire, but already he was going mad without her. In three years of marriage, they'd spent only a few nights apart. Even though their lovemaking had been sporadic since she'd taken ill in the autumn, he was still accustomed to their usual domestic routine: sitting before the fire together as she brushed her hair, discussing the day's events. If she didn't feel well, a kiss good night before they separated for their individual bedchambers.

James paused in the act of replacing the last ebony piece. "Fourteen hours . . . And I suppose you also know exactly how many minutes and seconds?"

With a small smile, Sebastian settled his queen upon her square and refused the urge to glance at the mantel clock over the sitting room hearth. Instead, his fingers reached below to the note he'd tucked away in the chair's crevice. There was no need to unfold it; he'd already read the words a dozen times, enough to memorize the few short sentences she'd written.

If he breathed deeply enough, he imagined he could smell her perfume rising from the well-worn paper, the same blended scent she used for her bath.

Lavender and vanilla.

Memories wrapped around him, warm and soothing and arousing. It had been a long time since Angela had allowed him to watch her bathe, but still he could remember the heady scent of lavender and vanilla upon her naked skin, the slosh of the bath water over the sides of the tub as she bucked beneath his touch.

The corner of the note twisted between his fingers.

James nudged the first pawn into play. "I know you have Parliamentary duties to attend to, but surely they would understand if you made it a priority to see to your wife's health first."

"They'll have to." Sebastian led his own pawn out. "I'm traveling to Hampshire in a week, whether the bill's resolved or not."

One week. Compared to fourteen hours, it seemed a hellish eternity.

Still, he looked forward to surprising Angela; she wasn't expecting him to arrive with their son for at least a fortnight. He might bring her a gift as well, perhaps a little house spaniel to keep her company when the weather forced her to remain indoors. Something to cheer her, to keep her from her melancholy. Regardless of how much he tried to attend to her, she seemed so lonely at times.

Her health had never been the same after Henry's birth, but recently she'd become more and more withdrawn. She continued to act the role of generous hostess while they were in Town, smiling and flirting as usual, but privately he could tell the London air was making matters worse. Sebastian could see it in her eyes when she looked at him. In the way the lightest touch of his fingers sometimes made her flinch, as if her skin was too fragile.

He didn't regret allowing Angela's departure to the countryside, but damned if he could stay away for even a week when she needed him.

Sebastian considered the row of ivory casualties at the side of the board, pieces fallen beneath James' advance. He moved his queen's bishop to counter James' rook. For the first time that evening, he actually felt like making an effort to win. "Make that three days instead."

James glanced up with a knowing look. "The night's young yet. I'm sure given a few more hours you'll be calling for the coach."

A crash of thunder outside echoed the anticipatory clamor of Sebastian's heart. He smiled. "Perhaps," he murmured, and captured one of James' knights.

The horses would have to ride hard through the storm, but he could very well reach the Wriothesly estate the next afternoon. It would be only a short while after Angela would have arrived, and to think he would be able to see her again so soon . . .

In a matter of minutes, Sebastian managed to eliminate piece after piece of the ebony set, including the king's bishop. "Check."

James tapped the table. "I seem to recall asking you to pretend to notice me. I never asked you to win."

Sebastian edged his chair away. "Hurry and make your move."

"Leaving so soon, are you?" James asked with a grin.

"Yes, damn you, now take my rook so I can—"

A knock sounded at the sitting room door.

"Enter," Sebastian called, glaring at James as he took his merry time in lifting his queen into the air, then slowly moved it toward the remaining white rook.

"My lord. A message has arrived for you."

Sebastian gestured absently in the direction of the butler, then, realizing how late it was, lifted his gaze to the doorway with a frown. "Who is it from, Wallace?"

"A Mr. Grigsby, my lord. I beg your pardon. I wouldn't have interrupted your game, but the messenger said it was most urgent."

"One moment." Sebastian turned to find his rook gone. With one last move, he shifted his queen across the board to trap James' king. "Checkmate."

"Yes, it's a great surprise, that one is," James muttered. Then with a wave of his hand toward the doorway, he added, "At least find what your mysterious message is about before you go."

"You're very generous as a loser, aren't you?"

With a faint smile at James' retorted oath, Sebastian beckoned for the folded parchment. It was cheap, the material coarse beneath his fingers, and spattered with raindrops. "A Mr. Grigsby, you said?" he asked without looking up.

"Yes, my lord."

"Hmm." Unfolding the letter, Sebastian bent it toward the light. He read slowly, his mind distracted by thoughts of Angela.

And then he saw her title.

Lady Wriothesly . . .

He read again, and again, and each time the words refused to coalesce into any meaningful coherence.

. . . identified by crest . . . carriage accident . . . coachman injured, man and woman killed . . . coachman informed . . . Lady Wriothesly . . . Mr. Ian George . . .

The letter began shaking before his eyes. No, his hand was shaking. The letter . . .

He must have said something, because he could hear James calling to him.

Angela was dead. His beautiful, sweet, beloved wife.
And Ian, too. His closest friend.
They were dead. Together.

Fragments of thought collided, then fused into a numbed comprehension. Sebastian stared at the letter, his thumb rubbing the ink until it smeared. He heard James' voice: "Sebastian, what is it?" Then the letter was gone.

And all he could think was:

She hadn't been lonely, after all.

Chapter 2

Are you aware, Mr. George, that I am a married
woman? A single kiss will not sway my heart ...
although perhaps two will do.

*I*n a way Sebastian could have defined his friendship
with Ian by the walks they'd taken together. Those first
midnight escapades when they roamed the grounds at
Eton, waiting for a light at the end of the chapel to appear and signal the arrival of Willie Foster's ghost. A few
years later, the hikes up the steep slopes around the
Wriothesly estate on summer holidays from Cambridge.
Then strolls through the park as they flirted with the ladies of the *ton*, trying to best each other with grand dem-
onstrations of gallantry.

It had been Ian he'd leaned on as they meandered
drunkenly through the streets of London the night before Sebastian's wedding, Ian who paced in the study
with him during Henry's birth.

Perhaps that was why Sebastian felt so peculiar now,
marching alongside Ian's coffin. The man with whom

he'd taken all those walks had been someone he knew and trusted, someone closer to him than even his own brother. But this man now, lying stiff and broken inside a box of polished oak and silver trimmings, meant nothing. His was the corpse of a stranger with the name of a friend. That was all.

The march from the church to the grave was short. It would have been over quickly, if not for the throng of mourners in the procession. Many had adored Ian; as at Angela's funeral, the fragmented sound of suppressed grief filled the air. Sobs which would not be given full breath, moans reduced to low gasps, tears which would have gone unnoticed except for the occasional sniffle or whimper.

Sebastian had not cried at Angela's funeral, but delayed until he'd reached the solitude of his own bedchamber. No tears would be shed for Ian—not now, and not anytime afterward.

As the procession approached, clods of heavy black earth tumbled from the edge of the grave into the empty pit below. Though the soil had been packed the day before, bits and pieces frayed by the morning dew collapsed into the void with each strike of their feet.

Soon the pulleys were set, and Sebastian stood nearby with the others as the workers lowered the black-enshrouded coffin into the ground. The final walk was over.

Sebastian jolted at the first thud of earth flung into the opening. At the second, he was seized with the irrational, contradictory impulse to either leverage the coffin out of the ground or wrench the shovel from the sexton's hands and bury Ian himself.

How dare he have loved her? To be the last person to see Angela's face, to even now be with her in death. She should have grown old by Sebastian's side, her beauty fading until it was only visible through the veil of kindness and generosity he'd always known. They would have had more children and eventually grandchildren. Her illness would have—

Yes, her bloody *illness*.

Sebastian flinched as a sob broke loose to his right.

God, how easily he'd been betrayed.

Minutes passed as the pile of dirt at the grave's side continued to dwindle. The sound of mourning became more pronounced. A black mass of crepe and bombazine huddled together, an ugly welt of pain and grief beneath the pristine blue morning sky.

And while they suffered, the rage inside Sebastian mounted to a nearly unbearable crescendo until, with the last shovel of earth, it finally turned from Ian and Angela to himself.

For there could exist no greater fool than he, to be so ignorant and trusting that he hadn't realized the truth of their betrayal. And now, even knowing what they had done, to still wish for both of them back.

As was customary of the ladies of the house, Leah didn't attend the funeral in the village near Rennell House. Instead, she stayed with Ian's mother for most of the day, consoling her as much as she could, only leaving when the viscountess remembered another task that must be seen to.

While Leah's tears had eventually dried the night she learned of the carriage accident, the grief of Lady Rennell was a relentless spring. No amount of handkerchiefs or cups of tea could stop it, and Leah's ears rang with the echoes of her sobs even after the viscount escorted his wife to her bedchamber for the night.

The following morning, Leah rose from bed when the first rays of sunshine paled the burgundy curtains to a pink mauve. She went to the window and sat, expecting to be summoned soon by the viscountess. After an hour passed and no maid entered to wake her or help her dress, she assumed she'd been given the day to grieve alone.

If only they knew how she'd mourned Ian's loss a year ago, when she'd discovered him with his head bent to Lady Wriothesly's bare breasts. Though she may have cried from shock the night of his death, her heart had already been broken. Even if she wanted to, she doubted she could make herself shed another tear.

Outside the window, the branch of an ash tree forked toward the sill. Leah watched as a small brown wren hopped up and down, chirping with glee. There was no mourning here, no thought of hushing his song in memory of the dead. And even though she was alone and no one could see her, she still felt ashamed for smiling at the bird's solitary parade along the branch. Guilty that she should take delight in such a thing, when the woman she'd been raised to be, the widow she'd now become, should have wallowed in misery rather than seek out pleasure. At least, that's what a proper widow should have done.

It was easy to stay inside the bedchamber all morning and avoid everyone's expectations. In here, she didn't have to substitute a veil for a widow's cap in order to hide the fact that her eyes weren't red-rimmed, her face not pale and worn. She needn't remember to keep her voice lowered and small so others would think it'd been strained from the effort of holding back her tears.

The room was a convenient cage, but eventually the wren flew away and Leah grew tired of pacing between the same four walls. Even though it meant facing the Rennells' entire household and their sympathetic glances, she drew a fortifying breath and called for her maid to help her dress.

Not five minutes after she'd departed the guest bed-chamber, a footman found her swathed in endless yards of wrinkled black crepe.

"Beg pardon, Mrs. George, but there's a gentleman here to see you."

Leah peered at the footman through the black shroud of her veil. It was beyond strange that someone should call on her, not only at her in-laws' house, but also so shortly after Ian's death. Not only come to call, but actually expect to see her.

"Who is it?" she asked quietly, lowering her gaze to the navy trim of the hallway runner.

"The Earl of Wriothesly, madam. He's been waiting in the drawing room for two hours. He wished me to convey his apologies, but says it's most urgent that he speak with you."

"Yes, of course." With a nod of dismissal, Leah reversed her direction and turned toward the drawing room. In truth, she was surprised Wriothesly had waited this long to seek her out. Every day since Ian's death she'd expected to see him, or to find a letter delivered at her door, at least. Not only because he'd been Ian's closest friend, but also because he must now know the truth of Ian's relationship with the Countess of Wriothesly.

God rest their souls.

Leah forced her fists to unclench as she entered the drawing room. Like all the other public rooms in the house, it still wore the mark of death: windows opened, blinds pulled down, the mirror covered in black cloth. The earl sat rigidly on the sofa, his gaze fixed on the opposite wall, the tea service before him untouched.

Here, Leah thought, was an example of true mourning. Although only his profile was visible from the doorway, grief was etched clearly on the stark planes of his face. His brow was pulled low, his lips tugged tightly inward, and the pale cast of his skin contrasted severely with the dark brown of his hair. Did he grieve for both of them? she wondered. If so, he was a far better Christian than she.

As her gaze touched upon the black ribbon tied around the hat he'd set to the side, his head swung toward her. He immediately stood and bowed. "Forgive me, Mrs. George. I wasn't aware of your presence."

Behind her veil, Leah's mouth almost curved. His execution of the niceties was exquisite, his countenance smoothing into all that was generous and hospitable, and yet his rebuke couldn't have been clearer: how dare she make a study of him while not announcing her arrival?

"Lord Wriothesly," she acknowledged with a curtsy. The distance between them was more than a matter of measurement; he seemed almost a stranger without Ian there as a bridge to provide them common ground. "You wished to speak with me?"

"Yes, I wanted to—" He stopped, frowning as his eyes narrowed on her veil.

Leah dropped her gaze accordingly, realizing belatedly that her voice had sounded a bit too bright.

"First, I wish to give you my condolences for your loss."

"And mine for yours," she returned, then watched as he inclined his head solemnly.

Oh, how well they each played their parts. Perhaps it was the requisite exchange of formalities, or the way Wriothesly appeared determined to skirt around a truth they both knew too well, but Leah suddenly found she didn't have the patience to continue this specific role. Not right now, not after spending the past year as the dutiful, perfect, and docile wife, pretending to everyone that all was as it should be. Even if he was in mourning, he needn't play this particular game of charades with her. After so much time spent in each other's homes, they'd moved past society's dictates for courteous acquaintances, hadn't they?

"Such a terrible accident, was it not?" she asked.

"Indeed." His mouth tightened, but he gave no other indication he heard the irreverence in her tone. Instead, he gestured toward the sofa behind him. "I believe this might be easiest if we sit."

Leah stared. He acted as if she needed coddling, to be prepared for distressing news. Surely he didn't think he needed to inform her of her own husband's infidelity?

"Mrs. George? Will you have a seat? Shall I ring a maid to pour the tea?"

She shook her head. "No tea, thank you." She walked forward, moving around him to sit on the sofa as he'd suggested, then waited as he lowered himself to the chair opposite. For a long moment, he made no move to speak, only adjusted the fitting of his black gloves. When he finally glanced at her again, Leah held up her hand. "Please, my lord, let's forsake this polite facade. I believe we're both aware of the nature of the relationship between Ian and Lady Wriothesly."

He blew out a harsh breath. "It wasn't a very discreet way to die, was it?"

"I agree. It was quite inconsiderate of them." Humor. It had been such a long time since she'd found anything to be amused by. How unfortunate that it happened to be at the expense of her dead husband and his lover.

Apparently this time Lord Wriothesly wasn't able to ignore the flippancy in her tone. Even through the safety of her veil, his eyes bored into hers, studying her until the black crepe seemed to have no more substance than the very air they breathed. Leah tilted her head and smiled.

His jaw clenched. "Either you've developed a very deep dislike for your husband in only a short time or you already knew of the affair."

"I believe it began four months after we were married, although I didn't find out until much later." And while she may have cursed him, screamed at him, she'd never found the strength to hate him. It had been easier to withdraw into herself, away from Ian, her family, all of society.

"Four months after . . . They've been having an affair for an entire *year*?" Wriothesly lurched to his feet and began pacing the room, one black glove burrowing through his hair. At length he halted at the other end of the drawing room, his back toward her, and stared at the closed blinds of the window.

Leah observed his agony from a distance. She wasn't without sympathy—God knew the hell she'd lived in when she too had discovered the truth. But she'd suppressed her own emotions for so long, it was almost embarrassing to see his put on such transparent display.

Then he lifted his arms, planted his hands against the wall, and bowed his head. As if he didn't have the strength to support himself.

Leah glanced away, only to find her gaze dragged back toward him a moment later. Perhaps she'd been mistaken to tell him, to draw him into the secret world she'd never shared with anyone else. Now, just by observing the slight tremble of his shoulders, she felt the wound she'd so carefully stitched together begin to unravel again.

She stood from the sofa, once more grateful for the veil's thin disguise. "Please excuse me, my lord. I should leave—"

"No." He whirled around, so quickly it took a moment for her to register the emotion on his face as not one of pain, but of rage. "You will not go."

Her spine instinctively straightened. "My lord?"

Wriothesly advanced toward her. "You should have told me when you realized what was going on between them. I had a right to know."

"Oh? And what was I to say? I beg your pardon, Lord Wriothesly, but your wife seems to have acquired a distinct liking for my husband's cock. Would you mind kindly retrieving her to your own bed?"

He froze. Stared at her.

Leah blinked. Dear Lord. She'd said *cock*.

Every sinew in her body thrummed with mortification and her throat ached with the need to stammer words of apology, but she pressed her lips together. The pleasure of that small act of rebellion surprised her, and as Wriothesly's eyes narrowed, Leah lifted her chin. A long moment passed in which they simply looked at each other. She was tempted to say it again, if only to see what his reaction would be to the second utterance.

Cock.

She tested the word in her mind. She'd never spoken it aloud before, didn't actually consider it a part of her vocabulary—just a sound relegated to a category of others too base and crude for a lady to use.

"I think we can both agree that Ian must have seduced her," Wriothesly ground out at last, his gaze flicking past her shoulder.

"Of course," she replied, disturbed by the contradiction between the opulence of his green irises and the scarcity of the eyelashes framing them. Although she still resented the countess, for a moment Leah could understand how easily Angela must have been swayed from her marriage vows. Compared to Ian's golden splendor and open charm, the earl would have appeared no more appealing than a mountain, all stark angles and planes, with nothing but the verdant color of his eyes to provide relief from his barren countenance.

"Regardless of exactly what transpired between them, or that you should have informed me of the affair when you discovered the truth, I've come to request a favor from you."

"Yes?"

He turned aside to pick up his hat. "Everyone believes Angela and Ian were traveling to Hampshire because she was ill."

"I've heard the story. Very well done, my lord. To have him, your dear and trusted friend, accompany her when you could not. And how convenient, isn't it, for Ian to have planned to visit our own house in Wiltshire after seeing the countess safely home?" Leah paused, attempted to swallow the bitterness from her tongue. She added softly, "You must have loved Lady Wriothesly very much, to care about her reputation even now."

Wriothesly drew the black ribbon of his hat between his thumb and forefinger. "I would appreciate if you could concur with your part of the story. The reason why you couldn't accompany her instead of Ian—"

"A headache, yes. Don't worry, my lord. I've carried their secret for this long now. I have no need of divulging yours."

He met her gaze steadily. "Still, I would ask your word."

Leah gave a small laugh. "You don't believe me?"

"Please."

"Very well. I promise. If someone asks me the details of that day, I won't contradict you. And I will ensure my servants believe the same."

"Thank you, Mrs. George."

"You're welcome."

And as when she had first entered the drawing room, Lord Wriothesly bowed and Leah returned the gesture with a curtsy. He placed his hat on his head, gave a short nod, and walked toward the doorway—only to stop and turn around a moment later.

"By the way, Mrs. George, I would advise you to wear a widow's cap while indoors. Remove the veil. It doesn't hide anything."

Then, with another nod, he pivoted and left the drawing room.

Chapter 3

*I must confess, I will never think of Lady
Waddington's music room in the same way ever
again.*

Two months later, Leah cursed the Earl of Wriothesly
for his advice. And herself as well, for taking it. Hiding the truth from her mother would have been far easier behind the refuge of a veil, no matter how unusual it
might have seemed to wear one indoors.

Trying to appear both wan and welcoming while the
ribbons of the widow's cap swayed against her cheeks,
Leah poured two cups of tea—one for her mother and
one for her sister, Beatrice. She'd dreaded their visit
even before returning to London three days ago. Her
mother doubtlessly expected to find her heartbroken
and miserable, and while Leah had always tried her best
to please her, her time away from society had made it
increasingly difficult to continue the dutiful role of
mourning widow.

The teapot rattled against the other china as she low-

ered it to the tray, the discordant sound impossibly loud
in the silence which had descended once they'd taken
their seats. Leah's heart sped, every nerve contracting.
As she'd done all her life, she waited for her mother to
speak.

Adelaide Hartwell sighed, her gaze returning from its
examination of the sitting room to settle on Leah's face.
"I admit it is very generous of the viscount to allow you
to continue using the town house and Linley Park, but
you must know we would prefer to have you home with
us. I worry for you, my dear, all alone with nothing but
your memories of him. At least if you returned to us, I
would be able to make certain you ate properly. I know
mourning takes a toll on one's appetite, but—" She
waved helplessly toward the platter of crumpets and biscuits, which Leah had yet to touch.

Ah, there it was. The first cut, so cleverly disguised as
maternal concern. And an old one, too. Whereas Adelaide and Beatrice Hartwell were the perfect portraits of
English beauty—rounded breasts and hips, pleasantly
full oval faces—Leah was the odd one. Too skinny. Too
few curves, too many angles. Too . . . lacking.

Leah lowered her lashes as she stirred sugar into
each of the teacups. "I've gained half a stone since the
funeral, Mother."

Adelaide accepted her cup and saucer with a tiny
pleat between her brows. "As you should, of course.
You've always been too frail. But I fear it isn't enough,
darling. You look like a starved crow in all that black
crepe. Have a biscuit. Just one, for my sake if nothing
else."

Leah glanced at Beatrice, seeking their usual exchange of sympathy. At seventeen, she was three years
younger than Leah, and except for her larger curves and
blue eyes, they'd always shared similar features and a
wary regard for their parents' instruction. But Beatrice

refused to meet her gaze, instead sipping at her tea. In fact, from the moment they'd entered the sitting room, she hadn't spoken one word. Leah looked at her mother, then again at Beatrice. Of course. Beatrice had spent two months in London alone with Adelaide while Leah had sought an escape from society. She must be glad for Leah to be the target of their mother's criticism, if only for an hour.

"Leah."

It was Adelaide's warning voice, a demand, and Leah didn't need to look to know her mother's gaze would be narrowed, the fine lines at the corners of her mouth carved with censure.

Like a whip to her back, the voice bent Leah's spine toward the platter of biscuits, her arm automatically outstretched. It was an obedient gesture from a dutiful daughter, and while she might now be jaded and skeptical as a result of her marriage, she'd always been dutiful, hadn't she?

Yet the moment before her elbow crooked and her fingers began their descent, she hesitated.

At Linley Park in Wiltshire, the George estate where she'd withdrawn after attending to Ian's parents, she'd become accustomed to obeying no one's wishes but her own. Maintaining a pretense of mourning was unnecessary with a small retinue of servants who made themselves invisible.

By day she did as she liked, following each and every whim as it occurred. She ate according to her own pleasure, dictating both the time and the substance; there was no need to plan menus to suit Ian's palate, or to guess whether he would actually appear for meals. She could curl up in a window seat all afternoon with a book or go for long, aimless walks over the chalk hills. Gone were the social calls which required her to chatter and smile on cue and agree indeed, she *was* the most fortunate woman to be married to Ian George. If she smiled while at Linley Park, it was only because she desired to do so. She could laugh or frown, grow angry or sulk, and there was no one about to whose expectations she must bow. For a while, she was able to distance herself from the loneliness that had begun after the discovery of Ian's affair.

And the evenings—the unmitigated *joy* of each night. To be free of that accursed canopy in the London town house and the rich, cloying smell of *her* perfume on Ian's skin. The stars were Leah's canopy instead, the innocent fragrance of daisies sweet upon the night air. Many nights she spent simply sitting in the garden, sometimes with a shawl wrapped around her shoulders to ward off the breeze, sometimes letting the soft spring rain cascade down her face. For the first time in her life, she finally discovered the art of indulging her own happiness.

Unfortunately, now that she was back in London and again the subject of her mother's frivolous demands, Leah realized that once developed, such a habit of selfishness became nearly impossible to break.

With a very small smile—she was still in mourning, after all—Leah withdrew her arm and straightened. "No, thank you. I'm not in the least hungry."

Across the tea service, Beatrice widened her eyes and mouthed a warning. Something about eating the bloody biscuit, Leah thought.

Ever poised, Adelaide merely raised a brow and reached for another spoonful of sugar. "Is there a reason you decided to wear crepe for your mourning clothes? When your grandfather died, I preferred to wear bombazine the entire time."

"I've had gowns made of both."

Adelaide placed the spoon aside and lifted her teacup and saucer. "I see." She took a sip. "I must say, though, the wrinkles in that crepe are dreadful."

Leah breathed deeply, desperately wishing again for her canopy of stars. "Is there a reason you asked for me to return to London, Mother?"

"Why, I told you in my letters, dearest. I've missed you, and worried for you. Now that you're a widow, you have no one to guide you or provide for you—"

"As you know, Viscount Rennell offered an annual allowance and the use of both this town house and Linley Park as long as I like. He's always had a great fondness for me."

"Yes, but I'm sure he won't abide by that decision indefinitely. He must expect you to marry again, or to see if . . ." Adelaide's gaze slid to Leah's stomach.

Leah swallowed, her hand involuntarily moving to cover the flat expanse above her waist. She glanced at Beatrice, then cleared her throat. "There's a possibility, but nothing's certain." Although her monthly courses had come precisely on time, their duration had been remarkably shortened. And then there was the fact that she'd gained half a stone in two months. She'd come to London at her mother's request, yes, but also because Lord Rennell had arranged for her to meet with his physician and be examined.

Tomorrow. She would know tomorrow if she was with child. If all those nights of waiting for Ian to come to her bed, of enduring his patient, thorough lovemaking, had been enough.

"An heir," Adelaide breathed.

A baby, Leah silently corrected. *Her* child, to love and adore.

"But this is an even greater reason why you must return home with us," her mother continued. "You cannot think to live alone. You are far too young, and vulnerable. Ian protected and took care of you when he was alive. And of course you loved him, darling, but he's gone now. You must come with us. Without a husband, you—"

"Stop." Leah's shoulders trembled, her hand curling at her waist. Her fingertips dug deep, crushing the gown and marking her palm with little indents of pain.

Adelaide paused, her lips still parted. Then her features drew taut, pinching until every wrinkle she worked so hard to erase ruched like lines of enemy soldiers at the corners of her eyes and mouth. "Leah, dearest—"

"No." The syllable came out shaken, quiet, and Leah hated that she was still trying to please her mother, to be the demure and dignified little mouse. "I don't *need* a husband," she continued, stronger now. "In fact, I think I will do quite well without one. And I'm sorry, but I also don't need my mother to tell me each step to make, to tell me if I should eat, or sleep, or what clothes I should wear!" The last word hovered in the air with a shrill defiance, the echo of her anger loud and insolent.

Adelaide glared at her; Beatrice's eyes had gone impossibly wide. Leah felt a thrill of satisfaction even as her head throbbed, the pins from the widow's cap stabbing into her scalp. She met Adelaide's gaze. Her voice was calm and steady when she spoke again, her conviction replacing any need to raise her voice. "I may have only twenty years, but I am not a child. I'm not an innocent. I'm a widow, Mother, and if being married has taught me nothing else, I've learned that I'm fully capable of managing my own life."

Leah waited, the quiet into which her breath rushed nearly tomblike. Adelaide's face resumed its expression of serenity. Slowly, she placed her cup and saucer down and rose to her feet. "Come along, Beatrice. Your father will be wondering why we've been absent for so long."

She turned toward the door, her spine the same rigid perfection Leah had achieved years ago. Beatrice obeyed at once.

Leah firmed her jaw and stared across the room. Minutes elapsed as she listened to their footsteps receding to the front hall below, more as she waited for the sound of movement from the coach outside.

She was fairly certain her mother expected her to run after them, to make an apology and beg for forgiveness.

The horses began their steady clop along the cobble-stoned street. Heedless of the pins secured in her hair, Leah wrenched the widow's cap from her head.

She'd spent nearly two years as the dutiful, obedient wife, even after learning of Ian's unfaithfulness. It was time to cease playing the dutiful, obedient daughter as well.

The next day, Viscount Rennell's physician gave her the news: There was no baby. She wasn't with child.

For more than a week afterward, Leah had no diffi-culty acting the grieving widow.

Sebastian knocked and took a step back. It felt strange to visit the George residence, knowing that he would no longer find Ian inside. He also found it odd for Leah George to send a note requesting to see him, but still he'd come, desperate to leave his own house.

Three months had passed since Angela's death, and yet Henry continued to ask after her. Sebastian had left it to his son's nurse to deal with the news of Angela's death as she saw fit, but Henry didn't seem to under-stand. He had hoped a boy of eighteen months would have forgotten by now, but on the occasions when Se-bastian entered the nursery, Henry always straightened from his toys and smiled, then looked behind him in search of his mother.

Sebastian blinked as a footman swung the entrance door wide and beckoned him inside. Giving his card, he said, "I believe Mrs. George is expecting me."

The footman bowed. "Of course, my lord. If you would follow me, please."

Instead of leading him to one of the more formal receiving rooms as he'd expected, the servant continued up the staircase to the second floor, toward the bedchambers. As they reached the landing, Sebastian could hear Leah's voice, strong and clear, so different from Angela's soft, dulcet speech.

"That one to charity. No, not the striped one—the footmen can look over it first. And the hat—yes, the one with the red band. My God, how many hats does one man need?"

The footman halted before what appeared to be the master's bedchamber. "The Earl of Wriothesly, madam."

There was a noticeable silence, and Sebastian wondered whether she'd forgotten about the message she'd sent. Then: "Oh, yes. Please come in, my lord. It will be only a moment."

Pausing at the threshold, Sebastian peered inside. While the room might indeed have once been assigned the role of bedchamber, it now resembled little more than a storage closet. Waistcoats, jackets, top hats, trousers—every article of a gentleman's wardrobe was separated into haphazard piles, with some thrown onto the bed, others embraced by the chairs in front of the hearth, and even more scattered on the floor. As he watched, a short line of footmen and maids exited the dressing room, each carrying another stack of clothing. These were dumped at the foot at the bed, which seemed to be the only space unoccupied in the room.

Mrs. George came at the end, her arms wrapped around a tower of bandboxes, her head peeking around the side as she walked. After tumbling them into the center of the new pile, she turned around, dusted her hands together, then curtsied. "My lord."

He should never have told her to remove the veil. Her eyes were too bright—dear God, *sparkling* even—

her cheeks flushed, her lips creased in an upward curve which appeared inclined toward permanence.

Sebastian would have preferred tears. Torrents of them, in fact.

"You're not wearing a widow's cap," he said.

She grimaced. "Yes, of course you would say something." Gesturing toward the servants sorting behind her, she said, "I've decided it's unnecessary. My clothes declare me to be in mourning, and the widow's cap was only making me feel like a mare with blinders on. Besides, I'm in my own home, with no one to see me except the servants. And, well, you." She paused, her lips tilting upward again in that annoying little manner. "I hope I haven't offended you."

Of course, she wasn't sincere. Nothing about her appearance or tone could convince him that his opinion mattered in the least.

She was so damned *happy*, a novelty in his misery-shadowed world of the past three months. His servants, his brother, the other lords at Parliament—everyone tiptoed around him, careful not to speak too loudly or laugh in his presence. Only Henry dared to smile at him, his childish innocence leaving him oblivious to the despair which had settled over the house and all of its occupants.

But Leah George wasn't a child who didn't know any better. And even if she'd known of the affair months ago—even if she despised Ian for it—she should at least have the decency to be miserable, too. If not for his death, then for the knowledge that she'd been betrayed. For the sudden change in the life that she knew. For not being able to wear anything other than black, for the balls and soirees and musicales it was now inappropriate for her to attend. God, for *anything*, as long as she didn't smile like that.

Sebastian responded with an emphatic frown, dismissing her as he glanced over her shoulder. "I see you're cleaning."

None of his maids had been sent into Angela's rooms; he had yet to venture into her bedchamber himself. The temptation to sit there with her fragrance surrounding him, pretending as if she would soon walk through the door, as if none of it had ever happened, was too much. It was nearly as strong as the temptation to destroy everything and set fire to her memory.

Clearly Leah, however, showed no struggle in moving on.

She followed his gaze, shrugging. "Preparations for my return to Linley Park. For the servants and then for charity—much better than indulging the moths and rats, I thought. But come," she said, moving toward a door at the side, "I know you must be impatient to learn why I asked you here."

Silently Sebastian followed Leah through the adjoining door into another bedchamber—*her* bedchamber, by all appearances. Except for the large canopied bed swathed in dark blue drapes in the middle of the room, the decorations were decidedly feminine. Not the rose and cream femininity Angela had favored, but a delicate palette of light blue and yellow. Comforting instead of sensuous, the textures and furniture more practical than luxurious, and yet Sebastian couldn't help but feel awkward as he entered. This was an intimacy he didn't welcome, a view into her private life he didn't care to see.

His gaze fell to Leah, who had already bent over a stack of odds and ends farther in the room. No servants traipsed back and forth here; only the voices emanating through the open door kept them from complete isolation.

With a glance over his shoulder, Sebastian moved closer until he could be assured only she would hear his voice. "We had an agreement, damn you."

Her head shot up, her hands pausing in their reach toward the pile. Her gaze narrowed, she looked him up and down—a bloody measuring of his worth, it seemed—then returned to her search. "I recall. I've told no one the truth."

"No? Perhaps you believe your servants are both blind and deaf, then. That they don't realize how unnaturally happy you are a mere three months after your husband's death. I don't give a damn what you wear or say or how you act when you're alone, but at least show some degree of decorum in front of others. If not—"

"Thank you, my lord." She cut him off without looking up. "I believe I understand your meaning."

"If not, people will begin to wonder why you aren't mourning your husband, then try to discover a reason. It wouldn't take long for anyone to suspect the truth, given the circumstances of their deaths—"

"Dear Lord," she exclaimed, rising to her feet. "Have you always been this overbearing?"

Sebastian snapped his mouth shut as she turned around, hating the fact that everything about her reminded him of Angela—not in similarities, but in contrasts. Her voice, her decorating style, and now, with only a foot between them, her scent. Rather than the warm, sultry combination of lavender and vanilla, he breathed in the artless aroma of soap: earthy, subtle, its only fragrance a slight hint of seawater.

He edged away, to the opposite side of the pile on the floor. Unclenching his jaw, he snapped, "Only to those who behave in such an obstinate and reckless manner."

He should have felt contrite; he'd never spoken to a woman without the greatest deference. He'd certainly never cursed at one as he'd done earlier. But no guilt seeped into his conscience. Standing before Ian's widow, this woman who served only to remind him of his loss,

there was nothing but anger and frustration and an irrational desperation to flee.

Then she laughed, and there was also a great deal of
annoyance.

"You think me obstinate?" she asked.

"Yes."

"And reckless?"

He hesitated, for her smile had grown wide at his response. Above all else, he didn't want to do anything to
make her any goddamned *happier*. Yet he refused to re-
tract the words. Slowly, warily, he nodded.

The sun could have lost some of its brilliance, for all
the pleasure radiating from her face.

Sebastian scowled. "You are quite contrary."

"Oh, come, Lord Wriothesly," she said as she knelt
once more to the floor. "Wouldn't you agree that 'obstinate and reckless' is much better than being obedient
and wretched?"

"Recklessness can make one wretched as well."

She glanced at him from beneath her lashes. With
Angela, the gesture would have been seductive. Leah
George, however, appeared only mischievous and sly.

Sebastian cursed. "As I said before, I don't care what
you do privately, but with others I expect you to act per
society's rules, lest the truth become known."

"And I've already promised not to reveal your secret." She chose an item from the stack of odds and ends,
a small leather-bound book. "I am curious, however,
what you think would constitute doing something reckless in private. Embroidering upside down? Reading the
Bible in the bath?"

"Are you curious, or simply looking for ideas?"

Again, that blasted smile. "Here you are, my lord,"
she said as she handed the book to him.

He held it by the tips of his fingers. "I assume it's
Ian's?"

"I've read only a few pages, but it seems to be a journal from when he was younger. For a while I doubted whether I should send for you, but I thought you should be the one to decide whether you'd like to have any of his things. He mentioned you in there."

Sebastian stared blankly at the brown cover, the color faded in patches, the edge worn and frayed.

"And here's a pin from Eton. Several newspaper clippings about legislature you've supported in Parliament. A rather strange-looking rock, although I don't suppose you'd want that, would you?"

The rock appeared above the journal, a dull gray stone tipped with brown, centered in the palm of her black-gloved hand.

It had been a stupid jest at the time. They'd been drunk—thoroughly soused, in fact—and meandering through the alleys of Cambridge in celebration of leaving university. They'd stopped to piss against a wall, and when they finished Ian stumbled over the rock. After weaving back and forth and swiping air with his hand the first several tries, he eventually managed to pick it up. His headstone, he'd called it, and they both thought it hilarious, in that giddy, unfocused drunken way.

Sebastian shook his head. "No, I don't want it. I don't want any of it." Shoving the journal into her hands, he turned away. Bloody hell. He didn't want these memories, memories that had been buried and fogged with time. He swung back around. "Was this meant as some sort of amusement for you? Did you honestly believe I would want—"

"My lord," she interrupted quietly, and inclined her head toward the open door, where her servants could still be heard sorting through Ian's clothing and other accoutrements. "You were his closest friend," she continued, "and I thought to at least ask before—"

"Is that all you wanted?" he asked, his voice low and controlled now. "Is this the reason you sent for me?"

She stood and smoothed her skirts. A long minute passed as she stared at him, the right side of her lower lip caught between her teeth. At last, her smile had disappeared.

"Mrs. George?" He ground out her name.

"No," she said, "there's something else." Sweeping toward the other side of the bed, Leah went to a writing table and opened one of the top drawers. Her return to him was slower, almost reluctant. When she at last stood before him, she averted her eyes. "I also found these, hidden away in his bedchamber. I thought you might want them."

Sebastian flinched as she held out a packet of letters wrapped in a pink satin ribbon. Lavender and vanilla permeated the air. Hanging from the packet, suspended by her finger, swayed a gold locket encrusted with diamonds.

"Her portrait," Leah whispered.

Breathing became a laborious effort, a struggle to move enough oxygen through his nostrils and into his lungs. Sebastian choked. "Did you read them?"

She shook her head, her eyes lifting to meet his.

"Why not?"

"She was your wife. You should read them first, since Lady Wriothesly wrote—"

Sebastian flung out his arm. The letters and the locket went flying from Leah's hand. They scattered across the floor, the pink ribbon loosening until the corner of only one letter lay within its satin grasp.

He stared, seconds passing as he realized what he'd done. His gaze shifted to Leah, despising her wide eyes, the guilt which finally managed to sneak its way in.

"Burn them," he said, and left.

Chapter 4

*Come to me. Sebastian's gone to the ball and I pled
illness again. Mary will let you in through the
study window.*

Leah knelt and gathered the letters strewn across the
floor. She envied Wriothesly the ability to walk away
without reading them. If only she possessed such
strength. As soon as she'd found them tucked away with
Ian's pocket watches and cravat pins, they'd called to
her, tempting her even though she knew the contents
might shatter her heart again.

She sat on the edge of the bed, the pink ribbon and
locket strung through the fingers of one hand and the
letters clasped in the palm of the other. There were
eleven letters. She'd counted them, over and over, reasoning with herself on why she shouldn't read them.

It was done with, after all. Ian and Angela were dead,
the affair ended. There would be no more nights listening for him to come home, no more attempts to empty
her mind as he touched her and filled her body, no more

weeks passing by in strained silence as they waited for the absence of her courses. What benefit was there in reading the letters? Surely they held only reminders of her heartbreak and disillusionment. Did she wish to wallow yet again in her own ignorance and foolishness?

Leah lifted her head and stared at the opposite wall with its blue flower script and yellow trim. She looked at the beige and gold Savonnerie rug, the rosewood chairs upholstered in damask jacquard. How she hated this room, and everything she'd done within its confines. Even with a low fire burning in the middle of summer, the air was cold. Images from the past haunted her, from their first four blissful months of marriage.

There, on the chair, she'd sat as Ian slipped her dressing gown off her shoulders.

And there, against the wall, he'd taken her—pinning her with her legs around his waist.

On the floor, bent over like an animal—oh, how decadently sinful and tempting she'd believed herself to be.

Leah closed her eyes.

And here, on this bed, after she'd discovered Ian and Angela together. For months she'd lain beneath him, trying to ignore the sensations created by his hands and mouth. She'd bitten her lip until it bled to suppress the moans that rose unbidden from her throat. And she'd allowed him to take her . . . over and over and over again.

Soulless. That's what she'd resigned herself to become. A pale mirror image without control, without strength. After discovering him with Angela, she swore she would never give Ian another piece of her heart . . . but in the end, without even realizing, she'd given him everything.

Lord Wriothesly didn't understand her behavior. He expected her to abide by society's expectations for mourning, to act the way she'd been before: obedient, submissive. But she couldn't. She'd tried to be a good wife and daughter in the past and she'd lost herself. And now, after Ian's death, she didn't know if she could survive relinquishing the independence she'd found.

Leah looked down at her hands. Moving them to her sides, she released the locket, the ribbon, the eleven love letters. Lord Wriothesly had been correct in one instance at least: burning them was an excellent idea.

Leah nodded at the footman holding the door open to the George town house. A weary smile lifted her lips; she could almost feel the circles beneath her eyes from acting as hostess of the dinner party the night before and then getting up early this morning to have breakfast with her mother.

At the thought of her mother, her shoulders went rigid, and Leah deliberately loosened her muscles, turning her head to stretch her neck from side to side. It didn't matter how many times Adelaide had indirectly criticized her this morning in front of the other women or insulted her more than once by interrupting Leah when she spoke. She was home now, and her bed was beckoning.

But first, Ian.

The weary smile shifted, a subtle transformation from a pleasantly polite expression to one of happiness.

Ian.

He'd said he would be home today to review estate business for Linley Park—admitted it with that singular pout that always reminded her of a schoolboy admonished to come in out of the dirt and sunshine to a dull and dreary classroom. But when she knocked on his study, no answer came. Peeking inside, she discovered the room was empty, his chair turned away from the desk as if he couldn't bother straightening it before he left.

"Roberts," she said to the footman at the door. "Has Mr. George gone out? Do you know when he'll return?"

"No, ma'am. He's gone upstairs. Lady Wriothesly came by to retrieve the shawl she left last night and he went to meet her." Roberts' eyes were focused above her head, not meeting her gaze, and Leah had the urge to jump up and down, forcing his attention to her.

She didn't, of course, merely murmured a "thank you" and climbed up the stairs to the drawing room where she'd found Angela's burgundy shawl last night once everyone had left. The soft wool had touched the bare, vulnerable skin between her gloves and the sleeves of her gown as she folded it, and she wished—for a fleeting, embarrassing moment—that she might be as lovely as Angela. To never hear her mother's comments again on her figure, hair, or complexion; to be able to wear violet without fear of her skin turning sallow; to have the confidence of a woman whom the entire world considered beautiful.

But she cast the thought away, ashamed of her momentary envy. If anything, she should be jealous of Angela's sincere and sweet nature which drew people to her like flowers opening to the sun. Leah wanted to have that effect, too, to be like the sun—only she had no real desire to be sweet or sincere. Unlike Angela, she couldn't listen to Miss York drone on and on about the fate of spinsterhood or sit patiently beside Lord Dowbry as he wheezed and snorted, all the while sneaking glances at her bosom. Not to mention that Leah didn't even have much of a bosom; it was to her woe that Lord Dowbry seemed happy to leer at small chests as well as large ones.

There was no doubt: Angela was the angelic one, and her reward for being beautiful, kind, and all things wonderful was to have Lord Wriothesly as her doting husband. Leah, on the other hand, was above average on the plain side and veering toward sarcasm rather than kindness. However, she was fortunate enough to have won Mr. Ian George through an arranged marriage. And he loved her.

Leah's smile grew wider as she approached the drawing room. In truth, there wasn't any reason at all to envy Angela.

She heard Angela's voice carry through the half-open door, and Leah called a cheery, "Good afternoon!" as she walked inside.

No, she'd meant to say it, but the words became lodged in the back of her throat, words that she couldn't breathe around, words that spoke altogether too much of her innocence and her belief in love, friendship, and the rightness of the world.

She stared at her husband, his golden head lowered to Angela's breast, pleasuring her with his lips and tongue as Leah watched. Angela's bodice hung at her waist, her hands clutching Ian's hair, her features twisted in ecstasy. On any other woman it would have appeared as a grimace. On Angela, however, the expression simply transformed her from a seraph to a full flesh-and-blood seductress.

Was it strange that the first thing Leah did was to think what her mother would do? She probably would have turned around without making a sound and gone on to pretend as if nothing had happened.

But Leah couldn't. She stood, transfixed by the sight, her hand lifting toward her mouth of its own volition. Oh, but of course. She was shocked, horrified. Yes, that's why her eyes were widening, filling with tears. And now she would dislodge the words from her throat, and instead of "Good afternoon!" they would be "Goddamn you!" and "I hate you!"

She would throw things—that vase of tulips, or the ormolu clock sitting on the mantel. She would race around the perimeter of the room, hurling heavy objects at their heads while screaming at the top of her lungs like the fiercest banshee.

The scene played out in her mind as she watched Ian

shift his attention to Angela's other breast, then move up to bury his mouth at her throat—all while the tears streamed down Leah's face. And the words that finally escaped were not curses or angry accusations, but a quiet whisper, so soft she was surprised to gain their attention. They both startled and looked at her. Leah would never forget Ian's face at that moment: his pleasure erased swiftly, the chagrin in his eyes branding him with his own guilt.

"How could you?" she repeated in a small, bruised voice.

Angela jerked her gaze away, covering herself as a deep blush ran crimson up her throat and over her face. And Ian—Leah sobbed; oh, God, how pathetic she was. Ian, her dear, beloved husband, stepped in front of Angela. Shielded her from Leah's gaze. Protected *her.*

"I'm sorry," he said.

She wasn't fierce at all. She was weak, and small, and she'd been a fool to ever believe he loved her. With an anguished cry, Leah whirled around and fled the drawing room.

"May I help you?"

Leah yanked her finger away from tracing over the dress patterns and looked at the modiste's assistant. "I'd like to look at the designs you have for mourning."

The girl curtsied and disappeared again into the back of the shop. Leah's gaze returned to the patterns laid out on the counter before her: tea dresses and ball gowns and riding habits sketched with bows and flounces, in muslin and velvet, silk and taffeta. Despite her inward chastisement, her hand lifted again and touched upon the yellow tea dress trimmed with white lace. Her heart gave a tiny, aching lurch inside her chest. Not until next spring would she be able to wear something so pretty again.

"Everything we have is in here," said the assistant as she returned. Leah snatched her hand away and buried it in her skirts, feeling like a child caught trying to steal a biscuit.

"Thank you." She almost smiled in an effort to hide her guilt.

A week had passed since Lord Wriothesly's visit; an entire seven days for loneliness to set in again. She'd felt it hovering after the physician told her she wasn't carrying, but was able to keep it at bay by staying busy sorting through Ian's things. But in the last week it had closed in on her, suffocating, until she could no longer stand one more moment inside the town house.

The seamstress stepped aside to sort through bolts of cloth while Leah surveyed the offerings. It was all the same. Bombazine. Bombazine. Crepe. Bombazine. Oh, and more crepe. All black. All dull, without even one tassel as a token of frivolity. Eight months she'd spent wrapped up and packaged, her actions restrained and emotions bottled while she lived as Ian's wife, alone in her despair. Even now she couldn't escape her obligation to him, but must turn herself into a dreary black memorial for his sake.

Leah flipped the book of widow's patterns closed and looked up. She smiled, but quickly composed herself as the seamstress met her gaze.

A smile. Only a simple smile. It wasn't what a proper widow would do; and she'd learned all the proprieties at the behest of her mother. It wasn't what a woman who wanted to keep her secrets should do, as Lord Wriothesly had pointed out to her in his best aristocratic tone. With all the restrictions and rules burdening her shoulders, it was a wonder she was even able to stand up straight.

"I don't think I want to order any of these today," she said.

Wariness writ itself across the assistant's brows—possibly due to the low, secretive whisper Leah used. "No, madam?"

"I'd like to see your fabric. Black, of course. But do you have anything other than crepe or bombazine?"

The girl's eyes lowered, her lips pursing to the side. "Just a moment, please."

Leah glanced around the room as she waited: at the shell pink upholstered chairs with a table between, at the piles of pattern books at the end of the counter. The walls were papered a blue-and-white Oriental theme, clean but peeling at the seams. A tapping sound echoed in her ears, and she glanced down at the nervous drum of her fingers on the counter. Taking a breath, she forced them still and watched the back curtains part to reveal the seamstress again.

In her arms she carried a bolt of black organza, shimmering like the darkest blue in waves of light as she walked. "Ordered for a ball gown, but the other lady decided not to use it."

There was no reason Leah's heart should have sped like it did; it was only a piece of fabric, and still black. She wouldn't be able to adorn it with bows or beads, or have it cut into one of the fashionable patterns. If she wore it, it would be made into a widow's garment, proper and respectable and without any hope of gaiety.

And yet, as she reached out and slid her hand over the organza, the material rasping beneath her black kid glove, she was unable to resist. It was a small rebellion, but it was enough.

"I've changed my mind," she murmured, unable to take her eyes off of the blue-black material. "I would like a dress made, after all."

"Which pattern, madam?"

Leah flipped the pattern book open and found a random dress which looked exactly like any of her other two dozen mourning gowns. "This one is fine."

"Would you like to have your measurements taken now?"

"Yes." Leah stood straight, reluctantly drawing her arm away. "When will it be ready?" she asked, then almost laughed. It wasn't as if she'd be wearing it anywhere except in her own house. As a recent widow, no one sent her invitations or expected her to attend balls or dinner parties. She certainly didn't expect her mother or Beatrice to come calling anytime soon. And the friends she'd once visited with over tea had all been Ian's admirers; yes, they'd sent the requisite sympathy cards, but otherwise they had no use for her anymore. They'd only needed her in order to flirt with Ian.

Still, when the girl said, "Is a week acceptable?" Leah actually gave a little twirl. She didn't think about it, analyze the propriety of the action or its repercussions, how it would make her mother feel or reflect on her husband. She just twirled.

And when she turned back around and found the seamstress staring at her, Leah smiled at her through the veil.

Smiling. Twirling. Black organza. All in one day. Oh, but it was only a small exercise in independence. From now on, she wanted so much more.

That evening, Leah wandered from room to room. She tried reading, but even Thackeray couldn't hold her attention. She attempted to amuse herself on the pianoforte, but found herself sitting still, her hands resting idly on the keys after only a few notes. Her feet tapped out a restless rhythm down the halls on the ground floor, the first floor, even up to the second. After a while, the servants began to send her curious glances.

For her entire life, she'd been bound by the restrictions set on her by her mother, by society's expectations. She'd never thought to rebel against those rules; she'd been content to play along, believing that her reward was to marry a nice man, hopefully someone who loved her, and have children. But being obedient had brought her nothing but misery so far.

Leah spun on her heel, her skirts lashing against the chair. It was almost as if the room was closing in on her, the silence overwhelming. She'd been alone with Ian's secret for so long, afraid to allow herself close to anyone lest they see the truth in her eyes. But now that he was dead, why should she accept the loneliness anymore? She shouldn't have to become a pariah because she was a widow. She understood that no one sent her invitations because they expected her to be consumed by her grief, but she wasn't.

She paced across her bedchamber, her gaze running to the walls, the floor, the various bric-a-brac she had set around her room not because it pleased her, but because she had wanted the room to appear like she expected a lady's bedchamber should. The perfume bottles on the vanity, with a comb placed precisely on the table—not resting haphazardly, but exactly straight and centered. The landscaped paintings on the walls, fields of dotted violets and peaceful pastures. No, if she had obeyed her own desires, she would have chosen the bold brush-strokes of Delacroix, or Géricault: bold, vivid life flung across the canvas instead of settling for a passive tableau.

She whirled again and spied her writing table set against the opposite wall. Inside were the letters Angela had written to Ian. No matter how many times she'd picked them up and held them out over the fire, she couldn't burn them. Their secrets wouldn't let her alone.

Pulling out the drawer, Leah lifted the letters in their pink silk ribbon. Though the vanilla and lavender scent was fainter now, it still stung her senses. A flare of memory, of watching Ian climb into her bed, of smelling the same perfume on his skin, slashed across her mind.

Her hand gave a slight tremble, itching to fling the packet away. Instead, she clutched them more securely and turned toward the chair near the hearth. A trickle of sweat inched down her temple as she sat, but she didn't ring for someone to douse the flames inside.

She held the letters so tightly in her hands that she could feel the moisture from her palms soak into the parchment. She breathed. In. Out. In. Out. Great shuddering breaths, as if she'd run up the stairs a few minutes ago instead of climbing them at a dignified pace.

The sweat trailed down her cheek and over her chin, along her neck and beneath her fichu to trace the line of her collarbone.

With hands still shaking, Leah loosened the ribbon and drew out a random letter from the stack. It could have been the first letter Angela had written or the last; it didn't matter. She didn't know what she was searching for, or even why she was reading one.

Tucking the others at her side, she opened the letter.

The parchment became like thin tissue, damp and worn between her fingers as her eyes focused first on the salutation.

My dearest love.

Leah waited for her eyes to burn and her throat to thicken with tears, but none came. She couldn't deny the sense of betrayal at seeing another woman refer to her husband in such a manner, but it didn't crush her. Her heart was no longer a delicate, fragile thing, and she was relieved by the realization that it wouldn't be broken again so easily.

> *Thank you for the flowers. They were beautiful. I do not even remember telling you that orchids are my favorite. They're in my bedroom now, and whenever I see them, I think of you and smile.*
> *However, I must insist that you stop sending me*

gifts. I had to explain to Sebastian that they were from my cousin Gertrude, meant to brighten my spirits. I don't want him to grow suspicious, and I do despise lying to him. Sometimes I can't remember what I've already told him. Two days ago I claimed to have a headache, and he nearly sent for a physician again because I'd told him earlier that my stomach was ill. I wish I didn't have to continue deceiving him with this ruse of sickness, but I can't bear the thought of him touching me any longer.

Leah paused, sucking in a breath. Lord Wriothesly had been right in refusing to read the letters.

Would that I had met you first, or that you would have been born an earl's son instead of a viscount's. Every day I wonder . . . but no, I know there is no use for such thoughts. I love you, my darling. You asked me before and I wouldn't admit it, but yes—I am jealous of her. When we're apart, I think of you together. How I wish that I could be the one to see you every day. I imagine sitting quietly in the evenings, working on my embroidery while you read. Quite the domestic scene, I know. Our children would sit at our feet and listen to you. You would make them smile, and laugh, as you make dear Henry laugh. And then when it becomes late, you would take my hand and lead me to your bedchamber.

My dearest Ian, I would write more, but . . . I will save the words until I see you again.

How long the days are without you.

I love you.

Eternally yours,
Angela

Leah held her breath. Her eyes unfocused, the dark ink becoming a blur. Her shoulders slumped, her fingers releasing their death grip on the letter. It shifted in her lap, almost forlorn in its abandonment.

They'd been in love. Or at least, Angela had loved him.

She'd assumed lust, yes, and probably a little obsession, but ... not love. Not the way she'd loved Ian. Half of her had been hoping the letter was nothing more than a vulgar mechanism to spout passion words. It would have been difficult to read any fantasies of lovemaking, but then any remaining anger or bitterness over their betrayal would have been justified. Now ...

They had all lost, hadn't they?

Leah stood from the chair, the letter falling from her lap to the floor. She took half a dozen harried steps before realizing and turning around, going back to tie the letters back together.

But perhaps Ian and Angela hadn't lost, not precisely. They'd done what they could to be together; they hadn't allow society's expectations—moral or otherwise—to rule their lives. Angela's letter bore echoes of her misery and loneliness when they'd been apart, but if her writing was any indication, her desolation was only more acute because of the joy they'd shared when they were together.

Leah opened the drawer again and slid the letters inside, the scent of vanilla and lavender no longer an offensive stench to her senses. It was something more. A reminder she would not forget. An encouragement she hadn't known she needed.

A dare.

Chapter 5

*Don't tell me you know how I feel. Do you know
the joy in my heart when you're near, or the
desolation when you depart? No, I fear you do not,
and I am alone in my heartache.*

Sebastian took a slow breath as he surveyed the room.
It stank of old titles and little wealth, the heavy fog
of cigar smoke lining his lungs as he inhaled.

"I regret it already," he murmured to James. He
hadn't ventured into the gentleman's club since Angela's death. It wasn't that he didn't welcome the sight of
people, or company; James had made himself such a
fixture in the town house that Sebastian was surprised
the maids hadn't begun polishing him along with all the
other furniture. No, it was the normalcy of the club, the
same reason he now avoided dinner parties and musicales. It was as if Ian's and Angela's deaths had never
occurred, as if his life hadn't collided with the somber
coldness of reality four months prior.

"You may regret it all you wish," James answered as

they moved to a table in the center of the room. Not one in the corner—God forbid—but directly in the middle of things. "Just be thankful I didn't tie you to my horse and drag you through the streets to get here. It was a tempting thought."

Around them, conversations carried over the usual currencies: weather, politics, war on the Continent and, with greater enthusiasm—women. The chair at Sebastian's back was too soft and cushioned; he longed for rigidity, for punishment. Hands curled over his knees, he watched James motion a server for drinks.

His brother sat back across from him and smiled, one arm resting on the table in front of him, the other hanging lazily at his side. "God, you look like hell."

"I'm not sure why you insisted on a change of scenery if all you mean to do is insult me wherever we are."

"I enjoy insulting you. It's one of my greatest pleasures in life."

Sebastian pressed his lips together as the server set the drinks before them. His gaze flicked to the scotch, a pale gold, then moved away. James sipped at his glass and stared at him in much the same way he'd been staring at him for months—with a patent expression of patience, only slightly marred by the frustrated slash of his mouth.

To Sebastian's left, Mr. Alfred Dunlop was speaking with the young Baron Cooper-Giles. "I must go. I don't care if there's a scandal. Walter told me that Miss Pettigrew would be there."

"The banker heiress?" he heard Cooper-Giles ask.

"Yes," Mr. Dunlop replied. The word held a grim note to it. "Lost the shipping investment a week ago when the *Reynard* sank. By the end of the week, I intend to have a marriage acceptance in hand."

Sebastian shifted his gaze over James' other shoulder and listened to Lord Derryhow spew on about his new

Thoroughbred, a dark roan hunter. James' sigh swept across the table, and Sebastian met his gaze with a half smile. It seemed the more he practiced those, the easier they became.

"Perhaps all I need is a woman," he said.

"A woman?"

"Yes."

"To bed?"

Sebastian nodded.

"You want to bed a woman?" James' voice increased in incredulity, and Sebastian scowled. Had his little brother always been able to see through him so easily?

Yes, he wanted a mindless fuck, someone to erase Angela's memory from his arms. Someone else's skin and scent and hands. But at the thought, his body rebelled, his muscles tensing and his lungs seeming to cave in. His breath spasmed, caught on that ever-constant, silent whisper of her name. Angela.

"Never mind." He turned toward the large window facing the street, over the heads of Baron Cooper-Giles and Mr. Dunlop. They were talking about a house party now.

But James continued to play along, his voice tinged with amusement. "Shall I send one to you tonight? Or perhaps we should leave now, and I'll do my best to find Lady Carroway. You did fancy her a few years ago, didn't you?"

"Goddamn it, James, I said—" The rebuke died in his throat as he heard a name spoken at the other table. His gaze fixed on Mr. Dunlop.

"Of course," James said, "the widow Carroway is quite a bit older than she once was. I suppose some men would be put off by the gray hair. Myself, for example."

Sebastian cast him a speaking glance, then stood and stepped toward the other table.

Mr. Dunlop halted in midsentence and looked up. "Lord Wriothesly."

"Good day." He inclined his head to Dunlop, then Cooper-Giles. Civilities. Those also became easier when practiced. The impulse to rage and destroy was weaker now than it had been a few months ago. A broken chair, a shattered window, walls forever indented with the impression of his fists. The fire poker hurled across his bedchamber after he'd resisted burning Angela's portrait. These days, his rage was more controlled. Only the mangled ruins of his cravats in the mornings bore evidence of the anger still lurking beneath the gentleman's exterior.

Sebastian looked at Dunlop. "I believe I heard mention of a house party?"

Dunlop exchanged an uneasy glance with Baron Cooper-Giles, and immediately Sebastian knew. He hadn't misheard. "Whose party is it, if I may ask?"

Dunlop didn't quite meet his eyes. "The widow George, my lord. We're leaving tomorrow . . . We were leaving tomorrow for Wiltshire . . ." His voice trailed away. Likely he expected Sebastian to be upset; even though Dunlop couldn't know of the affair between Ian and Angela and Sebastian's subsequent agreement with Leah to keep it quiet, the idea of the recent widow of Sebastian's close friend hosting a house party was absurd enough.

All thoughts of Angela fled, replaced by an image of the smiling, dark-haired deceiver. Three weeks. That's how long it had taken for Leah George to betray her promise.

"Ah, of course." He paused, calculating how long it would take for them to travel to the George estate. He nodded again, then turned back to the table where James sat.

"Sebastian?" James took another leisurely drink of

his scotch. "Is everything all right? Your face is turning that lovely scarlet shade I so enjoy—"

"It appears Mrs. George is hosting a house party," he bit out quietly. The tips of his fingers brushed the edge of the table. Not gripping, but a feather-soft touch to the dark polished wood—a testament to his control.

"Four months," James mused. "That seems quite early."

"Yes, and no one will be able to resist the scandal of it. The meek and mild Mrs. George, recent widow, hosting her own country house party."

He could well imagine how the first scene would unfold: Leah greeting her guests as they arrived, sans widow's cap, one of her bloody ridiculous smiles spread across her face. She might have even forsaken mourning clothes by now, dressed instead in a cheerful yellow or a provocative crimson that proclaimed to the world the joy of her new independence.

Reckless.

How she'd loved the word—*feasted* on it—her entire countenance lighting with glee. Had she already begun planning the house party when he'd visited her town house, or had he unknowingly sparked the idea with the use of those two little syllables?

But it made no difference. Whether she stood by her semantics of not directly *telling anyone of the affair*, the end result was that her actions risked the revelation of the truth. It didn't matter that he would be revealed as a lovesick fool, the doting husband who'd never suspected he was being cuckolded. That gossip would eventually pass, and his pride would heal. No, there was another thought he could not bear for others to echo, one that haunted him every single time he looked at Henry: the doubt of his son's legitimacy.

If only Henry could have had brown hair or green eyes. If only his face wasn't rounded and he wasn't so young, then he might show some feature or mannerism which would clearly mark him as Sebastian's son. But all Sebastian saw now when he stared at Henry was a perfect little boy with Angela's sweet, innocent face, his hair the same color as Angela's . . . and Ian's as well.

Ignoring the ache in his chest, Sebastian sat down heavily and reached for his untouched glass of scotch. He didn't drink spirits often, but it seemed necessary to fortify himself for the rumors which would doubtlessly soon begin.

Why would the young widow George not mourn the husband so beloved by others? What could he have done to earn such disdain?

There seemed no possible answer *but* the truth.

Across the table, James raised a brow. "When is the party to be held?"

"In two days."

Which meant Leah had already left London in preparation. He would never have enough time to travel to Wiltshire to convince her to rescind the invitations. And even if he could reach Linley Park early enough, there was little he could do. The scandal had already begun.

Sebastian set the glass down carefully; no thud against wood betrayed his masked calm. She must have known he'd disapprove of the house party. She also must have known he'd find out about it. Perhaps she didn't think he'd been serious when he warned her about being reckless.

Unfortunately, now the time had come for Leah George to learn from her mistakes.

Not six hours into her house party, Leah already regretted inviting these random acquaintances to come into her home and gawk at her. Oh, they were more discreet than that, of course, their curious glances furtively concealed whenever she looked in their direction. Nevertheless, she had to suppress the impulse to have the butler dismiss them all.

She wasn't accustomed to drawing such focused attention; even when she tried to play hostess, Ian had always been the one to entertain their guests. And despite the risks she'd taken in hosting the house party, even after nearly four months of widowed isolation, she was temptingly close to abandoning this next rebellion in exchange for the return of simple, blessed obscurity.

Looking down both sides of the dining table, Leah smiled. "I must beg your forgiveness, gentlemen, for requesting you forsake your cigars tonight. Instead, shall we all adjourn to the drawing room? I have an announcement to make before I tell you of our special entertainment this evening."

With uplifted brows and veiled glances, her guests rose from their chairs. Leah led the way up the stairs, no escort at her side. After she had issued more than thirty invitations, only eight had come—and honestly, that was eight more than she'd expected. But perhaps they assumed she'd arranged the numbers unevenly on purpose, to emphasize her eccentricity amid the rumors caused by hosting a house party so soon after Ian's death.

Once inside the drawing room, she waited for her guests to be seated. Although theirs were all familiar faces, none were particularly close friends to either her or Ian. Some were probably intrigued by the hint of scandal, some on the fringes of society and simply happy to receive an invitation. They might whisper about her and criticize her actions, but she'd made certain not to invite anyone who knew Ian well, or who might consider asking her uncomfortable questions.

With her heart fluttering wildly and her palms beginning to dampen with perspiration, Leah reminded herself that they were here for her amusement, nothing more. Taking a deep breath, she gestured to the large portrait of Ian beside her, the one she'd had removed from the gallery. "Thank you all for coming," she began, a signal to quiet their murmurs of speculation. "I realize—"

Herrod, her butler, caught her eye at the doorway. "Excuse me for one moment," she said, then slipped from the room, desperately grateful for the unexpected reprieve.

"I apologize for interrupting, madam, but a gentleman has arrived. The Earl of Wriothesly. He insists on seeing you at once."

Wriothesly. She'd hoped he wouldn't find out about the house party until it was over, to spare them both any attempt of his to restrain her. But he'd come. To berate her, to lecture her, to make her feel as miserable as he did, no doubt.

Immediately Leah's nerves calmed, her heart steadying, her breath slowing. She might not be her best in front of others, but the challenge of Lord Wriothesly was another matter altogether. He meant to test her independence, though she doubted he had any idea of the strength she'd acquired since Ian's death.

"Thank you, Herrod. Please see if my guests require anything while they wait," she said, then nearly skipped down the stairs in her haste.

Now she looked forward to seeing him, the earl of the impossibly green eyes and the severe, brooding countenance. She was curious to see how she would respond this time to his requests, how she would ply her courage and stand firm in her defiance.

In a way, she pitied him. Although she continued trying to move forward, to distance herself from the person she'd become while married to Ian, she couldn't forget the earl's anguish when he'd visited the George town house, the fury when he'd sent Angela's letters flying to the floor. Wriothesly clung to his misery, while she did everything she could to escape it.

How horrified he would be to discover she pitied him—probably even more so should he realize he helped strengthen her resolve. Regardless of what he said tonight, she wouldn't bend to his wishes for her obedience—no matter that he was an earl, nor that part of her heart sank whenever she witnessed the despair in his eyes.

Wriothesly stood inside the front doorway with a valise at each side. Scowling, as usual. Leah felt rather a perverse creature for taking pleasure in the way his expression darkened as she approached. Although a smile pulled at her lips, she subdued the motion and curtsied.

"My Lord Wriothesly. I wasn't aware you intended to come. The house party has already begun and we're now—"

"Consider my arrival a response to the rumors you've created." He took her hand, even though it had been clasped with the other in front of her waist, and lifted it toward his lips. While he disguised the movement as a courtly gesture, Leah was more than conscious of the heated iron of his grip, the velvet-soft threat of his kiss as his mouth swept across her glove. The air of desolation surrounding him was gone, replaced only by anger.

For the first time in their acquaintance of three years, she realized that the Earl of Wriothesly finally saw her. Not as another random society twit, not as Ian's wife or widow, but as Leah George, individual and separate. Removed from the great horde of women who were not the seemingly perfect Lady Angela Wriothesly and placed into a much more specific category of one: Leah George. Despised. Loathsome. Enemy.

Perhaps pitying him had been a mistake.

Wriothesly released her hand. "I fear I've done you a

grave disservice, Mrs. George. It appears I've overesti-
mated your intelligence."

Leah winced as she flexed her fingers, noting how he
didn't apologize for grinding her joints together. Now
that his grief seemed to have given way for the moment,
all his energy appeared to be focused on scolding her.

She tilted her head. "Are you sulking because you
came too late for dinner?"

"I thought I made my request for you to avoid a scandal clear enough for even a simpleton to understand,
and yet here we are."

"Yes," she murmured. "Here we are. Even though I
never sent you an invitation."

"I suppose I should be pleased you've decided to
continue wearing proper mourning clothes, widow's cap
and all."

"I decided to leave the silk night rail for my midnight
tryst."

"And that you've maintained some sense of decorum
by not walking about grinning like—"

He broke off, treating her with a remarkably malevo-
lent glare as she smiled from ear to ear. Leah reached up
and patted his clenched jaw. It was a mistake, an action
made only on impulse, and one that she regretted as
soon as she touched him. But she couldn't retreat now.
"My poor Lord Wriothesly. It's wrong of me to torture
you, isn't it? Please, come with me. I was about to make
an announcement to our guests when you arrived."

"Our guests?" he echoed as she walked away.

She began the ascent up the staircase, her back
straight as she listened for his footsteps. Halfway up, he
still hadn't moved.

"*Our* guests?" he asked again when her feet touched
the landing, his voice closer this time.

Leah glanced over her shoulder, prepared to deny

she'd ever said such a thing and provoke him into following after her.

He stood at the bottom of the stairs, one hand clutching the newel post, his mouth formed in a narrow, demanding line. Recently it had been easy enough to relegate him to a masculine version of her mother: autocratic, impatient, unwilling to swerve from the strictures of society. But she possessed memories of Wriothesly before the carriage accident. The sound of his and Ian's laughter drifting through the town house. The way he used to watch his wife with such love and tenderness, oblivious to the looks passed between Angela and Ian. The delight on his face when he paraded Henry in front of guests, and his pride when Henry first gave Leah a short, distracted imitation of a bow in exchange for her curtsy.

They'd both been changed by the betrayal. Leah liked to think she'd learned her lesson and though the pain was still great, had become the better for it. Perhaps she could exercise her independence without making him suffer; perhaps, in her defiance, she could somehow help him.

Sighing, she retraced her steps until she stood only a few stairs above him, a slight advantage which placed them eye to eye. "I know you wouldn't be here if not for your fear that I might incite gossip about Ian and Angela. I know you'd prefer that I send everyone home, and then you could return to the misery you've created for yourself the last few months. But if you could consider this house party as a chance to enjoy life again, if you would allow me to help you, you would understand why I decided to—"

"I do not need your help," he growled.

She shouldn't have said anything. She'd known he wouldn't welcome her interference, and yet still she'd done it anyway. "Perhaps not, but . . ."

She faltered as his gaze flickered over her face, animosity flaring in his eyes. "Is this how he was with you?" he asked.

Leah frowned. "I—I'm not sure what you mean."

"Ian. Was he patronizing? Did he treat you like a child?" The words were spoken softly, sorrowfully, as if he were the one who pitied her. She stood silent, uncertain where his questioning might lead, unable to look away from the ruthless curve of his mouth.

"My poor Mrs. George," he murmured, lifting his hand to brush the backs of his fingers across her cheek.

She knew he meant it as a mockery of her earlier gesture, but the slide of his leather glove across her skin felt too much like a caress, and she could no more halt the blush that rose to enflame her face than she could retreat from his touch.

His hand stilled along the line of her jaw and he tilted her chin up. Only the challenge in his eyes kept her from snapping at his fingers.

"You were always his quiet little shadow, weren't you? Content to echo Ian's every word and movement. And I see you've studied him well, although your attempt at mimicry is somewhat tedious. I am not a child, Mrs. George. I do not need your help."

"I assure you, my lord, it isn't my intent to act condescending. If it weren't for the circumstances of Ian's death, I wouldn't have anything to do with you at all. In fact, I believe it might be best if you leave. Your presence here is neither required nor desired."

And he could go rot in hell, for all she cared.

Wriothesly returned his hand to his side. "Alas, leaving you alone is no longer an option. And do not think to send the guests home, either. Doing so now would only cause more gossip. The party will continue, and with the least amount of scandal."

"You believe you can control me," she said, crossing

her arms, then uncrossing them because it felt like something a little girl would do. How had he taken the power away from her so easily?

He edged around her skirts and began climbing the stairs. "No, madam. I *will* control you, by whatever means necessary."

Leah stared at the vase of pansies on the table across from the staircase, her fingers slowly uncurling from the fists she'd formed. No matter how deeply she breathed, she couldn't seem to steady herself. A movement caught her attention by the door, and she turned to find a footman standing near the earl's valises, waiting for her direction.

"You may take his lordship's things to the blue room," she said, although she was far more inclined to order them destroyed.

She then returned to the drawing room, glancing neither right nor left as she moved toward the portrait. Ian stared at her, his mouth drawn in that perpetual hint of a smile. Perhaps his charm had occasionally come across as patronizing in the last months, but that was probably because his shining armor had been reduced to nothing more than dented, rusty tin in her eyes. Yet even if he'd been condescending, even though he'd given her plenty of cause to be hurt, humiliated, and angry, he had never intentionally insulted her.

Not, she thought blackly, *like Wriothesly did*.

Leah signaled for a footman to bring her a glass of the wine Herrod had supplied to her guests in her absence, then turned and waited for everyone to quiet. As before, her heart thudded rapidly against her chest, but this time it wasn't from anxiety. Her gaze skipped around the room until she found the earl, sitting near William Meyer and Baron Cooper-Giles. A warning glinted in his eyes as he nodded his acknowledgment, and Leah raised her glass toward him, well aware that everyone in the room observed their exchange.

"Ladies and gentlemen," she began, "I realize hosting a house party so soon after the death of my husband is rather unorthodox. Some might call it scandalous, even." Lifting a brow, she allowed her gaze to drift from Wriothesly to the others in the room. "However, if you knew Ian at all, you also know that he was a man who deserves more than our tears and grief. He had a way of living that many of us envied—myself included. He laughed, he danced, he debated politics, and he recited literature, all with a passion that somehow seemed too great to be contained in one man. And yet it was."

Leah glanced at his portrait. It was meant to be a touching moment, one where everyone assumed she'd become too emotional to continue speaking. Although no tears came, she well remembered the man she spoke of, how easy it had been to fall in love with him . . . how, once upon a time, she thought he'd loved her as well.

After a moment, she lifted her gaze and stared at the top of Lady Elliot's head, seeking to remember the rest of her speech.

"For the next week, I would request that instead of mourning, we celebrate Ian's life. You will find the meals prepared with many of his favorite dishes, and I have already planned several activities in the coming days which he particularly enjoyed. Ian's dearest friend, the Earl of Wriothesly"—she gestured with a wave of her hand, not bothering to hide her smile—"has also joined the house party so he might make further suggestions. For now, I propose a toast. To my beloved husband, friend, and one of the greatest men I ever knew—to Ian George."

One by one, glasses were raised across the room. "To Ian," they echoed again, then drank. Leah glanced to-

ward Wriothesly. Although his mouth touched the rim
of his glass, the liquid inside remained placid, the glass
level. The stillness extended to his expression, a pale
mask of studied politeness; only the sharp cut of his eyes
toward her revealed surprise and a promise of retribution.

Satisfied, Leah took another sip of her wine before
motioning toward Herrod. "And now, as promised,
please allow me to present our special guest, who will
entertain us with several of Ian's favorite songs: Miss
Victoria Lind."

As the enthusiastic murmurs of approval dwindled to a
hush and the opera singer opened her mouth for the
first soaring note, Sebastian tilted his glass and swallowed. A toast—not to Ian, but to his widow. Like Leah
George, the liquid was deceptively sweet, hiding the
truth of its strength in its delicate, innocent overtones.

With the opera singer situated at the far end of the
drawing room, it was impossible to keep Leah in sight
while pretending to give Ms. Lind the proper attention.
Even so, he could feel Leah's presence beyond his left
shoulder, a force he would no longer underestimate.

He wished he could continue thinking of her as a
young widow who wanted to explore her sudden freedom through any outrageous means possible. A widow
who was likely to take a dozen lovers simply because
she could, or act the eccentric because she had no husband to attract and no one to impress. While indiscreet
and irresponsible, her behavior would have made sense.
Given a few quiet moments without the thunder of train
or carriage wheels and a head clear of liquor, Sebastian
could have predicted her next course of action. He could
have endeavored to find a way to forestall whichever
ridiculous plan she devised next.

But she was more cunning than he had anticipated,

and the motivations he'd so quickly ascribed to her now seemed little more than his own foolish assumptions. She hosted a party, but she wore full widow's clothing— including a widow's cap—and had invited a mixture of bachelors, married couples, and a young woman with her companion. Certainly it wasn't anything to violate one's sense of morality. She'd even managed to turn any gossip on its head by arranging everything as a tribute to Ian's memory. How could anyone ever forget how *devoted* she'd sounded during that oh so touching speech of hers?

However, though the party itself was the only scandalous behavior she'd engaged in so far, Sebastian wasn't convinced. He might not yet understand her method or even her motivation, but he knew she wasn't as selfless as she appeared. Leah George wanted to be reckless. And although he'd misjudged her cleverness and the reason for her rebellion before, he would be sure not to make the same mistake again.

When the first song ended and everyone applauded, Sebastian looked over his shoulder, found Leah's gaze, and smiled. By the lift of her chin, he knew she understood the meaning of his expression: not as pleasure, not as happiness, but a warning.

Chapter 6

*Tell me again, darling. Tell me a hundred times, a
thousand. I will never forget the first time you
whispered it in my ear. It will never be enough. Tell
me you love me.*

It could have been a beautiful day. The late-morning
sun shone brightly overhead. A fleet of pristine white
clouds drifted lazily across the sky. An early autumnal
wind swayed the leaves on their branches, quietly stirred
the water, and sifted gently through Sebastian's hair.

It *would* have been a beautiful day, if not for the black
figure marring his view of the landscape: the formerly
inconsequential Leah George, who'd quickly managed
to make herself into a pestilence.

How innocent she appeared, from the tip of her black
parasol to the hem of her black skirts. In fact, he could
have applauded her—she used the widow's veil to add
to her facade of quiet rectitude, the crepe lending her
solemnity while lies issued one after another from her
mouth.

"...boating at Linley Park was one of his favorite pastimes...

"...and we thought he'd gone missing, only to discover he'd spent the entire afternoon on the lake."

His gaze followed her gesture toward the four wooden skiffs bobbing at the lake's edge. Various male servants had been summoned from the house to attend to the guests, and each one stood with a rope in his hands, mooring the boats to the shore.

"Once he was gone, I found a few pieces of poetry he must have written while he was out here. About a bird landing on the bow, of the different colors of the water throughout each of the seasons. Of the immense peace he felt in his soul when he was alone on the lake."

Head swiveling, Sebastian stared incredulously at Leah. There were lies, and then there were gaudy, excessive leaps of imagination. Ian might have been known for his recitations of poetry and literature, but he did it solely to gain favor with the ladies. The only poem Sebastian had ever known him to write was a limerick about a sailor's whore and a wooden dick.

"Oh, how lovely they sound," Mrs. Meyer said, the other ladies concurring with her. "Perhaps you might read them to us this evening?"

"I..." Leah made an inarticulate noise. Though the others likely assumed she'd been overcome with emotion, Sebastian preferred to think it was the sound of sputtering. "Yes, of course. Perhaps. But I've spoken for too long. With four boats, I believe it best to split everyone into two groups of two and two groups of three, with the gentlemen as the oarsmen."

She paused, and even with the parasol mostly obscuring her profile, he could see the calculating tilt of her head as she determined how to divide the guests. No matter where she placed him, he planned on refusing her direction. Besides being curious bits of fancy, her lies made it clear he couldn't trust any decisions she made.

Boating. *Ian's favorite pastime*, for God's sake.

"Miss Pettigrew, Mrs. Thompson, why don't you join Mr. Dunlop?" she directed. "Lord Elliot and Mrs. Meyer in the next boat. Mr. Meyer, Lady Elliot, and Lord Wriothesly. Which then leaves myself and Lord Cooper-Giles." Her parasol shifted, and a beam of sunlight pierced through her veil to expose the small smile she aimed at the baron. "That is, if you don't mind listening to me reminisce about Mr. George for a while."

"Of course not, madam," Cooper-Giles replied. "It would be my pleasure."

Sebastian crossed his arms and frowned. It wasn't that the unmarried Cooper-Giles was a scoundrel who might influence Leah to further corruption and scandal; in fact, besides his proclivity for gossip, the young baron probably had the truest moral compass of them all. No, it was Leah he worried about. No matter how well she tried to pretend, he doubted five minutes would pass before Cooper-Giles discovered how singularly happy she was to have a dead husband rather than a live one.

"I apologize, Mrs. George," Sebastian said, stepping forward. "If I had known about the boating excursion earlier, I would have spared you some trouble. You see, I'm afraid I can't join you. Motion sickness, you understand. But I don't mind standing here—alone—and watching. I'm sure it will be just as amusing."

The sun highlighted the corner of her mouth and the curve of her cheek as her chin slowly lifted toward him. Her eyes remained shadowed behind the veil. "Why, Lord Wriothesly. I'm very sorry. How dreadful a malady."

"Yes, it is."

"My cousin Herbert is exactly the same way," Mrs. Meyer volunteered. Sebastian smiled at her.

"Is he?" Leah asked. "I must confess, I'd heard of becoming ill at sea, but never on an inland body of water."

"Oh, yes. Even the smallest waves upset him terribly."

"How extraordinary," Leah murmured before looking once again at Sebastian. "Of course we understand, Lord Wriothesly, but I wouldn't dream of asking you to stay here by yourself. Perhaps you would prefer to retire to the house until the boating ends?"

Sebastian waved his hand. "No, no. I'll be fine, as long as I don't go on the lake." Glancing around at the other guests, he added, "Please, enjoy yourselves. I'll just stay here."

Miss Pettigrew looked hesitantly at Leah, then at Sebastian. "Mrs. Thompson and I would be happy to keep you company, if you like."

Almost immediately Mr. Dunlop, who had been assigned as the oarsman for Miss Pettigrew and her companion, offered, "I will stay as well."

Sebastian raised a brow. Mr. Dunlop wasn't being very subtle in his pursuit of Miss Pettigrew. Sebastian sighed and shook his head. "But I wouldn't wish to spoil the day," he said. "Mrs. George clearly wished for her guests to enjoy boating on the lake . . . just as Ian did."

As Mrs. Meyer opened her mouth to speak, Sebastian suspected everyone might soon return to the house. After all, an earl still curried more favor and ingratiation than the lower-ranking widow of a viscount's son, regardless of how eloquently she spoke of her deceased spouse.

But Leah interceded. "Nonsense. I will stay here with you, Lord Wriothesly. Miss Pettigrew, Mrs. Thompson, and Mr. Dunlop will go boating as planned. Lord Elliot, Mr. Meyer, and Mrs. Meyer will go in the second boat, with Lord Cooper-Giles and Lady Elliot in the third."

Sebastian gave her a nod. "Thank you, Mrs. George. That's very kind."

"Please, my lord," she murmured. "You were Ian's closest friend, so dear to him. How could I ever abandon you? He would think I had betrayed your friendship, something he would never have done."

Sebastian stiffened. How sweet and beguiling her tone as she fired the first volley. A reminder of Ian's betrayal, of the reason Sebastian had to endure her presence during this little house party: to conceal both his friend's and his wife's unfaithfulness. It had been meant to wound, and she had met her mark.

Although he couldn't help but flinch at her words, he was careful to maintain a polite expression before the others. Once they turned toward the lake, he followed Leah to a stone bench shaded by the meandering branches of a yew tree, ducking beneath her parasol when it would have pierced his eye—and not accidentally, he suspected. The other guests stepped into the boats with the help of the servants. Baron Cooper-Giles looked remarkably relieved, he noticed, to not have to listen to Leah muse on and on about Ian for the next hour or so.

Beside him, Leah cleared her throat. "I should apologize," she said quietly.

Sebastian watched a servant give the third boat a push from the shore.

"I was very much looking forward to the boating. I didn't expect you to sabotage me."

"Did you not satisfy him in bed?" Sebastian asked abruptly. Needing to place the blame somewhere. Wanting to hurt her as well.

He sensed her go rigid, saw her hand grip the parasol tighter out of the corner of his eye. "If you are implying he sought out Lady Wriothesly because I—"

"That's exactly what I'm implying." He shouldn't have sat so close to her. He could smell her again, that clean, soapy, strictly unfeminine scent. "It's a valid assumption, since you've never had children. Could he not bear to touch you? You're not beautiful like she was, or soft and womanly. And you're loud. Hell, you don't even smell like a proper woman. Angela—"

"Yes, my lord? I'm sure you mean to continue telling me how she was the ideal wife? A paragon of virtue, perhaps?"

"She . . ." Sebastian set his jaw. When would he cease thinking of Angela as the woman he'd wanted her to be?

He refused to look at Leah. But he could feel her stare, and twin lines of heat scored his upper cheeks. No other person had ever made him so easily ashamed; then again, he'd never had reason to regret his behavior before. She'd meant to apologize, and he hadn't even allowed her that courtesy. He forgot to leash his fury around her, forgot to be a gentleman.

"I suppose I could ask whether you satisfied Lady Wriothesly as well," Leah continued, "but I truly don't want to know."

Sebastian watched Mr. Meyer and Lord Elliot attempt to synchronize their oar strokes.

He and Leah sat beside each other on the stone bench, the sun sneaking through the tree's cover to dapple the ground with random beams of soft, golden light. One minute after another passed, until the sound of her breathing next to him seemed to enter his subconscious with a quiet permanence, and he could predict the spacing of each slow inhalation.

Out on the lake, Miss Pettigrew laughed prettily at something Mr. Dunlop said.

Sebastian shifted, uneasy with the silence beneath the yew tree, one that became even louder after the echoes of laughter died away. Even strained and oppressive, it felt too intimate. He might be curious about her motives, might need to know why she behaved as she did so he could prevent her future foolishness, but he didn't want to know her like this. Not her scent, nor the pattern of her breathing, nor even the calm dignity she maintained when responding to an undeserved attack.

In the end, it was she who spoke first, her voice light and ironic. As if they were simply two ordinary people engaging in an ordinary conversation. "With your illness, I assume you didn't go boating with Ian much."

Sebastian turned his head toward her, his posture easing as he gave her a small smile. "No, not quite."

She, too, looked at him, and this close, even with her veil as a mask, he could see her face. The sherry tint of her brown eyes. The slim point of her nose. The overfull decadence of her mouth, as if God had felt guilty for not giving her any feminine curves elsewhere.

Grimacing at this detailed analysis of her features, Sebastian focused again on her eyes. Her rather plain, *unexceptional* brown eyes. "In fact, I don't remember going boating with Ian at all. Or seeing him go boating. Or hearing of him boating. Rather, I distinctly recall Ian telling me how he feared any body of water larger than a stream after his near-drowning incident as a boy."

Leah blinked. "Oh. Well, that's most unfortunate."

"Unfortunate that he didn't like boating, or that I caught you in a lie?"

"The first, of course. Then again, you're the only one here who would have known. I made sure to invite only those who weren't close to Ian. And obviously even I didn't know him as well as I thought, since he never confided his fear to me."

He'd never told anyone else, as far as Sebastian knew. Ian only informed him when Sebastian had found him shivering and crying after the Eton masters made everyone participate in a swimming competition one day.

"And the poetry . . ."

Cocking her head to the side, she gave her parasol a lazy twirl. "I suppose I did get carried away, didn't I?"

Then her mouth curled upward in a coy, flirtatious little smile. He stared, discomfited by the realization that Leah George knew *how* to give a coy, flirtatious smile.

Shrugging, she looked out over the lake again. "As I said, I wanted to go boating."

"I see. Dare I ask what's next in store for us? Did Ian also like to knit, or paint watercolors, or compose hymns in his spare time?"

She slid him a sidelong glance from behind the veil. "Tarot cards. He loved to read tarot cards."

He groaned, and she laughed.

"I can be quite magnanimous, though. As his dearest friend, you're more than welcome to suggest activities Ian preferred."

Activities Ian preferred . . . Well, there was fishing, and hunting. Dancing and playing cards. And then there was fucking Sebastian's wife.

"No," he said.

Leah nodded, her gaze settled once again on the others. "Miss Pettigrew and Mr. Dunlop seem to get along rather well, don't you agree?"

He didn't give a damn about Miss Pettigrew and her potential suitor, not when his mind had suddenly become too busy torturing him with lurid images of Angela and Ian—of him pleasuring her with his hands, of her bucking beneath his thrusts. The good mood he'd been inclined to indulge in abruptly disappeared. "Tell me, Mrs. George. If you wanted to go boating, why not simply go boating? You have servants to accompany you. Why invite scandal by hosting a house party? Why disregard my request for *this*?"

She didn't speak.

"I am not accustomed to being ignored."

Without warning, she stood and strode from the bench. Sebastian followed. As he opened his mouth to question her again, she whirled toward him.

"My apologies, my lord. I believe the boating excursion is almost over, and our picnic—" She took a deep breath, then smiled. It was a small, polite gesture, and for once, Sebastian found himself missing the grand, obscenely extravagant curve of her lips. "I do hope you enjoy it," she finished, then turned away.

There weren't many trees on this side of the Linley Park estate. Near the chalk hills, the land was mostly rolling grassland, with only a few oaks and yews dotting the landscape.

To keep the guests shaded during the picnic, the servants constructed an awning and laid out food on tables below: lobster tails, poached chicken, iced champagne, berry tarts, fresh custard with cream, and more. Satisfied, Leah dismissed the servants and returned the few yards' distance to the lake.

Wriothesly was helping Lady Elliot and Baron Cooper-Giles out of their boat, with the other two vessels rowing to shore close behind. Though she stood still as she waited, a slight breeze lifting and teasing the hem of her veil, her heart continued to thump erratically inside her chest.

It wouldn't be difficult to tell him the reason why she'd decided to host the house party. After the welt of humiliation from being compared to Angela, explaining her loneliness couldn't have made the wound to her pride any more painful. If he would be willing to listen, he might appreciate the careful thought she'd given to how she could host the party with the least amount of scandal possible, how she'd even written Viscount Rennell for his permission first. Yes, she might have planned the activities for her own pleasure, but everyone believed she did it to honor Ian's memory. In terms of reprehensible behavior, she had a far way to go to either disgracing herself or raising suspicion about the affair.

Still, even though the truth might appease him, she couldn't help wanting to keep a little of herself locked away. For two years she'd given while Ian took. Although she'd tried after a while to hide her feelings from him, to show him nothing but polite courtesy, she knew by the regretful way he looked at her sometimes and the thoroughness of his lovemaking that he saw everything. Her anger, her sadness, the fading hope that one day he would end the affair and return to her. Even if it was only loneliness she felt now, didn't she have a right to leave that small piece of vulnerability unspoken?

"What a marvelous idea," Lady Elliot exclaimed as she caught sight of Leah. "I can well understand why Mr. George enjoyed boating here so much."

With the same smile she'd pasted on for Wriothesly, Leah gestured toward their makeshift pavilion. "I'm so glad you liked it, my lady. It's such a beautiful day, I thought we might also have a picnic."

Lady Elliot, middle-aged with an inquisitive beak of a nose and a wry pinch at the corners of her mouth, leaned in. "If I may be honest, Mrs. George . . ."

"Please," she said, her shoulders stiffening. God knew how much more brutal honesty she could handle today.

"You aren't quite the scandal I expected."

Leah's smile turned genuine. If only she had spoken loudly enough for Wriothesly to overhear. "I'm very sorry to disappoint."

"Yes, well . . ." Lady Elliot smoothed her skirts as they began walking toward the awning. "Although it's not quite the amusement I had hoped for, your devotion to the late Mr. George is most touching. I'd like to think Lord Elliot would do the same for me were I to pass before him, but I can't imagine he'd do anything more than lift a glass of whiskey in my name. Perhaps light a cigar. Or tumble one of the housemaids."

Leah's breath caught. "I'm sure he wouldn't—"

Laughing, Lady Elliot waved her off. "No, of course not. He'd be too afraid I would come back and haunt him. But this—well, Mrs. George, let's just say that you've almost made me believe in love again."

"My husband was . . . a very special man," Leah said, lowering her eyes to the ground. Somehow the lies didn't roll off her tongue as easily when she was alone with one of her guests. Hoping to bring someone else into their conversation, she glanced over her shoulder.

Lord Wriothesly walked behind them with the Meyers and Lord Elliot. And he was staring directly at her.

Flushing, Leah jerked her gaze ahead. Strange how she'd always been able to dismiss her mother's criticisms so easily, but Wriothesly's outburst had made her doubt herself. Even now, with the knowledge of his proximity and how he looked at her, she couldn't help being acutely aware of the straight, unswerving line of her body—from the slimness of her shoulders to the narrowed angles of her hips.

Perhaps Ian thought her as plain as the earl did, but he'd made her feel beautiful. Not just with words, but with the way he looked at her, with the way he touched her. Until she'd realized how deceitful even his silence had been.

Thankfully, they reached the awning before the exchange with Lady Elliot necessitated further adulation for Ian on Leah's part. In a short while, the women had arranged themselves on the blankets while the men strolled about doing their bidding: fetching plates of food, pouring glasses of champagne, and chasing after Mrs. Thompson's parasol when the wind sent it spiraling toward the lake.

Leah breathed a sigh of relief when Wriothesly planted himself on the opposite side of the blankets. With Mr. Meyers and Lord Cooper-Giles' heads between them, it appeared possible to pass the entire picnic without having to see his face.

"I think I'll have to make a regular trip to Wiltshire from now on," Mrs. Meyer declared. "The weather is much more hospitable here than it is in Northumberland."

Leah swallowed a spoonful of custard. "You should come in April. There are woods to the northwest of the house where the lavender covers every inch of ground for weeks."

Mrs. Meyer shook her head. "We only have snow in Northumberland in April," she said mournfully, then leaned in. "Mr. Meyer continues to be stubborn, but I have hope yet of convincing him to let a town house in London the year-round. Even with the stench and heat, it would be far preferable."

Lady Elliot waved this away with her glass of champagne, the liquid swirling dangerously near the top. "You must go to the sea for at least a few weeks during the summer. Not Bath—it's not quite the place it used to be. Lord Elliot and I thought about going to Italy this year, but someone told us there's still a bit of unrest since the revolutions."

Leah took another bite of custard. How wonderful it would be, to be able to explore the Continent at will—or even England for that matter. To choose where one wanted to go, not because so-and-so was hosting a party or because that's where the fashionable set went on holiday, but simply because she was free to do as she pleased.

Perhaps she would do just that after the party ended. She could go to Cornwall, or Sussex, or even Northumberland. Ireland wasn't very far away, either. And, oh, how her mother would have an apoplexy if she were to go to Ireland.

Beyond Mrs. Meyer's shoulder, Miss Pettigrew stood from where she'd been engaged in conversation with Mrs. Thompson, Mr. Dunlop, and Lord Cooper-Giles. "I believe I'll go for a walk," she said. Although both gentlemen immediately rose to escort her, she turned toward Leah. "Mrs. George, would you mind accompanying me?"

With Cooper-Giles having moved from his position, Leah could see Lord Wriothesly once again, his arms stretched out behind him, idly chatting with Lord Elliot and Mr. Meyer. Even though he continued speaking to his companions, his eyes once again settled on her. That intense green gaze flickered over her face, studying her, as if he stared long enough he might understand all of her thoughts and secrets.

Leah stumbled a little as she stood. "A walk would be delightful, Miss Pettigrew."

The girl was quiet as they strolled away from the picnic. She was probably only a couple of years younger, but Leah found it difficult to think of her as a woman with the soft innocence that seemed to permeate the air around her.

Once they'd walked for a few minutes, Miss Pettigrew stooped to pick a wildflower. "I meant to thank you for inviting me to your house party, Mrs. George. Linley Park is quite beautiful."

"I'm pleased you came."

With Miss Pettigrew carrying the flower in her hand, they meandered around the edges of the lake. "I'm sure it's not *de rigueur* to say this, but this is the first house party I've ever been invited to."

"That's not unusual. If this is your first Season—"

"Third," Miss Pettigrew muttered.

Leah blinked; they were actually of the same age.

"My father hired Mrs. Thompson as my companion, thinking that she'd be able to transform me into a proper gentlewoman. But all the *ton* ladies see is the daughter of a banker, and the fact that I'm wealthy does nothing to win their favor. Even Mrs. Thompson is barely able to conceal her dislike."

"Surely that's not true," Leah said. "I've seen her with you, and she—"

"Is a very good actress," Miss Pettigrew finished, her gaze fixed on the water. "When we're alone, she can hardly bring herself to speak to me."

"I'm sorry to hear that," Leah said. She probably expected Leah to give her some sort of advice to help her change the situation. After all, hadn't she spent the past twenty years being groomed and lectured on how to be a proper lady, how to become a desirable wife to a lord and a hostess that all the women envied? Leah tried to hide her amusement as Miss Pettigrew bent for another flower. Now she was more likely to suggest the young woman run off to explore Ireland with her, society be damned.

But Miss Pettigrew didn't ask her advice; she only acknowledged Leah's sympathy with a slight nod of her head. When she straightened and faced Leah, her blue eyes shone feverishly, a remarkable contrast to the paleness of her cheeks, the demure clasp of her hands. "I believe I might be in love, Mrs. George."

"Oh." Well, that hadn't taken long. "With Mr. Dunlop?"

"No."

"Baron Cooper-Giles?"

"Oh, no. No one suitable at all." Miss Pettigrew darted a glance across the lake where the others were picnicking. Leah followed her gaze, curious at her silence.

No one suitable. If not the two bachelors, then that left the married gentlemen, Mr. Meyer and Lord Elliot. While certainly inappropriate, Leah couldn't believe that Miss Pettigrew would find either particularly charming or attractive. Not with Mr. Meyer's thinning blond hair and slight lisp and Lord Elliot's whale of a stomach.

Of course, a recent widower might be considered unsuitable . . .

True, Lord Wriothesly wasn't bosom-heaving handsome in the way Ian had been, but Leah knew very well how easily he could mesmerize a woman with his eyes, creating an illusion of intimacy with nothing more than the touch of his gaze and the stroke of his voice. It was that illusion which made it easy to forget he'd designated her as his enemy, that intimacy which had made his earlier insults seem particularly vicious.

"I believe he's still in love with his wife," she told Miss Pettigrew.

"Who?"

"Lord Wriothesly."

"Oh, it's not him either," Miss Pettigrew said with a little laugh. "No, that would be too convenient—loving someone my father might actually approve of. Shall I tell you my secret, Mrs. George? Will you promise not to tell anyone?"

Leah tore her gaze away from the picnickers. "If you truly wish—"

"His name is William Price. He's one of Father's clerks."

"You're right. I don't suppose he's very suitable at all, is he?"

Miss Pettigrew smiled sadly and stared down at the flowers. A short while later, she said, "I'd like to know how you did it."

Leah lifted her skirts as they walked around a particularly muddy area toward the low end of the lake. "What did I do?"

"How you made Mr. George love you. That's why I wanted to walk with you. And to thank you for inviting

me here, of course. But the love you seemed to share—
I've never heard of anyone doing something like this.
You must have loved him very much, and he you. Tell
me, how did you convince him to marry you?"

"I . . . I—" Leah looked ahead. Thank God. The picnic area was only a short distance away. "Honestly, I
married him because it's what my parents desired. And
I believe his family wanted the match, also."

"Oh." Miss Pettigrew nodded glumly at her flowers.
"I beg your pardon, Mrs. George, for being so forward.
I'm afraid Mrs. Thompson would be quite embarrassed
for me."

"But I did love him," Leah added. It felt like a hundred years ago . . . another time. Another Leah. But she
had. She couldn't deny it. He'd been the fulfillment of
her girlhood dreams, her golden knight come to rescue
her from her mother, from herself and her own fears
that she'd never be enough. And she'd loved him for
that, for making her enough. Just as much as she'd hated
him for revealing her dreams to be nothing but lies.

"And he loved you," Miss Pettigrew said, sighing
wistfully.

It was a statement, not a question, for which Leah
was thankful. Although she'd become rather adept at
falsehoods of late, she couldn't have attempted to answer that one . . . especially when even she didn't know
the truth.

As they climbed the hill back to the pavilion, Miss
Pettigrew handed her one of the flowers she'd picked—a
dainty pink cerise bud. "You won't tell anyone of my
secret, will you, Mrs. George?"

"No, I promise."

"Thank you."

Miss Pettigrew returned to Mrs. Thompson's side,
where Mr. Dunlop and Lord Cooper-Giles soon found
her again. Clutching the flower in her hand, Leah headed

toward the bucket of iced champagne for another glass. She smiled at the guests as she passed. They each smiled back, all except for Lord Wriothesly.

He stared at her until she looked away.

Sebastian lifted the heavy glass globe, shifted it from hand to hand, then replaced the paperweight on Ian's desk.

No matter how many times he'd visited Linley Park, he'd never seen Ian in this study. He couldn't even imagine him sitting behind the desk, his head bent to the estate accounts or some other paperwork. He knew Ian must have maintained his responsibilities at his father's request, but he hadn't enjoyed them. Instead, Ian had preferred to lend his mind and his charm toward other things, such as—

Sebastian pivoted away from the desk. Not tonight. He'd done enough dwelling on the subject; tonight, at least, he wouldn't think of them together.

Besides, it was thoughts of Henry which had kept him awake. This in itself surprised him. He hadn't expected the longing to see his son's face, to discover which new words Henry had learned while he was gone. He'd been away from Henry before, of course, for weeks at a time. But not since Angela's death. And somehow although it had seemed fine before for a little boy to spend all day with his nurse, now Sebastian was jealous of those moments. He wanted to see his son, to play with him . . . to be reassured when he threw his arms around Sebastian's neck that yes, Henry did belong to him. But instead of being able to return to Henry now, Sebastian was forced to watch over Ian's widow.

A faint light flickered in the corridor outside the study. Sebastian moved to pull the door completely shut; it was well past midnight, and he didn't want anyone to enter and ask questions about his intrusion into Ian's private office. Even he wasn't sure why he'd chosen to come here. There was nothing to find, no papers or clue to indicate why Ian had betrayed him. Everything was neat and orderly. Clean. Unused.

He paused before the door could latch. Perhaps it was intuition, or he'd somehow smelled her particular scent, but he opened the door again and quietly slipped out, certain he would find Leah doing something she shouldn't.

As he crept down the corridor, the light fled before him, until he was no longer chasing the light but the shadows it cast on the wall in its wake. Footsteps sounded on the staircase, and he rounded the corner to see her climbing to the next floor, the lamp swaying in her grip.

She wore no widow's cap or veil, and her cloak was a deep royal blue instead of black, but still he knew it was her. He'd spent enough time watching her today, searching to discover the secrets she refused to reveal. From their time at the lake, at dinner, and through two tedious hours of charades afterward, he'd studied her until he could have closed his eyes and envisioned her face, could have predicted the nervous habit she had of rubbing her third finger and thumb together on her right hand.

And now Sebastian knew the truth. He should have realized it before, from the first time he saw Leah after Ian's funeral. She'd been almost happy to see him, although at the time he'd attributed it to a sordid relief that Ian was dead.

Again at the George town house, when she'd invited him to look through Ian's things, she might have been in good spirits when he arrived, but she didn't smile until she saw him.

And earlier today, among her guests at the picnic, her face lit up when in conversation with the ladies sitting around her. She jested and laughed, offered her opinions and even roused the others to join her in what she declared was Ian's favorite song. That is, when she wasn't stealing glances at Sebastian, trying to see if he still stared at her.

But he did stare—and he studied her. He was rewarded that evening during the charades, when he finally realized that Leah's attentiveness to her guests was something he'd never noticed before. All the times in the past when he and Angela had visited the George residence for a party or dance, Leah had stayed in the background, only speaking when someone addressed her. But now she purposefully engaged others, and the quiet wallflower he'd once known shone like a rare diamond, newly polished and cleaned.

Why would a recent widow who'd never before violated any rule of etiquette suddenly invite all manner of rumors by defying society's unspoken rules? Instead of the expected flirtations and outrageous behavior, why would she invite respectable men and women to her country house party and try to justify it as a celebration of her dead husband's life?

The answer was obvious; Sebastian had simply needed to wait for her to reveal herself.

Leah George was lonely.

Three months spent isolated in her widow's weeds, following a year of keeping the secret burden of Ian and Angela's affair all to herself. No wonder she scoffed at his lecture on obedience being better than recklessness; she'd nearly been entombed in her own adherence to society's expectations.

He might have been inclined to feel sympathy for her, or to applaud her courage, if not for the fact that she threatened both Sebastian and Henry with her actions. But he understood her better now, which meant that as long as he could help assuage her loneliness, he might be able to keep her from further scandal.

The only question that remained now was why she refused to admit it to him.

Sebastian stepped forward, his foot landing on the first stair as Leah reached the top. He started to call out.

But though his tongue touched the roof of his mouth for the first syllable of her name, no sound emerged. He let her escape without even demanding to know where she'd been, or where she was going. Instead, he remained frozen on the bottom step, the air where she'd just passed swirling around him, surrounding him.

Taking another breath, Sebastian discovered not the scent of soap, slightly stringent and unapologetic, but . . .

He inhaled again, and wondered.

. . . roses.

Chapter 7

*Did she say anything to you? How can you be
certain she won't tell him?*

"Yesterday Lord Wriothesly informed me that he and
Mr. George shared an affinity for painting. Watercolors, to be exact." Leah gestured toward the five easels
set up on the east side of the house and tried to hide any
betraying expression of smugness. "From this view, the
gentlemen may paint the first rise of the chalk hills, the
Linley Park evergreen garden, or any other subject
which catches your eye."

"The gentlemen, you say?" Mr. Meyer interjected.
"What of the ladies? What will you be doing?"

Leah smiled. "Archery."

Lord Elliot tugged on his ear. "I beg your pardon,
Mrs. George, but I don't know how to paint. And watercolors—"

Beside him, Lady Elliot harrumphed.

"No need to worry," Leah said. "I'm certain Lord
Wriothesly will be more than pleased to assist you in

your first lesson. You will help the others, will you not, my lord?"

For the first time since their conversation the previous day at the lake, she addressed the earl directly. That was one benefit of the eight other guests: with so many people claiming her attention, no one noticed when she avoided him for an entire evening.

Leaning back against the house, Wriothesly crossed his arms over his chest and observed her lazily. "The painting is not an issue, madam. But I must confess to being a bit concerned with the prospect of the ladies practicing archery alone. I shouldn't like for any of you to become hurt."

Over Miss Pettigrew's muttered protest and Mrs. Thompson's subsequent hush, Leah said, "You do remind me of him so much sometimes, my lord. Ian also was very chivalrous. Why, do you remember the time we were walking along the Serpentine and Lady Wriothesly stumbled, injuring her foot? Ian insisted she—"

"I remember," Wriothesly said sharply, straightening away from the wall. Even through her veil, Leah could see the flare of warning in his narrowed eyes. But there was also surprise. She wondered if he was thinking back to all the times the four of them were together, if he was now questioning every seemingly innocent interaction between Ian and Angela.

Not wanting to see the torment from such knowledge on his face, Leah turned her attention back to the women. "Shall we go, ladies?"

"Perhaps I should join them," she heard Mr. Dunlop mutter behind them as they began to walk away.

"Leave them be," replied Lord Cooper-Giles. "If the rest of us must paint watercolors, then you shall, too."

The women strolled down the hill, southeast of the men, toward the open field where the servants were preparing the targets.

"I've never shot a bow and arrow before," Miss Pettigrew confessed.

"Oh, it's quite fun," said Lady Elliot. "Simply imagine the bull's-eye as someone you dislike. I've had the greatest accuracy that way."

Mrs. Meyer grinned and nudged Lady Elliot's shoulder. "It also makes living with one's husband tolerable again, once you've imagined an arrow shot through his forehead."

"My, aren't we a bloodthirsty group?" Leah murmured, smiling. "Who shall you imagine on the target, Mrs. Thompson?"

Though she couldn't have been more than ten years Leah's senior, the severity of her expression often made the other widow appear nearly as old as Mrs. Meyer and Lady Elliot. For a moment she remained quiet, and Leah turned to Miss Pettigrew to save Mrs. Thompson undue embarrassment. But then she spoke . . . or, rather, spat: "Lord Massey."

Leah exchanged curious glances with Mrs. Meyer and Lady Elliot.

But when Mrs. Thompson offered nothing further, Lady Elliot turned to Leah. "And you, Mrs. George? Who will you be shooting today?"

"Unlike the rest of you, I'm quite civilized, thank you," Leah answered. "I merely enjoy archery for the sake of the game."

"Well done," Miss Pettigrew murmured.

"Nonsense," Lady Elliot declared, her brow rising slyly. "What of the earl?"

The rate at which Leah's heart began to race was frankly inexcusable. "The earl?"

"I believe she means Lord Wriothesly," Mrs. Meyer said.

Lady Elliot shifted her parasol to her other shoulder.

"Yes, there seems to be some sort of enmity brewing between the two of you."

Apparently she hadn't been as discreet in avoiding the earl as she'd thought, or as subtle in speech. With her heart threatening to break loose of its restraints and fly out of her chest, Leah sighed and lowered her voice. "I'm afraid Lord Wriothesly doesn't approve of the house party. He'd rather mourn my husband in private, along with Lady Wriothesly, than have such a public spectacle."

There, that was one truth for the day. Of course, it wasn't the entire truth: she didn't mention how she alternated between taking pleasure from provoking him and then feeling distressed when she realized she'd gone too far. Neither did she mention his very clear dislike for her, or that she refused to acquiesce to his demands to act the quiet, mournful little widow.

"But then why did he come?" Miss Pettigrew asked as they neared the table where the archery instruments were laid out for their selection.

Leah shrugged. "He felt it was his duty, I suppose."

"Well, if you truly don't wish to pin him on your target," Lady Elliot said, "then you have my permission to imagine Lord Elliot on yours as well."

"Such generosity, my lady."

Lady Elliot winked. "Fortunately, there's plenty of him to spare."

With laughter and a faint blush from Miss Pettigrew, the women each selected their bows and arrows, then spread out in a row before the targets. A few yards away, Mrs. Meyer instructed Miss Pettigrew on how to position her arrow. Lifting the veil over her head, Leah lined up her target in sight and pulled back her arm.

"A little to the left."

Her fingers slipped. The arrow went flying, then

landed on the ground several feet to the right of the target.

Whirling around, Leah glared at Wriothesly, who nodded toward the stray arrow and smirked. "As I said, you should have aimed farther left." He lifted a brow. "Or perhaps you need proper instruction on how to hold your bow?"

Leah smiled sweetly. "Perhaps you should go stand beside the target and show me exactly where to aim."

He chuckled, and despite still being upset at his words the previous day, Leah couldn't help but be inordinately pleased with herself. It was the first time she'd heard him laugh since the accident.

"Haven't you painting to do?" she asked, reaching for another arrow and turning around again.

"It's the strangest thing," he drawled over her shoulder, so close her fingers fumbled as she attempted to notch the arrow. "I find I haven't the faintest idea how to paint watercolors. My instruction of the other men only leads to formless blobs, and the colors end up running together like mud. Odd, isn't it, considering how much both Ian and I enjoyed the pastime?"

Her elbow made contact with his midsection as she drew back her arm, and although he stepped aside immediately, her entire body froze for at least ten seconds.

Leah narrowed her gaze on the target. "If you mean to forfeit so quickly—"

"Forfeit?" Moving beside her, his fingers wrapped around the arrow, holding it immobile. "Is this a game we are playing, Mrs. George?"

She arched a brow. "I don't believe I said—"

"If it is, I can assure you I will win each challenge. Boating, painting, or any other amusements you have planned. Even though you seemed to have forgotten the fact that you are now a widow, I haven't. And unfortunately, to ensure your proper behavior, I can't allow you to be alone with the other guests."

"I outgrew my nanny when I was six years old, Lord Wriothesly. I hardly think I need another one now."

He opened his mouth as if to speak, then closed it. With a twist of his lips he released the arrow and stepped back. "An opponent, then." He gave a short bow, pivoted, then turned back once more. "Oh, and Mrs. George?"

"Hmm?"

"Do not threaten me again with memories of Ian and Angela. Or you may find that I can best you at that game, as well."

As he walked away, Leah shot the second arrow . . . and gritted her teeth when it glided to a halt on the ground next to the first.

Instead of notching another one, she waited for a footman to retrieve the arrows while she watched Wriothesly approach Miss Pettigrew and Mrs. Meyer out of the corner of her eye.

She could only make out the sound of their voices, but it was clear from the way Miss Pettigrew's face lit up that he'd said something charming.

Then he moved on to Lady Elliot. Then Mrs. Thompson, holding her quiver of arrows as she selected one, leaning over her and managing to say something which made even the straitlaced companion laugh.

Finally, he retreated back toward the easels, not looking once in Leah's direction.

Soon the ladies surrounded Leah.

"Shall we return, then?" Lady Elliot asked.

Miss Pettigrew looked at her companion. "Mrs. Thompson, do you think it's all right?"

"I can't imagine why not. There's certainly nothing improper about the suggestion."

Leah frowned. "What did Lord Wriothesly say?"

Mrs. Meyer glanced toward the gentlemen and smiled. "The men say they need greater inspiration for their artistry than the landscape. They request to paint our portraits."

"How . . . charming," Leah managed, struggling for a gracious tone. Thus Wriothesly ruined another of her amusements by playing on the women's vanity. And, of course, she couldn't stay here and continue with the archery, not if she wished to be a good hostess. "How could we resist such a compliment? The targets may wait."

As they climbed back up the hill, Miss Pettigrew murmured to Mrs. Thompson, "Mr. Dunlop specifically requested me as his subject. Is that not good news?"

"Yes, and I'm supposed to sit for Lord Cooper-Giles," Mrs. Thompson replied. "The baron may have interest in you as well, if he is trying to cozy up to me."

Leah found Wriothesly standing before the easels as they crested the hill, his hands behind his back, feet spread, a curl of amusement on his mouth. Waiting. He'd known they'd come, the devious bastard.

"Well, I don't know what he's up to, but Lord Elliot wants me for his painting," Lady Elliot said, then more softly: "The romantic old fool."

Leah's steps slowed. It was expected for the bachelors to vie for the attention of Miss Pettigrew. Even though she didn't come from the best background, she was very pretty, with her dark curls and wide blue eyes. And she was an heiress, which even gentlemen with the most discriminating of tastes couldn't afford to overlook. But it was quite unusual for a married couple to be paired together.

"It *is* romantic, isn't it?" Mrs. Meyer said to Lady Elliot.

Then she sighed. And it was a very pleased, contented sound.

"May I ask who you'll be sitting for, Mrs. Meyer?"

Leah asked, with only a halfhearted attempt to keep the dread from her voice.

"Why, Mr. Meyer, of course," came the happy reply.

Leah glanced at Wriothesly, who returned her gaze with a smugness she deemed as another of his many, many flaws. She scowled. "Of course."

"Do stop glaring, Mrs. George," Sebastian coaxed, his pencil pausing on the curve of her right cheek. He peered down at the sketch. "How am I to be inspired if you insist on frowning?"

Like the others who had scattered along the east side of the house, Sebastian had chosen a more becoming background to his portrait than the open sky. Positioned at the juncture of the evergreen garden wall, Leah sat surrounded by white laurel shrubs and red-berried holly. Although the setting was beautiful, the ill-tempered widow in the center left much to be desired.

Behind the easel, Sebastian smiled. "Perhaps you could lift your brows a bit, so they're not crouched down as low on your forehead? And if you could not purse your mouth quite so—"

"How is this?"

Sebastian leaned to the side to discover that she had pulled her veil back down over her face. Every feature was obscured; only the whiteness of her skin could be glimpsed behind the dark shadow.

Tapping the pencil against the easel's frame, he said, "I begin to think, my dear Mrs. George, that you have no desire to be painted."

"Not at all, Lord Wriothesly. It's only that I fear my appearance is too offensive to you. How do I know that if I sit here for an hour, it is my portrait you will have painted and not that of your wife? It's difficult to sit here for such a length of time, knowing I will continue being compared to a paragon."

"Ah," he said, their conversation from yesterday surfacing in his mind. The one he had tried throughout the night to forget. "You seek an apology for my rudeness."

"No, I've accepted the fact that rudeness is inherent to your nature. Like your other flaws, it must be difficult for you to resist."

Setting the pencil down, Sebastian slid his stool away from the easel so he could see her without obstruction. His fingers twitched with the impulse to remove her veil; all of a sudden he wanted to see if the mouth which had been so persistent in sulking earlier now tugged upward with her own wit. "My flaws, you say?"

"Are you surprised to hear the plural?"

"Yes, in fact. I wasn't aware I had any."

She snorted, which elicited the beginning of a chuckle from his throat. Stifling his laughter, he said, "Please, do go on." Then he held up his hand. "Wait. Will it take very long to recite this list of the multitude defects in my character?"

The veil swayed as her head tilted to the side. "I'm not certain. I may not be able to remember all of them at the moment."

"But you shall try."

She nodded.

"And I shall paint." He stood and walked across the garden path, the small rocks crunching beneath his feet. Even though he couldn't see her eyes, he bent until they were at the same level. Reaching forward, he grasped the hem of her veil in his fingertips and raised his arms. Slowly, without any reason for such hesitation. Over the slender arch of her bodice, past the pale ivory column of her throat. Her mouth—he paused when it was revealed, pretending to lose hold of the hem. He stared at the bountiful curve of her lips, so full and lush that the small indent at the top of her upper lip was almost nonexistent.

He would never tell her that Angela's mouth had not once entranced him like this.

Clenching the crepe between his fingers, he pulled the veil above her nose, the delicate sculpture of her cheeks. His eyes met hers, and he could no longer pretend they were a plain, ordinary brown. This close, amber striations glinted in their sherry depths, the color made even more stunning by the frame of her dark eyelashes, lavishly thick. Her breath drifted across his lips, an involuntary, invisible kiss, and Sebastian shook, his gloved fingers grazing the slope of her forehead as he dragged the hem over her head.

Immediately he spun upon his heel and returned to the easel, away from her wary gaze. Unable to deny how the breath surged from his chest and the blood pounded in his veins. Disturbed by the sudden, arousing effect of Leah George's unveiling.

"Besides not letting me be alone with my guests, I suppose you don't trust me to lift my own veil, either?" she asked. Her voice had lightened with an idle curiosity, and he could feel her watching him as he settled once more behind the easel.

"Consider it one of my flaws," he said, striving for indifference. As if nothing untoward had happened. "You were going to enumerate them, remember?"

"Ah, yes. I believe I shall begin with . . . controlling."

Sebastian stared at the sketch. Several outlines of leaves, the top of the garden wall, the curve of her cheek. No detail was yet given to her face, but he could imagine each feature, from the stubborn rounding of her chin to the hint of a widow's peak revealed by her veil. Whether he wished it or not, every little aspect of her countenance was imprinted on his vision with startling clarity.

Speak, he commanded himself. She was silent, waiting for him to respond to her comment.

"If I am controlling, it's only to counterbalance the recklessness of your behavior."

"Recklessness?" Her voice came from in front of the easel. "You mean my desire to go boating and practice my archery?"

"The house party. You know it's inappropriate."

"Hmm."

He could almost see her accompanying shrug. But nothing could compel him to glance around the easel at the moment; he'd rather prefer her to be invisible than admit this physical attraction. Instead, he focused on drawing the lines of the brick wall.

"Another one, then," she said a moment later. "You're also very quick-tempered."

"Rarely," he amended, then frowned at the sketch. "And only with you."

"No, no. You can't blame me for your faults, Lord Wriothesly."

"Yet you are the only cause for my aggravation." Moving from the wall, he began the delineation of each leaf on the shrub to her right.

"I see. You refuse to accept responsibility for your own behavior. Shall the next flaw be cowardice?"

Even knowing she meant to provoke him, Sebastian couldn't help the stiffening of his shoulders. "When may I begin to recount the list of your flaws, Mrs. George?" he asked, his gaze flickering to the blank expanse of her face on his portrait.

She laughed softly, and Sebastian closed his eyes. He shouldn't be here. He should be in London with Henry, or now that it was August, moved to the country estate in Hampshire. He wasn't supposed to be in Wiltshire with her, wishing she would confide her secrets to him, listening to the delight in her quiet chuckles, discovering an unexpected allure in her once rather ordinary appearance.

"You may begin now if you like," she said, humor touching her voice the way he imagined it also lit her eyes. "But I can assure you that I'm already well familiar with each of them."

With a deep breath, Sebastian lifted his pencil again, quickly finishing the shrub before he moved on to the next plant. "There is the difference between you and me, Mrs. George. I've learned from my mistakes. While you do not hesitate to recite my faults, I'm far too polite to do the same for you, though I may be sorely tempted."

He waited, then smiled at the following silence. He rather enjoyed the feeling of putting her in her place.

"Self-righteous."

The tip of his pencil stuttered, a long line marring the sketch.

"That's another of your flaws," she said. "In addition to being controlling, quick-tempered, and cowardly."

Unaccountably, the smile stretched wider across his face as he tried to erase the stray mark. "Is that so?"

"Oh, but I forgot the rudeness. That's how we began this conversation, after all."

Sebastian selected his first watercolor, unable to stop smiling. "Tell me, Mrs. George. Is there anything at all in my character to recommend me?"

Again, silence followed his question.

"You know, this is where your habit of lying might be useful," he said.

Another moment passed. "You have nice eyes," she said at last, almost begrudgingly.

"Thank you. But I must point out that my eyes have nothing to do with my character."

"Yes, well, that's all I could think of. For the most part, I find you very irritating."

Before he could stop himself, Sebastian leaned to the side to look at her. "That's comforting to hear, for I don't have very much regard for you, either."

It was a mistake. Immediately, as his eyes met hers and he saw the reluctance in her matching smile, the futility of creating a faceless portrait became clear. Her features were still committed to his memory. His unanticipated and inappropriate attraction to her still remained.

"We've admitted it, then," he said. "Neither of us likes the other. You will continue to do as you please, and I will continue trying to ensure your actions don't lead to speculation about the truth. We are opponents."

She nodded, her smile fading, her gaze never wavering. "Yes," she replied firmly. "Enemies."

Chapter 8

*Tonight was a mistake. If Lord F— hadn't
consumed three glasses of sherry at dinner, I'm
certain he would have seen us hiding there. Oh, but
how I despise these clandestine meetings. Still,
every stolen moment with you is worth a thousand
scandals.*

Later that night, after dinner and three rounds of whist,
after everyone had retired for the evening, Leah lay
awake. For nearly three hours, she'd been unable to
erase from her mind the look in Lord Wriothesly's eyes
when he lifted her veil in the garden. She told herself
she was unsure about what she'd seen. She told herself
she had to be wrong. Most of all, she argued that she
hadn't felt the same awareness of him, either.

As she prepared to turn to her right side yet again, a
quiet knock came at the door. Leah gladly answered the
summons.

It was the butler, Herrod, a lamp lighting the crags at
the corner of his mouth and the hint of jowls sagging

from his chin. "Pardon me, Mrs. George, but it appears one of the guests has availed himself of the late Mr. George's brandy. He's in the study, and became quite surly when I suggested he retire for the night. Would you like me to leave him?"

Leah pulled her wrapper tighter around her waist. "Who is it?" she asked, although she already suspected his identity.

"Lord Wriothesly."

Nodding, she grabbed another lamp from her escritoire and prepared to leave, then thought better of it. "You may go on, Herrod. I'll attend to his lordship in a moment."

"Very good, madam."

Closing the door, she set the lamp aside and searched for a cloak to wear over her wrapper, a pair of shoes to slip on her feet, and a handful of pins to secure her hair in a bun at her neck.

Then she checked the mirror to ensure there was nothing improper in her appearance, reached for the lamp again, and headed downstairs.

Wriothesly was sitting upon the sofa before the fire when she arrived. At the sound of the door opening, his head turned toward her. She didn't know what she'd planned on saying to him, but at the sight of his fevered eyes and flushed cheeks, she faltered.

"Lord Wriothesly?"

He didn't answer.

"Are you—are you quite all right? Herrod told me you were here."

She inched toward the sofa, unnerved by the way the flames and shadows reflected in his eyes, setting an unholy gleam in his gaze. She would have welcomed any words to break the silence, even if it meant another lecture. But he only continued to stare, watching with a savage intensity as she approached.

She came to a halt a few feet from him, at the end of the sofa. "Would you like me to retrieve a footman?" she asked. "Do you need assistance returning to—"

"Come closer."

The words were low, not slurred as she'd expected. Still, she spied a brandy decanter clutched in one hand and a snifter in the other. The decanter was nearly two-thirds empty.

"Come, Mrs. George. Do not act the timid waif with me now. I've been waiting for you."

She remained firmly in place. Even though she wouldn't ordinarily consider Wriothesly a dangerous man, something about the way he looked at her made her think that she had a right to be timid tonight. In fact, she should probably run back to her bedchamber and let him drown his grief and anger with the liquor. But although she didn't take a step forward as he requested, neither did she retreat.

"Why have you been waiting for me?" she asked, folding her arms across her waist as if it could provide a buffer from his gaze. As much as she loathed her widow's entrapments, she wished for the security of her veil tonight.

His eyes narrowed at her disobedience, but then he shrugged and poured himself another finger of brandy. He consumed it with one swallow, tilting his head back so that the firelight stroked across the muscles of his throat as he drank.

Leah averted her gaze to the decanter, concentrated on the side-to-side swirl of liquid as it slowly steadied. When the snifter lowered beside the bottle on his lap, she looked at him again.

He was smiling, but it wasn't a real smile. Only one side of his mouth angled upward, his lips stretched not with humor but with a challenge. "Come closer, Mrs. George," he repeated. "I wish to smell you."

Yes, he's drunk, she decided. Fortified by this conclusion, she laughed and lowered her arms. Leaning against the arm of the sofa, she asked, "Smell me, my lord? Haven't you already said I don't smell like a woman? Surely there's no reason—"

He waved her off with the decanter. "I don't remember what you smelled like in the garden today. I want to know if you're wearing the rose perfume again."

Leah shook her head. "My lord, I know that you're inebriated, but I don't understand your meaning."

"Last night. I saw you, in that same cloak, walking up the stairs. You smelled like roses, and I thought . . ." His brow lowered, and he looked away, into the fire.

"I was in the flower garden."

"Yes. Of course you were."

"The roses are in bloom."

He nodded, then poured more brandy into his glass.

"But . . ." She gave a disbelieving laugh. "You thought I wore rose perfume for you? Because of what you said?"

He swallowed the entire amount again.

"My lord, I do believe I shall have to add 'arrogant' to your list of flaws."

Looking down at the brandy, he muttered, "I don't like to drink."

"Yes, I can see that," she said dryly. Moving toward him, she removed the snifter and decanter from his grip and set them atop the mantel. "I'm going to ring for someone to help you up the stairs."

"Don't. I want to stay here, with you. I want to . . . talk with you."

Leah strode toward the bellpull. "It's past two, my lord, and—"

"What did the letters say?"

She stilled, her fingers tight around the rope. She glanced over her shoulder.

A pin loosened at the sudden movement, a lock falling to lie against her neck.

Wriothesly had sprawled on the sofa: one arm was thrown across the curved back, the other dangling carelessly over the edge. His legs were spread wide, his head laid against the leather cushions as he stared at the ceiling. Never before had she seen him submit to such casual abandonment.

"You did read them, didn't you?" he asked.

Her first instinct was to deny it; but the quiet bleakness of his tone kept the lie still on her tongue.

"Mrs. George?"

"Yes, I read the letters. Not all of them, but a few."

"Did you burn them afterward?"

"No. I kept them."

He sighed. "Why should I be surprised?"

"They're in my desk. Would you like me to retrieve them? I could read them to you if you like."

"No." He lifted his arm and draped it across his eyes. "Thank you, but I want you to tell me."

Leah strolled toward him and sat on the opposite end of the sofa, her hands on her knees. Another pin came loose as she looked into the fire, and a long silence passed as she tried to tuck her hair back into the bun.

"Does this mean you refuse?" he drawled.

"Just one moment." Despite her best efforts, the same stray locks kept falling down. She knew if she couldn't pin them up again, the entire bun would soon unravel about her shoulders. And although the earl had accused her of courting scandal with her behavior, her desire for independence didn't slip into this realm of impropriety. And certainly not with him.

"Here, allow me." His weight shifted, making her sink toward him as she fought for balance. His breath blew across her ear as he took the pins from her fingers.

"I don't need your help," she protested, twisting to

reclaim them. Then she turned back around immediately, for he was unbearably close, so close her nose had
nearly brushed against his.

"Be still. I would hate to accidentally stab you. I've
had quite a bit of brandy, you know."

Leah barely breathed when his fingertips swept
across the nape of her neck. And despite the heat of the
fire and the warmth emanating from his body, she shiv-
ered at the touch of his hand on her head as he secured
the pins in place. Likely he wasn't aware of what he was
doing; surely he wouldn't have taken such a liberty had
he not been drunk.

He patted her hair on both sides of the bun, then
pulled away to settle himself in his former position, his
arm flung over his eyes. Leah took a long breath, her
equilibrium slowly returning.

"The letters," he prompted.

She shifted to face him, warily watching should he
find another reason to advance toward her. "What
would you like to know?"

"I want you to tell me it was just lust."

Leah sucked in a breath at his frankness, at the quiet
plea in his words. She wanted to lie to him. In fact, it
would be rather easy to do so. But she couldn't. "I believe she loved him." When he didn't speak, she added,
"Of course, I don't have any letters that Ian wrote, but
the words that Lady Wriothesly penned made me
think the affair was . . . It wasn't only about the physical act."

He made a low sound in his throat, one that brought
to mind an animal in pain. "Did she explicitly say she
loved him?" Leah winced at the hoarseness in his voice,
even though the words were spoken matter-of-factly.

"Yes."

"That's not enough." Drawing his arm away, he lifted

his head and met her gaze. "Lovers often confess their love, even when it's not true. I could say I loved you right now and try to seduce you."

"I would never fall prey to such tricks. And we both know you wouldn't try to seduce me." The idea of anyone touching her like Ian had was too foreign. The thought of *Wriothesly* touching her was ... disturbing. Her breath caught, much the same way it had when he lifted her veil earlier in the garden, when his fingers had played in her hair as he fixed the pins. Even though his features might hold a certain appeal, she no longer desired such false intimacies from anyone. Not after offering her soulless body to Ian again and again.

He stared at her, the fire sending shadows to flicker across his eyes. Then his mouth tilted in a hint of a smile. "No, I wouldn't," he said.

One thing was certain: he did have a rather unique talent for making her feel unattractive.

Laying his head back, he asked, "What more was there?"

Leah hesitated. "Perhaps you should read the letters, if you wish to see the proof yourself."

"If you fear my wrath toward you for being the bearer of bad news, you have nothing to worry about. I'm asking you to tell me."

When she said nothing, he flicked his hand. "Go on."

"She wanted to leave you," she said in a rush, then paused, waiting for his reaction. He didn't move; for a moment, it seemed even his chest would not rise with breath. "They were making plans to flee England—"

"To go where?"

"France. Paris first, then—"

"The fools. I would have followed them."

"They were to go into hiding."

He pulled himself up from the sprawl, his movements

now rigid. "I would have found them," he said, then cut his eyes toward her as if demanding she acknowledge it as truth.

Leah spread her hands wide. "As I said, they appeared to be in love, my lord."

"And I suppose that's better?"

She began to nod, but something in his expression stopped her. He needed her to tell the truth, just as she'd needed to see his grief and anger after he'd first learned of their betrayal. To know she wasn't alone.

She looked away. "Perhaps not. But it makes me feel . . . less unworthy."

Silence lengthened between them, and she could feel him watching her. "I am sorry for my comments at the lake," he finally said. "I shouldn't have compared you to her. I shouldn't have been rude. Actually, you're quite pretty—"

Laughing, she turned to him. "Please. There's no need for flattery. I didn't mean unworthy in that sense."

In fact, it was almost more of an insult for him to believe he needed to shore up her self-esteem.

His lips pressed together, as if he were deciding whether to respond. Instead, he stood from the sofa. "I need another drink."

"My lord—"

"You still haven't told me the truth, Mrs. George."

"Which truth?" she asked, tensing when he weaved back and forth.

Returning to sit, he filled the glass. But this time, he sipped at it slowly, closing his eyes as he swallowed. Holding out the snifter toward her, he said, "Why you decided to host a house party."

She shook her head and pushed his hand away. "As I said, I wanted to help you."

"Liar. You're much too selfish. For some strange reason it's one of the things I like best about you."

Leah tilted her chin and smiled. "I thought we disliked each other."

"Oh, we do," he said, taking another sip. "I detest you quite thoroughly. Especially when you smile."

Her lips flattened. "Do you?"

He gestured toward her with the drink, the liquid sloshing out the side to drip over his thigh. Leah's gaze followed the brandy's path where it darkened on his trousers, then jerked upward again as he spoke. "You're too bloody happy. It's very offensive."

"Indeed?" she said, trying not to smile again.

"And there it is." He scowled, then swallowed the rest of the brandy. "If you wish to be a competent hostess, you will endeavor to be miserable. I might detest you less if you acted a bit more pathetic now and then."

"I see." She paused as he bent to set the decanter and snifter on the floor. "It will pass, you know. Eventually."

"I should mention that I also disapprove of optimism."

She laughed, disarmed by this drunken, jaunty version of Lord Wriothesly. Without the brandy, he would have almost resembled the man she remembered prior to Ian's death.

"And now I believe I shall put my head on you," he announced. "The room has started to spin, and it's been a very long time since I've laid my head in a woman's lap."

Leah ceased laughing as he twisted and began to lie back. "No, my lord." His shoulders landed on her outstretched arms. "Sebastian! Let me up."

He groaned as she struggled against him. "I was beginning to wonder if you remembered my name. Please, be quiet. Just a moment." Reaching behind his head, he caught her hand and moved it to his mouth, where he pressed a kiss against her bare skin. "Only a moment, until the world turns itself aright again."

Leah snatched her hand back, irritated by the lingering sensation left by his lips. He then took advantage by leveraging his weight against her, forcing her to allow him to lie down.

With her hands pressed tightly against her chest—for there was nowhere else to put them—she stared down at him, bemused.

His head was turned toward the fire, his eyes closed. "Thank you," he said, and sighed. "I believe I might fall asleep."

"If you do, I promise to shove you off."

He chuckled, and her gaze skipped over the crook of his lips, noting the faint shadow of stubble extending across his jaw.

Leah glanced at the mantel clock over the hearth. "I'll give you five minutes, nothing more," she said.

"You are a generous woman, Mrs. George."

As the minutes ticked by, she tried to keep herself occupied by watching the fire. It was burning down, only the smallest of flames licking now at the coals. Soon it would be nothing more than embers, waiting for a servant to enter before dawn and stir it to life again.

Yet, as much as she sought to dwell on the fire, her gaze kept returning to the man laid prostrate across her lap, his head pillowed upon her thighs. She noted the meager crescent of his eyelashes, the straight blade of his nose. His hair was a deep, dark brown, growing thickly and trimmed neatly at the ends.

She was well aware when the five minutes passed, and yet she didn't speak. A low rumble sounded from his chest as it began to rise and fall in a slow, steady motion.

After a while one hand drifted toward his hair—of its own accord, she decided—and sifted through the dark, silken strands. She smoothed his hair away from his ear, dragged her fingers down to his nape, caressed the skin there with the pad of her thumb.

If he had stirred she would have yanked her hands away, pretending that he'd dreamed her touch. But he didn't wake, and she continued combing her fingers through his hair, finding a sensual contentment in the repetition of each soft stroke against the flesh of her palm.

At last her arm grew weary and she withdrew, tucking her hand against her side. Though her eyelids felt leaden and the heat of his body was comforting after so many nights spent alone, she couldn't fall asleep with him. In only a few hours the servants would waken. She didn't want them to find her with Wriothesly. Neither did she welcome the sort of familiarity that came with having a man pressed against her through the night, even though the circumstances were entirely innocent.

"Sebastian," she whispered, and touched his shoulder.

His chest paused at a rise, then fell sharply.

"Sebastian," she murmured, shaking him slightly. "Wake up."

His head turned away from the fire, facing upward on her lap.

She sighed. "Sebastian—"

Then his eyes opened, slowly, and met hers. His splendid, forest-depths green eyes. Eyes that one might never tire of looking into.

And Leah realized she'd become far more affected by him than she wished.

Chapter 9

*I'm sorry. He changed his mind at the last minute
and decided not to go. He said he wanted my
company tonight. Don't worry. He didn't touch
me. I miss you.*

The next afternoon, while the guests sorted through
wigs and costumes and props for the forthcoming
tableaux vivants, Leah excused herself to see to her cor-
respondence.

Her first inclination as she sat at the small desk in her
bedchamber was to fold her arms and lay her head
down. She hadn't slept much the previous night, even
after seeing that Wriothesly was escorted to his bedchamber.

Though she tried to forget, she kept recalling the feel
of his hair beneath her fingers, the unexpected comfort
of having him lie against her while she watched him
sleep. Nor could she erase the memory of his breath on
her ear and neck as he replaced the pins, or the warm
press of his lips against her bare hand. She'd enjoyed his

company, drunk though he was, just as much as she'd taken pleasure in his nearness and the way he touched her. It was the knowledge of the latter that tugged at her thoughts and turned her limbs restless so that she tossed from side to side. It was the realization of her own physical response to him that made her . . . frightened.

Only when the sun had risen did her body finally succumb to exhaustion, her mind allowed a brief reprieve for precisely five hours before a maid came to wake her.

She missed breakfast, but apparently so did the earl. Nor did he join her and the other guests when they took a morning ride over the grounds. When he didn't appear for lunch and a servant reported that no answer had been given to his knock, she could only assume that he was still sleeping off the effects of the liquor. Privately, she hoped he remained secluded in his bedchamber for the rest of the day.

With a tired sigh, Leah straightened her posture and reached for the first envelope on the desk. The aggressive slant of her mother's handwriting laced across the front. That one could wait, then. Adelaide had probably heard of the house party and demanded to know why Leah had decided to disgrace herself, her mother and father, her sister, all of her extended relatives, and so on.

It was the next four letters that Leah had been waiting for, responses to her invitations for the dinner party on the last night of the house party. There would be dancing afterward—one of the few activities planned for the house party that Ian had actually enjoyed. It would also be her first opportunity to dance since the carriage accident—a self-test.

Even now, after four months of being relegated to the periphery of society, after examining her heretofore dedication to all the rules and obligations and deciding that her own happiness was more important than obedience, a part of her still balked at the idea of violating the mourning rituals to such an extent. Yes, the very thought of dancing cotillions, quadrilles, and waltzes hour after hour set her blood to racing with anticipation, but dancing was far different from boating on a lake, practicing archery, or even being so bold as to host a house party so soon after her husband's death.

Besides the fact that it was possible no one would want to be her partner, she still wasn't certain if she wanted to invite that kind of scandal. Not because she feared Lord Wriothesly or his predictions about her behavior risking the revelation of Ian and Angela's affair, but simply because, despite her wish for independence to do as she wished, it remained difficult to free herself from her role of quiet observer. The woman who watched everyone else live their lives, who analyzed their speech and actions, who admired the vivacity and charm of women like Angela but was content to allow someone else such a place of prominence.

But the dinner party was three days away, and she had until then to make her decision. Regardless of whether she danced or not, the others could enjoy themselves, and the house party would end with a fitting farewell. One last tribute to Ian's memory, as her guests believed.

Sorting through the four final responses she'd received this morning, Leah found only one to be a note declining the invitation. In all, then, there would be nine more guests, mostly local Wiltshire gentry who favored the company of the aristocracy. In truth, it was a much better response than she'd expected.

Rising from the desk, she sent a look of longing toward her bed. A good hostess would return to her guests at once; it wouldn't be very polite to leave them alone for more than a half hour, as she'd done already.

But they *were* occupied getting ready for the presentation of the *tableaux vivants* the next day, and as a recent widow she could now be excused far more easily than she would have been otherwise. Leah thought of Wriothesly, still asleep in his bed. If nothing else, she was much more tired than he was.

Walking to the bellpull, she rang for a servant to take a message to the guests downstairs.

God, his head ached. Sebastian nodded, wincing, as Miss Pettigrew went on about the part she wanted him to act in her scene for the *tableaux vivants*. Unlike the others, she hadn't selected a famous painting to portray, but the stabbing scene from Shakespeare's *Julius Caesar*. Thus, Sebastian was supposed to kneel on the floor while Lord Baron-Giles and Mr. Dunlop aimed knives at his torso.

A spectacular fun time, that's what it would be.

And where was Leah?

For the past two hours he'd been pulled back and forth across the rose salon by each of the ladies, all claiming they needed his assistance to play a part in this pastoral scene or that painting of God's retribution on earth. Various wigs had been shoved onto his head—men's and ladies' alike; garters and hose had been tossed at his feet, a doublet and a bow and arrow thrust into his hands. And from the looks of it, he wasn't alone. The other men appeared to be suffering the same fate. Sebastian wasn't sure whether Leah had planned the *tableaux vivants* as amusement or torture for her male guests.

She was supposed to have a headache. That's what Herrod had announced shortly after Sebastian had joined the others downstairs. The ladies had murmured their concern and cast glances back and forth, their thoughts more than transparent.

Surely, their expressions said, Mrs. George must be suffering a bout of grief over Mr. George. The poor, dear thing.

Sebastian was more inclined to believe she was avoiding him. Unfortunately, he wasn't exactly certain about the reason. He didn't remember everything that had occurred in Ian's study the previous evening, but he remembered enough. Drinking far too much brandy. Speaking about Ian and Angela. A fascination he seemed to have developed for Leah's nape as his fingers reveled in the softness of her hair.

Although he couldn't recall much of their discussion about Ian and Angela beyond Leah's claim that they had meant to run away together, and he was still trying to figure out why he had touched her hair, beyond either of these he was far more disturbed by the memory of laying his head upon her lap. *That* he remembered, and much too well.

He recalled not only lying down and feeling the surprising softness of her thighs beneath his head, but falling asleep to the rhythm of her breathing and the gentle strokes of her fingers in his hair. Waking to the mildly exasperated but low and throaty sound of her voice, thinking as he stared into her tired brown eyes above him that he never wanted to move again.

Earlier, when Herrod had first sent her regrets that she wouldn't be able to return for a while due to her headache, Sebastian had been relieved. He didn't want to see her again. Inside, where she wore a widow's cap instead of a veil, it would be easier to read her expression. And God, but he didn't want to see the same acknowledgment in her eyes that he'd been forced to make that morning when he woke. The same realization that there was more between them now than only Ian and Angela's secret.

"Here you are, Lord Wriothesly," Miss Pettigrew said, appearing before him again with some sort of wreath in her hands. Sebastian peered down at the evergreen and the little red beads meant to represent holly berries. "For your head," she said, reaching upward.

Sebastian stilled the movement and took the wreath away. "I don't believe this is the sort of thing the Romans wore on their heads."

She bit her lip and nodded reluctantly. "Yes, but it was all I could find."

"I've agreed to wear a toga, Miss Pettigrew."

She beamed, her expression a mastery of sincerity and innocence. "I can't thank you enough, my lord, for your help—"

"A *toga*." He arched a brow.

Miss Pettigrew's smile faded. "Yes, you're right, of course." She removed the wreath from his grip. "This headpiece won't do at all."

As she turned away, Sebastian glanced at Lord Elliot on the opposite side of the room. He wore a brown robe belted around his abundant waist, a forked tree branch held as a shepherd's crook in his right hand. Mr. Meyer stood nearby, his head bent to accommodate Lady Elliot as she painted his cheeks with charcoal. Sebastian cast both men a commiserating look. The only two who appeared to enjoy the attention were Cooper-Giles and Dunlop, though perhaps they were more enamored of the beatific smile Miss Pettigrew showered upon them as she passed rather than the particular roles they'd each been assigned.

Yes, at first Sebastian had been relieved to find Leah absent, but that had been two hours ago. Now he was simply irritated. He waited until Mrs. Meyer approached Lord Elliot with a pair of worn old shoes that, with a few more holes in them, might have resembled sandals. Then Sebastian caught her before she could return to the trunks. He drew her to the side, a few feet away from the others.

"I'm beginning to become concerned about Mrs. George," he said, keeping his voice low. "I know she confessed to having a headache, but in all the time I've known her since she married Mr. George, never once do I recall her neglecting her guests in this manner."

Mrs. Meyer clasped her hands at her waist and leaned forward. "But I don't believe she does have a headache, my lord," she whispered.

"No?"

She shook her head. "She seemed very pale this morning, and drawn. And her eyes were red."

Sebastian frowned at this description. Perhaps she *was* ill.

"I believe she's been crying, my lord," Mrs. Meyer said. "I fear she's still far from finished grieving for him. Although it was a nice gesture, perhaps having the house party and talking about everything Mr. George enjoyed was too much."

"Hmm. I agree. Thank you, Mrs. Meyer."

She curtsied, and then smiled up at him. "I must say, my lord, that toga is very fetching on you."

Sebastian did his best not to look annoyed. "I'm going to find a servant to look in on Mrs. George," he announced, then strode to the door.

"But, my lord . . ." Mrs. Meyer's voice followed him into the hallway, soon subsiding beneath the sound of his footsteps on the floor.

Sebastian found a housemaid who directed him to Herrod. "I would like to see Mrs. George," he told the butler.

"I'm sorry, my lord, but Mrs. George is currently unavailable."

"Yes, I know. That's why I would like to see her." If he had to endure being dressed and made to feel like a doll in the middle of a game of make-believe, then she damn well wasn't allowed to hide away in her room. Unless she was truly ill. And then Sebastian wanted to see the proof; he'd seen her play poor little widow far too many times not to be aware of her attempted acting skills.

Unfortunately, the butler merely stared at Sebastian with a mask of patient tolerance on his face. "Mrs. George is not to be disturbed," he said, his blue eyes turning to steel behind his spectacles.

Sebastian inclined his head. "Very well."

Then he turned and headed toward the staircase. True, he wasn't certain if she still kept the mistress' bedchamber, but he knew where the master bedchamber was, and the room next to it seemed like a fairly good place to start. Herrod followed him up the stairs.

"My lord."

Sebastian turned down the right side of the corridor, heading toward the fifth door on the left.

"My lord!"

He halted before the door and watched as Herrod approached, his breath wheezing from the effort of chasing after him. Sebastian lifted a brow. "Shall I enter, or would you like to speak to her first?"

"Neither!" the butler whispered furiously. "Mrs. George is unavailable to see her guests because she is sleep—"

Sebastian opened the door and stepped inside.

"—ing," Herrod finished with a sigh.

"Sleeping?" And indeed, it appeared to be true. Across the room, curled up in the center of the bed, Leah had her eyes closed, her mouth parted slightly, one hand flung out across the counterpane. Sebastian turned to the butler, frowning. "Is she ill? Has someone sent for a physician?"

No other glare had ever been so self-righteous. "I believe Mrs. George is simply tired, my lord," the butler said, both his voice and expression acerbic. "There was a problem with one of the guests quite late last night."

"Ah." And now he felt like a bastard.

Herrod nodded and waved his hand toward the hallway. "If you would come with me . . ."

"Yes, of course."

But before he could leave, her voice reached out and stopped him. "Sebastian?"

Not Lord Wriothesly, but Sebastian. Said in the same low, throaty tone—exhausted tone, he realized now—

from the previous night. And just as the sound of her speaking his name in the study had caught him off balance as he'd tried to lay his head upon her lap, he found himself turning around, looking to her to set the world to rights again.

She was struggling to sit up, the bedspread tangled about her torso. "What are you doing here?" she asked, her gaze skipping behind him—to Herrod, he presumed.

"My apologies, madam," the butler said. "I was just escorting Lord Wriothesly out."

She blinked, pushing her hair behind her shoulders, tucking it behind her ears. Sebastian stared, enchanted by the simple, almost childlike gesture, watching as the sleep-induced confusion cleared from her eyes and she narrowed her gaze at him.

"The guests are downstairs. Am I now to understand you don't trust me to be alone in my bedchamber, my lord?" she asked, lifting her chin. "Or is sleeping in the middle of the day considered reckless behavior?"

"I beg your pardon, Mrs. George," Herrod tried again from behind Sebastian. "Lord Wriothesly and I will leave you to—"

Sebastian smiled and stepped forward until he stood at the foot of the bed. "Would you believe that I was worried about you?"

She gave a little huff of disbelief. "No." Then, as if she were suddenly aware of more than his presence, of her state of undress in the bed while he stood only a few feet away, she scowled. "Turn around."

Sebastian made a point of studying first her unbound hair, then the lace edges of the nightgown which peeked out from the counterpane and swathed her neck and wrists. Finally, the violet-adorned bedspread which covered everything from her chest to the tips of her toes. "It's too late," he drawled. "I think I've already been compromised."

Herrod cleared his throat at the door.

"Oh, for heaven's sake," Leah exclaimed, then reached behind her and threw a pillow at Sebastian.

"I'm glad to see your strength hasn't waned," he said. His gaze followed the path of the pillow, which had missed by about a foot and now lay well beyond his left shoulder. He looked back at her. "I thought you might be ill."

He could almost hear her grinding her teeth. "I'm not."

"Are you certain? Your face appears flushed. Perhaps I should feel your forehead to see if you have a fever—"

"Herrod . . ." Though she spoke to her servant, she saved the murderous glare for Sebastian alone. He felt rather flattered.

"Yes, Mrs. George." This time, the butler actually took hold of Sebastian's arm.

"We shall see you soon, then?" Sebastian asked as he was steered toward the corridor.

Another pillow hit the back of his knee.

"Much better," he called. "It's clear you're improving—"

Herrod shut the door and released his arm. "Does your lordship need assistance in finding the rose salon again?" he asked, the thin veneer of politeness doing nothing to conceal his displeasure.

"No, thank you. I believe I know the way."

The butler smiled tightly and tipped his head toward the staircase. "As you wish, my lord."

Sebastian strolled down the corridor, well aware Herrod followed him a few paces behind. As he descended the staircase, he found Mrs. Meyer, Lady Elliot, and a housemaid climbing up.

"Oh, there you are, my lord," Mrs. Meyer said. "Did a servant see to Mrs. George? Is she well?"

He nodded solemnly. "As well as can be expected. I

fear you were correct in your assumption, Mrs. Meyer. The grief . . ."

"Oh, dear."

Lady Elliot pursed her lips.

"Well, let us return to the salon and continue preparing the *tableaux vivants*," Sebastian suggested. "Perhaps Mrs. George will join us in a little while, and I'd like her to see how far we've come."

As one, they started down the steps again, Mrs. Meyer murmuring beneath her breath, "Poor Mrs. George. Oh, the poor dear."

There was something about being awakened by Lord Wriothesly's voice earlier in the afternoon that banished Leah's exhaustion for the rest of the day, even though she'd had only a few hours of sleep. When it was time for the evening's entertainment after dinner, she cheerfully led everyone out the front door and across the lawn.

At the crest of the hill where it evened out before descending toward the lake, the servants had arranged a surfeit of blankets and cushions upon the ground. One footman remained to the side, near an iced bucket of champagne. On the other side stood a low table on which perched the object of honor for the night: a telescope.

She'd had an opportunity to toy with it only a few times since buying it in London before the house party, and she was looking forward to searching for the constellations again, hopefully with the aid of someone who had more experience with such instruments.

Setting her lamp on the table beside the telescope, she turned to the guests. She wore no veil tonight, for it was difficult enough to see in the darkness without it before her face. Even with the backlight of the house in the distance and the lamps on either side of the blankets, the guests were little more than outlines and shadows beneath the velvet night sky.

Leah smiled and extinguished her lamp, leaving only the light from the footman on the far side. Somewhere in the middle of the group, someone squealed. Mrs. Meyer, probably; for despite Miss Pettigrew's innocent act she seemed far too sensible, and Leah doubted Lady Elliot would cry out even if a bat winged down from the sky and brushed across her head.

Out of the dark came Lord Wriothesly's droll voice. "Oh yes, astronomy. I had forgotten how much Ian liked to gaze upon the stars."

Unperturbed, Leah replied, "It was by far one of his favorite hobbies." Tilting her head up, she twirled in a slow circle. "I remember the many times we would come out here and lie on the grass for hours. Ian would name each constellation, one by one, and recite the myths lest I forget the beauty behind the science."

It was something she dreamed of doing now, though the man beside her in her imagination was nameless, his face made invisible by the night. At times she wondered whether there would ever be someone else; after Ian, she found it difficult to believe she could find enough faith to bestow upon another man.

"Mr. Dunlop, Mrs. Thompson," she said. "Would you like to be the first to take a turn at the telescope?"

Soon everyone else had spread out on the ground, some with glasses of champagne in their hands. The dark shapes of Mr. Dunlop's and Mrs. Thompson's heads bent over the telescope.

Leah curled her legs beneath her skirts and leaned back against a cushion. Apart from the flower garden, this was one of the loveliest places at Linley Park in the evening. On the crest of the hill, one could look out over the lake and see the moon and stars reflected on its silvered surface. And while the smoke and fog clouded the sky in London, out here the air was so piercingly clear that it ached in one's lungs and made it possible to believe that every single star was visible to the naked eye, with no need for a man-made instrument.

Nearby, she could hear Lord and Lady Elliot debating good-naturedly the name of the constellation formed by a cluster of stars which hung like a brilliant white sapphire over the lake. Leah took a sip of her champagne and sighed quietly.

This was what she'd wanted. This was the reason why she'd decided to host the house party. Shared pleasure in the things that made her happy; company to ease her loneliness without intruding upon any other emotion. The simplicity of amusement for amusement's sake, and the freedom to choose who she would be in the future while yet still clothed in the black regrets and memories of her dead husband.

After a while Mr. Dunlop and Mrs. Thompson sat down, and Baron Cooper-Giles and Miss Pettigrew moved to the telescope.

A large shape sat down beside her. Now that her eyes were accustomed to the darkness, she could see it was Lord Wriothesly.

"I'm glad to see you're feeling better," he said, moving a cushion so he could recline and stretch out his legs. Lowering his voice, he added, "Although next time I would advise you to lock your door."

Leah gave him a mocking smile. "What an excellent idea. However, I assure you that if I had any reason to believe someone would enter uninvited, it would have been locked."

He nodded and looked up at the sky, giving her the impression that he wasn't quite paying attention to her. "I think this is the best idea so far," he said. "When I was a boy, my father would take me out into the garden and have me point out the constellations. He wanted to make sure I was attending to my lessons."

A moment passed, and then he chuckled. "Of course,

each time I would have to recite them in different languages. Latin, French, Italian. I was a very well-rounded little astronomer."

Leah looked at him. "I'm sure you—"

She entirely forgot the words she'd meant to say. The lamplight at the side cast a golden glow over his features, and though she shouldn't have found him appealing, the wistful expression on his face as he stared up at the sky made her breath catch in her throat. Then it seemed only natural for her gaze to trace over the line of his jaw and down his neck, over the long, lean planes of his torso.

"This is actually something Ian would have enjoyed, you know," he said, and Leah looked upward just as he turned toward her with a crook of his lips.

She shifted away, darting a glance toward Miss Pettigrew and the baron. "Yes, I know. That's precisely why I chose to do it."

"Hmm." The sound was partial consideration, partial disbelief.

Leah sat up. Even having moved a few inches away from him, their positions beside each other on the cushions was too close, too . . . disconcerting. She waited a few more moments, and although he didn't say anything else, it was still too much.

She stood and went to the telescope, leaving the earl behind without a word.

Lord Cooper-Giles was adjusting the eyepieces. "There, have another try."

Miss Pettigrew bent over, peering through the lens. "Oh, there it is. I can see Orion now." Glancing up, she spied Leah. "Here, Mrs. George, you should look, too. Quickly, lest I lose the angle."

Leah stepped forward as Miss Pettigrew moved aside. "Thank you," she murmured absently, then stooped to look through the telescope. "Oh, yes, I see it," she said.

In truth, her eyes refused to focus on any pattern. Even though she had no reason to believe he was staring at her, still she imagined Wriothesly watching every movement she made. She swung the scope in an arc, searching for any likely shape or form which she could name as a constellation. But as the minutes lapsed and the scope moved in every direction the mount would allow, her mind refused to make sense of the images she saw. All she was aware of was the presence of Wriothesly nearby, and the thought that he might or might not be presently looking at her. Silently cursing, Leah straightened and gestured for Miss Pettigrew to take the telescope.

Once again, the Earl of Wriothesly had managed to ruin one of her most-treasured amusements.

Sebastian sat in a chair before the hearth in his bed-chamber. The constellation viewing had ended a few hours ago, and he should have been asleep in his bed like everyone else.

And he had tried. He'd undressed and climbed beneath the sheets. He had even closed his eyes and measured his breathing until it reached a slow, even pace. But nothing could induce him to fall asleep when images of Leah continued teasing his mind.

The fact that she'd nearly all but run away from him during the evening's entertainment should have set him at ease. If nothing else, it told him that she neither wanted nor welcomed his friendship, nor anything else beyond a polite acquaintance. But though he should have been content with her reaction and allowed it to distract his own wayward attraction to her, he found he wanted nothing more than to pursue.

He wanted to investigate her vulnerabilities, to understand the mystery of Leah George that kept him fascinated when by all rights he should dismiss her as nothing more than a source of aggravation. He wanted to get close enough to see through every layer, then satisfy his curiosity and walk away.

He shouldn't be sitting here, dwelling on the sweet curve of her mouth. And his attraction to her shouldn't make him question whether the woman he'd loved for more than three years had only been a beautiful facade that he'd invented to match his own desires.

The chair toppled over as Sebastian stood. Scrubbing his hands over his face and then into his hair, he strode from one side of the room to the other.

He'd loved *Angela*, not some caricatured ideal his imagination had conjured. He knew it with every breath he breathed, every beat of his heart, with all the certainty of his own existence. He had loved her, and if he had known about the affair, he would have done everything he could to make Angela choose him. If he'd known, he would have won her back, no matter the cost, and she wouldn't now be dead. Nor Ian, either. And he, Angela, and Henry would be together again, with Ian and Leah somewhere hundreds of miles away.

Sebastian swung around, sweat beginning to bead on his brow from the humidity of the summer evening. Moving toward the window, he braced his forehead against the pane, but it was hardly cooler than the bedchamber. With a low curse, he found the lock on the window and started to push it open, when a sight below in the flower garden arrested his attention.

Leah, sitting on a bench, the telescope perched beside her on a low table. The moon and the starlight limned her features as her head lay tilted back, the hood of her cloak open to reveal the sweep of her unbound hair.

Sebastian pivoted away from the window, his mouth set in a grim line. Damn the consequences. This would end now.

Chapter 10

I read the Romeo and Juliet sonnet you gave me every day. I fear the paper is now stained with my tears. I will forever be yours as well, "in longest night, or in the shortest day," "in heaven, in earth, or else in hell."

She continued looking at the sky as he approached. For some reason, Sebastian found this annoying. Though they were in the middle of the countryside, she was out in the middle of the night, with only a lamp and presumably no weapon aside from the heavy brass telescope sitting nearby. He could have been anyone.

He halted a foot away from the bench, directly opposite from her, and waited for her to acknowledge him.

Leah lowered her head, nodded, and pointed to a nearby rosebush. "I might smell like roses again," she warned him. When he didn't respond, she returned her gaze to the sky and said, "I found Orion. And Hydra. Cassiopeia. Aries."

"I know why you decided to host the house party."

"Do you? And what conclusion have you drawn?"

Sebastian was silent, entranced by the pale skin of her throat and the movement of her lips as she looked up, as though she were waiting for a kiss to be dropped from the heavens.

She met his gaze and gave a halfhearted smile. "Did you decide that I was lonely, my lord? Is that why you're here?"

Sebastian sat down beside her.

"Why are you here?" she repeated. He noticed she shifted away, pressing as far as she could into the corner of the bench.

"*Are* you lonely?" he countered. There was something about witnessing Leah pull her invisible armor about herself that made him not want to push as hard. The frustration of a moment before subsided in her presence. He wanted to draw her out, little by little; he wouldn't accuse or force her to tell him, for suddenly he desired Leah's trust just as much as he sought to understand her.

"Not at the moment, but thank you." Her voice was distant, courteous, the most polite it had ever been when addressed to him.

He ignored the hint and stayed. "I couldn't sleep," he said. Turning toward her, he set his back against the arm of the bench and studied her profile. Then he tilted his head back toward the sky. "You said you found Cassiopeia?"

Her arm lifted into his vision, one slender finger guiding his gaze. "There, to the left," she said.

"Ah. Now I see."

They sat together for a long time, silently searching out the stars. Sebastian waited, listening to the leaves on the rosebushes rustle together beneath a slight wind. He found the constellations Hydra and Orion, and was looking for Aries when she finally spoke.

"The ninth of April last year. That's when I found them together." She said it slowly, each syllable precise, almost as if she were reciting the words.

"You never told me what happened," Sebastian said, returning his gaze to her. He paused. "Never mind. I don't want to know."

Her hand reached out toward the telescope, and she began tracing her fingers over the cabriole legs. Up and down. Up and down. "Sometimes I wish I hadn't learned the truth until the carriage accident, like you did. I would have liked to be angry, too. I would probably have been able to grieve, then, for his death. But I spent most of my tears a year ago, in those first few weeks of April."

She sighed, the sound forlorn, a piercing contrast to her stalwart attempt at keeping her voice devoid of any emotion.

"Leah . . ." he began, apologetically. He had no right to cause her this pain, no matter how much everything about her pulled and tugged at him with a visceral desire to reveal her deepest secrets.

She waved him off. "Yes, I was lonely. I wasn't able to cry in front of anyone—they would have asked questions. And I stayed away from Ian . . . as much as I could."

"Did you confront him?"

She shook her head. "I found them together. They both saw me. There was no use for a confrontation." Her fingers paused on the telescope. "I didn't want anyone to know. Not my family—especially my mother, who believed she'd made the perfect match for me. Not any friends or acquaintances I had, who were mostly his friends and acquaintances, in any case. They all envied me, believing I was the most fortunate woman alive to marry *the* Ian George. And you—"

Taking a deep breath, she reached up and fiddled with the scope. Sebastian watched her hand, slender and small, surprisingly graceful.

"Perhaps I should have told you, but I was ashamed. Back then, it was easy to blame myself. I must have done something wrong, I thought. I was boring, too plain, or"—she cast a sideways glance at him from beneath her lashes, then looked away again, folding her hands in her lap—"as you suggested, I didn't satisfy him in our . . . marital relations."

Sebastian cleared his throat, silently willing her to continue. Apart from his remaining guilt for having ever said such a thing, he was beginning to find it difficult to think of Ian and Leah as lovers. In fact, it was easier to picture Ian and Angela together, so much time had he spent torturing himself with his own imagination. But Ian and Leah . . . they were too different. She was dark while he was blond, short while he was tall, quiet while he was outspoken. How could anyone have ever thought they belonged together?

"Although I was surrounded by people—servants, Ian, all of London society—I was completely alone. I had no one to confide in, no one to talk to about how awful it was. Then Ian tried to speak to me about it, and it became even worse. He forced me to have a conversation, when I wanted nothing more than to be left alone, to pretend that I never cared about him."

She became silent, then opened her mouth, then closed it once again.

"Tell me," Sebastian urged, thinking perhaps Ian had threatened her, yelled at her, hit her. After all, if he hadn't known Ian well enough to realize that he would betray him with Angela, then it was possible he was capable of even worse. Sebastian felt a sudden impulse to examine Leah himself and search for bruises, even though they would have all faded by now.

But she refused to answer. "No, there's no need to tell you everything."

"At least tell me if he hurt you."

She swung her head toward him, her eyes wide. "No. Ian would never . . . No, nothing like that."

Sebastian swallowed, releasing a long breath.

She began to speak again, this time faster, her tone almost blithe. "For an entire year I never spoke a word of their affair to anyone. Until the accident, and then there was you. But, of course, you didn't want to speak of it. You wanted to hide it from everyone."

"Surely you understand my reasoning."

"I do," she said. "I don't blame you. After all, I didn't want anyone to know because of my own shame."

"I'm not ashamed, Leah. I—"

She turned to him, covered his mouth with her hand. "Would you like me to finish?"

Her hand was soft and warm against his lips, the scent of soap fainter. Sebastian was tempted to close his eyes and hold his hand against hers, press a kiss to her palm. Instead, he nodded silently, and she pulled her arm away.

"I was about to say that I didn't want to be alone anymore. Not after the carriage accident. I know you're still angry, but I've spent the past year and more of my life being wretched because of them. You're right in saying that I could go boating or do anything else I wished by myself, but I don't want to. And if the only way that I can be happy and not be alone is to pretend to still be in love with Ian and carry out some farce of a celebration in his memory, then so be it."

She tilted her head up again, toward the stars, her mouth parting as she breathed. Her chest rose and fell rapidly, and he could see the quick pulse of her heartbeat at her throat, made visible by the light cast from the lamp at her feet.

"And did you achieve what you wanted?" he asked.

She rolled her head toward him silently, an unspoken question.

"Now that you're hosting the party, do you still feel alone?"

Her lashes lowered, avoiding his gaze, and he thought that single motion was to be her answer. He prepared to ask again. But then she lifted her eyes to his, and her lips curved into a small, mocking smile. "Not when I'm with you."

There was nothing alluring or seductive about her tone; indeed, it sounded more like a reluctant admission, as if she didn't want him to be the one to ease her loneliness. Yet all the same, Sebastian found himself leaning nearer, unable to keep his distance, his hand reaching out to stroke her unbound hair.

God, it was soft. Like water running through his fingers, unbelievably fine and silken. He drew it away from her face, then watched it tumble like a waterfall against her cheek and throat.

She made a sound, something hushed and tentative, as if she pleaded with him. To stop, or to continue? Sebastian looked in her eyes and found her gaze wary, worried. But then her eyelashes fell, her lids closing. It was all the permission he needed.

He held his hand against the side of her face, feeling the delicate edge of her jaw beneath his palm. For a long moment he remained still, absorbing the heat of her cheek in contrast to the coolness of her throat, reveling in the lush texture of her skin.

Then his thumb stole across to the corner of her mouth, and as soon as he brushed against the bold, lavish swell of her upper lip, he could feel his blood begin to quicken with desire. Unable to stop himself, he toyed with her mouth. Rubbing the pad of his thumb over it until her lips parted, drawing the lower lip down, touching his thumb against the hot, velvet pink tip of her tongue.

And when she flicked her tongue against the edge of his thumb—not one, but two small, hesitant licks—with her eyes still closed and her hands clasped tightly on her lap, Sebastian could do nothing but draw his thumb away and wait for her eyes to open, wait for her to acknowledge him and admit she wanted more.

After a moment, her lashes lifted finally. Sebastian held her gaze as he bent forward, his hand gently tilting her chin up, and kissed her.

Leah stiffened as soon as Sebastian's lips touched hers. A kiss—that was more than a simple caress, more than the experimental tongue play with his hand. She'd known he meant to kiss her when she opened her eyes to find his bright and burning, the green depths betraying his intent. And she'd allowed him to lean over her, thinking—mistakenly—that she wanted this.

His mouth moved across hers, slowly at first; then he began to try to tease her lips apart. Nipping at the corners of her mouth, pulling her lower lip between his teeth, using his tongue as a means of persuasion.

And it was too much. Although she tried, she couldn't return his kiss. She sat there, her eyes open, waiting for it to be over. Just as she'd done again and again, night after night, with Ian.

But he continued kissing her, and his fingers began stroking the side of her throat, and oh God it felt good, but now she was suffocating in his embrace, unable to escape.

Leah shoved him away and lurched to her feet, knocking the lamp over in her panic. The light extinguished, leaving them alone with only the night and the shadows created by the moon and stars overhead.

She whirled toward him, her arms and legs trembling. "*Don't* touch me again."

She could see him lean forward, his hands upon his knees. "Leah . . ."

Swallowing, she stooped to retrieve the lamp, her fingers fumbling over the ground for the iron handle. It took a moment, quite a few agonizing silent moments as her fingernails scraped over the soil and rock, but soon she grasped it and straightened, hugging it close to her side.

Her feet urged her to turn and flee, but she couldn't. She stared at him through the darkness, unable to see his expression. "Why did you kiss me?" she asked, her voice little more than a whisper. *Don't tell me that you want me; don't tell me that you desire me. Please don't lie to me.*

She waited for a very long time. He didn't speak.

"Was it for revenge?"

"I'm not certain what you mean." Now his voice was cold and distant. Once again, they were nothing more than passing acquaintances, their only common ground the affair of their spouses.

"You're angry with Ian and Angela," she said quietly. "Did you hope to take your vengeance by using me? By betraying them just as they betrayed—"

"That's enough, Mrs. George."

"Tell me," she insisted, feeling rather foolish for staying when it was clear he wanted her to go. When *she* wanted so much to leave. "You asked why I held the house party, why I was lonely. And I told you. Do I not deserve to know why you kissed me?" She hesitated, then repeated, "Was it for revenge, my lord?"

He leaned back and crossed his ankle over his knee—shadows merging, shaping, separating. "Yes," he said finally, his voice low and careless. "I did it because I was angry. I kissed you for revenge."

Leah nodded and edged toward the telescope, scooping it beneath her other arm. "Don't touch me again."

"You already said that."

"But you understand—"

"Yes, I heard you perfectly. Don't fear, Mrs. George, I won't make the mistake again."

"Thank you." Leah moved onto the garden path. "Good night, Lord Wriothesly," she said, then quickly made her way to the house, the telescope swinging awkwardly against her leg and tangling in her skirt with each step.

Chapter 11

*Don't ask it of me again. I cannot leave him. I am
his mother.*

Apparently it had been too much to hope that Leah
would enter the drawing room the next morning to
find Sebastian gone, to hear that he'd departed from
Linley Park at dawn. Instead he stood speaking to Mr.
Meyer and the other gentlemen at the windows, his back
to the door, his legs impossibly longer and his shoulders
broader than she remembered. She'd spent all night trying to diminish him in her mind, to no avail. Not only
was his physical presence overwhelming, but the memory of his kiss was still vivid, the pleasure he'd induced
still tangled with the fear of letting go, of losing herself
to him as she had with Ian.

Summoning a smile from her reserves, Leah walked
toward the ladies sitting in the middle of the room.
"Good morning."

"Good morning," Miss Pettigrew returned. "Are you
feeling well? We didn't see you at breakfast."

No, she hadn't attended breakfast for the past few days, ever since Sebastian arrived. He tied her stomach in knots and kept her mind too busy to sleep until the first rays of sunlight. If she saw her mother again and Adelaide said anything about Leah's weight, it would be Sebastian she would blame.

"Oh, I'm fine, but thank you for your concern. There were some details regarding the dinner party on Friday that needed my attention." Encompassing Lady Elliot, Mrs. Thompson, and Mrs. Meyer with her smile, she asked, "Are we ready for today's activities?"

Lady Elliot stood, an orange russet gown highlighting the faint rouge she'd swept across her cheekbones. Rather than a youthful glow, the color revealed the skeletal structure of her face and the papered texture of her skin. "Indeed we are, Mrs. George. Here, let me walk with you to gather the gentlemen. I've been meaning to tell you about my cousin Anne's first husband. He reminded me a lot of your Ian."

Allowing Lady Elliot to link arms with her, Leah pretended to pay attention as they approached the gentlemen. She pretended, because in all actuality she couldn't draw her gaze away from Sebastian. He stood in profile to her now, at least a head above the other men. His posture was more confident compared to theirs, his waist leaner, his nose straight and his mouth too thin at the top and too full at the bottom to be defined as anything other than sulky.

A mouth to be kissed. A mouth she had kissed.

Sebastian answered a question from Baron Cooper-Giles, his head turning toward her. Leah recalled once likening him to a mountain, but she'd been mistaken; he resembled a jaguar, his dark hair and green eyes entrancing when they should have elicited nothing more than a passive glance from her.

"My dear."

Leah's gaze darted back to Lady Elliot. The older woman's eyes held a warning. "Do try not to be so obvious in your attraction."

Leah's heart sank to the pit of her stomach and beat there, a dull, heavy thing. "I beg your pardon, Lady Elliot. I misunderstood what you—"

"I agree that Lord Wriothesly presents a fine appearance, but it's unbecoming of you to eye him as if he were a pheasant laid out on your best china."

Leah swallowed. "Lord Wriothesly was my husband's best friend. I assure you, my lady, although I have the highest regard for the earl, I do not esteem him in the manner you suggest."

They were about to reach the gentlemen's end of the room, but Lady Elliot tugged her arm and they continued walking the perimeter, passing the other ladies again. "I know we do not know each other well," Lady Elliot said after a moment, her voice low. "And you seem to have courage in spades to think to risk the censure of polite society to host this house party. But if you will indulge me, Mrs. George, I would advise you not to entertain further scandal by meeting with Wriothesly at night in the garden anymore."

Leah went deathly pale; she could feel it, the blood draining from her face, the light-headedness that came at the peak of an illness. It was a reaction of shame, of embarrassment, immediate and instinctive. "You saw." The words scratched her throat as she spoke, low and hoarse.

Lady Elliot tightened her arm around Leah's, as if she feared Leah would fall in a faint. "Yes, and I saw you run away, as you should have. If it weren't for Howard's snoring, I probably wouldn't have witnessed anything. I enjoy gossip, Mrs. George, and there's nothing I would like more than to be the bearer of your little tête-à-tête to all my friends. But I also like you. Take this as a warning, my dear, for although I admire your fearlessness, I can't say that I'll be able to restrain myself next time."

Her tone was friendly, not in the least malicious, but Leah understood her perfectly. Lady Elliot did as she pleased, the sort who used her influence to turn debutantes into spinsters if they offended her, who transformed wallflowers into belles for amusement's sake. She reminded Leah of her mother, though Lady Elliot was more direct in her threats and kinder with her words. Leah had no desire to influence others but, like Lady Elliot, she would do as she pleased. No longer did she have any reason to care about being ashamed or embarrassed over her actions.

"I appreciate your concern, my lady. Please allow me to assure you once again that I have no interest in the earl. But if I did, and if indeed I wanted to meet with him in dark corners, I would have no regrets. I am a widow—a reputation is of no use to me now."

Lady Elliot laughed, the sound both amused and disbelieving. "A woman must always guard her reputation. It's the only thing we have."

"Forgive me, my lady, but I disagree. I would give up my reputation at once if it were ever an obstacle to my independence or happiness."

Lady Elliot raised her brows as they neared the gentlemen again. "Then give it up, my dear. But please—tell me before you do so I may be the first to inform everyone else."

The problem with telling yourself you didn't want something, Sebastian discovered, was that soon you desired it even more. After spending the night trying to convince himself to stay away from Leah, he found that every promise and affirmation that she meant nothing to him were quickly revealed as fanciful lies when he saw her the next day.

Perhaps if Leah had made an effort to avoid him, she might have roused his sympathies enough that he would have left her alone ... Perhaps, but she never gave him the chance to do so. For she didn't avoid him; to the contrary, she treated him with the same politeness and courtesy as she did all of her guests. She talked with him, laughed with him, even challenged him and his horse to a jumping competition as the group rode across the Linley Park estate that afternoon. In short, she pretended as if the previous evening, the kiss they'd shared, and her subsequent retreat had never happened.

And perhaps it was for this reason, because she seemed so intent in forgetting everything, that Sebastian couldn't.

That evening, at the sound of the dinner gong, Sebastian offered Leah his arm. As the highest-ranking peer at the house party, he had the pleasure of escorting her to meals. If he hadn't been studying her so closely he might have missed it, but it was there, flashing across her face for an instant before her expression of eternal cheer and politeness fell into place again: alarm.

Not fear, exactly. And not awareness. But something in between.

"Good evening," he said. It was the first he'd spoken to her in relative solitude that day, the others behind them drowning out his words to any ears but hers.

She glanced at him and gave a smile that was more of an impression on her lips than anything else, quick to rise and quick to fade. "Good evening, my lord." A blush rose on her cheeks, the first he'd seen from her. The splash of color on her pale skin made her appear younger, more innocent—too young to be wearing widow's weeds.

Before he could say anything else, she began walking, her pace urging him toward the staircase and the descent to the dining room. Sebastian kept his steps slow, drawing out their time together . . . enjoying the realization that despite her pretense, it was indeed difficult for her to act as if she hadn't been affected by his kiss the night before.

"I'm looking forward to the *tableaux vivants* tonight," he said, then paused. "Actually, perhaps I should require that the scene from *Julius Caesar* only include paper knives. I've seen Mr. Dunlop with a rifle before, and if his aim with a knife is equally as bad, I might have cause to fear for my life."

Even though he gave her an opportunity to say something, to nod her head or even add a noncommittal hum, Leah made no reply. The pressure of her gloved hand over his arm was light, almost like a whisper. She'd asked him not to touch her again. How it must aggravate her, to be expected to touch him in front of the others as social customs mandated.

Sebastian angled his chin and turned his head slightly, his height putting him at the advantage where his mouth could hover near the top of her ear. "I begin to think you're ignoring me, Leah," he murmured.

She recoiled; a stiffening of her shoulders, a reflexive jerking of her arm where it lay on top of his. Oh, if only she knew how that little response encouraged him. How interesting, that she didn't respond to the man he played in public, the gentleman earl who appeased all, who had won London's prized beauty with his gallant manners and considerate nature.

No, Leah George preferred his darker side. The man who teased and provoked, the low voice that hinted at passion and pleasure and broken rules.

"Does it bother you for me to call you by your Christian name?" he asked, watching her profile for any sign of reaction. Other than the rapid rise and fall of her chest, nothing seemed to change.

"As you wish, my lord."

"Ah, she speaks."

"I have full faculties. That includes the use of my tongue."

"Yes, I remember well the use of your tongue last night. But how wicked of you to remind me, Mrs. George."

He heard her swift intake of breath, and she darted a glance at him, a frown appearing on her lips. Her mouth, of which he'd had only a taste before she denied him.

"If you hadn't run away so quickly last night, I would have enjoyed learning more of your tongue and its uses."

This time she gave him her full attention, the ribbons of her widow's cap slapping against her cheeks and her shoulders squaring indignantly. "I am a widow, my lord. May I remind you that my husband died only four months ago?"

Behind them, other conservations quieted at Sebastian's laughter. Oh, but he could not help himself. She looked so self-righteous, her cheeks burning, her eyes sparking fire. It was almost as if she believed the conviction in her own words. Soon the others began speaking again and Sebastian, unable to keep the sly curve from his mouth, raised a brow as he guided her down the last step of the staircase. "I do apologize, madam. It is obvious that your clothes and aspect present a careful reminder of your status. I can only plead your forgiveness, and argue my case by pointing out how pretty a widow you do make."

"Stop teasing me." The words were quiet, her blush higher. "Stop acting as if this is all nothing but a source of amusement to you."

"If it's not meant to be amusing, this farce created in tribute to Ian's memory, your flirtation with the edge of scandal, then tell me—what is it?"

She turned her eyes on him again—those great amber eyes. Intelligent, compelling. Mesmerizing. "It's a choice."

"A choice?"

"A test for myself."

They reached the dining room, and Sebastian again slowed his steps, trying to prolong their quiet conversation. For as soon as they reached the table, no private words would be allowed in the presence of Lord and Lady Elliot and Baron Cooper-Giles.

"And what sort of test do you seek?" he asked, his lips coming close to her ear. Not touching, though he was tempted to brush his mouth against the soft shell. To gain another reaction, whether it meant she flinched away like last night or—more doubtful—leaned in toward him.

But also to test himself. This attraction to her, this pull between them that presented a physical temptation and something more as well. A meeting of the minds, a close affinity that they both seemed reluctant to admit.

However, she continued along until he was forced to escort her to her chair. "I do hope you enjoy tonight's menu, my lord," she said brightly, her voice risen for the others to hear.

This was the Leah she wanted him to know, the Leah she pretended to be for the others present. But he'd seen something more, and he was no longer content to settle for this token offering. It still amazed him that, along with everyone else, she'd fooled him into believing she was nothing more than a wallflower, peeled away and brought to life only through Ian's doing.

They sat down for the meal, Leah at the side of the empty head of the table—another tribute to Ian—and Sebastian across from her. He watched as she conversed with Lord Elliot and Lady Elliot.

During the house party she'd begun to show a little of herself to the others, but not everything. They'd glimpsed her kindness and her quick wit, but he alone had measured her strength, her vulnerability. It was an interesting feeling, to contain someone else's secrets and to know that they kept yours. Not just the knowledge they shared of Ian and Angela's affair, but an understanding of the layered depths hidden from the rest of the world. It was likely that he knew more of Leah than he'd ever sought to discover in his own wife. And whether he liked it or not, she knew more of him than he'd ever wished to reveal to anyone else. His every emotional state: his anger, his sadness, his offenses and curses brought on by despair. And now she knew, though he would have chosen otherwise, how he hungered for her.

A footman moved forward to pour more claret into Leah's glass, and she sat back, her hands folded in her lap. She made the mistake of looking across the table and meeting Sebastian's gaze. Lifting his own glass, he gave her a silent toast before bringing the wine to his lips. He stared at her over the rim as the footman stepped away. And he was glad he studied her so closely, for it was in that moment that everything changed.

He saw it in her eyes. Not hidden, not buried, not rejected by fear. It was there, plain when she should have kept it secret from him, a truth acknowledged by the stark craving in her gaze.

Leah George desired him as well.

After dinner, Leah rose from her chair and spoke to her guests. "If you'll excuse me, I'll follow you back to the drawing room shortly."

"Is something wrong?" Lady Elliot asked, her gaze sliding from Leah to Sebastian.

"No, just a small household matter," Leah assured her. She smiled as everyone left—including Sebastian.

A moment. She just needed one minute of reprieve before she had to return to the drawing room and endure being stripped bare by Sebastian's eyes again. Any enjoyment she'd received from the house party was gone; all she looked forward to now was seeing him depart. She couldn't bear being near him any longer. The unspoken questions between them, the inclination her body seemed to have in leaning toward him whenever he stood beside her, the way her pulse rebelled against her attempts to act calm and unmoved.

Leah asked Herrod to summon Mrs. Kemble. At the sound of her footsteps approaching from the hall, Leah left the dining room to meet her.

Sebastian was there, against the far wall, his arms crossed over his chest. Waiting for her.

With her heartbeat thrumming in her ears, Leah gestured to Mrs. Kemble. "I remembered an item that needs to be changed on the menu for the dinner party," she said. "Instead of the quail, ask Chef to cook a duck in a raisin compote."

"Yes, madam." Mrs. Kemble scribbled a note on the little book she carried around with her everywhere, as much a part of her person as the round of keys she wore at her waist.

Leah moved slightly until her back was fully turned toward Sebastian and she could no longer see him in her periphery. It didn't matter, however; her body was still attuned to his presence, aware of his gaze on her. Another blush heated beneath her skin. "Oh, and one more. For dessert, add a blackberry tart."

"Is there anything else, madam?"

Leah shifted from one foot to the other. Perhaps if she changed the entire menu, enough time would elapse that he would leave. "No, that will be all."

"Very good. I'll alert Chef to the changes immediately. Thank you, madam." With a curtsy, Mrs. Kemble turned and bustled away, her notebook tucked beneath her arm.

Taking a deep breath, Leah turned and faced Sebastian. Though tempted to sail straight past him without a word, she cloaked herself in the polite control to which she was accustomed and gave him her most winsome smile. "Have the guests become impatient? Did they send you out to find me?"

He ignored her questions and stepped forward. Only a foot away. "I wanted to speak to you alone."

Leah raised her brows and started walking, creating a more comfortable distance between them. "Perhaps another time. The others are waiting, and it's sure to be a long evening. You have to change into your costume as Julius Caesar, do you not?"

Oh, God. And now an image of Sebastian clothed in nothing but a toga seared her mind.

"You're trying to avoid me." His strides matched hers, making her attempt to preserve distance between them impossible. "I'm disappointed, Leah. You did so well earlier today." His voice deepened, taunting her.

She stared straight ahead. Had she not made it clear enough the night before? She didn't want him. "On the contrary, my lord. I shall be happy to speak with you in the drawing room, but I refuse to be rude to everyone el—"

He grabbed her arm and whirled her toward him at the foot of the stairs. "Allow me to apologize for last evening's mistake. You have no need to fear me, Leah."

She glanced up the staircase, toward the voices she could hear coming from the drawing room, then back. "I don't fear you," she said, steadily meeting his gaze, daring him to repeat it again.

"Then why did you run away?"

"Please remove your hand from my arm."

He looked down and stared at the place where his fingers wrapped around her wrist. Instead of releasing her, he turned his grip into a caress, easing beneath the sleeve of her widow's gown to stroke her skin.

Leah yanked away, trying to ignore the fire spreading

from the inside of her wrist to her chest, the inside of her thighs. "Damn you, Sebastian," she breathed, then turned and began climbing up the stairs. Her spine was straight, her steps steady and graceful. A dignified departure, but they both knew she was running away again.

Halfway up, Sebastian's voice, hushed but still strong enough to set tremors racing through her body, carried to her from below. "I lied last night, Mrs. George."

Clutching her skirts more tightly, Leah continued up the stairs.

"I didn't kiss you because I wanted revenge on Ian or Angela."

Leah faltered, almost losing her balance as her slipper caught the hem of her dress. Reaching out toward the banister, she kept her eyes on the landing above. On the landscape Ian's great-grandmother had painted of Linley Park, on the two rose-patterned chairs positioned below.

His voice followed her, unrelenting. Defiant. "I kissed you because I wanted to. Because I wanted *you*."

Her legs trembling beneath her, Leah ran to the top. Her breath shuddered as she turned toward the drawing room.

"Leah."

She glanced down at the sound of her name, long enough to meet his eyes, to see the desire written clearly across his face. Then, with a low gasp, she fled—away from Sebastian and the reflection of her own need.

Chapter 12

*I will send you a reply tomorrow. I found this two
days ago, and thought of you. No matter what
happens—I love you. "My bounty is as boundless
as the sea, my love as deep; the more I give to thee,
the more I have, for both are infinite."*

The next day, Leah changed the structure of the house
party. Instead of the group activities she had scheduled, she encouraged the men to go out and enjoy the
more traditional amusements of a country house party:
fishing, hunting, riding. She let them choose, as she didn't
care what they decided as long as it kept Sebastian far
away from her. The ladies stayed mostly indoors: chatting, knitting, and playing instruments in the music
room. When they did venture outside in the late afternoon, it was to take long walks in the gardens, areas
where Leah knew the men would not be.

At dinner Leah urged the most talkative of the
guests—Lady Elliot and Mr. Dunlop—to regale the rest
of the table with gossip they'd heard toward the end of

the Season, and bits that were currently making the rounds from house party to house party.

Afterward, when she suggested an evening of cards, Leah made certain she remained occupied on the opposite side of the room from Sebastian. Though they both knew she was avoiding him, he surprised her when he made no effort to stay close or even to make sure she didn't have an opportunity to be alone with the guests.

Apparently he trusted her now, although he would soon learn it to be a mistake.

The following morning, the day of the dinner party and the last day of the house party itself, Leah finally rose early enough to find everyone else still at breakfast. However, instead of having a plate readied for herself, she stood before the table and made an announcement.

"I apologize for my absence, but I've prepared a surprise for the dinner party tonight which requires me to journey to Swindon."

"Oh, I do like surprises," Mrs. Meyer said, looking at her husband. He nodded in agreement.

"Unfortunately, I'll be gone for several hours." Leah motioned to Herrod. She gave him a list she'd penned the night of the *tableaux vivants*, one which had kept her busy from thinking of Sebastian's words that evening . . . and the handsome tragedy he'd presented as Julius Caesar. "But I encourage you to look at the paper I've provided Herrod. It lists several more activities which Ian enjoyed."

Though the expressions of the guests were curious, no one pressed her for further details. Even Sebastian abstained from questioning her, though she could feel his gaze on her back as she excused herself and walked out the door.

Once inside the coach, Leah tried to relax in the seat and prepare for the ride which would take well over an hour. She glanced across to the opposite side, where the black organza gown she'd never intended to wear in front of anyone else now lay neatly folded inside a long, rectangular box.

Leah—recent widow, self-made rebel—had decided to dance.

A test, that's what she'd told Sebastian the other evening. The entire house party, from the beginning when she first thought of hosting it, to sending out the invitations, to planning events which pleased her and her alone, was meant to be a test to her new determination to live as she wanted. Her choice, to not bow to the expectations of others, but to find her own happiness through the independence she'd gained after Ian's death.

And if she wanted to dance at her dinner party when most of society would agree that such a thing was wholly inappropriate for a widow in mourning, she would do it. And if she wanted to not only wear the black organza dress that was more a mockery of her widowhood than a symbol, but also to alter it into a scandalous style, then that was her choice. As she'd told Lady Elliot before, the happiness she created for herself now was for more important to her than the prison of her own reputation.

There would be consequences—she wasn't naive to think she could escape unscathed—but for the first time in her life, Leah wasn't afraid to discover what those consequences might be.

Watching the hills roll by, with the thickets of trees few and far between, Leah idly wondered at Sebastian's response to the news that there would be dancing after dinner that evening.

She'd meant to tell everyone that morning, as she knew the ladies would be thrilled at the prospect, but after Sebastian's kiss in the garden and their subsequently frayed relationship, she thought better of it. Instead, she would tell them later this afternoon, before

they began preparing to dress for the meal. Then it
would be too late for Sebastian to try to cancel the party,
as the other guests from the surrounding area would already be preparing at their own houses.

The more interesting thought, of course, was what Sebastian would do when he realized she meant to dance
along with the other guests, especially when he saw what
she wore.

He would be furious, that was certain.

But no matter his reaction, she didn't plan to dance
for him, and she didn't intend to wear the gown for him.
If she'd learned nothing else from the garden incident
and the way she kept running from Sebastian, it was that
part of her was still locked away with Ian in the past.
And tonight, at last, she meant to be free.

The coach swung roughly around a corner, sending
the dress box sliding across the opposite seat. Leah
stretched forward to save it from falling to the floor.
Catching it with both hands, she dragged it onto her lap.
It remained there, held tightly beneath her arms, until
they reached Swindon.

The dressmaker, Mrs. Neville, met her at the door of
the shop. Much smaller than any modiste's shop in London, Mrs. Neville's business had only one assistant, and
Leah saw her head bent low over a skirt as the dressmaker escorted her into the back room.

Mrs. Neville looked Leah over from head to toe, taking in her veil, dusty black skirts, and no doubt wondering at her widow's weeds. Soon, however, the dressmaker
held out her arms. "I assume this is the gown you mentioned in your note?"

Leah hesitated, almost reluctant now to give her
the box.

"Madam? You do still wish me to make the alterations by tonight, yes?"

With a sense of stepping over an invisible line she'd

only previously contemplated, Leah nodded and placed the box in Mrs. Neville's hands. "Yes."

"Helen," Mrs. Neville called to the girl at the other end of the room. "Put down that skirt for now. Please help Mrs. George undress."

Leah submitted as the assistant removed her veil and bonnet, then unbuttoned and pulled the dull black dress over her head.

At a table in a nearby corner, Mrs. Neville clucked her tongue appreciatively as she opened the box and lifted Leah's gown out. She turned to Leah with a sly smile, her hands smoothing over the fabric. "I believe I'm beginning to understand what you wish, Mrs. George."

Soon, with Helen's help, they lowered the organza gown over her head. Even without the alterations made, Leah couldn't help but be pleased as she glanced in a mirror set against the opposite wall. Although it was black like all of the other dresses she'd worn since the carriage accident, the customary white trimmings were missing from the high neck and around the wrists. The organza wasn't crisp against her skin like bombazine or wrinkled like crepe; it was soft, the skirt shimmering blue with the light, fluid and supple in her hands. In contrast, the petticoats beneath felt too stiff, too restrictive.

Mrs. Neville began taking measurements around her waist. As she moved to the back, Leah could feel her fingers skimming over the long line of pearl buttons. "What would you like me to do with these, madam? I could sew them around the edge, if you like."

Leah considered the mirror and the bold woman within. For the first time in a very long while, she met her own gaze without flinching away. "I think that's a wonderful idea, Mrs. Neville."

After half an hour, the dressmaker finished with the other measurements to the bodice and shoulders and stepped back. "Very good, Mrs. George. I don't believe it will take me long. I'll have it delivered to you by six."

Leah nodded, took one last glance into the mirror, and smiled.

"She's a fine mare, but no better than Lord Derryhow's. I saw her at Ascot last year, when her left leg turned lame shortly after the first turn . . ." Any words Sebastian had meant to say next disappeared as Leah walked into the drawing room.

"But her bloodlines are far superior. Why, her sire was—"

Sebastian blocked out the sound of the voice of Baron Cooper-Giles, who apparently hadn't yet seen the beautiful woman who'd just entered.

"Lord Wriothesly?"

Sebastian gestured toward the doorway. "I believe Mrs. George has returned from preparing her surprise for this evening."

A surprise that required her to leave her guests for most of the morning and early afternoon. Whatever she'd done, she appeared quite pleased about it, her eyes sparkling despite her attempt to match the somber tone of her mourning clothes. Sebastian turned his head, fingering the curtain of the window he leaned against as he glanced outside. No matter how much he'd tried to stay away from her yesterday, his memory teased him mercilessly with reminders of their kiss and the desire he'd witnessed in her eyes. Sebastian released the curtain to look at Leah. Or perhaps he'd only imagined the desire; he certainly hadn't seen any evidence of it since.

"I apologize for not telling you before now," she said, "but I wanted to make sure all the details were in place. Tonight, after dinner, I've arranged for musicians to come. We'll finish both the dinner party and the house party with dancing."

Although murmurs had risen when she appeared in the drawing room, guesses made regarding the surprise for the evening, her announcement about dancing withered every voice in the room. Each moment of silence pulsated with the question in everyone's minds: would she dance as well?

Jaw clenched, Sebastian waited with them for the answer, although he already suspected the truth. While he understood Leah's quest for freedom and might have encouraged it otherwise, if she did decide to dance, the rumors created in the wake of the scandal could escalate dangerously. It was possible they wouldn't extend to Ian and Angela, nor then to Henry's legitimacy. Possible, but Sebastian wasn't comfortable with the idea of *possible*.

Leah inclined her head, the ribbons of her widow's cap swaying with the motion. Her posture, her expression, every movement she made bespoke modesty and meekness. Sebastian crossed his arms and watched her, looking for any nuance that would give her thoughts away.

"As I said before, I know this isn't a usual house party, but with this being the last night, I wanted to do something to express my appreciation for your presence. Ian always enjoyed dancing. Tonight, I hope you will, too."

Sebastian narrowed his eyes. She focused on *their* enjoyment, *their* dancing, but she didn't say she wouldn't be joining them.

"Now, if you will excuse me, I believe our other guests will be arriving in a little over an hour. I must get ready for dinner."

As Leah turned and exited the drawing room, he had to admit it was very well done. In only a few sentences, she'd been able to raise even more speculation: she would attend the dinner—that much was clear—but would she also attend the dancing? And if so, would she participate or simply observe?

It was the perfect way to heighten excitement about the evening. Unfortunately for her, it was also the perfect way to ensure he would corner her before the dinner began and discover her true intentions.

Almost as soon as Leah left, the other women departed for their own preparations. The men took the opportunity to lounge about and chat about horses and the upcoming fox hunting season before they had to return to their rooms as well.

Sebastian didn't wait, however. Excusing himself, he made his way to the opposite wing and shortly found the mistress' bedchamber. Looking down both ends of the corridor to make sure no one saw him at Leah's door, he knocked once, then twice more.

As if to torture him, an image of Leah undressing immediately arose in his mind.

Grimacing, he knocked again, then stepped to the side when he heard footsteps near the door. Even though it was likely one of her maids, he didn't want to take the chance of accidentally spying Leah in her undergarments. Or, God forbid, seeing even one inch of her bare skin beyond her face and hands.

He heard the door unlatch; then a round face peeked out at him from around the doorframe. Her lady's maid blinked. "Yes, my lord? How may I be of assistance?"

Sebastian straightened away from the wall. "Please tell Mrs. George—"

"Oh, is that Lord Wriothesly?" he heard her call from inside the room.

The maid peered over her shoulder. "Yes, madam."

There was a rustling sound, and soon the lady's maid disappeared. Leah appeared in her place, wearing another of her ordinary black crepe mourning gowns. However, no widow's cap covered her head. Instead, most of her hair was hanging down, as if the maid had just begun to work on it. Light brown locks gleaming like golden amber flowed over her shoulders and caressed the side of her face. The same locks he'd made the mistake of touching only a few nights ago.

Leah smiled as she looked at him, all of the vulnerability and insecurity she'd revealed to him before now hidden behind the curve of her lips. Sebastian suppressed the urge to reach out and touch her hair again, to stroke her mouth with his thumb, to see the pretense of her expression fade away.

"I expect you want to know if I'll be dancing with everyone else tonight," she said, her gaze meeting his evenly.

"Are my thoughts so transparent?" He studied her face, willing himself to find Angela in the contrasts between their features. He could see Angela clearly when he was alone; though he tried to dismiss her memory, she was everywhere he looked. He would spy her profile in the pattern on the wallpaper, or imagine her reclined on his bed at night, the voluptuous curve of her back turned toward him. If he attempted to squeeze his eyes shut and block her from his thoughts, her image clung to the black slate of his vision, taunting him, refusing to let him forget her.

But the picture of Angela that came to his mind now was faint, less than a shadow, disappearing before it could fully form. All he saw was Leah, slender and pale, too exuberant and full of life to be suffocated by the expected mourning rituals. The rituals he would now ask her to continue observing.

"Not transparent," she answered, tilting her head to the side, "but you have become rather predictable."

"Have I?" he asked, searching her eyes to find the awareness she hid so well behind this disguise of polite cheer. If her maid weren't there behind her, he would have backed her into the bedchamber and kissed her again.

"As to the question of whether I'll be dancing to-night . . ." Her smile grew wider and she leaned in—only a few inches, but Sebastian felt the air quickly become thinner, her presence stealing the oxygen from his lungs. "The answer is yes," she said, then turned and shut the door. The lock clicked loudly into place.

Sebastian stared at the door, gritted his teeth, and raised his fist to knock once more. No answer came. "Mrs. George," he said quietly through the door, glancing down the corridor again. Still no answer. "Mrs. George," he called, this time a little more loudly, his tone more strident. "Mrs. Geo—"

A noise came from somewhere toward the end of the hallway, and Sebastian stepped back. No good would come of him being caught outside Leah's bedchamber, especially if it was a scandal he wanted to prevent.

With a final glare at her door, he pivoted and strode to his own guest chamber to prepare for the dinner. Leah might have convinced herself she would dance to-night, but she would find it impossible to do so when no partner offered his hand.

Dinner was a success. All of Leah's guests were witty and charming, the women dressed in gorgeous gowns and the men handsome in their evening wear. When they moved to the salon for the dancing, the musicians played better than any she'd ever heard before. Even without her organza gown on yet, the night had taken on a glittering, dreamlike luster to Leah. It was a night that she had never imagined orchestrating, a night she'd never imagined at all, one in which she defied all the rules.

From the time she was a little girl, her mother had told her stories each night when she brushed her hair. These weren't bedtime stories to fill a girl's head with princes and princesses and happily ever afters. They were stories about other little girls, daughters of Adelaide's friends who had done something wrong. One had been caught playing in the mud with her brothers, another hiding a puppy beneath her bedcovers. As the years passed, Leah learned not only what was expected of her, but also what was frowned upon by her mother, who seemed the moral representative of all of England.

One must not stare. One must not belch. A lady should brush her hair no more and no less than one hundred strokes every night. Never be alone with a gentleman. Always sit up straight. Wear white for your debutante ball and black for an entire year when in mourning. Maintain a proper figure—not too plump and not too skinny. Smile when you don't feel like smiling, dance when you don't feel like dancing—but no more than twice with the same man—and practice perfection until you achieve it.

And never, ever—ever—break the rules.

Tonight, Leah's only intention was to break the rules.

She smiled up at Sebastian, not because she felt like smiling but because she simply couldn't help herself. Tonight she didn't try to ignore the wonderful feeling that burned low in her stomach when his eyes held hers; she didn't try to escape from his presence—at least, she wouldn't right now. With one foot tapping the floor and the taste of the wine from dinner still sweet on her tongue, she felt as light as air. Happy. Free. And for once, she believed the lie in his eyes that said she was desirable. Tonight, it was the truth.

"You should go dance," she told him as they watched the other guests in a reel.

"I prefer to stay beside you."

Leah laughed; he didn't even try to hide the suspicion in his voice, although his words were lovely. "Is my company so appealing, then, my lord?'

His head turned from the dance floor, his gaze landing on her mouth before rising to her eyes. "It is every-thing about you that is appealing, Mrs. George."

Leah pressed her lips together, ignoring the blush that was surely spreading all the way to her fingertips, She watched Miss Pettigrew dance with Mr. Dunlop. "You're very handsome tonight, my lord."

"What's this? A compliment from the lovely widow?"

"A mere observation."

"Why do I suspect that you had too much to drink at dinner?"

A corner of her mouth lifted, and she looked at him sideways beneath her lashes. "Perhaps I did. Or perhaps I'm finally being honest."

Her words erased all amusement from his face. He leaned close, and she opened her mouth to warn him not to incite gossip, but he spoke first. "Be careful, Leah, or I'll start being honest as well."

Her pulse leapt as she remembered his speech on the stairs about wanting her. He stood so close now that his arm almost brushed against hers. Leah lifted her hand and pretended to wipe a fallen hair from his shoulder. Just a little touch to indulge herself—one that before she couldn't even admit she needed. "I've been careful all my life. It's begun to grow a bit dull, I'm afraid."

Then she swept away just as Baron Cooper-Giles stopped to talk to Sebastian, knowing Sebastian would try to chase after her soon. Leah nodded at Lady Elliot and Mrs. Meyer as she walked past. Everyone else ex-cept for Mrs. Thompson was dancing, the skirts of the ladies swirling about their feet as the gentlemen led them through the patterns. Leah kept to the edge of the salon, their ballroom for the evening. Every minute or so, she caught a glimpse of Sebastian as she peered past the dancers. He may not be following her yet, but he was trailing her with his eyes.

As the reel ended, Leah saw Lord Elliot and Mr. Halladay walk toward Sebastian and Baron Cooper-Giles. Miss Pettigrew and Miss Sanders, the daughter of a third cousin twice removed of the Viscount Parbury, gathered around Leah.

"Oh, I was just about to leave," Leah said.

"Leave?" Miss Pettigrew exclaimed, her cheeks flushed, a sheen of perspiration shining on her forehead. Leah nodded and lifted her skirt an inch off the floor to reveal the hem she'd first cut with scissors and then tore with her hands before dinner.

"My foot somehow snagged on my dress. I'll be back soon, though."

"Would you like some company while you get it repaired?" Miss Sanders asked, but her head was already turned, craning toward Baron Cooper-Giles who had left Sebastian's side and was presently strolling in their direction.

"Oh, no. Thank you. Just keep dancing." With a smile at Miss Pettigrew, Leah glanced again at Sebastian to make sure he wasn't watching, then hurried out of the salon.

Once in her bedchamber, she gestured to Agatha who sat waiting in one of the chairs before the fire. "Come, we must hurry."

As her maid unlaced her crepe dress, Leah removed the pins from her widow's cap to reveal the braids Agatha had worked to perfect earlier that evening. Looking in the mirror, Leah smoothed her fingers over a braid at the crown of her head. "I think this one is coming undone."

"It'll take me only a minute to fix it, madam."

"No, not to worry. There isn't time. I want to be back down in time for the waltz."

Part of her hoped that Sebastian would be so stunned by the dress that he would forgive her for the scandal and ask her to waltz with him, regardless of the opinions of her other guests. But if he didn't, the most important moment would be when she entered the salon in the organza gown, having made the decision to dance no matter the censure she would endure. If no one asked her to dance, she would still have successfully claimed her freedom, her new identity. She was no longer a slave to propriety, no longer obedient to another's whims, no longer the slip of a girl who hid behind her mother's criticisms and her husband's infidelity.

Leah stepped out of the crepe dress, then walked toward the organza gown laid out on the bed. It was exquisite; Mrs. Neville had outdone herself. With the back open, the neck was wide enough for Agatha to slip the dress over Leah's head without displacing any of her braids. Even though Mrs. Neville had taken her measurements and Leah knew it fit perfectly, the sensation of air at her back made the gown feel too loose, the material a sensual slide across her skin.

Leah sat at the dressing table and picked up the diamond pendant earrings. "I cannot believe I am doing this," she whispered to her reflection as she put one earring on, then the other. She waited as Agatha slipped the matching diamond necklace around her neck. Compared to the free movement of the dress, the clasp felt heavy at her nape, the end of the silver chain cool at the top of her spine.

Her maid moved back, and Leah stood. As when she'd first bought the organza, she held out her arms and twirled, smiling. "Do you approve, Agatha?"

The maid smiled in return, her round cheeks threatening to hide her eyes. "You're beautiful, madam."

"Thank you," Leah said, lowering her arms. But tonight it wasn't important that she look beautiful. Tonight, all she wanted was to no longer look like a widow.

Chapter 13

How can I hope for more? It was wicked of you to tease me, to make me believe it is possible.

Sebastian was pacing outside the salon when Leah appeared from the other wing.

Dear God.

Bloody hell.

Both seemed apt phrases, appealing to the heavens and cursing the lower dominions as he ground his jaw together.

The widow he'd known for the past four months had completely transformed. Her widow's cap was gone, revealing a braided coiffure which complemented the angles of her face. She wore diamonds, not the usual somber, black ornamentation allowed. And although her dress appeared black at first glimpse, it became clear as she walked that blue threads were interwoven into the material, for the gown shimmered and reflected the light, alternating between blue and black with each step.

Still, thank God the dress was modest. Her sleeves

were pulled to her wrists, the line of the bodice high at her neck. Any illicit thoughts he had as she walked toward him were inspired by his own imagination, not by the cut of her gown.

She slowed as she neared him, the smile on her face fading. "You weren't supposed to see me yet."

Sebastian moved toward her. He told himself it was to block her path to the salon, but in reality he simply wanted to be closer to her. "Return to your chamber," he said. "Change back into the dress you were wearing before. And please, don't try to dance tonight."

She shook her head and tried to step around him, but he extended his arm. Her chest lifted as she inhaled, pushing against him. She turned her head and met his gaze. "I need to do this."

"If you do, you risk hurting Henry. I can't allow you—"

"Please, Sebastian. It's rather far-fetched to believe anything I do will cause rumors about Ian or Angela."

"Perhaps it is. I might be concerned for nothing. But if the truth does come out, even if it's just a rumor that no one can confirm, what do you believe will happen to Henry? How soon until you think people will begin to question his legitimacy?"

"Then they'd be fools," she said slowly, considering him as if in doubt of his sanity. "Sebastian, he looks just like you."

"Does he? What of his hair? His eyes?" Sebastian dropped his arm and stepped closer to her, the scent of her soap like an aphrodisiac to his senses. "Some days it's perfectly clear that he's my son. Other days I look and look, searching for some resemblance, unable to find any. All I ask is that you think of Henry. If he is mine, allow him to grow older until there's no doubt. If he isn't—" Sebastian exhaled harshly, lifting his hand to her face, cupping her cheek. "He's still my son. Don't do this, Leah. Don't take the chance."

She closed her eyes, and for a moment, Sebastian thought he'd convinced her to give up her plan. But then she shook her head again and opened her eyes, a small, regretful smile on her lips. "I'm sorry," she whispered, and then ran past him, her sleeve slipping through his fingers as he tried to catch her.

Leah paused at the door to the salon, glancing back over her shoulder to see Sebastian following behind. His eyes widened as he spied the open V at the back of her gown.

Moving forward, Leah edged to the side of the room to stand near Lord Elliot and Mr. Meyer as she waited for the next dance—the waltz—to begin.

Her ears buzzed too loudly for her to understand their conversation, but she was aware after a few moments of the absence of speech; Lord Elliot was no longer talking, but staring at her, his brow wrinkled. Leah offered him a smile and curtsied, then did the same as Mr. Meyer turned to look.

Second by second passed, and one by one the guests turned from their small groups toward her. Eventually the dancers in the middle of the floor stopped dancing, and the musicians in the corner of the room ceased playing in turn.

Sebastian's gloved hand was warm at the small of her back as he came up behind her. "You wanted to dance, yes?" he murmured, a smile in his voice. As he walked around to face her, she could see that the smile was more a gritting of teeth.

Leah placed her hand on his arm and lifted her chin. "Yes, my lord, I would love to dance." With a nod to the musicians, she called, "A waltz, please."

Sebastian guided her to the center of the room and they took their positions as they waited for the music to begin: her hand on his shoulder, his on her waist, their other hands clasped together. All around them, from ev-

ery corner of the room, she heard the swell of voices.
Then the music started, and they began to waltz.

Leah remembered that she'd danced with Sebastian a
few times since her first Season. She couldn't recall the
specific times, or the specific places, but she knew she'd
danced with him before. How was it, then, that this
dance seemed so incredibly intimate, each movement of
their bodies a flirtation, an unspoken question waiting
to be answered by the other?

"When the waltz is over, I suggest you make an apology. Make an excuse about this being for Ian—they probably won't believe it, but any reason is better than none."
His hand tightened on hers, his lips thinning as he glanced
over her head. "Of course, you had to wear that dress."

"Do you like the dress?"

"Do I like it? No. Do I want to tear it off of you? Yes."
His gaze returned to hers, and she found herself caught
in their green depths, tangled in his desire. "For more
than one reason, Leah."

"Mrs. George," she reminded him quietly, for his sake.

They continued dancing, Sebastian leading her as
they turned about the floor. Leah swallowed as she
glanced around; by the way no one else came out to join
the waltz, but just stood and stared at them, she sur-
mised that her attempt at breaking the rules had gone
over quite well.

Instead of feeling a flush of embarrassment rise over
her as might have happened in the past, Leah looked up
at Sebastian and smiled. "Thank you," she said, "for
dancing with me."

"I assure you, Mrs. George, it's entirely selfish. If I
were to leave you alone the consequences would be
much worse. In truth, I don't know if I've succeeded, but
I hope by waltzing with you to make it appear as if this
was planned. God help me, I hope they believe it. Just
explain when you make the apology—"

"I'm not going to apologize, Sebastian," she said, then amended, "My lord."

He turned her with him at the corner, and a wall of faces flashed by her vision. He dipped his head. "You've already created cause for a scandal," he said urgently in her ear, "but you can still minimize it."

"This is what I wanted. I won't apologize."

He drew back. "And what of Henry?"

"He's your son. It's obvious, even if you have doubts. He'll be fine." Leah forced herself to believe the words, forced herself to believe that even if Sebastian didn't understand or forgive her now, he would someday.

"Very well," he said, his shoulder stiffening beneath her touch. "Be aware, then, that once this waltz ends, I will be the first to spurn you. I will not acknowledge you again, nor will I defend you should anyone ask me the reason for your actions. In the future, if something should happen and you should ever think to ask for my assistance—no matter your situation—be assured that you will be sent away without a hearing."

The hand at her waist pressed in, guiding her through another turn.

"Do you understand?"

Her heartbeat became faint. His words threatened to topple her resolution, but she remained strong. "I understand you very well, my lord."

"Good."

She looked in his eyes, and even though no more words came, a host of unspoken emotions passed between them. There was anger in his gaze. His desire for her that she could no longer hide from. Also, resignation and regret.

She had made her choice, and he had made his. Just as Ian's and Angela's deaths had drawn them together, her actions now ensured that they were returned to a more formal relationship. Not even the polite acquaintance they had once shared, but something closer in resemblance to an aloof enmity. At last, they were the enemies they'd pledged to become.

As the last note of the waltz faded, Sebastian brought them to a halt. He withdrew his arms and stepped away. Then, without making a bow or any other gesture of courtesy, he turned his back on her and strode from the drawing room.

Breathe, she told herself. *Breathe.*

She wouldn't faint. She wouldn't vomit. No matter how inclined her body seemed toward those measures at the moment, after Sebastian gave her the cut direct in front of the entire party of guests and as those same guests stared at her in horror and salacious disbelief, she held her head up and kept her shoulders straight. If she'd learned nothing else from her mother, it was the carriage of confidence.

She pasted a smile on her face and strolled from the dancing area. The musicians began to play another tune. Yet no one moved to dance, and as she walked forward, guests edged away so that she felt like Moses parting the Red Sea. A part of her found this humorous, since every step she made created a space of three feet in distance between her and the nearest guest. But another part could not help but be mortified.

After all, after having been taught to please others for so long, it was natural that she should feel discomfort at being the object of their criticism, wasn't it?

Looking around, she spied Miss Pettigrew sneaking a glance at her. With a deep breath, Leah smiled wider. Miss Pettigrew answered with a glimmer of a smile and moved to step forward, but her arm was caught in the grip of Mrs. Thompson. The companion stared at Leah and murmured something to Miss Pettigrew. With an abashed gaze, Miss Pettigrew turned her back on Leah and began speaking with Miss Sanders.

So it was for the next half hour. Covert glances were thrown Leah's way, but no one dared approach her, and the guests' voices rose until it became clear none meant to shield their comments from her ears.

"I suspected she wasn't truly sorry about his death . . ."

"It doesn't matter if she was. She should have some sort of decency . . ."

Eventually the musicians stuttered to a halt, and the lead violinist caught her gaze. She nodded, and they played again. Not a dancing tune, but a performance piece. They'd been paid, after all, and at least the music would partially drown the overwhelming condemnation of her guests.

Finally Lady Elliot approached. "Mrs. George," she acknowledged, arching her brow. "I thought you were to tell me before you created a scandal."

Leah's smile turned genuine at the viscountess' admonition. "Please accept my apologies, my lady. I meant to surprise you."

"Oh, you did, my dear. But you do know I have no intention of keeping this quiet, don't you?"

"I rather suspected you wouldn't."

Lady Elliot nodded, her gaze approving. "Good for you," she murmured. Then, more loudly, "I'm afraid Lord Elliot and I cannot stay throughout the evening. We won't be leaving in the morning. We shall leave now."

With one last look at Leah, she whirled and placed her hand on her husband's arm. As the music played behind them and the other guests watched, Lord and Lady Elliot departed the drawing room.

Soon it became apparent that Lady Elliot would be the only one to even attempt to say good-bye. In the following minutes the others began trickling out, slowly at first, then with greater haste until a line formed to leave through the drawing room door.

Leah sighed, then moved across the room toward a

settee which had been pushed against the wall. The quartet continued to play as she sat on the sofa. Her guests' voices receded down the hall, and she listened to the wheels of their various conveyances rumble across the drive as they departed.

She might have predicted it would end this way. After all, if she had been one of the guests and her hostess had done something similar, Leah would have felt compelled to leave. Then again, with the hint of scandal surrounding such a house party, she probably wouldn't have attended in the first place.

Yet even with Sebastian's disappointment and the knowledge that she would soon become a social pariah, she felt no remorse. She'd broken the rules, did as she pleased, and for tonight at least, she would enjoy her freedom.

Every few miles Sebastian decided he would stop the carriage and have the coachman return to Linley Park. He would return to the salon, grab ahold of Leah, and demand that she return to her senses.

Then he would kiss her.

But even though he lifted his arm toward the roof of the carriage numerous times, he always ended up lowering it before he could pound on the ceiling and make his wishes known.

They had come to a standstill, he and Leah. She had made her decisions, and he must do what he could to now protect Henry from the consequences. Perhaps if he had stressed the importance of not creating a scandal before . . . but no, he'd tried. He simply hadn't told her what the consequences would mean to him, or to Henry. Even if he had, he had no reason to believe it would have changed her actions, not when she'd so readily dismissed his concerns earlier tonight.

Goddamn it.

The coachman drove the carriage on, past the chalk hills, past the rolling lines of trees that were thick, tangled shadows beneath the moonless sky. Sebastian lowered his head into his hands, the image of Leah imprinted on his mind after she'd entered the salon. Her chin lifted, head held high, more regal than Queen Victoria herself.

And the absurdity of it all was, for an instant in the corridor, he'd been glad to see her—happy that finally, even though she was wearing black, it wasn't the customary widow's weeds. In that moment, she'd seemed free. He hadn't felt guilty for wanting her so soon after Angela's death, and he hadn't felt guilty because she was Ian's wife. Everything had seemed right, their future together unclear, but certainly something possible outside of his lust-filled fantasies.

Sebastian's fist pounded at the roof before he had time to hesitate and retrieve it back to his side. The carriage slowed, the horses snuffling as the reins tightened.

His breath came faster, anticipation filling him at the prospect of turning around and returning to her. Soon the coachman climbed down and knocked on the door.

"You may open it."

The coachman's round face appeared, whiskers thickly striped along his jaw. "Ye signaled, milord?"

Sebastian inhaled. He thought of Leah.

He exhaled. And he thought of Henry.

"Never mind," he said. "It was a mistake." Turning his head, he stared out the window again. At the countryside that would soon disappear, changing into the city landscape, taking him closer to his son and farther away from Leah. "Drive on."

Four days had passed since the infamous end of her country house party. All the guests had left the night of the dinner, so that when Leah woke the next morning it was to a quiet house, completely silent except for the movements of the servants around her. It was almost as it had been after Ian had first died, when she'd retreated to Linley Park in order to escape everyone.

Leah was in the flower garden, walking among the roses in the afternoon, when she heard the sound of a vehicle approaching on the drive. She already suspected who it would be. Out of all the people who might have been upset at her behavior the other night, it was the Viscount and Viscountess Rennell whom she regretted disappointing the most.

Clutching her skirts in her hands, she left the garden and walked through the doors of the conservatory, then into the hall, pausing to pat down her hair in a mirror as she passed. No widow's cap. No veil. She'd even stopped wearing black. If they hadn't heard the rumors, her appearance would tell them all they needed to know.

Herrod appeared at the top of the stairs as she started her ascent. "Madam, Lord Rennell—"

"In the drawing room?"

He inclined his head. "Yes, madam. The viscount has already requested tea and biscuits."

"Of course. And send in those cherry tarts his lordship is so fond of as well."

Bowing deeply, Herrod disappeared. Leah climbed the stairs to the drawing room. Her hands trembled at her sides as she paused outside the doorway. She took a deep breath, straightened her shoulders, then walked in.

"My lord Rennell. My la—" She paused, frozen in the middle of her curtsy. Lady Rennell was not present.

The viscount came to his feet and gave a perfunctory bow. "Leah, please. Have a seat."

Thirty seconds. That's all it took for it to be clear that he was the master of Linley Park, that she was at his mercy for her shelter, her food, and her amusements.

Leah sat.

A maid entered at that moment with the tea service, and neither spoke as she arranged the tray between them. When she left, Leah leaned forward and poured two cups of tea. "Milk and sugar as usual, my lord?" she asked.

"Yes, thank you. And I see you sent for cherry tarts." A small smile crossed his mouth as he selected one of the pastries.

Leah passed him the cup of tea, proud of the surety of her hands. Not one ripple marred the surface of the liquid. However, when she stirred in her own sugar and removed her own cup of tea from the tray, it nearly tipped over and scalded her lap.

"I've come to request that you leave Linley Park within a fortnight," Lord Rennell said a moment later. "I will give you a small purse of coin—"

"Thank you, my lord."

"—but afterward, you will no longer be welcome at any of our homes, nor will we continue to support your livelihood."

Leah met his eyes, then looked down. She nodded. "I understand."

A few elongated, terrible moments of silence followed, in which she alternated between sipping at her tea and listening to the sound of Lord Rennell eating his cherry tart.

Finally, she heard him set his cup on the tray. "Leah," he said softly. She glanced up. "Do you think that we didn't know?"

She stared. "The party . . . You did receive my letter, didn't you?"

"Not the party. About Ian. He was our son. And you, even in such a short time, have become like our daughter."

"My lord . . . I'm sorry—"

"No, don't apologize." His mouth quirked, and it re-

minded her of Ian. "We both know you wouldn't mean
it, anyway. I daresay you deserve to be happy now. God
knows Lady Rennell and I both regretted seeing you so
downtrodden with Ian's faithlessness."

"How long did you know?" she asked, her grip tightening on her teacup. The wonderful part of keeping her
husband's affair a secret was her belief that no one else
had been privy to her humiliation. She realized her own
strength and confidence now, but the viscount and viscountess must have witnessed her at her worst: small
and weak, stripped of her pride.

"Something changed in you. You ceased looking at
Ian as if he were a king and became more reserved, even
toward us." He paused. "We would have liked you to
continue as our daughter, if only in name. We do care for
you, my dear, and would have done anything for you.
But now . . ."

She nodded.

"We cannot ignore the rumors. It would make us appear ignorant and foolish. Also, I suspect you knew the
consequences of your actions before you carried them
out."

"I did, although I regret bringing shame upon you
and Lady Rennell."

The viscount waved a hand. "It's done now." He
stood, and she followed. He smiled across at her, then
reached out to take her hand. Leah lowered her gaze,
watched as he enfolded it between his. It was one of the
most comforting gestures she had ever known and, not
for the first time, she found herself jealous of Ian for
having the sort of parents she'd always dreamed of.

"We wish you the best, Leah." The viscount withdrew
his hands. "You have a fortnight. No more. I will see that
the purse I spoke of is delivered to Herrod shortly." He
gave her another bow. "Good day, Mrs. George."

Leah curtsied. "Good day, my lord." She watched him

walk away, and just before he strode from the room, added, "And thank you."

"Be careful," Sebastian warned.

Henry paid no heed, teetering on the bench before the pianoforte as he leaned over and banged on the keys. Grinning, he looked at Sebastian and said, "Play, play, play!" before turning back and once again serenading Sebastian with his masterpiece.

Sebastian shifted, his elbows moving to his knees, his hands open and ready to catch Henry if he should fall.

Henry swiped his hand down the pianoforte and pivoted toward Sebastian, moving his hands up and down in the air on an invisible instrument. His foot slid to the edge of the bench and Sebastian swept forward, his arms outstretched and his heart beating madly in his chest as he tried to catch his son.

But Henry righted his balance and turned back to the pianoforte, unconcerned.

"Sit down," Sebastian said, pointing to the bench. Henry didn't respond.

Scooping his legs out from under him, Sebastian planted Henry on the seat, then scooted beside him. His arm supported Henry's back in case he decided to fall sideways and scare Sebastian again.

Henry grinned up at Sebastian and pointed to the pianoforte. "Papa play."

Sebastian smiled and touched one key, leaving his hand at rest until the note died. Then, as Henry watched, he moved his finger over each key, all the way down and back up, faster and faster.

"Hooray!" Henry shouted when he was finished, clapping his hands.

"Hooray!" Sebastian echoed, glancing at the half-open door to the music room, his voice not quite as loud.

He feared that was as well as he could do; he'd never

been offered music lessons, and he'd never had any interest in playing the pianoforte. For some reason, though, he was fairly certain Leah knew how to play the instrument, if not many others. She was capable, intelligent, trained to act the perfect Victorian lady; it seemed only natural that she would excel at nearly everything.

A week had passed, and though it seemed the rest of the *ton* had deserted London in favor of their country estates, Sebastian had kept Henry in the city.

Why?

It was a question he asked himself at least ten times a day.

Because he thought—he hoped—Leah would return to London after the disastrous end to her house party. Because, even though another new rumor spread every day and he knew it was only a matter of time before he heard one about Ian and Angela, he couldn't stop thinking of Leah.

He had no reason to believe she would come to him—he'd specifically told her not to—and yet he stayed, looking through the post as soon as the butler brought it to him each day, wandering toward the front door whenever he thought he heard someone knock.

Henry pushed his arm away and climbed down off the bench, and Sebastian turned on the seat to watch him. Henry went first to a plant and fiddled with its leaves, then crouched down and poked his finger in the soil. "No," Sebastian said when it appeared his son might stick his finger in his mouth.

Henry glanced at him over his shoulder with a look that could be described only as mischievous. It reminded Sebastian of Leah. Hell, he admitted silently, raking his hand through his hair, everything reminded him of Leah. He looked for her everywhere, tried to see her in everything, even dreamed of her at night.

Henry meandered from the potted plant to the sofa,

climbing up onto the cushions and then attempting to hoist himself over the back. Sebastian stood to rescue him again.

It was time to move on. He was exhausting himself, and Henry needed the countryside to play. He needed the wide-open fields to run in and soft grass to tumble on. Sebastian couldn't rescue Leah. And it was clear that she didn't want him to, for she hadn't come, nor had she written him.

It was time he saw her as she saw herself: a widow with no need for anyone else.

Sebastian crouched low and hurried behind the sofa. First he saw Henry's hand reach over the top, then the crop of his blond hair. Sebastian growled, then jumped up and snagged Henry in his arms, holding the squealing, giggling boy tight. "Come," he said, striding to the door. "It's time to go to Hampshire."

Chapter 14

When I lie in your arms, the entire world stills. The night fades, and the sun doesn't dare to show its face. My life seems to exist in moments like these, in the short hours I am with you.

Leah stood as her mother entered the room.

"I thought your message said you've be arriving earlier this morning."

"The train was delayed."

"I see." Her mother's expression was one of both disapproval and victory. How glad she was, Leah thought, to see that her errant child must be forced to come under her wing. Even though Leah's reputation was ruined, all that mattered was Adelaide's satisfaction.

"I've had a footman take your things up to your old bedchamber. I haven't changed anything since your wedding, so everything should be as it was before. However, I believe we need to discuss the expectations your father and I have for you, now that you've returned home. Namely, the expectations we have now that you have threatened the reputation of the Hartwell name."

Leah remained silent. There was nothing to say, after all. She'd taken control of her life, but that control had resulted in her losing her independence to her mother again. She wore black once more, had donned her veil for the journey home. Would that the coin purse from Viscount Rennell had been but a little larger. Then she would have had enough to travel somewhere else, where her reputation wouldn't have preceded her. In Ireland or Europe, or even in America, she might have been able to find a decent position as a governess or companion with the benefit of her speech and education.

Adelaide moved to the sofa opposite of Leah and tucked her skirts beneath her as she sat down. Pursing her lips, she scanned Leah's appearance. As always, the direct evaluation was quite tedious. Leah didn't squirm, however, nor did she avert her eyes; she met her mother's gaze evenly, her chin lifted. She might have nowhere to go but her family's home, but she was more confident now. She would not be cowed by the same steely glance that had once caused her to scrub her face until it was raw when she was younger, just in case her mother might comment upon the dullness of her complexion.

"You've lost weight again." It was difficult to tell whether Adelaide was more pleased or disappointed at her daughter's failure.

Leah's fingers twitched in her lap. It was what she'd expected after missing breakfasts during the house party, but she couldn't explain the reason behind her lack of appetite. It hurt too much to think of Sebastian, and she could never speak of him to her mother. He would be her secret, his words and their time spent together to be examined over and over again only in the darkness of her own bedchamber.

"I shall eat twice as much at dinner," she replied, hoping at least that they could move on to a different topic quickly.

Her mother seemed happy with her response. "I've already decided what we must do in order to halt the rumors and remove you from the scandal you've created."

Hopefully it would be to sequester her in a nunnery. Right now that idea sounded much more appealing than living beneath her mother's roof once more.

"You will continue to wear your mourning clothes, of course, although I think you should have more bombazine dresses. You are fortunate that it's autumn and we're no longer in London. Otherwise I would forbid you to go outside. However, you will have a servant with you at all times should you decide to go for a walk or a ride—and if you do make such a decision, you will act as the lady I have instructed you to be."

"You believe the scandal will die down simply because I begin to act like a regular widow once again? That if we ignore the rumors, my reputation might be saved?"

"Of course not." Adelaide gave a small humph. "I'm only telling you these things because I fear if I don't mention them you will believe that you have the freedom to do otherwise. No, my dear, I fear the only thing that will save our family's name now is for you to marry again once your time of mourning is finished."

This time, Leah was unable to keep herself detached. Her entire body flinched at her mother's words, and she felt her stomach roll—not once, but twice.

"Since the Season has ended, we don't have very many choices, but do not worry, my dear. I've already selected two potential candidates for your next husband. Fortunately, they both live nearby so that your courting may be done as expediently as possible. You will be engaged quietly, the banns announced as soon as it's appropriate, and when you are married again, you won't have to live so far away from us."

"Mother, I . . . I cannot marry again."

Adelaide stared at her, a frown marring her smooth forehead. "You cannot marry again?" she asked, her tone bemused. Too quiet.

"Perhaps later, after a few years. When I've—I've—" Leah stammered to a halt, unable to comprehend the possibility of lying together with another man. So quickly after Ian's death, and so soon after she had gained her independence from the marital bed. Even a few years seemed too short of a time. "I will not marry again," she said, then added when her mother's frown turned into a reproving glare: "Not right now, at least."

"Hmm. Well, darling, I'm afraid it's the only choice you have. While I would thoroughly enjoy you staying with us for as long as you wish, I fear that the little party you gave has made that impossible. We can only work to improve your situation. As you said, ignoring the rumors will do no good, and there is nothing else that can be done to stop them except for you to marry again. Then the gossipmongers will see that you have been taken in hand by another husband, and they will find something else to speak of."

Leah swallowed, her heartbeat deafening as it pounded in her ears. "Then, if I understand you correctly, you mean to say that if I do not agree to either one of your suggested husbands, I may not be allowed to live here?"

Adelaide tilted her head to the side, blinking. "I'm sorry, Leah, but there's no other choice. If you cannot do this, you must realize your scandal will soon spread to your father and me. Of course, we would not care as much, but it would also affect Beatrice. You wouldn't ruin her opportunities at such a wonderful marriage as you had with Ian, would you?"

"Beatrice," Leah repeated.

"Your sister." Her mother gave a small smile, the width of which did nothing to hide her growing satisfaction. Satisfaction that she had caught Leah in her trap, that she would once again direct Leah's life?

Inhaling, Leah forced her shoulders to relax. "May I ask who the two men are whom you've already selected as candidates for my next husband? And how do you know that they will be amenable to courting me? Will they not have been dissuaded by my actions?"

"Not at all. Your father has seen fit to provide you with another dowry. A smaller one than you had when you married Ian, to be sure, but a decent one, nonetheless."

Leah's smile felt brittle. Idly, she wondered if she laughed now whether she would break apart into a thousand tiny pieces. "But it's not a dowry, is it? You mean to pay someone to take me."

Her mother raised an eyebrow. "Your reputation is ruined, Leah. We are merely providing necessary inducement for the gentlemen to court you."

"Again, may I ask who these men are?"

"Of course. You know both of them well. First, there is Mr. Grimmons—"

"Mr. Grimmons? The vicar?"

Her mother shrugged. "Clergymen need money, too, my dear. I believe his sister and her husband were helping with part of his support, but apparently that has ended."

"But my reputation—"

"Does not matter to him. I've assured Mr. Grimmons that you have learned the error of your ways and are more repentant. He believes it is grief which led you to behave so wickedly. And what better way to assure everyone that you are still my good and proper daughter than for you to marry a vicar?"

Leah inwardly sighed. "And the other?"

"Mr. Hapersby."

Leah stared. "Mother."

Adelaide waved her hand. "No, no. He's an excellent match as well. I might have exaggerated when I called him a gentleman, but butchery is good, somber work. And you cannot be mistaken for a frivolous young woman when you're helping your husband carve and sell meats."

Leah continued staring.

Finally, her mother had the grace to look abashed. "I must admit, I did try to convince Lord Sommers that you would make a fine wife, but he wanted assurance that you could breed in order to take you on, and since you had no children with Ian—"

"I understand." Thank God. For once, thank God she'd never borne a child. Lord Sommers was at least eighty years of age, with a bulbous nose and bulbous eyes and a neck that sagged to the middle of his chest. She might have had to endure Ian's lovemaking, but at least she hadn't been physically repulsed by him.

"Well? Do you agree that you must marry one of these men? Will you act in good faith when they come to call on you?"

Perhaps it was the frighteningly cheerful lilt of her mother's voice, or simply that she'd observed too many of Adelaide's schemes, but dread crept up Leah's spine at the last of her questions. She didn't know if she could do this. "And . . . when might they begin calling on me, Mother?"

Adelaide smiled. "Why, Mr. Grimmons is coming to dinner tonight, my dear."

Sebastian lay on his stomach at the edge of the blanket, his elbows propping him up as he moved one of the yellow blocks to the fore of the castle. Of course, Henry had no idea it was a castle. To him, it was simply a pile of wooden blocks to be built up and then knocked down again when it became so high he couldn't resist.

Reaching for a blue block, Sebastian locked eyes with Henry and smiled conspiratorially as he lodged this one at the top of the castle. With an answering grin, Henry stepped forward, wobbling a bit as his foot caught on a fold of the blanket, and swiped his arm against the structure, toppling it all but the two lowest sections. Sebastian lifted his arm in the air, and Henry mimicked him, turning in circles and crying out, "Again, Papa, again!"

For more than a fortnight they'd been in Hampshire at the Wriothesly estate. The countryside seemed to do Henry well. Every day, Sebastian would rescue him from his nurse after going over business with the steward, and they'd roam about the manor or the grounds.

They played hide-and-seek on the lower floor, where Sebastian chased Henry around and around the sofa in his study, pretending to lose his breath and hobbling like an old man. Where he listened to Henry giggle as he rounded the sofa again and caught Sebastian by his legs.

They went for walks over the meadows, Sebastian pointing out the various insects and flowers that Henry kept stopping to look at and touch. Sebastian even allowed Henry to sit on the pony he'd bought him for his second birthday. By the time Henry was five, he'd no doubt be jumping fences.

Yet even though Henry appeared to enjoy himself, and Sebastian did everything he could to amuse and distract him, in the evenings when they said their good nights Henry still wrapped his little arms around Sebastian's neck. Clinging, he would ask in the hushed whisper his nurse taught him was used at bedtime, "When is Mama here?"

Sebastian separated the blocks by colors as they prepared to build up the castle again. This time, he would try to make the tower ten blocks high. Henry seemed to squeal louder the taller it became.

"Here. Put the red one on," he instructed, then watched as Henry took it from his hand and turned toward the castle ruins, his knees bending, leaning forward in that serious, determined little boy way.

After placing the red block on top, he held out his hand again to Sebastian. "Blue, Papa."

Sebastian tried to give him a yellow block, but Henry closed his fist and shook his head. "No. Blue block."

Grinning, Sebastian held up a green one. "Is this it?"

"No."

He held up an orange one. "This one, you mean?"

Henry stared; then his cheeks rounded as he smiled. "No, Papa. Blue block." Stepping forward, he reached for the blue pile, but Sebastian grabbed him beneath his arms and swung him about, laying him faceup on the blanket. He lifted the green one again.

"This is blue," he said.

Henry giggled and shook his head. "Green."

Sebastian tickled him, and Henry rolled from side to side, kicking his legs as he laughed.

"Blue. Admit it," Sebastian threatened, "or I'll continue to tickle you."

"Green!" Henry shouted, and laughed again.

Black boots appeared at the edge of Sebastian's vision. "What insolent cur is this, to contradict and attack his lordship? Never fear, Viscount Maddows, I will protect you."

"Uncle Jamie!" Henry screamed with delight as James pulled him loose from Sebastian's grasp and swung him around and around.

Climbing to his feet, Sebastian nudged the blocks into the center of the blanket. After a few more moments of spinning, James set Henry back on the ground. The boy ran to Sebastian, his grin wide, and hugged Sebastian's legs.

Sebastian looked at James. "This is a pleasant surprise."

The smile on James' face faded. "I have news."

*　　*　　*

That evening, after dinner and after Sebastian had said good night to Henry, he and James sat in his study. James drank whiskey. Sebastian had nothing. Ever since the experience of being drunk in front of Leah, he had no inclination to imbibe. Even the sting of liquor reminded him of her.

"There are rumors going around."

Sebastian shrugged. "There are always rumors going around."

"It's about Ian's widow. Mrs. George."

Although he tried not to show his reaction, Sebastian couldn't keep his gaze from flying to meet James'. "I'm not surprised about that, either. I told you what happened at the house party. She's brought this on herself."

James' foot scuffed against the rug below his chair. "Then this might get your attention, because you are now included in those rumors, dear brother."

Sebastian straightened. "Go on."

"It appears that several of the guests at the house party are now convinced that you and Mrs. George are . . . How should I put it?"

"Damn it, James, stop this dithering around. What are they saying?"

"The rumor is you and she are . . . involved. If not lovers, then close." James looked down at his whiskey, swirling it around. "Although I suspect soon the gossip will take that final leap."

Sebastian clenched his jaw. It was of no use to point out that he'd been the first one to leave the party, or that he'd gone solely to keep her from creating a scandal. The gossipmongers wouldn't care; in fact, it would probably only feed the fire for him to defend himself. The best thing he could do for the entire situation—for himself, for Leah, and for Henry—was to ignore it.

Exhaling slowly, he leaned back against his chair. His

hands curved over the end of the polished oak arms. "Let them talk as they wish. It will pass eventually—before fox hunting season, if not sooner, I predict. I have no plans to see Mrs. George again, so anything she does now will be on her shoulders alone."

James nodded and sipped from his glass. "I trust you are right." He paused, sipped again. "But if you're not?"

Sebastian shrugged, annoyed at their conversation and the reminder of Leah, when he had tried so hard to put her from his mind. "There's nothing to be done. Let them gossip. It means nothing to me."

A month passed, and as the days went by, Leah's desperation to escape grew stronger and stronger. Especially in moments like these, when she was required to spend time with one of her two suitors. Of the two, Mr. Grimmons the vicar was the least bothersome. He was severe in his appearance and his manners, but he also seemed quite uncomfortable around her, which made the afternoons easier for her. Mr. Hapersby, on the other hand, leered at her the entire time they were together. After having spent twenty years without being the object of lust, his ogling tempted her to do whatever she must to scare him away. But she couldn't—she knew they both reported to Adelaide after each session, and Leah knew her mother well enough to understand that her threats were not idle. If she didn't cooperate, she would be required to leave the house. And she had nowhere else to go.

As she walked sedately beside Mr. Grimmons in the garden, Leah plucked a late-blooming rose from its stem and twirled it between her fingers. Without intending to, she remembered the night she'd found Lord Wriothesly in Ian's study, and how he'd told her she smelled like roses.

Hiding her smile, Leah slid a glance at Mr. Grimmons from beneath her lashes. "Do you like roses, sir?"

The young vicar startled—apparently he'd been lost

in one of his reveries again—and looked at her, blinking beneath the glare of the sunlight. "I enjoy all of God's creation, Mrs. George. Do you not?"

"Of course," she murmured. "But I have a particular affinity for roses."

"Oh." They walked a few more moments in silence; then Mr. Grimmons halted. "Wait here, please," he said. He turned to the side, where a white rosebush bloomed, and snapped off a partially open flower midstem. "For you, Mrs. George."

"Thank you." She looked at him, but he said nothing more. No compliment to compare her skin to the rose, nothing to emphasize his regard for her. He didn't even blush—as she might have expected—or meet her gaze with his limpid brown eyes that were two inches too close together.

Instead he stared straight ahead, his arms stiff at his sides. Sighing, Leah held the white rose he'd given her in her hand and dropped the red one to the ground.

"Mrs. George."

Leah waited, but he didn't say anything else. "Yes, Mr. Grimmons?"

"I would like to discuss a matter with you. But out of respect to your sensibilities after so recently losing your husband . . ."

Oh, how she was tempted to tell him that she'd never grieved at all. Would he be horrified? No, he'd probably take that as encouragement. But if she pretended to weep, would he try to comfort her? Leah glanced at his profile—the stern pull of his mouth, the angular line of his jaw. Probably not.

She sniffed, just to see.

He looked at her, concern in his expression, and stepped closer to her.

Oh, God. Leah gave a weak smile. "I think I might be growing ill."

He stilled, then subtly stepped back to his side of the garden path. "Perhaps we should go inside. And if you are feeling better tomorrow, would you mind if I call on you again? I would like to . . . discuss something with you."

Inwardly sighing, Leah came to a halt. "Do you intend to ask me to marry you?" Let it be done today, then, so she didn't spend half the night fearing what the words out of his mouth would be the next afternoon.

Mr. Grimmons stumbled, then whirled around to face her. This time his cheeks did flush and his mouth hung open. "I—"

"If that is your intent, sir, then it seems that it might be best to spare us both the time in waiting."

His mouth closed, his eyes narrowed, and Mr. Grimmons looked at her as if she were a creature that had, if not crawled from the bowels of hell, then dropped from some bewildering place below heaven. "In truth, Mrs. George, I understand it is your mother's wish that we might wed, but I do not believe you are the one God has chosen for me."

Leah stared, feeling her own cheeks heat. "Oh."

"I wanted to ask you about your sister. Miss Beatrice."

"Oh."

"I wished to discuss my intention of asking for Miss Beatrice's hand. Although I'm sure you would bring honor and respect to your next husband—"

He seemed to choke on the words "honor and respect." Leah smiled, wondering if he was thinking about the rumors of her and the house party.

"—I have known Miss Beatrice much longer, and I have formed quite an attachment to her. I sincerely apologize if this news distresses you, but—"

"Mr. Grimmons."

His gaze returned from somewhere above her head, and he met her eyes.

"I will speak to Beatrice, if you wish."

He blushed again—and it softened his intense, earnest expression, making him appear almost charming. "Thank you, Mrs. George."

Leah stretched out her arm and handed the white rose to him. She winked. "Beatrice's favorite flower is the calla lily."

As she'd done every week since her mother gave her the ultimatum of marrying or leaving the house, Leah pored over Beatrice's women's magazine, searching in vain for a job which didn't require skills she didn't possess or a reputation she no longer had.

A knock came at her bedchamber door. Before Leah could call out the door swung open and her mother strode in. She shut the door quietly behind her. "What have you done?" Adelaide asked.

Leah flipped to another page in the magazine, to an innocent spread on the latest fashions. "Perhaps you could elaborate, Mother. I'm not sure—"

"I was expecting Mr. Grimmons to come again today and take you riding, but instead of waiting for you to come downstairs—which I noticed you never did—he asked for me. Do you pretend not to know what he said?"

Leah sat up on the bed. "He's not interested in marrying me."

Her mother's gaze narrowed shrewdly. "No. He wants to marry Beatrice."

"Unfortunately," Leah said, "when I spoke to Beatrice of it, she didn't seem very enthusiastic."

"You spoke to Beatrice?"

Leah nodded, her breath shortening as her mother approached the bedside.

Adelaide's lips pursed, then flattened, then pursed again. Her nostrils flared. "Of course," she said softly, "I told him Beatrice was too young for marriage. The fool, thinking I would give my daughter to him."

Her new favorite daughter, she doubtless meant. Though her mother had refused to settle for anything less than a title with Leah's first husband, it seemed any man would do now as long as his status wasn't lower than the village butcher's.

"Mr. Grimmons was not pleased when I told him Beatrice couldn't marry him. When I asked him if he would not reconsider marrying you, would you like to know what he said?"

Leah waited.

"He said you were too forward. What did you do, Leah?"

She shrugged. "I simply asked him if he meant to marry me." Leah's gaze fell to her mother's side, where her hand twitched. Tensing, she waited for Adelaide's arm to rise, for her palm to attempt to strike, but Adelaide instead stepped back with a smile.

"Well, since you have ruined any chance you had with the vicar, I suppose that means only one thing. I was going to allow you the choice of either man, but I know Mr. Hapersby planned to ask for you later this week. Now I will tell him you are all his."

Leah rose from the bed to stand beside her mother. They were close in height, although Leah had a slight advantage. "And if I do not wish to marry him?"

Adelaide's gaze flickered, but no sign of sympathy or remorse entered her expression. "Then you are welcome to leave. Would you like me to ring a maid to help you pack?"

"No," Leah said. She would do it herself.

Chapter 15

*She pretends well. How happy she appeared
tonight at your side. And yes, if you must know,
how jealous I was to watch you together.*

As he'd done every Sunday since returning to Hampshire, Sebastian sat on the front pew of the church and listened to the vicar's sermon. Today, it was about adultery. Not particularly something that he wanted to hear, but they'd been going through the Ten Commandments for the past few weeks. Vicar Peters had seemed most enthused about taking the Lord's name in vain, but today the topic of adultery managed to excite him to red-faced proportions.

His voice became louder and louder as he spoke, until Sebastian began cringing away. It was even difficult to allow his thoughts to drift with the man's voice booming within the small confines of the church.

Sebastian straightened in the pew. If Henry were here, he'd no doubt be covering his ears by now. But after bringing the boy to church a few weeks ago, Sebas-

tian had learned his lesson. Henry wasn't frightened of
Vicar Peters, Sebastian, or God, for every attempt at
keeping him quiet and still had been ignored. No, he was
at home. Blessed, peaceful home, with his nurse attending to him.

"And that is why the Lord God demands that we are
faithful. For just as we are faithful to our spouses, He
expects us to be faithful to Him. Was He not faithful on
the cross? Did he not—"

Sebastian winced, ducking his head to avoid a further
assault on his ears. Thankfully, the sermon was soon
over, the completion of the remaining rituals signaling it
was time to leave.

Standing, he took a breath and prepared to greet his
fellow parishioners. Once the rumors had begun regarding an affair with Leah, he'd made every point of being
friendly and polite, disregarding their curious glances
and sly whispers.

"Mr. Powell," he greeted. "Mrs. Powell. A pleasure to
see you this fine Sunday morning."

Mr. Powell made a similar, inconsequential greeting
in return, and Sebastian was about to turn away toward
the Byars family when he saw Mrs. Powell shaking her
head, tears in her eyes.

"Mrs. Powell?"

"Oh, Lord Wriothesly," she said, reaching out but not
quite touching him, her hand hovering above his arm. "I
saw you over there in your pew. How today's subject
must have wounded you. If there's anything Mr. Powell
or I can do . . ."

Sebastian inclined his head, looking down at her in
bemusement. "I apologize, Mrs. Powell, I'm not sure—"

Glancing at her husband who gave a short nod, she
edged nearer, stood on her toes, and whispered—loudly.
"We've all heard the news of Lady Wriothesly and Mr.
George. Of their . . . being together."

Sebastian stiffened. "Surely it can't be recent news that my wife and my friend were together in the carriage accident which killed them both." He stared at her, his jaw firm. "That is what you're implying, is it not?"

Mrs. Powell's eyes grew wide. "I—"

"Martha," Mr. Powell said, taking more heed to Sebastian's warning than his wife appeared inclined to do, for she continued talking.

"But . . . if it isn't true, my lord—which of course I now realize it couldn't be. It's just shameful how quickly such rumors can spread. Was Mr. Peters not speaking of the evil of gossip only a while ago?" She smiled, a faltering curve of her lips, and lowered herself from her toes. She shook her head ruefully. "But it's just as well you know, my lord. So you can be prepared should someone else mention it."

"Thank you, Mrs. Powell. How fortunate I heard it first from you."

Mrs. Powell nodded slowly. She appeared as if she might add something else, but her husband took her elbow and began leading her away.

"A fine day to you, Lord Wriothesly," he said.

"And to you as well. A fine day."

Goddamn it. How in the hell had the rumor started? How could he not have known about it earlier? Now it was clear why Vicar Peters had continued looking at him during his sermon—not because of the rumors of an affair with Leah, but because he, too, must have heard the gossip about Angela and Ian.

"Lord Wriothesly. How is little Henry?" Mrs. Harrell asked, pulling her two little towheaded girls behind her.

"Very well, thank you." Sebastian looked at the girls, their names escaping his mind. Everything escaping except the reminder of Henry and the threat to him if the rumor about Angela and Ian was allowed to grow and mutate into something even darker. Thank God he hadn't brought Henry, or the parishioners might have seen the blond boy sitting beside Sebastian and begun to wonder at the difference in their appearances.

Mrs. Harrell was saying something, but Sebastian didn't hear a word.

"I beg your pardon, Mrs. Harrell, but I must go. Henry isn't feeling well, and although his nurse is taking care of him, I promised to look in after him as soon as the service was over."

"Oh, but I thought you said he was well."

Sebastian had begun walking way, but paused to look back over his shoulder. "He is. I mean, better than before."

"Well, then." Mrs. Harrell smiled politely, though her wrinkled brow attested to her confusion. "Please give him our best wishes. We will be praying for him."

"Thank you. Yes, of course. I will."

Damn it. Sebastian wove his way through the throng of churchgoers as he headed toward the doors, acknowledging various greetings with a dip of his head and a smile. Damn it. Where had the gossip spread by now? Surely James would have alerted him to it if he'd heard anything in London. Passing through the doors, Sebastian looked at the line of people waiting to say their farewells to the vicar. Cursing beneath his breath, he stepped to the side and walked past them.

"Lord Wriothesly," he heard Vicar Peters call.

Sebastian halted and turned, gritting his teeth. "My apologies, Vicar, but I must return home. Henry is ill today."

He eyed the sky—a normal gray. Anytime. God would send a bolt of lightning down to strike him at any moment for lying to a clergyman. Perhaps two lightning bolts, since he'd also lied to Mrs. Harrell inside the church. Sebastian moved a little to the left, out of the shadow of the eave, creating a clear path from the heav-

ens to where he stood. Then again, it could be a boon for
God to strike him dead in front of the church, here before dozens of witnesses. That news, at least, might shift
the attention away from Ian and Angela.

Vicar Peters frowned. "I understand," he said. But his
expression revealed more than godly concern; there was
also pity there, deep in his gaze. He, too, believed the
rumor about Ian and Angela.

Sebastian nodded and swung away, cursing beneath
his breath. There was only one person to blame for this.

Leah George.

Sebastian stared at the sketch he'd begun in the evergreen garden at Linley Park. The surrounding details
were filled in and painted now, but her face was yet to be
completed. Over the past two months he'd drawn the
slender arch of her eyebrows, the firmness of her chin,
the straight slope of her nose. But her eyes and lips remained invisible, his mind unable, or perhaps unwilling,
to commit them to canvas.

Working on her portrait was the only time he allowed
himself to think of her. These moments late at night
when Henry was in bed and even all the servants had
gone to sleep were the only ones where he allowed his
doubts to surface, allowed his lingering thoughts of Angela to fade as he imagined talking with Leah, smiling
with Leah . . . kissing Leah.

Although he didn't know how the rumors had
skipped from their supposed affair to the affair between
Ian and Angela, he knew that Leah was tied in to that
speculation. No one else knew that he hadn't arranged
for Ian to escort Angela to Hampshire; James only knew
the truth because Sebastian had told him.

And while he'd been fairly sure the rumors about
Leah and himself would die down—and they had, for
the most part—he had no idea how long it would take,

or what damages would be done, before the gossip about Ian and Angela had run its course.

Sebastian reached out to the unfinished portrait, his fingers hovering over the faint line of Leah's cheek. Slowly, he withdrew his arm and let it hang again at his side.

There were several things he could do. He could ignore the rumors, as he'd done with the ones about Leah. He could also deny Ian and Angela's affair. But neither of those routes would cease the gossip immediately. And each day it continued, there was a chance that the next extension of the rumors would turn to speculation about Henry's parentage.

Before even acknowledging the third idea as a fully formed thought in his mind, Sebastian wondered if it was actually something valid that would help stop the rumors, or if it occurred to him only because he desired it as an excuse.

But no—why would he want to seek her out, when he had worked so hard to forget her? When she had made it clear more than once that his attentions weren't welcome. When, although he'd tried to forget Angela as well, he was still wounded by her betrayal.

Yet of the three ideas which came to him, it was this last one which appealed to him the most. Sebastian sat in his chair and studied the portrait, his mind readily supplying Leah George's extraordinary brown eyes and decadent mouth.

Tomorrow, he would leave Hampshire and find her.

Leah smiled at the seamstress who had first showed her the organza. She didn't even know her name, which she regretted now. Surely it would have been better to call her by something other than "Miss" when searching for employment.

"Good afternoon," she said brightly, aware that the

assistant probably believed she was there for another gown since she was wearing a day dress of green poplin—nothing so serviceable as a worker's attire.

Perhaps she should have gone around back and knocked on the door there? Swallowing, Leah placed her hands on the counter, then lowered them to her waist.

"I'm not sure if you remember me," she began.

"Of course, Mrs. George. We remember all of our clients." The seamstress smiled politely. "How may I help you today?"

"Actually, I've come to apply for a job." There, she said it.

The smile on the assistant's face remained in place, though her brows knit. "I beg your pardon—"

"I sew quite well. In fact, quite a few pieces of embroidery have been admired by the queen herself."

"You are looking for a job, Mrs. George?"

Leah sighed, smiling again. A friendly smile, not her polite smile which hid all of her teeth. "Yes. I would like to join your little shop as a seamstress."

As soon as the words escaped her mouth, the assistant's mouth narrowed, her eyes losing some of their kindness. Oh no. Had that seemed patronizing? Little shop?

"I've much admired your work in the past, and I think, with a little instruction, I could learn to make beautiful dresses."

The seamstress stared at her.

"And other things, of course. I needn't be limited to gowns. I could make chemises and cloaks. Those wouldn't be as hard, would they?"

"You want to be a seamstress?"

"Yes." Leah looked about the shop, at the piles of books, the cluttered bolts of cloth. Everything had appeared so clean before when she'd come to buy a dress, but now that she really looked, she could see how an-

other hand could help organize the front better. And if
the front was just a little messy, she couldn't begin to
imagine what the back of the shop must look like, where
they did all the work. "Or I could clean," she suggested.
"Keep things tidy. More menial labor before I improved
enough to become a seamstress."

The assistant crossed her arms. "I'm sorry, Mrs.
George, but we do not need another seamstress."

Leah shifted to her other foot. "Perhaps if I could
talk to the modiste ..."

"She's busy with a customer."

"Oh, I see. Hmm." Leah tapped her fingers against
her skirt.

"Good day, Mrs. George." And just like that, she was
being dismissed.

Leah tried to swallow, but a lump of pride caught in
her throat. With an attempt at a smile, she turned toward
the door. "Thank you, Miss—" She stopped and looked
at the assistant. "Excuse me. What is your name?"

"Elaine. My name is Elaine."

Leah nodded and smiled again. "Thank you, Elaine.
Good day to you as well."

The stench of manure took her breath away as she
opened the door. Odd, but her senses had never seemed
so overwhelmed by London before, when she had more
money and a secure future. Now there was a beggar every few feet, their appearances only distinguishable by
the limbs they were missing.

The sounds were louder as well: the jostling of horse
harnesses, the hawking of the vendors. As Leah walked
away from the shop, she recoiled at a drunken man who
stepped into her path, the narrow slits of his eyes focused on her bodice. His breath reeked of spirits, his
clothes of urine. He didn't say anything, though, instead
crossing the street without giving heed to where he was
going. When an oncoming cart nearly trampled him,

Leah flinched, her arms outstretching as if she could reach him and pull him to safety.

How had she been so blind before? Nothing had changed about her except her station in life. She still wore the clothes of a lady; she still moved and spoke with dignity. Nothing about her was different. . . .

Except now she had no one to wait on her, no one to assure her safety. Her world which had previously been one of wealth and privilege was now mired right along with the other less fortunates of the city.

On the lookout for the muck which would ruin her skirts, Leah kept her head down as she walked toward her next destination: the milliner's where she'd once bought her hats. She'd taken only a few steps, however, when she collided with someone. A woman who, when compared to the other people crowding the area, smelled sweeter than a valley of daisies.

"Mrs. George!"

Leah lifted her head. "Miss Pettigrew." At last, a friendly face. "How are you?"

"I'm fine, thank you." The other woman took her elbow and they edged to the side to allow a businessman to pass. "I'm wonderful, actually. Mrs. Thompson resigned from the post of companion two days ago."

"Oh. Did she?" Leah's heart thrilled with hope.

"Yes. Apparently she and Father had a discussion after we returned from Linley Park. After Father heard about . . ." Miss Pettigrew scrunched her nose.

"Me?" Leah supplied, her tone dry.

"Well, yes. You. After Father heard about what you did the night of the dinner party, he said he couldn't understand how a real lady could have advised her young charge to attend a house party hosted by a recent widow in the first place. They argued. Father threatened. I thought Mrs. Thompson meant to stay on. She tried, God knows, although I prayed every night she would leave."

Leah smiled as Miss Pettigrew chattered on. The shy, pretty girl who had been so unsure of herself in Wiltshire had suddenly transformed into a lovely and vengeful chatterbox.

"Of course, Father accused me of deliberately misbehaving when I poured tea on Mrs. Thompson's lap instead of into her teacup. But she wasn't burnt! I wouldn't have gone that far."

"Miss Pettigrew," Leah chastised. "I always suspected you had a mischievous streak." Miss Pettigrew shrugged, her mouth curved slyly. "Yes, well, now Father's made me return to London so he can find me another companion. And I'm so happy, Mrs. George. I've seen Will twice already in the past week."

"Will?"

"The bank clerk. Remember?"

Ah, yes. The object of Miss Pettigrew's affection. "Has your father hired another companion for you yet?" she asked, sending up a silent prayer.

"No, not yet." Miss Pettigrew slid her arm through Leah's and tugged her along. "There are interviews today and tomorrow, but I hope he doesn't find one he likes for a while. I'd rather stay in London with a chance to see Will than be sent to the countryside to begin the tour of house parties again."

Leah took a deep breath and crossed her fingers at her side. "I know your father was upset about the house party—"

"Oh, yes. He was furious. Said I'd never catch a proper lord if I became associated with such scandal."

"But it was only a dress," Leah protested, even though she knew better. It was much more than a dress. It had been a denouncement of polite society.

"It was a scandalous dress. But it was very beautiful," Miss Pettigrew said.

Leah gave her a weak smile. "Thank you." She paused,

then added, "I don't suppose he would ever consider me for the position of companion?"

Miss Pettigrew stopped and turned, clasping Leah's free hand. "Oh, Mrs. George, that would be wonderful!" Then she frowned, letting go. "But no, I'm afraid he would never hire you. In fact, he'd probably throw a tirade just at the sight of you, and you'd have to stand there for half an hour as he ranted about impressionable young ladies—even though we're practically the same age."

"I see." Leah glanced down as her foot sank into something soft and warm. She sighed. Of course. A pile of manure.

"But I do know someone who might be interested in having you as a companion," Miss Pettigrew offered a moment later.

How easily her hopes were raised. Even with muck on her shoe. "Oh?"

"Yes. She's a widow also, so she's less likely to be as stringent. Her name is Mrs. Campbell. I've known her since I was a little girl. She's one of my mother's closest friends. Her husband owned a few of the textile mills in Birmingham."

"And you believe she needs a companion?"

"Oh, not to instruct her or chaperone her, of course. Only to keep her from becoming too lonely."

"Would you mind introducing us, then?"

Miss Pettigrew squeezed her arm. "Mrs. George, it would be my pleasure."

The Hartwell butler escorted Sebastian up the stairs and to the drawing room. From the rumors abounding about Leah, Sebastian knew that Viscount Rennell had required her to leave Linley Park and had disassociated himself from her completely, forcing her to move in with her family.

Mrs. Hartwell and Leah's sister were already sitting in the drawing room when he entered.

"The Earl of Wriothesly," the butler announced, and both Hartwell ladies rose to their feet with curtsies.

Sebastian's gaze roamed the room but didn't find Leah. Striding forward, he bowed over her mother's hand, then her sister's. "Mrs. Hartwell. Miss Beatrice."

"What a pleasure it is to have you visit us, Lord Wriothesly," Mrs. Hartwell said, smiling. It was the same polite smile he'd seen Leah use when she was nervous or lying. Nothing at all like the wide, uninhibited smile he'd become accustomed to.

"I'm glad to see you again," Sebastian said, following her gesture to sit down. He and the Hartwells had never had much interaction, even though they moved in the same social circles. If not for Ian's affiliation with them through Leah, he probably wouldn't have known them out of the other hundreds of distant relations to the aristocracy.

At that moment, a maid entered with a tea service. Sebastian watched and waited patiently as Mrs. Hartwell poured the tea. "I don't believe I've had the chance to tell you, my lord, but you have our deepest sympathies for the loss of your wife."

Sebastian inclined his head. "Thank you," he said, then added, "Neither," when she motioned to the pots of cream and sugar.

Mrs. Hartwell nodded toward Leah's sister, who sat pretty and quiet on the sofa beside her. "This past Season was dear Beatrice's first. Were you aware, my lord, that she's already had two offers of marriage?"

"Indeed, I was not," Sebastian answered, his hand beginning to tap against his thigh. He stilled it. "As you know, I was at the Linley Park country house party."

Mrs. Hartwell's lips thinned. "I must apologize for my elder daughter's behavior, my lord. Grief seems to have changed her more than I would like."

"I was wondering if Mrs. George will be joining us. I'd like to speak to her, to make certain she's all right. As you know, Ian was one of my closest friends. Although her behavior has certainly seemed strange, I feel a duty to see—"

Mrs. Hartwell's teacup clattered against her saucer. "I fear my daughter is no longer in residence, my lord."

Sebastian paused, staring. If she was no longer being granted Rennell's hospitality, and she wasn't staying with her family . . . "Would you mind telling me where she's gone?"

Mrs. Hartwell bent her head and poured another two spoons of sugar into her tea. Even though she stirred it vigorously, the surplus of white grains swirled at the top of the liquid. "I'm afraid I can't."

Sebastian frowned. "If you would, Mrs. Hartwell, she—" He thought of the letters. "She has something which I believe belongs to me."

Mrs. Hartwell's head snapped upward. "Do not tell me Leah stole from you."

"No, not at all. She has something which was in Ian's possession, something which she once offered to give me and I refused. Besides making sure she's all right, I'd like to take it now."

Mrs. Hartwell lifted the teacup to her lips and sipped, her eyes lowered. "I'm afraid, my lord," she said, looking up to meet his gaze, "it's not a matter of refusing your request. I do not know where my daughter has gone."

"You don't?"

"No. As you know, she's been acting quite oddly of late. She didn't see fit to tell me her destination when she left."

Sebastian narrowed his eyes. There was something in the way she said it that made him believe Leah's mother had a part in her disappearance. "I see," he said. Setting down his cup, he rose to his feet and bowed. "I do apologize for leaving so soon, but I must go now."

Both Mrs. Hartwell and Miss Beatrice stood. "We would love to have you stay for dinner," Leah's mother said. "And afterward, Beatrice could play a tune for you. She truly is quite lovely on the pianoforte."

"Thank you, but I can't stay." With a brisk nod, he turned and quit the drawing room. He descended the stairs and was heading toward the front door when he heard a pattering of footsteps behind him.

"Lord Wriothesly!"

He halted and turned to find Leah's sister hurrying toward him. She came to a stop three feet away, her cheeks flushed and her eyes bright. "Leah is in London," she half whispered, sending a glance over her shoulder. "She ran away after Mother threatened to make her marry the village butcher."

"In London," Sebastian interrupted. "Who is she staying with? A friend? A cousin? Where is she?"

Miss Beatrice shook her head. "She's working."

"Working?" Of course. She had no support from her family or otherwise; she was a social outcast.

Her sister leaned forward. "She's a companion to Mrs. Campbell. She walks her dog, a little spaniel named Minnie, and . . ."

"How do you know this? Is she corresponding with you?" Sebastian motioned toward the nearby footman. He put on his hat and overcoat.

"Yes. Mother knows, but she won't admit that her daughter must work. Sometimes it seems she'd rather assume she's dead, actually. No, I didn't mean that—"

"She lied to me."

Miss Beatrice began to nod, then stopped, blushing. "I'm sure Mother would never purposefully deceive you, my lord."

"Mrs. Campbell, you said?"

She hesitated. "Yes."

"Thank you, Miss Beatrice. Good day to you."

"Good day, my lord."

Leah loved her days off. Not that she was entirely free on Sundays. She was still required to attend church with Mrs. Campbell in the morning, and she still had to take Minnie for a walk in the morning when the spaniel had to "do her duty," as Mrs. Campbell called it, and then again in the evening before the sun set.

It had been odd at first going out with no footman or maid to accompany her, but the walks with Minnie soon became Leah's favorite part of the day. When she was alone except for the dog, it was the greatest amount of independence she had. But now the morning walk was done, the church service ended an hour ago, and Mrs. Campbell consulted to see if she required anything else of her for the afternoon.

Humming to herself, Leah changed from her nicer black church dress to one that was easier to walk about in. She sighed, thinking how lovely it would be to go for a ride in the park. Most of the leaves had fallen to the ground and there was a brisk chill to the air, but the sun was out and shining, providing enough warmth to make it a beautiful autumn day. Although she and Mrs. Campbell got along quite well, there was a fine line between them as mistress and companion. Though she might look longingly toward the mews, Leah imagined it would be a while before she asked if she could borrow one of the horses.

Instead, today she planned to go shopping, something it felt like she hadn't done in ages. She'd been paid her first wages, and she was itching to join the great mass of people who descended upon the shops on Sunday afternoons.

"Leah? Are you ready?" Christine, Mrs. Campbell's lady's maid, knocked and opened the door. Most of the female servants had to share small, cramped bedchambers, but Leah, Christine, and Mrs. Beesley all had their own rooms—although those were also small and cramped.

Shoving a pin into her black bonnet to keep it in place, Leah pulled her veil over her face and turned. "I feel like buying something ridiculously frivolous today."

Christine, who came from a middle-class family in Yorkshire, gave her a disbelieving look. "Something frivolous? You?"

"And not black."

"It best be for your undergarments, then, or Mrs. Campbell will have a fit."

"Yes, I know." Even though Mrs. Campbell had called Leah a friend once Miss Pettigrew introduced them, she'd made it clear that she'd heard the rumors of Leah's behavior and expected her to behave with all propriety as her companion. Though she'd been born of the lower class, Mrs. Campbell acted like the women of the aristocracy. She kept Leah at a distance and never engaged her in conversations beyond the subject of Minnie. They never spoke of their previous lives, their dead husbands, or of widowhood. If not for Christine, Leah would have been lonelier than she'd been when Ian was alive.

"Perhaps a new handkerchief," Leah said. She couldn't afford a new chemise.

Shutting the door behind her, she walked beside Christine as they went down the servants' stairs. The only time she used the front portion of the house was in the company of Mrs. Campbell.

"I mean to buy the scarf today," Christine said as they walked through the kitchen.

"The blue one with the lace edging you showed me last time?"

Christine nodded and held the back door open for her. They walked along the side of the house, toward the public path at the front.

Leah gave Christine a sly look. "There's also the hat. I'm sure Robert would appreciate it when you go walking later."

Christine blushed at the mention of the first footman. "He's only a friend. As I've told you before. A hundred times."

They began to walk along the street, away from the house. A carriage passed by. "And that's why you're blushing, of course."

Christine humphed and looked away pointedly. "If I blush, it's only because you enjoy teasing me so."

They heard the coachman of the carriage call the horses to halt behind them. Leah glanced over her shoulder, though she couldn't make out the crest on the side. "Overton again?" she asked.

Christine shook her head. "No, Mrs. Thompson finished with him. Trahern, most likely."

Leah arched a brow and turned around. "Trahern? I thought she despised him."

"Maybe so, but he's quite easy on the eye. And there's no need to talk when they're in bed."

"Christine Farrell. How deceitful that innocent appearance is."

Christine laughed quietly. "Hush, now. I've tried very hard to—"

"Leah?" A man's voice called her name. "Mrs. George?"

A voice that had become as familiar as Ian's once was. A voice that, in truth, she never thought to hear again. Leah paused midstep, her gaze pinned on the street ahead.

Christine wasn't as discreet. She looked behind again.

"Leah," she whispered. "It's the man from the carriage. Not Trahern. He's looking at you."

"Yes, I know," she answered, uncertain whether she wanted to turn around. "Lord Wriothesly."

"You know him, then?"

"He—he was friends with my husband."

"Oh. Well, he's coming this way."

Leah swallowed. Indeed, she could hear his footsteps, so sure and steady, purposeful. Only she had no idea why he would seek her out, not after he'd said he would never acknowledge her again.

"Good day," he said.

Christine swung around to face him, bending in a low curtsy. "My lord."

"And good day to you, Mrs. George. I'm not mistaken, am I? It is you?"

Leah slowly turned toward him, lifting her chin and her pride along with it. She didn't bother to curtsy. "What do you want?"

Christine smothered a gasp.

Leah didn't know what she expected Sebastian to do; she wanted to make him angry, or see him put on a show of arrogance at the public slight. Anything to keep him from witnessing the vulnerability that had suddenly surfaced upon hearing his voice, the pleasure that nearly stole her breath at seeing him again.

Oh, but how she wanted to drown in his gaze, to bury herself against him as his green eyes roved over her face. He was handsome, terribly so, taller than she remembered and very well-dressed. The fine fit of his gray trousers and jacket, the silken cloth of his navy waistcoat, all served to remind her of the present differences in their stations. He was still a lord, an earl, but she was no longer a lady.

Leah glanced away. Surely he wouldn't be able to see

that she'd once been weak. That once she'd walked Minnie to the park across from his London town house and stood watching it for what seemed like hours. Knowing he wouldn't be there, but wishing he was all the same.

"Mrs. George."

She couldn't help but look at him. She wanted him to treat her coldly, to give her a greater reason than the ones she'd created to dismiss him from her memory. But he had to be contrary. Instead of frowning or glaring at her, he smiled.

"I'd like to speak to you for a moment." With a courteous nod at Christine, he added, "Privately."

Leah crossed her arms. "You may speak now. But please make it short. We were headed for the shops."

He inclined his head, his mouth still curved at the ends. "As you wish." Then he stepped forward, took one of her hands, looked into her eyes, and said, "Mrs. George, would you please do me the honor of becoming my wife?"

Chapter 16

Meet me on Thursday afternoon at 2 o'clock, near the watches.

Leah jerked her hand out of his grip. "Christine, would you mind—"

"Not at all. I will see you before Mrs. Campbell's dinner." The lady's maid turned and began to walk in the direction of the shops by herself. Very slowly, Leah noticed. No doubt she hoped to eavesdrop.

Leah stared up at Sebastian, searching his expression for some hint of what he was thinking. His green eyes returned her stare, undaunted, humorless. He'd asked her to marry him, and he'd meant it. "I don't understand. You want to marry me?"

"Shall we take a walk in the park together?" he asked, gesturing across the street.

Numbed and bewildered, she nodded her head and allowed him to escort her to the park, where they began walking along the path. "I don't want to marry you," she said, her voice low, her heart secretly pounding.

"Yes, I'm not surprised," he answered, sounding remarkably cheerful, as if her response didn't deter him for a moment. "However, something has happened which necessitates my request."

She looked at him. He walked easily along the path, his frame relaxed, his eyes focused on the trees ahead. Only the firmness of his jaw betrayed any anxiety on his part. "Are you aware that, since your actions at the country house party, rumors have been circulating that you and I are having an affair?"

Heat trailed into her cheeks as she remembered his kiss in the garden, and she turned her head away. "Yes."

"And are you also aware that, more recently, rumors of Ian and Angela's affair have surfaced?"

Leah stumbled, and Sebastian reached over, his grip warm on her upper arm as he steadied her. "No, my lord, I didn't realize ..."

"I warned you, didn't I?" he asked quietly, his hand slow to remove itself from her person.

Leah lifted her chin. "There is a possibility the rumors would have begun regardless of anything I did."

"Yes, you're correct. It is possible. But unlikely."

"If you please, my lord, I'm not in the mood to be scolded. Tell me why you asked to marry me so I can refuse and we may go our separate ways once again."

"I believe the best chance we have of silencing the rumors about Ian and Angela is to redirect the gossipmongers back in our direction. Allow them to believe that we are lovers, and confirm that belief by marrying. If all goes well, they will stop speculating about Ian and Angela and focus all of their attention on us, until eventually we will be rid of those rumors as well."

"If the talk has already begun, my lord, why not allow it to run its course? Is your pride so very great that you cannot stand to be thought of as a cuckold? Are you trying to protect Angela?" Leah hesitated, then continued, her heart quickening. "Are you still in love with her?"

He looked at her, his expression grim. "You've left out the greatest reason," he said.

He hadn't answered her question about Angela. "And what reason is that?"

"Henry."

"Oh." Leah started. "Of course. But you must believe me, Sebastian—he looks like you. I can't believe that he's not your son."

Sebastian nodded without acknowledging her words. "I want to protect him at all costs."

"Even if you believe your best option is to marry me." Leah watched one of the last remaining leaves of the season drift to the ground. "I'm sorry, my lord, but agreeing to marriage seems wholly unnecessary. Henry is a wonderful little boy, but—"

"He also . . . needs a mother."

And just like that, he pulled one of the strings on her heart, causing it to shudder and jerk and dance inside her chest all at once. "Here's another possibility, my lord. Find someone else to marry. It will end the rumors about us having an affair, might also end the rumors of Ian and Angela, and also provide Henry a new mother. There's no need for me to be involved."

"Your sister told me that you've become Mrs. Campbell's companion."

"Ah. Beatrice. I'd wondered how you found me." A vendor pushing his cart passed them along the path, his back bowed.

"Do you enjoy walking her dog?"

"Yes," she answered. "Minnie is quite enjoyable company." She said this in such a way that he'd have to be daft not to understand the inference that in contrast, his company was not so pleasant.

"At Linley Park you spoke of freedom and independence. I can't imagine you have much of either here, being summoned here and ordered there at the whim of your mistress, someone to whom you're actually more than an equal."

Leah smiled. "If you're trying to convince me that I would have more independence as a married woman, my lord, please do not trouble yourself. I'm well aware of the shackles that brings."

"I would allow you—"

"Precisely. You would 'allow' me. Does that not imply that you would be my master, and my independence would be dependent upon your wishes entirely?"

His lips pressed together. "I will phrase it another way, then. If you were to marry me and become Henry's mother, your only requirement would be to see to his maternal needs. Otherwise, you would be free to do as you wish. Go riding, practice your archery, go boating, walk in the garden at midnight. Whatever pleases you."

"And if I wished to never see you?" she asked. Not because she was considering his proposal. Simply because she was curious to see how far he would take the conversation.

"We might go on outings together with Henry, but otherwise, there is no need for you to suffer my company." He paused, then turned to her with a small smile. "Or I yours."

Leah couldn't help smiling a little back at him.

Abruptly, Sebastian looked ahead again. "And because it needs to be said," he continued, "that would include any interactions which might be expected to occur in the bedchamber."

Leah swallowed. "You mean you would not require a consummation?"

"No."

"You wouldn't wish to engage in marital relations."

"No."

"Our marriage would be in name only? If neither of us dies early and we are married for the next thirty years, you would never try to bed me?"

She thought she heard him choke. "No."

"You would take a mistress, then."

He glanced at her, his gaze sharp, the grooves at the edges of his mouth deep. "I will be loyal to you."

Leah laughed, although there was no joy in the sound. "Come, my lord. You mean to tell me that you would remain celibate for the rest of your life, if only I would agree to marry you?"

His green gaze, so deep and intense, darkened. "I will be celibate for as long as you wish it. Until you decide that you want me in your bed."

Her throat thickened, tightened. She tried to laugh again, but the sound came out hoarse and strained. "How confident you are, my lord. But what if, by chance, I never desire you? Indeed, what if I find someone else I wish to take to my bed?"

"We have both experienced the pain of adulterous spouses. Even if ours is not a love match, if you cannot commit to faithfulness now, then there is no need to continue having this discussion."

"I don't want to marry you," she repeated. And yet this time it left her lips as a whisper, as if uncertain.

He stopped in the middle of the path and turned to face her. He didn't take her hand again, or come close, but they were alone, the distant sounds of the city surrounding them but not interfering. Leah resisted the urge to step back, to escape the moment of intimacy.

"Then allow me to tell you why I want to marry you, Leah."

Not Mrs. George, but Leah. How she'd missed hearing her name on his lips. She shouldn't have missed it at all.

"I know why you want to marry me. To redirect the scandal."

"Yes."

"To have a mother for Henry."

He inclined his head. "Yes. And as you told me, I might find any other woman to help me do the same. But I want to marry you, Leah George, not someone else. You see, I've become rather accustomed to your smile. Even if it angers me when I'm so determined to be miserable. And I've grown to anticipate your devilish antics—it seems I like watching you enjoy your freedom as much as you like exploring it. You already know Henry. I've seen you interact with him before, and I believe the relationship between the two of you could quickly develop into something more. And . . ."

His gaze moved beyond her head. Leah waited, then prodded when it appeared he wouldn't finish. "And?"

He looked at her again, his expression guarded. "When I'm with you, somehow I'm able to forget about Angela and Ian. I can't even picture her face, because all I see is you. And I think—if for no other reason—that's why I need you."

"You want me to help you forget your wife."

He shook his head, muttering a curse. Then he stepped closer. "You foolish woman," he whispered, his expression tortured. His hand cupped her cheek. "Do you not remember when I said it before? No matter. I'll say it again. I want you." His thumb swept across her upper lip, much as it had done before he'd kissed her in the garden. "I desire you." His hand left her cheek, his fingers stroking over the ends of her brows, across her eyelashes as she closed her eyes, meandering down her face until he held her chin.

She opened her eyes when he made no other movement. He withdrew his arm and stepped back. "But I will keep my word. I won't require you to suffer my company unless we're together with Henry, and I won't seek to come to your bed unless you ask me. Beyond my own desires, I will give you your freedom. Help me to protect Henry. Be a mother to my son. If you say yes, you will never be lonely again."

Leah started breathing again, not knowing until the first breath rushed from her lungs that she'd even stopped. She crossed her arms over her chest and looked away, pretending to study a squirrel as it skittered from one tree to the next. "I will think about it," she said, even though she knew she should refuse him now.

"Thank you," he said, and she could tell by the relief in his voice that he'd expected another answer entirely. "When should I call on you again?"

How polite he was, asking for her preference instead of telling her when he would come. But she wished he wouldn't have asked at all. She didn't want to give him a definite answer. Perhaps, if she said nothing, he wouldn't return.

"Next Sunday," she said, before she knew she even meant to say the words. "The same time. I'll give my answer then."

He nodded and offered his arm. She placed her hand over his wrist. Together, they walked silently back to Mrs. Campbell's house.

Over the following days, Leah wished she hadn't given Sebastian an entire week. It was too long, and although she knew that her answer would be negative, part of her kept wavering and considering all that he'd said.

She didn't care about covering up the scandal of Ian and Angela, although if it meant protecting Henry, then it was certainly worthwhile. The thought of being able to act as a mother to Sebastian's son was overwhelming. She couldn't help but think how wonderful it would be to lavish her attention on him, to love him with all of her heart. But she wondered if he could ever truly be hers, or if he could ever satisfy the longing in her heart for a child of her own.

Despite Sebastian's assurances, she wasn't certain how much freedom she'd be able to have if she married him. Certainly working as the companion to Mrs. Campbell— and also, Mrs. Campbell's dog—wasn't something she looked forward to doing for the rest of her life, but at least she wasn't under her mother's roof, and she wasn't relegated to a miserable life simply because she'd made the mistake of marrying. But if she had her freedom as Sebastian claimed, she wouldn't be that miserable, would she? He said he desired her, but he wouldn't come to her bed. Still, what if her wish for a child of her own led her to request his presence, and then she might be in the same position she'd put herself in before. Her body violated, not by her husband, but by her own will.

On Saturday night, after both Mrs. Campbell and Minnie had retired for the evening, Leah sat on the edge of her bed. A week of consideration, and the doubts remained.

"I will say no," she said aloud as she imagined meeting Sebastian on the path in front of the house the next afternoon. She would stare into his lovely green eyes, ignore the way her body seemed to pull her toward him, and refuse his offer.

"No," she said again. Her voice still sounded weak. She stood and paced. She couldn't go very far in the narrow confines of her room, but the movement helped with some of her agitation.

By marrying her, Sebastian offered her a child to love, one she already knew she could grow to adore. It might be the only chance she ever had of becoming a mother without subjugating herself to the marriage bed and bearing one of her own.

But even though she couldn't deny her hope of becoming a mother, Sebastian had gone so far as to say he wanted to marry her because he desired her. Not just her company, but her. He wanted her in his bed.

As she'd done the rest of the week, Leah scoffed. She pivoted on her heel, wrapped her arms around her waist. After Angela, Sebastian thought he wanted her.

How many times when they were courting had Ian made her believe the same? How many times had he whispered to her heart before he could make love to her body? And she'd believed him. God, how foolish she'd been to believe him.

Sebastian said he wanted her, he desired her. He said she made him forget about Angela. Yet these could all be lies, meant to persuade her to agree so he could have his way.

Sebastian and Ian. They'd both wanted her for their own selfish reasons. Ian might have betrayed Sebastian, but they had been close friends. Were they not similar? They'd both said . . .

Leah stilled, her skirts swaying as she suddenly ceased her pacing. Ian had done everything to make her fall in love with him. He'd brought her presents, flowers, poems he'd copied. He'd written her love letters. He'd said he loved her.

Sebastian had simply stood there, logically listing each reason why they should marry. He hadn't brought her any gifts, and he hadn't tried to woo her. He hadn't even looked happy when he said he desired her—he'd appeared quite wretched, actually.

He hadn't lied, she realized. For, most importantly, Sebastian had never claimed to love her.

Sebastian arrived at the Campbell house half an hour early. It would have been an hour early, but he'd instructed his coachman to make circles around the park.

He was nervous, more so than he could ever remem-

ber being with Angela. She had known how to make a
man feel at ease. With her eyes, her voice, the little things
she said, she'd made it possible to feel like he was the
only person who mattered. Her attention demanded
confidence.

But with Leah ... He must have gone through six
different cravats that morning, his fingers suddenly too
large and fumbling to do the job properly. Since he'd
dismissed his valet once he married, Sebastian finally
had to call his butler to assist him with the neckwear.

Not that it mattered. Sebastian tugged at the cravat
now, unable to get it loose enough that he could fully
breathe. He didn't know why he'd returned. Everything
Leah had done last week, and everything she hadn't
done—her posture, the words she'd said and the words
which remained unspoken—it all led him to believe she
would refuse his offer. The only reason he'd taken a
chance and returned was because she'd told him she
would give him an answer today. She could have said no,
but she hadn't. There was a chance. And now that he'd
once again revealed he desired her in addition to needing her for Henry's sake, Sebastian couldn't return to
Hampshire without receiving her final response.

But no, even that wasn't the truth. Even if she refused
him, he still wanted to see her again. One last time.

He pulled back the curtain and stared out the carriage window, willing her to appear.

And then she did, walking around the corner of the
house from the back, taking the servants' route. But she
moved with her head held high and her back straight; no
stranger would ever have mistaken her for a servant.

As she approached the carriage, Sebastian knocked
on the roof. A footman promptly opened the door, and
Sebastian stepped out, his arm stretched toward her.
Though the day was cloudy and he couldn't see whether
she frowned beneath her veil, he smiled. "Would you

like to take a drive today?" He watched her shiver beneath her black cloak, resisting the temptation to point out how cold it was and order her inside.

"Yes, thank you," she said, and allowed him to assist her into the carriage. As he settled back against the seat, he wished he wouldn't have touched her. All week the memory of the slide of her skin beneath his gloved fingers had tortured him, and now he could feel the warm imprint of her hand against his palm.

"I've decided to accept your proposal," she said, even before the coachman had called for the horses to go on.

Sebastian clenched the same palm she had touched into a fist on his knee. "Are you certain?"

She laughed, a mirthless sound. "Would you like me to refuse instead?"

"No."

"In truth, my lord, I thought of one reason you neglected to mention that made me realize I would be a fool not to accept."

Sebastian shifted in his seat, unable to stop himself from leaning closer. Yes, there it was. Within the confines of the carriage, with the filth and coal smoke of London blocked outside, he could smell her scent, the same as before. God, how he'd missed it.

"What reason is that?"

Her hands lifted to the hem of her veil, and she drew it over her head, revealing a mischievous smile. "No more mourning clothes. No black, no crepe or bombazine, no widow's cap, and no veil."

He matched her smile, although he wanted to tell her how much he would like to again see the gown with the V at the back that she'd worn the last night of the house party. But he was careful not to say anything which might be construed as a demand or an order. He couldn't take the risk that she would see it as a threat to her independence and change her mind.

"Would you like to go to the modiste's now?" he asked.

Her mouth formed a rounded oval of surprise, and she shook her head. "No, but thank you."

"We didn't discuss this last time, of course, but would you rather I request a special license so we might get married immediately, or would you prefer that we have the banns published?"

"You seem to have taken my acceptance quite well," she jested.

Sebastian looked out the carriage window at the rows of houses. "I'm anxious to see Henry again."

"Will he not be at the wedding?"

He returned his gaze to her. "If you agree, I'd prefer for him to stay in the countryside. I'd like to introduce him to you again after we're married. I don't think he'll understand what's happening, anyway, and I hope to make this no more disruptive to his usual routine than it must be."

Leah tilted her head and studied him, two lines forming between her brows.

Sebastian forced his fist to finally relax. "Yes?"

"You seem very involved with him. Of course, I've seen you with him before, but I never realized . . ."

It didn't work. His hands balled into fists once again. "He's all I have."

She didn't say anything, but the lines between her brows smoothed and a small smile formed at the corners of her mouth. "A special license, then, I think. That way we can be on our way to Hampshire as soon as possible. However, I'll need to give Mrs. Campbell some notice so she can begin searching for a new companion."

"You'll be able to give Mrs. Campbell plenty of notice. While I agree that I would prefer a special license, I don't think we should create any further rumors by marrying so hastily. Publishing the banns with the announcement of our engagement will distract everyone easily enough. And don't forget the invitations," he reminded her.

"What invitations?"

"To your family and friends."

"This is part of redirecting the scandal, isn't it?" she asked.

"If you'd like, we can also invite the ones who probably began it all. Mr. and Mrs. Meyer, Mrs. Thompson, Miss Pettigrew. Mr. Dunlop and Lord Cooper-Giles. Lord Elliot and—"

"Lady Elliot. Yes, let's do. I'm certain it was mostly Lady Elliot, in any event. But we must make sure my mother receives the first invitation. Perhaps we should invite the entire *ton*, shouldn't we? As many as will fit. Then it will be upon everyone's lips at once."

Something in her voice made Sebastian narrow his eyes. "Perhaps I should be concerned that you've accepted my proposal. I find I'm suspicious now that you agreed so readily."

She shrugged. "It's simple, my lord. Do you love me?"

Sebastian froze. What did she expect him to say? If he answered honestly, would she demand he return her to Mrs. Campbell's?

They stared at each other, every wall securely in place at the same time every pretense was laid bare.

"No," he said at last, the lie pushed stiffly from his lips.

She nodded, her expression relieved. "And that is why I decided to marry you, my lord. For I don't love you, either."

Chapter 17

I know, my darling. I cannot believe it myself.
Soon!

As Leah stood before Sebastian on their wedding day, it was difficult not to think of her first wedding. It had been only a little over two years ago that she'd stood in front of a crowded church at St. Michael's, pledging to love and obey her husband until death should part them.

Leah looked up at Sebastian. Although his hands held hers, he was watching the priest, his expression solemn. Was he thinking of his wedding to Angela? How strange it was, to realize she'd once thought she and Ian would grow old together, have children and grandchildren. Yet here she was, not three years later, marrying his best friend. A man whom she knew only little better than she'd known Ian at the time.

He was dressed in a dark charcoal jacket and trousers, his black waistcoat threaded with silver, his cravat black as well. His hair had been combed straight back from his forehead, leaving his eyes all the more intense.

No, he wasn't as handsome as Ian, and he wasn't as charming, but for some reason she felt secure as he held her hands. And although she should know better, the fact that he hadn't lied about loving her made her trust him. She might regret that later, but for now it was a wonderful feeling, to look up at the man whose ring she would soon wear and realize that he deserved her faith.

The priest began reciting the vows and Sebastian held her gaze, his expression inscrutable. She tried, but she couldn't look away. The moment felt surreal, that she should surrender to another marriage so quickly.

Then it was her turn, and all she could think as she looked into his eyes was that he desired her. Suddenly the security of his hands disappeared, the comforting warmth turning into a blistering heat which nearly scorched her skin. She felt her fingers tremble with the urge to pull away, out of his grip. Perhaps he felt it, for his hands tightened around hers, holding her in place.

Her voice wavered. "I take thee, Sebastian Edward Thomas Madinger, to be . . . my husband." The last two words were nothing more than mere whispers. He squeezed her hands, and she looked down. How large his hands were; she'd never noticed before. Clad in dark gray gloves, they covered hers completely, his palms nearly twice the size of hers, the tips of his fingers brushing against the inside of her gloved wrists.

Leah took a deep breath and continued repeating her vows. With the rings exchanged, the priest announced them as wedded. Sebastian leaned forward, and Leah tensed; although they'd discussed this beforehand, talked about how they would make a show of it to convince their audience that theirs truly was a torrid affair, and although she'd tried to prepare herself for the past month, she still wasn't ready.

She closed her eyes as she waited for his mouth to meet hers. And then it did, warm and firm. And quick.

Her gaze flew to his face as he withdrew, but he'd already turned toward their guests, tucking her hand in the crook of his arm.

"Thank you," she whispered, but she didn't think he heard. Or, if he did, he ignored her. Instead, he drew her down the steps with him and through the church, to the carriage that would take them to the wedding breakfast prepared at his house. Once he'd helped her into the vehicle and sat across from her, she realized just how close a carriage could be. Much closer than this particular one had ever seemed before. She looked out the window.

As the carriage started toward his house, Sebastian glanced at Leah. He couldn't help but feel like a voyeur as he studied her, the knowledge that she was now his wife something which seemed too far-fetched to be real.

She was indescribably beautiful in her wedding gown, a light gray which reminded him of the gleam of a pearl. Even though it wasn't black like her mourning clothes, he wished she would have decided to wear another color instead. Blue perhaps. Something vibrant and joyful, something separating her from her life with Ian.

The gown accentuated her slender figure without making her appear overwhelmed by the yards of cloth. He longed to fit his hands about the curve of her waist, to see if she really would fit their span as it appeared. The bodice covered her chest so there was just a hint of soft flesh beneath, making it seem a mystery that waited to be discovered. And although he might have chosen a different color for her to wear, the shade complemented her fair skin, making her appear ethereal rather than fragile.

When he thought she would ignore him the entire drive to his house, she turned to him and said, "You didn't kiss me."

He lifted his brow. "Yes, I did."

Her cheeks blushed prettily, but she held his gaze. "It was different than what we had discussed. I expected . . . more."

For a moment, Sebastian allowed himself the fantasy of moving across the carriage and taking her mouth as he'd dreamed of doing ever since she'd first accepted his proposal. Without his permission, his eyes lowered to her lips, and he felt his heart begin to thud within his chest. "Tell me, Lady Wriothesly, is that an invitation?"

It might have been a seductive moment, if the sound of her new title hadn't stunned both of them. Lady Wriothesly. The name no longer belonged to Angela, but Leah. This time, Sebastian was the first to look away. But he heard her repeat the words she'd said inside the church.

"Thank you."

"Don't paint me as a good man for not kissing you as we'd planned. You simply appeared as if you might faint were I to do anything else."

"I wouldn't have fainted," she protested, sounding so much like the Leah he'd grown to know at the house party that he smiled.

He looked at her. "You went completely white, even your lips. Your hands were shaking in mine."

She lifted her chin, defiant. "And you weren't nervous at all?"

"No." Well, only to the extent that he'd feared she would turn and bolt out the church door. After her hands had trembled, he'd made sure to keep a tight grip on her.

Her mouth turned downward. "It occurs to me that I forgot to take your flaws into account before I agreed to marry you."

"Ah, but now it's too late, Lady Wriothesly." He said it again, purposefully, testing the sound of her name on his tongue. Somehow, it felt . . . perfect.

She stared at him for a moment, then looked down at her gloved hands, clasped together in her lap. "What will you do if the rumors about Ian and Angela don't abate now that we've married?"

"They will. I find it hard to believe that the gossip-mongers would continue with that line when we've proven to them their first speculation about us."

"But if they don't?" she pressed.

"I don't know," he bit off, then immediately regretted his tone. "I don't know," he said again, softer this time. "We'll ignore them, I suppose. After all, there's no evidence to confirm that they were having an affair."

"The letters."

Sebastian shook his head. "You have the ones from Angela, and though I searched for any from Ian in her room, I couldn't find any."

Leah didn't say anything for a moment. Then she lifted her gaze. "Will we be leaving for Hampshire after the breakfast, or will we be spending the night and departing in the morning?"

She asked so many questions. And God help him, he never knew what the right answer was. "Do you have a preference?"

"I . . . No. But if we do stay in town for the night, I'd like to know that I won't be staying in her room."

He'd spent the past month readying for the wedding once she'd accepted his proposal. This included finally venturing into Angela's room, looking for any letters from Ian, sorting through things he thought Henry might want later on. He'd instructed the maids to pack everything else and distribute her clothes as they saw fit. The room had been painted, new furniture purchased, aired out until he could no longer smell any trace of lavender and vanilla.

"Don't worry," he told Leah. "I planned to have you stay in one of the other rooms, the largest guest bed-chamber."

"Oh. Thank you. That was very thoughtful of you."

Sebastian smiled. "So you see, some of my flaws are balanced by my better attributes."

Leah tilted her head and returned his smile. "That, my lord, remains yet to be seen."

The carriage arrived shortly afterward at his town house, and they entered to a fete where all of the people who had once whispered about a supposed affair now celebrated their marriage.

Sebastian was aware, of course, that all of the whispers hadn't yet been silenced. Many of the guests sent them sly looks during the breakfast—probably confirming to one another their original suspicions. But that was as he'd expected, and as it should be.

To assist with the idea, he made sure to stay by Leah's side as much as possible. Although he never touched her, he would lean in toward her and murmur in her ear. He said things to make her blush while knowing his suggestions might never come to pass. These earned reproving glances from her, which pleased him to no end, as her eyes seemed to sparkle brighter and she laughed as a defense to her embarrassment. When her mother and sister approached them with their congratulations, she blushed even brighter. By the time the breakfast reception ended, Sebastian was certain most—if not all—of their guests believed the newly married couple to be shamefully in love. Or, at the very least, gloriously in lust.

As the guests made their way out four hours later, Lord and Lady Elliot approached, the last ones to leave. Lady Elliot wore a smile of knowing satisfaction. "Lord Wriothesly. Lady Wriothesly."

"How glad we are you could come to the wedding," Leah said warmly.

Sebastian glanced at her, but her expression seemed sincere.

"Of course. I wouldn't have missed it." Lady Elliot paused to look at her husband. "Even if it is close to fox hunting season."

She edged closer to Leah, and although she made a pretense of lowering her voice, Sebastian could still hear every word she spoke. "Do you remember at the house party when I asked if you imagined Lord Wriothesly on your target?"

Leah nodded. Sebastian raised a brow.

"I see I was correct," Lady Elliot said, peeking at Sebastian from beneath her lashes. "There's not much difference between anger and passion. Is there, my lord?" she asked her husband, elbowing him in the side.

Sebastian followed the man's gaze to a nearby plate of apple tarts. Lord Elliot started, disrupted from his reverie. "No, my dear, not at all. Anger and passion are very good things."

Lady Elliot sighed and gave Leah and Sebastian an exasperated look, then smiled fondly at her husband. "Let's go, my lord, and leave the newlyweds to themselves."

As they withdrew from the banquet room, Sebastian turned to Leah. "Target practice, was I?"

She shrugged. "At the time it seemed the most use I could make of you."

"Hmm. Perhaps I shouldn't allow you to spend too much time with Henry when we reach Hampshire."

Her lips curved into a mischievous smile before she turned away.

"Where are you going?"

"Upstairs," she said. "I believe I shall read for the rest of the day."

"The library's down the hall," he called after her.

"I brought books of my own."

Sebastian watched her stroll down the hallway and turn toward the stairs, realizing that she meant to exert her independence immediately. Wishing that she would have preferred to stay and talk with him.

Leah tried to read. But every time she began a sentence, the memory of Sebastian whispering inappropriate words in her ear returned, and she couldn't focus on the meaning, the construction of the sentence, let alone the spelling of the next word. The text was nothing more than black lines and dots, the memory of his voice much more real, as if he were there in her room with her.

She tried to take a nap. She convinced herself that if her mind could drift off into sleep, at least then she would escape him. But as soon as she lay upon the mattress, she began to remember his words about how he would lie her down on his bed, how he would undress her and cover her with satin sheets, how he would enjoy watching her move beneath him.

Even though she knew he'd said such things only for the benefit of their guests, to provoke blushes that would help solidify belief in their alleged affair, that knowledge didn't matter.

No more than two minutes passed before she leapt from the bed, her breathing heavy, her heart racing, and went to the window. She pressed her palm against the glass, then her forehead. Her cheek. Slowly—eventually—she could feel the flush on her skin begin to fade.

Who was this man that she'd married? When she believed him to be the gentleman earl, he defied her expectations and showed her another man, one who wasn't so refined, one who insisted on invoking passions she sought to keep buried. Yes, she knew she was attracted to him, and he'd made it clear he desired her, but to think that he had such power over her, that he could speak only a few words and leave her wanting, then desperate to escape him for fear she'd turn to him in need . . .

Leah sat on the settee before the hearth, holding the

book once again. She started to read aloud, trying to force her mind to focus on the words that came from her lips.

Tonight would be their wedding night.

Although they both knew there would be no consummation, she couldn't help the image that came to mind of Sebastian lying in bed that evening, only a few steps down the corridor. Would he be thinking of her? Would he be imagining all those things he had said?

He desired her.

Of all the love words Ian had ever murmured in her ear, none had ever been as powerful as Sebastian's declaration.

Leah pinched the next page of the book between her fingers, watched it shake as she turned it. One thing was certain: she must never let him know how much his words affected her. If he continued speaking to her in such a manner as before, she wasn't sure she could trust herself with him again.

Sebastian resigned himself to the fact that he would be eating alone at the dinner table that evening. He hadn't seen Leah all afternoon, and she didn't come to the sitting room before the meal was served so he could escort her inside.

He sat down at the table, alone, as he'd eaten nearly every meal since Angela's death. A footman placed a bowl of soup in front of him. Sebastian picked up his spoon, not even caring that he couldn't identify most of the contents. It was warm and it was good. That's all that mattered.

Then the door to the dining room opened and Leah swept in. "My apologies for being late," she breathed, smiling as the butler held out her seat.

Sebastian stared. No longer was she wearing black, or even the gray she'd worn as a wedding dress that morning. Instead, she was dressed in a dark blue evening gown. Finally free of Ian. Finally his.

"You're forgiven," he said, and ate another spoonful of soup. "Is that from your new wardrobe?"

"Yes."

She didn't say anything else as she, too, began eating the soup, and Sebastian alternated between watching to make sure his own spoon made it to his mouth and sneaking glances at her.

"Do you like it?" she asked a minute later. "I must admit, it feels a bit odd to be wearing something not so dreary. I almost feel guilty. Perhaps I should have waited a little longer—then I might have actually become accustomed to the role of widowhood."

"It's beautiful," he said, wishing he could say more, hating the fact that so much uncertainty existed between them now that they were more than simply Ian's best friend and Ian's wife.

But she wasn't Ian's wife any longer. No, she was his.

"Tell me, my lady, what does an independent married woman long to do with her time? Do you have any specific plans yet for when we reach Hampshire?"

She smiled at him over the table. "I don't know. I think that's part of freedom—not knowing what the future holds, but realizing that so many possibilities exist for you to take advantage of."

"How do you mean?"

"For example, when I was younger and living with my parents, Mother had every minute of the day planned for us, down to the exact hour. Getting dressed. Breakfast. Tutoring lessons—only the subjects varied from day to day. Lunch. Practice at the pianoforte. Singing. Dancing. Knitting. Afternoon calls—"

"But surely that must have changed after you married."

"It could have, I suppose. And the actual activities

were altered. But the pattern of plotting out my day to the last detail had become so ingrained that it seemed easiest to continue it. After I found out about Angela, I even scheduled each evening to include—"

She cut herself off and stared down at the soup.

Sebastian's grip tightened on the spoon, his jaw clenching. If it had to do with Ian at night, there could only be one thing she was referring to. "You don't have to tell me if you prefer, but I'd like to hear what you have to say whenever you're ready."

She nodded, glancing up at him briefly, then continued eating.

"As for routines," Sebastian said, "the only person who has a regular routine is Henry, and that's only for the mornings and the evenings. In the afternoons, he and I usually spend time together."

"What do you do?" she asked.

She sounded distracted, the question more polite than interested. Still, if it would help her become better adjusted once they reached the Hampshire estate, then Sebastian would tell her everything.

He smiled. "We play with blocks. We go on picnics and walks. He sits on his pony—"

"He has a pony already?"

"Yes, for him to get used to. If he wants to truly ride, he goes with me."

"Is he speaking yet?"

Sebastian frowned, realizing that the last time she'd seen him was before the carriage accident, when he'd had only a few words in his vocabulary, and most of those weren't clear. "A few sentences, nothing too complex. Let's just say that he knows how to get his way."

"You spoil him," she said, her tone indulgent.

"Perhaps." Sebastian set his spoon aside. Soon, a footman came to remove the bowl. "I suppose I find it difficult to be too harsh with him now."

He forced himself to remain still as she studied him, wondering what she saw when she looked at him. A man of strength or a man too easily given to sentiment?

After a moment, she too put down her spoon and said, "I think we all shall get along wonderfully." Then she added, "As long as you can keep up with mine and Henry's adventures."

"Adventures?"

"Oh, yes. I already have quite a few planned."

"I thought you said—"

She waved him away. "That was in regards to myself. I've been thinking all month how best Henry and I might get along."

She leaned forward, the table pressing against her bodice and revealing the lithe curve of her chest. Sebastian looked away, then back, then away again, clearing his throat. He signaled to the butler, and the next course was brought in.

"Of course I don't have any brothers," she continued, "so I might need your help in a few things, but I've always wanted to learn how to climb trees."

"It's too dangerous." The words spilled from Sebastian's mouth before he could think them through.

Her gaze narrowed. "I believe our agreement was that I might do whatever I wish."

Their first evening together, and they'd already begun arguing.

"First of all," he said, "Henry is my son, and if he's too young to ride a pony, he's certainly too young to start climbing trees."

"Well spoken, my lord. But if I still want to climb trees by myself?"

The subject of the conversation might have been comical, if Sebastian didn't think that she would do it just to prove a point to him. Still, even though he would try to restrain himself from giving her orders as much as possible, he couldn't imagine any sort of relationship where he didn't try to keep his wife from harm. "Your skirts are also a hazard. If they became tangled, or caught in a branch—"

"As I said, I will need your help for a few things. Finding a pair of trousers is the first task."

Sebastian tapped his fingers against the table. "If I provide a pair of trousers for you to use, will you agree that I must accompany you? In this, and any other dangerous endeavor you have in mind?"

"But you will have to suffer my company, my lord."

"I'm suffering it now, aren't I?"

She laughed, and Sebastian couldn't help but wonder if he'd somehow passed a test. It was the same as before, at the country house party; the more he thought he understood her, the more he came to realize that each layer he peeled back revealed a deeper mystery beneath.

He longed to ask her about the evening schedule with Ian that she'd alluded to earlier, to know every secret she tried so hard to keep hidden from him. But instead, he smiled along with her and attempted to think of another, easier topic of conversation. Then he realized that beyond the subjects of Henry, Ian, and Angela, there wasn't much that they had in common. This wife that he desired, that he felt a need to protect, was still little more than a stranger to him.

Leah shifted in her seat and pushed around the veal cutlet on her plate. "Why do you look at me so?" she asked.

His mouth curved upward on one side, but the attempt at a smile did nothing to mask the frank intensity of his eyes. He stared at her as if she were a puzzle and he were trying to figure out how best to solve her. She could tell him there was nothing to solve; she was simple, plain. All she wanted was to have a chance to pursue her own desires, and even those were mostly ordinary.

"I was thinking about how you would look in a pair of trousers," he said.

"Much like a boy, I imagine."

"No." His gaze dipped from her face to her bodice, then back up again. "Somehow I doubt you could ever look like a boy."

Leah struggled not to blush. Reaching forward, she lifted her glass and swallowed a mouthful of sherry. Perhaps she shouldn't have come down, after all. But something had seemed wrong with the idea of staying in her bedchamber all evening, almost as if she was ignoring him.

If truth be told, she was as curious about her new husband as he seemed to be about her. That curiosity began with his relationship with Henry and the time he spent with him when other fathers would have simply consigned Henry to the nursery all day long. But she also found as she watched across the table that her gaze drifted to other, more masculine aspects of him. The wide breadth of his shoulders, the formidable wall of his chest—it was nearly incomprehensible how he sat in his chair and didn't somehow make it appear as if he were a giant playing on a dwarf's stool.

Leah swallowed more sherry, determined to keep her eyes on her plate for the remainder of the meal. If nothing else revealed the awkwardness of their situation, it was this: the silence that descended over them, the realization that she didn't know what to say to him now that they'd spoken of Henry. Apparently he didn't know what to say, either, for he remained silent. Watching her, she assumed. She didn't look up, but she could feel his stare on her, warming her cheeks.

It had never been this way with Ian. He'd been

talkative—but not in a manner where he dominated the conversation. He made observations about the weather, the latest society *on dit*, his own personal foibles—anything to put the other person at ease. He asked questions, eliciting information which the other would probably never have been comfortable telling anyone else. He had a way of making one feel like the only person in the room—whether there were a hundred other guests present or simply a footman waiting at the sideboard.

At first, Leah had been grateful for Ian's gift of conversation, seeing as how she was more comfortable listening and observing than participating herself. And when he concentrated on her, she'd felt like the most beautiful woman in the world. After a while, though, she saw his charm for what it was—an attempt to ingratiate himself to the other person, to make them feel charitable toward him. Above all, Ian always wanted to be liked.

Apparently that wasn't the case with Sebastian . . . her new husband. He engaged in conversation well enough, of course, but he didn't seem to care that an uncomfortable silence had descended over them.

Leah glanced up and met his gaze. From the way he looked at her, she almost wondered whether he used the silence to his advantage, just as Ian had used words to his. For even though he didn't speak, the message in his eyes repeated what he'd said before, intimidating and arousing at the same time without one word being said: he desired her.

She didn't understand it, but she couldn't deny it, either. And while she believed he would keep his promise not to try to consummate their marriage unless she asked him to come to her bed, how soon until he began to chafe at their agreement, to resent her for refusing him? Better to be straightforward now and repeat her requirements, than for him to hold to the mistaken hope that one day she might weaken and go to him.

"Would it be possible to have the servants excused for a moment?" she asked.

He made a gesture, and soon they were alone in the dining room.

"I would make a request of you, my lord," she said.

"Sebastian," he corrected.

"Sebastian, then." Though she'd said it aloud before, he hadn't been her husband then. It felt different now, heavy and thick upon her tongue, almost exotic.

"Yes?"

"Sebastian," she repeated, simply to be able to say his name again. "As I said, I wish to make a request of you."

"Yes? Go on." He smiled, as though amused by her dawdling.

"I would like to expand my earlier condition of a marriage in name only to include that you will not look at me or speak to me as you've done today. It is—" Disarming. Terrifying. "Offensive."

Sebastian sat back, his gaze shuttered. "I apologize if I've offended you, my lady."

She opened her mouth, paused, then shut it again.

"No, please," he said. "Tell me what you were you about to say."

"If I call you Sebastian, shouldn't you address me as Leah?"

"I'm not certain," he said, and although his tone was polite enough, there was an undertone of emotion she couldn't identify. "We are married, yet it seems that you would have us remain as strangers. Should we not address each other as such, as well?"

"All I ask—"

He planted his hands on the table and rose to his feet. "I know what you ask, and I will respect it. You agreed to the marriage. We will each keep to our end of the bargain. However, I would ask your forgiveness in advance, my lady. I will attempt to control my speech and the way I look at you, but I don't know if I'll be able to control my thoughts. Would it offend you if I admit to fantasizing about stripping you bare, even here on this table, and kissing my way across the length of your body?"

Leah stood, lifting her chin though flags of heat emblazoned themselves on her cheeks. "Now you mock me?"

"No, I don't mock you," he said, a self-derisive smile curling his lips. "I mock myself. I loved my wife, more than I've ever loved anyone else. She betrayed me. She died. I should be raging at the heavens, cursing her name, wallowing still in the misery that you first saw me in. Instead, it is you I can't stop thinking of, you who haunts my dreams, you who have somehow managed to erase her face from my memory. By all rights I should despise you—not only for that, but also for your behavior which risked so much for Henry—and yet I married you."

He paused, and she watched as he appeared to collect himself, drawing his arms to his sides and straightening to his full height. He stared down at her, his eyes hooded, no emotion betrayed in their depths.

"I married you," he repeated, his tone dull. Weary. Then, inclining his head slightly, he pivoted and left her standing there alone.

Chapter 18

*I can't help but think America is too far. It might
be more difficult for him to find us, but my heart
aches at the thought of Henry living an ocean
away.*

They arrived at Sebastian's country estate in Hampshire late the next afternoon, tired, dusty, and wrinkled. However, looking at the estate, which she'd visited only once before, Leah still felt an overwhelming sense of awe.

It wasn't that the house was much grander than Linley Park; indeed, they appeared to be about the same size. No, it was the surrounding grounds that took her breath away. From the front circular drive, she could see a garden maze to her right, the greenery and shrubs interspersed with autumn flowers. To the left, a large rolling meadow. And all around, in every direction beyond, trees. Towering up to the sky, encroaching upon the civilized landscape, there were trees.

Viewing the estate as a visitor was entirely different

than viewing it as Sebastian's wife, with the realization that this was her home now, too.

"Come," Sebastian said in a low voice. It was the same polite tone he'd used throughout their journey, the same brevity. Since the previous evening, he'd spoken as few words as needed to communicate with her.

He escorted her up the front steps and inside the great door, where the servants had lined up in the entrance to greet them. Sebastian moved Leah along the row, introducing each servant by their name and position in the household. She nodded her head and murmured words which she couldn't remember a moment later.

Once they completed the line of servants, Sebastian directed a few of the footmen who were bringing in her things to take them to the southernmost guest chamber.

"I assume you do not wish to take Angela's bedchamber here, either?" he said when she raised her questioning gaze to his.

"No. Thank you," she answered, and looked quickly away. He'd held true to his word. Nothing today in his expression or his comments had made her believe he desired her—had ever desired her. Rather, he addressed her with as much distant courtesy as if she'd been a relative to the queen, and he a lowly courtier.

"May I see Henry now?" she asked. If there could be no middle ground between Sebastian and herself, then at least she could seek out the little boy's company.

Sebastian inclined his head. "As you wish."

Turning, he strode up the stairs, Leah only a few steps behind him. Henry's nursery was on the third floor. Rather than the narrow room which she'd been expecting, Sebastian guided her to a chamber which was at least the same size as her guest chamber at the Wriothesly town house in London, if not larger. The room was painted a bright, cheery yellow, and toys stacked end upon end littered two sides of the room. The other side was devoted to the boy's bed, a small table with children-sized chairs, and a rocking horse.

In the middle of the room, seated amidst a wrecked wooden train, was Henry.

Her son now.

Leah found it difficult to drag her gaze away from him as Sebastian sought to introduce her to Henry's nanny, a Mrs. Fowler.

"He seems to play very well by himself," she said a few moments later, admiring the short blond crop of his hair, which made him appear a little gentleman. His legs were tucked beneath him, his hands sure as he guided the wooden train around the tracks with an enthusiastic imitation of a train whistle.

It was the expression of stern determination on his face as he played that made Leah smile; except for his coloring, he was almost an exact miniature of Sebastian.

Leah was loath to disturb him, so absorbed was he in his play, not even glancing up to see who had entered.

But then Sebastian called to him. "Henry," he said, and the boy looked up, his concentration broken by a wide smile of delight, and hurtled toward his father's legs.

Sebastian picked him up and spun him around, then set him down and crouched before him. "Do you remember how to bow like I taught you?"

Henry nodded, sneaking a glance at Leah, his blue eyes wide.

"And do you remember Mrs. George?"

Again, Henry nodded, but this time with a pause of hesitation.

"Please say hello, then, and give her your best bow."

The boy turned toward Leah. "How do you do?" he said, his voice small and more than a little uncertain, and gave a short bow. Then he turned back to his father, almost hiding behind his shoulder.

Leah's heart gave a quick, hard thump in her chest.

She smiled. "Very well, thank you."

Sebastian smoothed his hand over the boy's hair. "Would you like Mrs. George to stay with us? She can play with you, and sing you songs." He looked up at Leah and gave her a wink, then returned his attention to Henry. "I've also been told that she has quite an affection for frogs."

Leah's brows lifted. Affection might be too strong a word—she was fondest of frogs and any other nonmammalian creatures when they stayed far away from her.

But then Henry peeked up at her from behind Sebastian's shoulder, his blue eyes round with awe, and she decided that she might be able to learn to like frogs a little bit more.

Henry looked at his father and nodded.

"Very good, then," Sebastian said, standing. "I'll see you after your dinner. Go along."

Henry wrapped his arms around Sebastian's neck, then turned and ran back to his trains. Leah watched him for a moment, then smiled at Mrs. Fowler and followed Sebastian out of the room.

"I hope you don't mind that I didn't tell him we're married yet," Sebastian said as they walked down the stairs to the second floor.

"No, not at all. I imagine that might be a bit much all at once."

Sebastian didn't say anything, and they turned down the stairs to the first floor. At the landing, he stopped and looked at her. Only, he didn't quite look at her, but somewhere above the top of her head.

"If you'll excuse me, I must see to some business. You're welcome to explore the house at your pleasure. The gong will be sounded when it's time for dinner."

Leah hesitated, then reached out to touch his sleeve. "Sebastian—"

She could feel him tense beneath her fingertips, and his gaze flew to hers. "Yes?"

"I . . ." She didn't know what she meant to say. That she wished he wouldn't treat her like some honored guest? That she wished they could return to the familiarity they'd achieved when they were at the house party? That she admired him and wanted . . .

She shook her head and removed her hand. "Never mind."

His mouth flattened, and he turned around. As he walked down the final set of stairs, he called back to her, "Your chamber is down the hall, fourth on your left."

She stood at the top of the steps, her hands clutching the banister, and watched him disappear from sight. As she turned around to find her room, she realized what she'd meant to say.

She wanted him to stay.

In the following days, Leah didn't see much of Sebastian. At each meal, she went down to the dining room hoping to find him there, only to be informed by the butler that he was eating while he worked in his study.

Neither was she invited by Sebastian to spend time with him and Henry. Twice she ventured to the nursery in the afternoon, when she knew he was free to play, only to be told by Mrs. Fowler that Henry had gone with Sebastian.

It seemed her new husband meant to give her much more independence and freedom than she could possibly desire.

Determined to enjoy herself despite Sebastian's aloofness, Leah found plenty to do. Although it was now mid-October and the weather had become quite cold, she took walks through the forest for hours at a time, listening to her feet crunch through the leaves, watching the squirrels scatter as she approached.

She borrowed a roan mare named Bluebonnet from the stables and went for a ride across the meadow, beyond the trees, where she discovered a fair-sized lake. Later she discovered that Bluebonnet had been Angela's mare. She chose a different horse the next time.

One day when it rained, she decided to explore the house as Sebastian had suggested, going room by room on each of the floors—skipping over the master's and mistress' bedchambers.

As she returned to the main floor, intent on trying to amuse herself by playing on the pianoforte in the music room, instead she found her footsteps advancing toward the study. It was late afternoon. Sebastian would have left Henry in the nursery for the day and isolated himself away from her.

With the suspicion that she'd be turned away if she knocked, Leah quietly opened the door and entered. Sebastian wasn't seated behind his desk, reviewing estate business or any other kind of work. He reclined on the sofa against the wall, a book settled on his chest as he read.

When he didn't turn toward her, Leah strolled over, crossed her arms, and stared down at him.

"Hullo, dear husband."

His gaze flickered up, then down. Then, with the greatest show of reluctance, he closed the book and sat up.

She took a seat beside him. "You said I wouldn't be lonely."

He stared across the room, saying nothing, then stood and retreated to his desk. For that's what it felt like—a retreat.

Leah followed him, refusing to let him make her feel like a leper. She strolled around the desk and stood beside him, so close her skirts brushed the arm of his chair. "Am I to understand that you've decided not to speak to me unless I invite you to my bed?"

He blew out a harsh breath, his palms flat against the surface of the desk. "No." He looked up at her and smiled. Or rather, it was an attempt at a smile. An abysmally poor attempt. "I apologize if I've left you to think so ill of me. I simply thought it would be best—for both of us—if I kept my distance."

"Because you regret marrying me." He'd all but said as much the night of their wedding.

"Would you like for me to be honest?" For a moment, Leah was tempted to shake her head. Instead, she nodded.

"Yes, I regret marrying you." He sighed, lifting his hand and plowing it through his hair. "I thought it was the perfect solution. Make the gossipmongers focus on us instead of the Ian and Angela. Provide a mother for Henry, to keep him from continuing to ask for her. Find a way to make you want me, to not reject my advances as you did before."

Leah swallowed.

Sebastian put his face in his hands, rubbing as if he hadn't slept enough. And when he pulled away, she saw that it was probably the truth; the skin beneath his eyes was dark, shadowed.

"And yes, I still believe the rumors about Ian and Angela will die down. And Henry still needs a mother. But I should have chosen someone else, as you suggested. Because I've tried, but I can't look at you and not want you. I haven't asked you to spend time with me and Henry because even then, as much as I desire the simple pleasure of your company, I know I will want more, and I won't be able to disguise it."

He leaned back in his chair and reached out, taking one of her ungloved hands between his. He stroked her palm with the pad of his thumb, slid his fingers against and in between hers. Leah took a deep breath, tried to calm the blood which suddenly leapt within her veins.

His lashes were lowered as he looked at their joined hands, his voice low when he spoke. "Do you see? Not five minutes, and I'm already touching you. But it shouldn't be your hand that I'm holding. It should be Angela's."

Leah tried to tug her hand away, but he held it tight.

"Sometimes I wonder if I'm drawn to you only because we share that secret. If she'd betrayed me with another man, would it be that widow that I turned to? Or perhaps not. Perhaps there's something in you that I can't resist. You are nothing like her, and perhaps that's why I'm like this, because I . . ." He looked up, his green eyes fatigued, faint lines indenting the corners of his mouth. "I never expected you."

He released her hand. Leah stepped away. Her heartbeat pounded in her ears.

"But it's not too late," he continued. "It's crossed my mind the past couple of days, and . . . since we haven't consummated the marriage, I could petition for an annulment."

"Is that what you want?" she asked. He'd said he couldn't resist her. He looked at her like he wanted her to go away but needed her to stay. As if she were his salvation and damnation combined.

"No. But neither can I stop myself from wanting you, and you've made it quite clear—"

Leah leaned forward, before she could think of all the reasons not to, bent her head, and kissed him.

Sebastian didn't move when Leah's lips met his. It was almost as if he was inside a dream. Never had he thought she would be the one to come to him, to touch him, to kiss him.

But there she was, her mouth on his, gently persistent, moving over his. Her hands cupping each side of his face. Her scent and warmth surrounding him.

He parted his mouth, just to see what she would do. When she bit down on his lower lip, he couldn't keep the groan from rising inside his chest, and his arms came up, his hands settling at her waist, pulling her closer.

Almost as soon as he touched her, she pulled away, panting. But her cheeks were flushed, her eyes hazed—almost as if she'd drunk too much—and she swayed as she placed her hands behind her, steadying herself against the desk.

They stared at each other, Sebastian's heart pounding in his chest, his body prepared to take her upon his lap and devour her. He'd never wanted like this before, almost as if she were his only hope of sustenance. Not even with Angela.

"I'm sorry," she said, her breathing broken. "I can only give you a kiss."

"But why? Why kiss me at all?"

She lifted her hand to her neck, her cheek, her hair, almost as if to assure herself that she was still whole. Did she believe he would destroy her if he came too close? "Because I . . . I wanted to."

Sebastian's chest rose sharply. "While I appreciate your gesture, I can't do it that way. I can't keep a firm control on myself all the time, and then have you suddenly come at me with your own desires. I'm not that good of a man."

Her hands lowered, twisting at her waist. Her lashes fell to her cheeks, then rose again. "Then just spend time with me," she said. "With Henry, if that's the way it must be."

"If I spend time with you, with or without Henry, I'm not going to be able to hide my desire for you."

"Then don't," she said, then paused, staring directly

into his eyes. "As long as you allow me to look my fill, also."

For several moments, Sebastian didn't breathe. A flush rose beneath his skin, heating his body, tightening his loins. He almost reached for her, almost told her that it was more than desire that drew him to her. Instead, he simply said her name, although it sounded more like a curse as it was torn from his throat. "Leah."

She darted away, as if she knew the dangers of remaining so close to him. "Perhaps if we spend more time together, one day I will be ready to . . ."

Sebastian took a deep breath, forcing his mind to clear. "We made an agreement. If you never wish to come to my bed, I will honor it. But I can promise you that I will continue to desire you, to imagine making love to you, no matter what you decide."

Her lips parted, softening from the line where she'd pressed them together.

"Should I not have spoken so?" he asked in a low voice, leaning forward.

"No . . . You may speak as you wish."

His gaze lifted from her lips back to her eyes. Rising from the chair, he crossed to the sofa and sat down. "Come here, then." When she didn't move, he added, "I won't touch you."

She followed his path, her steps small and hesitant. But she came.

"Sit down," he said, motioning to the opposite end of the sofa. To his surprise, she obeyed without saying a word. Wonder of wonders, his independent wife was allowing him to instruct her.

He shifted on the sofa so that his body was turned toward her. "No matter what I say, promise me that you won't look away or close your eyes."

A ripple slid down her throat as she swallowed, drawing his attention. He should have sat on the opposite side of the room. Already he wanted to cover her with his lips, to suck at the spot where her pulse throbbed at the base of her throat.

Then her chin lifted, and she said, her voice only slightly louder than a whisper, "I promise."

"It's the end of summer again. We're not at Linley Park, but here. We're outside. It's late at night, and the stars and the moon are the only light we have. The lamp is no longer lit. I've brought you out to the meadow with the pretense of looking at the sky through the telescope, to show you a constellation that can be seen only at this particular time. There is a blanket on the ground, and two glasses of champagne. It's much the same as it was at the country house party, only we are alone. Do you remember?"

"Yes."

"You're wearing the black dress you wore the last evening, the one that made a mockery of your widowhood. In the moonlight, your back gleams like a white pearl, like the ones on either side of the V. You're wearing black gloves also, and although it's dark outside and it's only the two of us, your mourning veil."

Sebastian looked down at Leah's hands and found them clenched tightly together in her lap. He returned his gaze to her eyes. "Neither of us can see the other through the shroud of your veil. I take your hand and guide you to sit down on the blanket. First I take off my gloves, and then I slide yours down your arms, my fingers trailing over each inch of pale skin that's revealed. You're warm to the touch, the inside of your wrists smooth, silken. I can feel your pulse beating against my thumb as I pause there, savoring the first feel of your flesh against mine."

Leah's gaze left his, moved to somewhere beyond his shoulder. "Don't look away," he ordered. She drew in a shaky breath, then looked at him again. Sebastian almost stopped there, arrested by the uncertainty in her eyes. But he didn't. He couldn't.

*   *   *

Leah's mind screamed for her to stand and run out the door. Every muscle was tensed, prepared to obey. Even her heart beat wildly inside her chest, each thud seeming to demand, "Go. Go. Go."

But she stayed. Not because she had promised— she'd broken promises before. But because, God help her, she wanted to know what came next.

"After I remove your gloves, I draw you down, until you're lying on the blanket, watching me. I push your skirts to the middle of your thighs. You're not wearing anything else—no corset, no petticoats, no chemise. No stockings. I stare at your legs, wanting to push your skirts higher, but I resist. I remove your shoes instead. I run my hands over your arches, your heels, curving around your calves. I lean over you and push my hands against the insides of your thighs, spreading your legs wide."

Sebastian stopped speaking and simply stared at her. Leah had to force herself not to cover her face with her hands, but to meet his gaze evenly, to see his desire glinting from the depths of his eyes. And she became aware of other things, too. Her thighs were pressed tightly together, as if to defend herself against the hands which spread them apart in his fantasy. She wasn't breathing. She was drinking the air. In the silence between them, she could hear her own rapid pants, pulling and pushing out oxygen as if she would never be able to get enough.

A corner of his mouth tilted, his eyes darkening. "Am I arousing you, Leah?"

A beam of afternoon sunlight penetrated through an opening in the window curtains, slicing between them. She shook her head, not daring to look away.

"Ah. Then I shall endeavor to do better."

She bit her tongue—unsure whether it was more inclined to urge him to continue or stop.

"Your legs are spread wide apart, and I settle between, kissing the insides of your knees, moving upward along your thighs. My hands push your skirts higher, ever higher as I continue kissing you—with my lips, with my tongue, biting at your tender flesh. But I stop at the top of your thighs, your skirts still hiding the view of your quim—"

Leah gasped, then swallowed. His gaze followed her hand as it lifted to her throat. She lowered it, but slowly, almost tempted to let it cover her breast, to have his eyes linger there.

"I've often wondered what you look like there," he said. "Your hair is light brown. Is the hair between your thighs lighter? Darker? Is it black?"

His voice was like an opiate, mesmerizing, his words not only seducing her imagination but her body as well. They slid along her limbs, making them heavy with desire. They moved inside her veins, along every nerve ending. With only his voice, she felt the pull at her nipples, as if he'd set his mouth there. She felt his words probe at her core, as deft as fingers. Stroking, heating, softening her.

"Leah?" He tilted his head, the question of her name drawing her out of the near trancelike state. "Would you like to tell me the color?"

She didn't think she could blush any more, but she did. Heat scoured her cheeks, as if a fever had overtaken her. "No," she choked out.

His mouth curved again, that knowing, sensual imitation of a smile. "Very well. I shall imagine that it's the same color as your hair. The dark amber of honey."

He paused, looking at her expectantly, but Leah wouldn't speak to either confirm or deny. Neither would she consider the use of honey as an innuendo for her taste. Or rather, she didn't want to consider it. But she did. And she felt a rush of heat between her thighs, dampening her flesh.

And still Sebastian continued his torture. "I've thought about how you would feel to the touch, the softness, beckoning me to search further. I imagine parting your lips, slipping my fingers inside to feel the heat, the wetness. My thumb would caress you until you came, while my index finger moved in and out, exploring your tightness, making love to you until you cried out for me to stop."

"Is—" Leah glanced away, then remembered and looked at him again. "Is this still happening when we're in the meadow?"

"Oh, no," he said softly, his voice dragging across her senses like velvet. "I'm imagining doing this to you right now."

Leah leapt to her feet.

He stood as well, although he didn't follow her as she ran toward the door. "We can go back to the meadow if you like," he said, in such a way she was convinced he taunted her. "I have yet to fully unclothe you." He took a step forward, and then another. "Don't you want to know what happens next?"

Leah leaned against the door, her hand gripping the handle. He continued strolling toward her. She should flee. And yet she didn't.

Reaching out, he took her hand in his.

"You said you wouldn't touch me."

"I'll let you go soon."

With a gentle pressure, he moved her away from the doorframe to the nearby wall. As promised, he released her hand. Leah flattened herself against the wall, the back of her head sliding against the silk wallpaper as he stood in front of her, only a few inches keeping his legs from brushing against her skirts. He lifted his arms and placed his hands on either side of her shoulders, then bent his head to her ear.

"I'm not touching you."

Chapter 19

*I won't cry again, I promise. You needn't worry
about me. This is what I want. You are what I want.*

Leah closed her eyes. He might as well have been
touching her, for the way his nearness affected her. If
she had thought his words dangerous, the scent of him,
the heat from his body was even more so.

It curled inside her, creating a longing she'd rather
ignore. It wasn't desire or a physical craving. It wasn't
lust but something more, something that she feared had
to do only with Sebastian. She'd thought she'd experienced it before with Ian, but now, now that Sebastian
stood before her, she realized that it had only been a
glimpse of a shadow.

"Leah." He said her name, and she breathed it in, the
sound filling her, expanding her lungs, warming her
hands and her feet and everything in between.

Without opening her eyes, she rose to her tiptoes and
leaned forward. Her lips found the side of his neck, the

warm skin above his cravat, his racing pulse. He stiffened.

She kept her eyes closed—perhaps if she didn't open
them, she wouldn't have to admit to what she was
doing—and lifted her chin, her mouth grazing over his
jaw, across his cheek, settling like a whisper on his lips.

He exhaled harshly, his arms leaving the wall beside
her to crush her against him. It was like the force of a
tide, surrounding her and pulling her under, a sweet,
heady rush.

Yes, this is what she wanted. To open her mouth, to
touch her tongue to his. Here there was no fear, no
weakness. It was only Sebastian and the comfort of his
touch, the realization of his desire for her that left her
legs shaking and filled her head with a wild, dizzying
rush. With a soft, pleased sound, she slid her arms up
over his chest, her hands gripping his shoulders. Before
she could link her hands around his neck, he broke free,
lurching back. His chest heaved as he held their hands
between them, his gaze tormented, wild, bewildered.

"Do you want me, Leah?" he asked. His voice rasped
across her senses, turning her skin to gooseflesh.

She tugged her hands from his grip and rubbed her
arms. "I . . ." She wanted him. She knew that without a
doubt. Sebastian. She wanted him to continue talking in
that voice, the one that made her come undone, that
made her feel as if she were something to be worshiped,
a siren who made him lost control. She wanted to hear
him laugh, to share his smiles, to soften her heart while
he played with Henry. She wanted to stare into his eyes
and realize, without trying to deceive herself that it was
something else, that he told the truth when he said he
desired her.

She wanted Sebastian. But did she want this? Could
she handle giving him everything; could she risk not
knowing whether she would ever gain it back?

Leah shook her head. "I'm sorry—"

He took another step back, his gaze shuttered, then pivoted and strode to the window. "Then go," he said. "Go right now, before I make the mistake again of testing my own strength."

"Sebastian—"

He looked over his shoulder, his mouth twisted. "Go, Leah."

She faltered, unable to move. Lifting her arm, she opened her mouth and reached toward him, but he had turned around. Ignoring her. Whirling, she did as he asked. She fled.

From that day forward, Sebastian determined to treat Leah as simply another member of his household. She would be a wife, but only as she'd wanted: one that shared his name but not his bed, someone to be a mother to Henry but who was free to come and go about the grounds as she pleased.

If they were ever in the same room alone, Sebastian found a reason to summon a servant or leave to see to some sort of business. Often the business entailed hours of staring down at ledgers his steward submitted to him while thinking about Leah, or pretending to read a book in his bedchamber while thinking about Leah, or half listening to James during one of his regular visits while thinking about Leah.

Perhaps if it was only desire that kept him tied to her, it would have been easier to dismiss this obsession. But it was more than the lush curve of her upper lip and the slender sway of her hips. It was the humor in her eyes as she discussed politics with him and James over dinner, the intelligent arguments she made when she was certain she was right, and then after she won a discussion, the easy manner in which she turned the conversation back to Sebastian as if she wanted to know what he would say next.

Angela, too, had been intelligent and kind. But if he tried to compare her to Leah, he could see now that Angela had always let him win their discussions; her kindness had actually been a means of placating him, her laughter meant more for his satisfaction that her own enjoyment.

Like Angela, Leah also had an air about her that she was trying to contain herself, to be as others expected. But where Angela had maintained that mask perfectly, Leah's continually slipped. More and more, her polite smiles were turning into grins, her sedate strolls into strides.

One day when frost layered the grass, he caught her dancing in the fields with Henry although she had said they were to go pick the late-blooming flowers.

Leah held Henry to her chest, one arm about his waist while her other hand clasped his, keeping a flower tucked inside his fist. As Sebastian strolled nearer, he could hear her humming a waltz as she danced across the field which served as their imaginary dance floor.

"What flower?" Henry asked, staring at their joined hands.

"I'm not sure. I believe it's a chrysanthemum, although we'd do better to ask the gardener. I know plenty about roses, but not much else."

Then she swung him in a tight circle—once, twice, three times as Henry let his head fall back and giggled at the autumn sky.

That made her laugh, and the sight of them together, hearing his son's laughter tangled with hers—if Sebastian wasn't certain he loved her before, there was no way he could deny it now.

Sebastian stopped a few feet away, hiding in the shadow of a large oak. Leah stopped spinning, and they weaved back and forth for a moment as she seemed to catch her balance.

"I must say, my lord Henry," she said breathlessly, "you are a very accomplished dancer."

Henry smiled at her and leaned over, pointing at the ground. "Flower."

"Yes, a few more flowers." Leah put him down, and took the flower he gave her from his hand before he bent to pick more. She crouched beside him, her hand brushing across his hair before settling at his back. Their voices were too low now; only murmurs came to Sebastian's ears as they studied the flowers and the grass.

Pushing away from the tree, Sebastian clasped his hands behind his back and walked forward. "Do you mind if I join you?" he asked, deliberately focusing his gaze on Henry.

Henry's head jerked up, his face brightening as he pointed at the ground. "Bug, Papa! Spider!"

"Ah. A spider is it? I thought we were looking at flowers." Sebastian glanced at Leah with a rueful twist of his mouth, telling himself not to notice how her face seemed to brighten at his presence, too.

She shook her head and stood to her feet, a hint of a smile playing at the corners of her mouth. "Apparently spiders are much more interesting than flowers, my lord. Eight legs? And they crawl? What little boy wouldn't be fascinated?"

"Indeed."

Leah withheld her sigh and forced herself to smile wider. Sebastian wasn't rude or unfriendly. He was simply ... aloof. Distant. She could tell he struggled with it— probably didn't want her to feel lonely, no doubt—but for all the times that he invited her opinion on something or flirted with her, there were an equal number of times that he allowed his gaze to drift away from hers when they were talking until they both fell silent, or found a reason to excuse himself from her presence when only a few minutes had passed in the same room together.

Therefore, as they were accustomed lately, instead of looking at each other they turned their gazes and looked at Henry.

Henry, who kept trying to get the spider to walk onto a blade of grass. Finally, ingeniously—he was Sebastian's son, after all—he plucked another blade of grass and scooped the spider up with the two together. "Look, Papa," he urged.

Sebastian bent down and put his hand on his chin, studying the small insect which scrabbled back and forth, from one edge to another. Then he gasped. "Look at its eyes!" he exclaimed.

Henry leaned forward, nearly dropping the grass in an attempt to bring the blades closer to his face. "He has four eyes!" he said, then looked at his father, his own blue eyes wide with wonder.

"Hmm. So he does. And look, do you see this black marking at the back?"

Henry nodded even before returning his gaze to the spider, and Leah smiled. How he loved Sebastian, and Sebastian adored him.

Leah had never realized that her dreams of having a child had been unfinished. Now, with Sebastian there, she understood that Ian had always been an addendum to those dreams, not an inherent part of them. But Sebastian—she couldn't imagine Sebastian not being here, not as part of the picture. She could have been the outsider, but he'd brought her into his family, to have the life she'd dreamed of having. She was now a mother and perhaps—one day, a day she couldn't foresee, but had hope it would come to pass—she would truly be a wife to Sebastian as well.

Sebastian and Henry studied the spider for a few moments longer. Then Sebastian stood and Henry hurriedly laid the blades of grass and the spider on the ground and lifted up his arms, his hands clenching and unclenching.

With a growl, Sebastian swooped him up and over his shoulders. Sebastian looked at Leah, pretending to ignore Henry's giggles as he hung upside down over his back. "What say you, my lady? Shall we return to the house?"

Leah bent and picked another flower, then stepped near to Sebastian. Meeting his gaze, she placed the flower in the buttonhole below his cravat. She stepped back, gave him a tentative smile. "Yes, let's go home."

Chapter 20

After I danced in your arms tonight, I realized it was the first time I ever remembered feeling like there was hope for us to be together.

"This one?"

"That's the one." Sebastian stopped beside Leah and looked up at the oak tree. It was one of the trees on the outskirts of the forest, its lowest branch only a few feet from the ground.

Leah turned to him, her brow lifted. "How kind of you to find the easiest tree for me to climb. I'm sure even Henry could climb it repeatedly without difficulty."

"Nonsense," Sebastian answered. "Henry's only climbed it once."

She glared at him, and he smiled as she stepped closer to the trunk. True to his word, he'd borrowed a pair of trousers and a shirt from the hall boy. Although the clothes fit her well enough, it was still disturbing—and arousing—to see Leah clad in men's clothes. When she walked a certain way, taking a full step, the trousers curved lovingly over her backside for a moment, leaving Sebastian's body aching and wanting.

Leah looked at him over her shoulder. "Shall I start?"

He inclined his head. "Whenever you're ready."

Placing one hand on the trunk, she lifted her foot high until it planted on the low branch, then gave a little jump with her other foot. However, instead of successfully landing on the branch, her first foot slipped. Sebastian leapt forward and caught her as she fell, his arms bracketing her waist.

"Are you all right?" he asked, his lips moving against her hair, his heart thudding hard in his chest.

"I'm fine. You may let me go."

"I'm not sure," he said, running his hands along her sides, skimming over her hips.

She escaped from his embrace and whirled to glower at him.

"You're so small and fragile," he teased. "Perhaps I should teach you how to climb up on my bed first. It's a little lower to the ground."

She narrowed her eyes and turned her back to him, but not before he spied a faint blush rising in her cheeks. As she lifted her first foot onto the branch again, Sebastian stepped beside her, putting his hand at her lower back for support.

"Yes, because that's very helpful," she said, not looking at him.

"This time, try swinging your leg completely over. Then, once you're straddling the branch, you can use the trunk to lever yourself up."

Her mouth pursed, but she did as he instructed. Sebastian kept his hand upon her as she moved to straddle the branch—first her back, then her waist and her thigh. When she placed her hands on either side of the trunk to stand, the material of her borrowed shirt stretched and pulled, revealing the slight curve of her breast. Sebastian's hand faltered, slipping from her leg.

Leah stood on the branch by herself and looked down at him. "Are you coming or not?"

It had been a long time since he'd climbed trees, but his body seemed to remember well, giving him the balance needed to straddle the branch then stand up without support of the trunk. He faced Leah. "Impressed?"

"Indeed. Especially since we've already established that even a child could climb this tree."

"Perhaps, but not quite as well." He pointed upward. "Keep going."

Leah continued climbing, Sebastian supporting her as best he could. She only slipped once more, when there was a gap a little wider than the length of her leg between two branches. After that, Sebastian made sure he climbed ahead of her, so that he was able to pull her up when she had troubles.

At last they sat upon a branch twenty feet above the ground, the highest one left that would support both their weights. Although it was cold, their exertion from climbing the tree had left them warm and breathing hard, their breath fogging the air as they exhaled.

"Congratulations, Lady Wriothesly. You have now climbed a tree."

She turned her face toward him, the widest smile upon her lips, wider even than when he'd first mentioned the word "reckless." "Thank you, my lord," she said, and leaned into him, her shoulder fitting against his side.

For a moment Sebastian didn't breathe, more than aware of the import of her voluntary action. She'd touched him. True, it wasn't another kiss, but it was something more. An act of trust—a small one, but one nonetheless.

"What happened with Ian? Did he do something to make you shy away from me at times, or is it simply me?" he asked, then cursed himself as she stiffened against him. He'd assumed she would draw away, but she didn't. She held still, though she averted her gaze. When she didn't speak for several minutes, he cursed himself again. "I apologize. I shouldn't have asked."

She made a slight motion with her head—almost a nod—and he could hear her deep, indrawn breath. "Do you remember when you compared me to Angela at Linley Park?"

"Leah . . ."

"You assumed Ian couldn't bear to come to my bed, that that's the reason we never had any children. You thought that was why he'd turned to Angela."

Sebastian remained silent. He might want to apologize a million times more, but it was clear she would always remember.

"The truth is, my lord—"

"Sebastian." He would at least remind her that he was her husband now. He was no longer her dead husband's betrayed friend, callous and vengeful, intent on hurting her to assuage his own pain.

"The truth is, Sebastian, Ian came to my bed every night."

Sebastian had once thought nothing could hurt him as much as the knowledge that Ian and Angela had both betrayed him. But he was wrong. Somehow, these words were worse.

"It wasn't long after I discovered the affair that Ian confronted me. It should have been the other way around, but . . . I didn't want to acknowledge it. Perhaps, I thought, if I didn't speak of it, then it would end, and he would return to me. He would love me again. But he made me discuss it. And he apologized. Profusely. I cried. He didn't. And I felt even more wretched because there I was, pouring my heart out to him, and none of it mattered. He didn't love me anymore."

Her voice was deadened, emotionless, dry as the fallen leaves scattered by the wind below the trees.

"I don't know why he did it—perhaps he thought it would make me feel better. And I let him, because I—" She laughed, a disbelieving sound. "I thought that, even though he couldn't say the words, that his lovemaking was proof he still felt something for me.

"When it was over, and he apologized again, this time for making love to me, I didn't know what to think. I was—confused. By him, by myself, by the entire situation. I told him that I didn't care about his affair with her, but that I wanted a baby, that I deserved a child of my own, to love and cherish. And it was true. I did want a baby—desperately so. I've wanted to be a mother since I was a child, playing house with Beatrice. But I still managed to convince myself that he couldn't agree to such a thing unless he still wanted me. Perhaps he didn't love me any longer, or at least he didn't think he did. But if he could come to my bed every night, at least I knew he desired me. It was a little piece of him, one I thought could be enough."

Sebastian glanced down, caught by the motion of Leah's hand curling into a fist on her thigh.

"He kept to his end of the agreement. A man of his word," she scoffed. "Every night, he would come to my bedchamber. He smelled of sex, of vanilla, and some other scent—"

"Lavender." Sebastian clenched his jaw.

Leah nodded. "Her scent. He smelled of Angela. And he would come to me, take off my chemise, kiss me, caress me. I wanted to think he took care to pleasure me because he wanted me, but . . . as weeks passed by, and his nightly visits were all that he gave me, I realized that he was trying to absolve himself of his sins. To make me feel better. Each time he made love to me, it was a silent apology.

"It didn't take long before I dreaded the nights. I could have turned him away, but I didn't. I wanted a child. A child. That was all that mattered. But I never carried, and—don't you understand? I became his whore. And he became mine. My body for a baby. His for repentance. God, how relieved I was when he died."

She was trembling against him. Trembling so hard that the side of his body she was leaning against started shaking as well. And he couldn't think of anything to say.

"I'm sorry, Leah." He lifted his hand from the branch, as if to put it around her shoulders, then lowered it again. "I'm so sorry."

"It's terrible, isn't it? That I'm not sorry? I never wished he would die. I accepted it for what it was, praying every day that I would conceive. And yet now that he's gone ..."

She inhaled, exhaled. He could feel every movement of her body. The gentle sulk of her shoulders as air escaped her lungs. He wished he could wrap his arms around her, that she would welcome his embrace. But, more than ever before, he didn't want her rejection. He would not be equated with Ian.

"He wasn't a monster," she continued quietly. "He could have treated me badly, but he didn't. He simply ... fell in love with someone else." She didn't say anything for a while, then tilted her head back and looked at him. "I'd like to climb back down now."

"All right."

And it was almost as if she'd never revealed any of her past with Ian. They climbed back down the way they had come, Sebastian going first to steady her. On the way to the house, she talked about Henry and how she looked forward to playing in the snow with him when the first snowstorm hit. She talked about what she and the housekeeper had planned for dinner that night. She talked about the birds flying overhead and how warm the house appeared, and she challenged him to race her the few remaining yards inside.

But she didn't speak of anything else that would help him see past the wall she'd reerected, and when she rushed through the front door, laughing as she pretended to shut him out, Sebastian felt another door—this one invisible—close between them.

As soon as Leah entered her bedchamber, she sat on the edge of her bed and buried her face in her hands. Why couldn't she let this fear go? She wanted Sebastian, knew he desired her.

She had a choice, just as she'd had a choice with hosting the house party, with wearing the organza dress, with leaving her parents' home rather than marrying the butcher. The repercussions of each of those choices had been greater, more uncertain. This one should be so simple.

She cried again, missing the strength of Sebastian's embrace. Her future with him was clear: she either chose to continue giving in to her vulnerability and the fear of losing herself again, or she chose him.

That evening, Leah met Sebastian in the drawing room as was their usual habit before dinner was served. She'd taken special care in her choice of gown: a dark rose-colored dress which sloped at the shoulders and curved at the middle of her chest. It was a modest dress in terms of evening gowns, but the way the material moved against her body didn't insinuate innocence as much as sensuality. There were few times in her life Leah had ever dressed for the sole purpose of attracting a man's attention. Tonight was one of those nights.

She smiled and chatted with him as he escorted her

into the dining room, and she tried very hard to focus on each course of the meal, but in the middle of pushing around the duck with turbot sauce, she realized Sebastian had ceased talking. And apparently he'd been staring at her for quite some time.

"Is something wrong?" he asked.

Leah set aside her fork and folded her hands in her lap. Biting her lip, she looked at the servants. Sebastian dismissed them with a motion of his hand.

"What is it?"

"I'm not hungry," she said.

"Are you ill?" he asked, a frown creasing his brow.

"No. I'd like to go to my bedchamber."

Although he still appeared bewildered, Sebastian stood as she rose to her feet. She stared at him.

"Leah?"

"I . . . I would like for you to go with me." They were only words, and yet once they were said, she felt as if all the strength had been drained from her body.

He didn't understand. She could tell by the way he came swiftly to her side, as if she might faint at any moment, wrapping his hand around her upper arm. "Shall I send for a physician?"

"No," she said, then straightened her shoulders as she drew in a breath. "I'm inviting you to come to my bed."

His fingers tightened on her arm, and his eyes lowered, concealing his reaction.

"Of course, I might shut you out at the door," she jested, and smiled when he looked up.

"Are you certain?"

"Yes," she said, her answer barely more than a whisper. "Yes," she repeated, her voice stronger, firmer.

He nodded and led her out the room, down the hall, and up the stairs. When they reached her bedchamber, he paused, and she knew he was waiting for her to change her mind.

"Open the door," she said. He did, sliding his other hand down her arm to twine his fingers with hers. He pulled her inside.

They faced each other at the foot of the bed, and she could hear his breathing, equally as loud as her own.

"Shall I undress you?" he asked. She nodded, and turned her back toward him. His hands were sure as he unfastened the buttons, steady unlike the faint trembling of her legs, and soon the gown gaped at her waist, her bodice dipping forward from her chest. Leah withdrew her arms from the sleeves and closed her eyes as she felt Sebastian reach low for her skirts and pull the gown over her head.

She kept her eyes closed as he continued to undress her. First her corset, her petticoats. Her shoes, her stockings, her drawers. Her chemise. Each article of clothing fell to the floor beside her, and she only moved at his direction.

"Lift your arms."

"Bend your knee."

"Move your foot."

He made his commands, and she obeyed him, imagining each order as if it came from her lady's maid. She didn't try to cover herself but retreated mentally, focusing on the darkness behind her eyelids, not speaking a word.

Then his fingers were in her hair, plucking out the pins, and heavy locks began to fall over her shoulders, down her back, across her naked breasts. She could feel him move around until he stood in front of her.

His hand cupped her cheek, warming her skin as he tilted her face upward. "Leah."

When she opened her eyes, she found herself staring directly into his.

"You're beautiful."

And she closed them again, for they were the echo of Ian's words, repeated by Sebastian's voice.

"I'm not going to do anything more unless you tell me to do it."

She nodded.

"And I won't do anything you tell me to do unless you look at me. It's me, Leah. Sebastian. I'm not Ian."

"I know," she said, and looked at him. It was a lie, however, for even though her eyes told her differently, her heart and mind were convinced that it would be just as it had been before, with Ian.

He stepped forward, not close enough that they touched, but enough that she could feel the heat of his body warming her own as he bent his head. "And I promise you," he murmured in her ear, "I want you more than he ever did. Much, much more."

"I believe you." Another lie.

He moved back and removed his evening jacket, his waistcoat, his cravat, his shirt. He held her gaze until he stood before her, bare to the waist. "Do I look like Ian?"

Leah allowed herself to admire him, to let her eyes trail over the carved contours of his shoulders and arms. A fine matting of dark hair covered his chest and spread downward across his abdomen which was defined by even more muscles. He was broad where Ian had been narrow, thick where Ian had been lean, dark where Ian had been golden.

"No." She returned her gaze to his. "You don't look like Ian."

"Touch me," he said. "Put your hand over my chest."

She did, placing her palm in the center, over his breastbone. The hair was surprisingly soft, and his hand was hot as he moved hers, until she could feel the beating of his heart.

He held his hand over hers, imprisoning her. "Do you feel how it pounds? How it races? Being this close to you is nearly unbearable. It's difficult to breathe, difficult to look at you, knowing that you don't desire me as I do you."

She moved her fingers, smoothed them over his skin as much as his hand would allow. "I do desire you," she said, staring at his chest.

"Do you?"

Heat rose to her cheeks, and she tried to pull away, but he held her fast. "I wouldn't have invited you here if I didn't."

"I see. It's not a test, then, to see how far you can push yourself?"

"No."

He released her hand, and it dropped back to her side. For the first time, Leah became fully aware of her nakedness, the aloofness and isolation she'd tried so hard to maintain suddenly disappearing. She would have attempted to cover her breasts and the juncture of her thighs, but he was watching her, his gaze knowing, as if he understood her better than she did herself.

"I said I wouldn't do anything unless you told me to," he said. "Tell me to touch you."

She lifted her chin, refusing to retreat from his challenge. "Touch me."

He started at the base of her throat, moving downward to her collarbone, then lower, circling the areola of one breast before going to the next.

"I suppose Ian touched you here?" he said, his gaze holding hers captive.

Leah frowned. "Yes, but I don't want to—" She gasped as he caught her nipple between his finger and thumb, tugging gently, then pinching.

"No, you don't want to talk about him. But I know you'll be thinking about him when I touch you, comparing us."

"I won't. I promise." Even as she said it, her mind

conjured an image of Ian leaning over her, the canopy beyond his head.

"Yes, you will. But after tonight, I promise you'll never think of him again when I'm with you. It will be only you and me."

"And are you thinking of Angela when you touch me now?"

"No." His eyes met hers evenly. "You've long ago chased away her memory, Leah." He paused, as if letting his words sink in. "Is there anything you and Ian didn't do together?"

Leah flushed. "I—I don't believe so."

Sebastian's eyes darkened. He knelt to the floor before her and braced his hands on either side of her hips. Leaning forward, he flicked his tongue against one nipple, then another. "Did he kiss you?" he murmured, then captured the hardened peak between his lips, biting softly, pleasure and pain melding together until he laved it with his tongue. His hand rose from her hip and cupped her breast, scalding her as he held her still while he sucked, his tongue continuing to lick at her.

Leah's hands hovered over his head, then dropped back to her sides.

Sebastian leaned back, looking up at her. "Did he kiss your breasts, Leah? Did he take your nipples into his mouth?"

"Yes," she said, her voice hoarse.

He trailed his mouth down her stomach, nibbling a path toward the crease at the top of her thigh. He moved slowly, torturing her, and Leah wanted to scream for him to hurry, to get it over with. To not make love to her like Ian had.

He pulled his mouth away, and his fingers touched the hair between her thighs. "Black," he murmured, tilting his head to give her a crooked, wicked smile. "I was wrong."

Leah couldn't contain her moan this time, and as if of their own will, her legs parted, waiting. But he moved on, teasing her as he smoothed his hands over her thighs, her calves, her ankles. He bent over, placing hot kisses on the insides of her legs, rising as he nibbled at the sides of her knees. She had to steady herself by putting her hands on his shoulders when he kissed the insides of her thighs, her mind succumbing to the heavy, languorous pull of pleasure as she realized he was acting out his fantasy.

Her legs slid farther apart. A silent plea.

When he pulled away once more, she nearly cried out in frustration. But his hands moved where his mouth should have been, soothing her dampened flesh with his fingers.

"Leah."

Her name was a command, and she obeyed, bending her head to see the flame of need in his eyes, the sulky want of his mouth.

"Did Ian touch you here?" he asked, and his thumb rubbed across the tender peak of her flesh.

"Yes," she choked out, clenching his shoulders. He pushed his middle finger inside her, and Leah whimpered.

"Did he put his mouth to you? Did he kiss you here? Did he lick and suck and bite you?"

"Goddamn you," she cried out, her knees beginning to buckle. "Yes, goddamn you."

His thumb worked steadily, his middle finger sliding in and out. "And did you come for him, Leah? Look at me," he ordered when her lids fell, their weight heavy as she tried to concentrate on the movement of his hand. "Answer me."

She glared at him. "Yes! I came. Over and over and over again."

"Then do it for me. Come for me now," he said softly, and with a flick of his thumb, she bowed over, every muscle stiffening, quivering, her hips jerking against his hand as he lightened his touch, bringing her down gently.

Leah's arm wrapped around his neck, her face buried against his shoulder, her breast pressed against his cheek. She panted. She might never be able to suck in enough air again. She felt Sebastian turn his head and place a kiss on the side of her breast; then he stood and scooped her into his arms.

"I don't like you," she murmured, resting her head against his chest.

He laid her on the bed and pulled the counterpane over her as she turned on her side. "That's all right," he said. "We're married. Sooner or later I'll convince you otherwise."

He moved away, and she heard the rustle of her gown as he picked it up off the ground.

"Are you leaving?"

"No."

The muffled thud of boots hit the floor, followed by what she presumed to be the removal of his trousers. The room fell dark except for the fire still flickering in the hearth. Her breath quickened again when she felt the slight dip of the mattress. She waited for him to pull her against him, to try to arouse her again, to adjust their bodies so he could enter her from behind. When minutes passed and he didn't touch her, she rolled onto her back and turned her head toward him.

He lay facing her on the opposite side of the bed, and she made out the glint of his green eyes by the firelight as he stared at her.

"Sebastian?"

He reached out and cupped her cheek, his thumb tracing over her mouth much the same as he'd done in the garden at Linley Park. "After he made love to you, did Ian stay here with you, or did he return to the master chamber?"

"He left," she said, her lips moving beneath his touch.

Sebastian withdrew his hand. "Then allow me to stay the night, if only to sleep beside you."

"You don't want . . . anything more?"

"No. Tonight, I just want to be with you."

She didn't know how to respond. She'd been prepared to see to his needs, but he didn't want anything else. She hesitated, then rolled back to her side and stared into the fire. "Good night, then."

"Good night."

She watched the fire die down until only embers remained. She tried to close her eyes, but couldn't fall asleep. She was too aware of him behind her, the memory of his touch and his mouth upon her skin.

He'd forced her to tell him what Ian had done, how he'd made love to her. But she hadn't told him that she'd never responded like that before. Sebastian's touch was different, eliciting something in her that had been far greater than simple pleasure.

Nothing at all had been the same.

Chapter 21

I must have packed and unpacked my valise a thousand times already. Truly, all I need to take with me is my portrait of Henry. Besides that, you are all I need.

The following morning when Leah woke up, Sebastian was gone. She fought a sense of disappointment as she sat in the middle of the bed and pulled her knees to her chest. She remembered waking up several times during the night and having him there beside her, the comfort and warmth of his arms. While some of her fear and doubts were still present, he'd made it possible to believe in herself a little more. He hadn't used her, but gave her pleasure without seeking his own. He'd then offered her comfort, when it must have cost him dearly to lie beside her, aching with need.

Sebastian.

Leah flopped back on the bed, turning her head toward the sunlight streaming in through the curtains. She smiled.

A knock sounded at the door, and Leah hurriedly pulled the blanket up to her chin. "Enter," she called.

A maid came in, balancing a tray against her hip. "Good morning, milady. His lordship has sent breakfast to you, as he's already eaten." She waited for Leah to sit up, then set the tray before her. "And I'm to give you this as well," she said, handing Leah a note.

"Thank you," she murmured, then waited for the maid to leave before quickly unfolding the paper.

> *I've taken Henry to the village with me today. Rest while you can, for he's already anxious to see you this morning. We'll miss you.*
>
> *—S*

Leah smoothed the parchment out beside her and re-read it repeatedly while she ate. She wondered what matter of importance called Sebastian into the nearby village, and why he'd taken Henry with him. And she wondered if Sebastian had labored over every single word writing it as she did reading, trying to decipher possible hidden meanings. Such as "We'll miss you." Had Henry told Sebastian that he would miss her, or had Sebastian simply included him because he didn't want to admit that he would miss her? The "we" made it seem more impersonal, somehow, although if it were the truth and they both would equally miss her, then that was something spectacular, actually.

Her husband and her son.

The thought of them made her chest ache, and already she wished they were home.

Leah tried to relax that morning—she truly did—but her ears kept listening for the sound of their return. None of the books she chose from the library held her attention, and she changed her morning dress twice, thinking about how Sebastian would look at her when he saw her again. So much between them had changed, but she was still uncertain where to go from here, or what he would expect from her.

When they hadn't returned by the lunch hour, Leah began to worry. Only a little. After all, the village was no more than an hour away, and not very large at that. What could they possibly be doing which would take them so long?

Trying not to fret, especially when she saw clouds moving in across the sky, Leah went to her writing table in her bedchamber and pulled out Angela's packet of letters. It had been a while since she'd read any, at least since before their wedding. In truth, she hadn't wanted to read any more after that, hadn't wanted to be reminded of Angela when she looked at Sebastian. But it was the only thing she could think of to distract her for a moment, and so she sat on the window seat and untied the ribbon, letting the letters fall into her lap as she glanced out the window.

Still no carriage.

Sighing, Leah picked up the first letter from the jumbled pile; she'd been too careless, and now they were out of order. She opened and folded one after another, placed them to the side as she tried to find one she hadn't read. Soon only one letter lay in her lap.

Leah picked up the letter and opened it.

My darling,
I've made the arrangements as we agreed. I haven't been able to sleep for fear that I will wake up and discover that I am dreaming. Two days! Two days until we're together. Two days until we never have to part again. Do you know how often I've dreamed about being able to wake up beside you? Soon, I will.

I know one day I'll see Henry again, and I love

you all the more for understanding my anguish. How I wish that he were yours, that I had met you first, that he could be our child. But as the heir, I know it's more likely for Sebastian not to try to follow us if I leave Henry... my dear, sweet boy. I pray that soon I'll be able to give you a son, and then you too can know this joy I hold deep in my heart. I will send you one more letter when I confirm the time, and then we will be together.

All my love,
Angela

Leah's fingers trembled as she folded the letter again, then tied them all with the pink satin ribbon.

Oh, Sebastian. Come home to me. Never again need he question whether Henry was his son.

Sebastian carried a tired, wet little boy in his arms up to the nursery early that evening. He deposited Henry in his nurse's lap, then turned to the door. "We'll be back in just a moment to say good night."

"I'll send for his supper right now, my lord."

Sebastian nodded, then went in search of his wife. He went from room to room on the ground and first floors, then finally turned toward her bedchamber, frowning. She didn't usually go to bed this early. She'd seemed fine last night, with no sign of illness. Perhaps she'd actually taken his suggestion and rested all day, although he'd doubted she would when he'd written the note that morning.

He gave a light knock, then opened the door to her bedchamber when he didn't receive an answer.

A sweet ache filled his chest as he spied her, asleep on the window seat, her cheek resting against her fist. Sebastian strode across the room and pushed a stray wisp of hair away from her face. Leah stirred at his touch. *"Shh,"* he said, bending forward to scoop her against his chest. He moved toward the bed, but when he laid her down, her eyes immediately widened and focused on him.

"Sebastian?"

He smiled and stroked her face, simply because he had to touch her. "I see that you've taken to following my orders well."

She blinked, then pushed herself up on one arm. "Where were you? Is everything all right? You were gone a long time."

"Missed me, did you?"

Already the sleep was clearing from her eyes. "I missed Henry, of course," she teased, then lifted to her knees and gave him a short, sweet kiss. Sebastian would have lengthened it, but she climbed off the bed and straightened her skirts.

"I missed you, too," he drawled, then took her hand and led her out the bedchamber. "Henry is almost asleep. I told him I'd have you come say good night before he went to bed."

"I was worried about you."

Sebastian turned his gaze to her, squeezed her hand. "I'm sorry. We would have returned sooner, but one of the wheels got stuck in the mud on the way back."

"Is Henry well?" she asked as they climbed the steps to the second floor, quickening her pace.

"He's fine, don't worry. Just tired. I took him with me to visit with all the tenants, and it took much longer than I expected, for he wanted to play with all of the children he met."

"Oh. Of course he would want to play, I suppose." She climbed the remaining steps ahead of him without a word, and Sebastian wondered whether she was thinking about other children, wishing she could give Henry a brother or sister to play with.

"Leah—"

She glanced over her shoulder and smiled. "I have something to tell you."

Sebastian gave an inward sigh of relief. "Oh?"

She nodded and waited for him to reach her at the top of the stairs; then they turned and walked toward the nursery together.

"Am I going to have to barter for your secret?" he asked, unprepared for the thrill of joy when she slipped her hand inside his. "A kiss for each word, perhaps?"

She gave him a mysterious smile, then placed a finger over his mouth as they stopped outside the nursery. "Soon," she promised, and walked inside.

Henry was at his small table, eating his supper. When he looked up and saw Leah, he scooted his chair backward and went to her. Leah lifted him up and kissed his cheek, then smoothed his hair.

"Hello, sweet boy," she said. "I missed you today."

"Missed you, too," he said, wrapping his arms around her neck. Then, spying Sebastian behind her, Henry held out his arms again.

Sebastian gave Leah an apologetic glance as he tucked Henry against his chest. "It's fine," she whispered, touching Henry's hair as he laid his head against Sebastian's shoulder.

She smiled and, at that moment, Sebastian fell in love with her again. How many times had he spurned spending time with Henry so he could be with Angela? This was how it should be, when he didn't have to choose between his wife and son. "Henry?" Sebastian said. "Are you ready to go to sleep?"

"I believe he already is," Mrs. Fowler said from across the room.

Sebastian moved toward Henry's bed and gently laid him down. Leah stepped close and pulled a blanket over his chest, then leaned forward to kiss his forehead. Sebastian touched Henry's hair, then followed her out the door. Once he closed it behind them, he pulled her into his arms and kissed her neck. "Thank you," he murmured against her skin.

Her hands came up to rest on his shoulders. "For what?"

"For loving him."

Leah laughed and pulled back. "How could I not?" she asked. "As I told you before, he's just like—" She stopped, closing her mouth, and looked away.

"Leah?"

"Do you recall that I had something to tell you?" She looked at him again. "I read another of Angela's letters today, the last one."

Sebastian tensed, his arms falling to his sides. "And?"

Leah smiled at him, her hand lifting to his jaw. "He's yours, Sebastian. She says it in her letter. Even if you don't think he looks like you, there's proof now. He's yours."

Sebastian's throat ached. He stared at her. "Are you sure?"

She nodded, reached for his hand. "Come, I'll show you. You can read it for yourself." He followed her blindly down the stairs, trying to resist the urge to run back to the nursery and look at Henry sleeping.

"I only wish I'd read this one first," Leah said as they entered her bedchamber. She hurried to the window seat and picked up a packet of letters lying between the cushion and the window, tied with the pink ribbon Sebastian remembered seeing before. She drew out the one on top, then thrust it at his chest. "Here. This is it."

Sebastian stared at it for a moment; then his fingers were fumbling as he unfolded the letter. It took a moment for his eyes to focus, and he skipped over the beginning, not seeing anything until he found Henry's name.

The laughter started inside his chest, then pushed its way out, and Sebastian reached for Leah, spun her around in a half circle. It was either laugh or cry, and . . . bloody hell, perhaps both.

He kissed her, pouring out his love and joy and gratitude with the sweep of his mouth. "Thank you for not listening to me, for not burning them. Thank you," he said. "I lo—" He caught himself and drew back, but she was laughing and crying, too. She hadn't even noticed.

It was amazing how quickly his heart turned to lead in his chest, just with the realization that he still had to fear her withdrawal if he told her the truth. Sebastian concentrated on the task of folding the letter again. His fist closed over it tightly. "Thank you," he repeated, then leaned forward and kissed a tear from her cheek. "Good night."

"Wait," she said as he turned toward the door. He closed his eyes, then glanced back with an attempted smile. He feared he failed. "Are you . . . Aren't you going to stay with me? We could have dinner in here tonight, and—"

Sebastian shook his head. "Not tonight, I'm sorry." He paused, wanting to erase the hurt from her eyes but not trusting himself to be the one to do it. "Thank you," he said again, lifting the letter in his hand, then turned and walked out, closing the door behind him.

In the corridor, he leaned against the wall beside her bedchamber. Last night he'd tried to show her how he felt with the strokes of his hands and the touch of his mouth. The very fact that she'd invited him to her bed had felt like a victory. But afterward as he'd held her in his arms, with a profession of love hovering on his tongue, he remembered her reason for accepting his marriage proposal.

And that is why I decided to marry you, my lord. For I don't love you, either.

Sebastian closed his eyes, his chin sinking toward his chest. How long he'd been trapped by those words, afraid to scare her away. How long he'd hoped that after she dealt with Ian's ghost she would one day turn to him. Her confession of her relationship with Ian while they sat in the tree had been one step, her willingness to let him pleasure her another, and yet still it wasn't enough. He wanted everything: her trust, her joy, her heart, her vulnerability.

If he continued waiting, would it mean she would come to love him? Would it take another month, a year? He could imagine them then, sharing each other's beds, acting the happy family with Henry and possibly another child on the way. But they might still be kept apart by her reluctance and fear.

No, he couldn't wait. Even if it meant she withdrew from him completely, he would tell her he loved her. She always spoke of wanting her independence; then let her decide how much it truly mattered.

Sebastian pushed away from the wall.

If she wouldn't surrender to him, then he would surrender to her.

Chapter 22

I've noticed that your kisses have been longer, sweeter recently. Is it because we know that soon we will have every minute of every day to be together, that there's no need to rush each moment now?

Three hours later, as Leah was preparing for bed, a knock came at the door from the hallway. Pulling her wrapper close around her night rail, she strolled across the rug and opened the door.

Sebastian stood on the other side in a black cloak. He held out his hand, palm facing upward. On it lay a small box, wrapped in plain brown paper.

"A gift for you," he said. "I may have neglected to tell you that, in addition to visiting the tenants, we also bought you something in the village."

"We?" Leah questioned, smiling. She wanted to ask him why he'd left as he had earlier, but it seemed the moment had passed. Everything was well between them again. Sebastian was here, his mouth curved charmingly, and her heart raced as a result. Yes, just like it should be.

He lifted a shoulder. "Henry actually chose it, though he used my coin. Therefore I suppose that yes, we bought it together."

Leah reached out and lifted the package from his hand. With a glance at him from beneath lowered lashes, she unwrapped the paper. Inside was a silver box. She shook it.

"Perhaps it's empty. Henry does like boxes, after all."

She raised a brow. "Oh, perhaps it is. What a beautiful box," she said, turning it around so she could gaze at it from all angles.

Sebastian chuckled and stepped forward, taking her hands between his. "However, I promise you that there is something inside this one."

Leah swallowed at his nearness, her skin overly sensitive at his touch.

"Open it," he urged, "else we'll be late."

"Late?" Leah pulled the lid from the box and peered inside, aware of Sebastian's hand brushing against her breast as she brought the gift closer. A blue ribbon lay at the bottom, its satin length edged by lace.

"Henry wanted to buy you a hair ribbon," Sebastian explained. "We searched for over an hour for the perfect gift, and this is what he chose. Although . . ." He paused, lowering his head to press a kiss to Leah's neck. "I must admit that when I saw it I thought of tying up things other than your hair."

Leah tilted her head. He kissed her again. "You should have let him give it to me."

"Perhaps. But I wanted a reason to come see you."

Her heart gave a lurch inside her chest. Leah closed the box and turned her head, meeting his mouth with her own.

"Now that I'm here," he said against her lips, "I want you to come with me."

"Where shall we go, my lord?" She tried to lean in to him, but he moved away, returning to the door.

"I've come to take you on a secret outing," he said, raising his brows. "An adventure, you might say."

Leah's gaze fell from the cloak across his shoulders to the width of his chest, the leanness of his waist and down the length of his legs. Of course she would go with him. He could ask to take her to France on a storm-swept sea in nothing more than a canoe, and she'd say yes.

"Just a moment," she said. "I have to—"

"*Shh.*" She glanced at him, her brows knit. Sebastian grinned and winked at her. "You must whisper, else we'll get caught."

Unable to stop herself from smiling again, she stepped back and closed the door. As soon as she donned a simple day dress and her own cloak, she joined him in the corridor. "Here I am, my lord."

"Perfect," he said, then swooped her over his shoulder.

"Sebastian!" she shrieked, kicking her legs ineffectually, as his arm was wrapped around her thighs. The hood of her cloak fell over her head, obscuring her vision. She grasped handfuls of his cloak, trying to steady herself as he descended the stairs.

"You're not being very quiet," he admonished her.

As he continued walking and her hood bobbed out and away from her face, Leah could see two footmen from the corner of her eye as they walked out the front door.

"Yes, and a lot of good it would do to be quiet when all the servants see the way you're absconding with me."

Sebastian patted her bottom as if she needed to be soothed. Then, as they fell outside the circle of lamplight from the house, his movement turned into a caress, circling across her buttocks.

"Sebastian," Leah warned, choking between a fit of laughter and the immediate flaring of desire.

"Before we were married, you said you wanted adventure. Do you remember?"

"Yes. I also recall saying that I wished for independence. Having a brute of an earl carry me over his shoulder does not make me feel very independent."

"My poor, dear wife. Well, we cannot have everything, can we?" With one arm still holding her pinned to his chest, she felt his other hand creep up her calf.

Leah let go of one fistful of his cloak and reached back, trying to swat him away. "Don't do that."

"Oh, this?" As if her hand was nothing more than a gentle breeze, his fingers continued their ascent, slipping over the back of her knees to tickle at her thighs.

Leah gasped. "Sebastian."

"We're here," he announced, and brought her down, sliding her down the front of his body, setting his hands at her hips to steady her as her feet hit the ground, holding her flush against him.

She'd been so concerned with being hauled away that she hadn't even paid attention—not that she could with her hood obscuring her vision, anyway—to where they were going.

The night air was cool on her flushed cheeks, but every other part was warm—burning—from him. He tipped her chin up with his finger and leaned down, gently kissing her.

Leah closed her eyes, savoring his touch as much as her own ease with it. She'd never thought to be able to enjoy a simple kiss again. But when his hands moved from her waist, up toward her breasts, she involuntarily tensed, then hated herself for doing it. His hands fell away, and with one last quick kiss, he stepped around her.

Leah turned, feeling deserted in his absence, as if a great gift had been stolen from her. She detested this wariness. She had no reason not to trust him, no reason not to give him everything. Time and again he'd proven he was nothing like Ian.

She wanted to apologize, but before she could open her mouth, her gaze landed behind Sebastian, on the small boat bobbing at the edge of the water. He'd brought her to the lake on the Wriothesly property. With no lamp, the only light given was the light from the moon and the stars above, and those were partially obscured by the clouds scudding across the sky. The water was cast half in shadow, half silvered by the faint light. A line of trees ringed the lake; from this perspective, it appeared that they were the only ones in existence, the trees shielding them from the outside world.

Leah brought her gaze back to Sebastian. He stood at the bow of the boat, a small smile on his lips.

"Because I ruined your plans the day you decided to go boating," he said, then stretched out his arm to her.

She stepped forward, even as questions rose to her lips. "It's too cold, isn't it?" His hand was warm as it enfolded hers. "And it's too dark. What if we tip over and fall in? Or hit something?"

His eyes were even darker as he steadied the boat with one hand and guided her in with the other. "I won't let you tip over."

Leah tilted her head back and looked up at the sky as she settled into the far end of the boat. "The clouds make it appear as if it might rain."

"Leah." His voice nudged her, brought her gaze back to him as he gave the boat a push, then vaulted over the side. "It's an adventure. If something terrible happens, then that's part of the amusement."

"Then you expect something terrible to happen?"

He laughed as he pushed off the rest of the way with the oars, sending them even farther out into the lake.

She smiled, unable to help it, and watched in the silvered moonlight the movement of his chest and shoulders, the play of muscles revealed by his parted cloak. She wrapped hers even tighter around her, wishing she was still being held in his embrace. Wishing, just for once, that she could let go and not think about anything except the pleasure she gave him and the pleasure he gave her.

After a few minutes, Sebastian pulled the oars out of the water and set them in their hooks. He stared across at her as the boat drifted at the lake's whim, a breeze tugging at the ends of his hair.

Leah gave him a halfhearted smile, curious at what they were meant to do next. He didn't smile back.

"Do you remember at the house party at Linley Park, when I kissed you in the garden, and you ran away?"

"Of course I do," she answered. It was the first time he'd touched her. Even now she felt the heat of a blush creep beneath her skin, suffusing her with warmth.

"I don't suppose you can run away now, can you?" he asked softly.

Leah stiffened at the quiet, murmured threat. "Sebastian?"

"There have been many ways that I've thought about telling you this—"

In her mind, she saw Ian bent at Angela's breast again. Leah gripped the bench at either side, waiting, unsure what he would say, but staggered by how much greater the pain was this time.

"—and many times as well, but I never felt like it was the right time." He looked down at the water, brought a hand up to scrub the length of his jaw. "In truth, I don't think it will ever feel like it's the right time."

"You don't want me anymore." That was the most obvious conclusion; easy enough to believe after the way he'd left her bedchamber earlier that evening.

His hand dropped away and he stared at her. "I love you, Leah." Even in the faint light from the moon, his expression was one of torment.

"I—I—" She stammered, and she suddenly felt hot all over, then cold. Then, because even though she had tried to escape her background, and because politeness was still ingrained into her very core, she said, "Thank you."

"Thank you?" He laughed, an incredulous sound. "Thank you?"

"I don't know what to say," she said, lowering her gaze.

He didn't say anything, either, and when she finally looked up after a long moment, she found him studying her, one corner of his mouth drawn into a tight, sad smile. "I made a mistake, didn't I? I was right at the beginning—I never should have asked you to marry me."

She clasped her hands together, hid them in folds of her cloak as she wrung them. "I . . . enjoy being married to you, Sebastian. I truly do. And I adore Henry—"

He cut her off, slashing his hand through the air angrily. "This isn't about Henry," he said. "This is about you, and me, and the fact that you will never forgive me."

"I have nothing to forgive you for—"

"You will never forgive Ian—"

"I have already forgiven him!" she shouted.

The boat rocked, the lake lapping little waves at the side. Despite her flushed cheeks, Leah was suddenly colder in the silence, and she huddled further into her cloak. "I have," she repeated. Then, feeling the need to defend herself, she said, "It's never been about Ian . . . well, at least, not all of it." She stared at her hands, clasped so tightly together in her lap that her knuckles turned white. She inhaled deeply, then released a sigh. She looked up, met his gaze, then looked away to the moon's reflection on the water. "It's always been Angela."

As she watched, she saw a ripple in the reflection of the moon. She thought it was a fish, but then another ripple marred the surface and she felt wetness splash against her cheek.

"Angela?" he asked, and although he didn't raise his voice, she could hear the bite of impatience, the confusion.

Leah examined the sky. Another raindrop, then another, spattered over her cheeks, landed right below her eye. "It's raining," she said, glancing at him. "We should go back."

"No. It's only a little drizzle. You're not running away this time."

Before he could even finish the sentence, a rumble of thunder poured from the sky, and at its pronouncement a sheet of rain fell from the heavens. "Fine," Sebastian said, raising his voice to be heard over the rain. He glared at her, as if she'd been the one to start the storm. "I'll row back, but we're not finished talking."

She nodded, relieved at least to have a momentary reprieve.

He unhooked the oars. "How do you mean it's about Angela?" Apparently he didn't intend on waiting until they returned to the house.

She thought about pretending she didn't hear him, but he only said her name louder.

"Leah? What do you mean—"

"Nothing. I shouldn't have said anything." She, too, raised her voice to be heard over the sound of the rain cascading down, repelling against the lake.

"Well, you did, so finish it." He glanced over his shoulder to steer them. His cloak gaped, revealing the front of his shirt already plastered to his chest by the rain.

"It's only—I'm not her, Sebastian."

He whipped his gaze around, fastening on her. He opened his mouth, but the boat ran aground, jerking her forward. Wind sent the rain slipping inside her hood, trailing down her cheeks and inside the collar of her dress. Sebastian climbed out, pulling the boat farther onto the shore, then waded into the water. Leah stood and held out her hands, but he picked her up by her waist and then cradled her, one arm behind her back and the other beneath her thighs as he carried her to dry land. As soon as he stepped on the soil, she said, "Put me down."

This time, he didn't refuse, but held on to her wrist when she would have pulled away. "I know you're not Angela," he shouted above the wind.

She shook her head. "From the beginning, you've compared me to her. I didn't smell like her, I didn't act like her."

He pulled her closer, not seeming to notice her resistance. "I apologized—"

"Yes, you did. But can't you see? You loved her. Ian loved her. She was everything I'm not." He tried to tug her to his chest, to wrap his cloak around her, but she wrenched free, her hood falling open. "I'm sorry, but I can't be the wife that you need."

She turned and ran, slipping in the sand now turned to mud.

"I don't care that you're not Angela," he called from behind her. "I'm glad you're not her!"

Now tears were pouring down her face, mixing with the rain as she struggled forward. "It doesn't matter! She'll always be there, between us. Just as she was there with Ian. You might not think it now, but you'll realize it soon. You'll wake up and miss her, wish that it was her with you instead of me. You'll—"

A hand caught her shoulder, twisting her around. Leah cried out as she lost her balance, but Sebastian caught her. Steadied her.

"Goddamn it, woman!" he shouted above the wind and rain. "Listen to me! It will always be you." Thunder roared again. His hands shifted from her waist to her shoulders. "You, Leah!" From her shoulders to her neck, cradling her head between his palms. "You!"

He kissed her. Hard. Leah dug her nails into his wrists to hold on against the onslaught of his mouth. He was savage, ruthless. Gone was the gentleman who'd pleasured her so thoroughly; gone was the understanding husband who'd held her all night in his arms. He demanded, and she gave; he pushed against the seam of her lips, and she opened, welcoming him. He was like a wave assaulting her senses, sweeping her under, away with the tide.

Leah couldn't think. The rain slicked her hair to her head, forcing her to close her eyes and simply feel. The warmth of his hands holding her head steady for his plunder, the heat of his body as she stepped forward and burrowed into him, unable to get close enough. The bruising of her mouth as he bit her lips, the tender give of his flesh as she bit his.

She tugged at his cloak, his shirt, great soaking handfuls of cloth that fought her attempts to strip them away. Her fingers fumbled at his waist, and he moaned against her mouth. She gave up, and stroked him through his trousers, molding her palm against the hot, rigid length of him.

His hands fell from her neck, but his mouth stayed. He continued kissing her, his tongue warring with hers as he touched her breasts, her stomach, tugged up her sodden skirts to her knees, then her thighs.

Leah broke their kiss, gasping. "Sebastian." He captured her mouth again as his finger filled her, and she sank onto the pleasure. He went with her until they were kneeling on the ground, streams of water running past. She lay down, tugging him with her, bucking her hips as he inserted two fingers, then withdrew. Again and again. She tossed her head and wrapped her arms around his waist, pulling him toward her, over her. She succeeded in loosening his trousers and filled her hand with his cock, hot and heavy in her grip. He broke away from their kiss, his fingers halting their slick slide inside her.

Leah opened her eyes. He was above, staring down at

her, water dripping from his face. Looking into his gaze, Leah shoved his arm away and spread her legs, offering herself to him. Not a soulless offering to a man who didn't want her, but a willing sacrifice to a man who did. She lifted her hips even as she felt hot tears escape from the corners of her eyes. "I love you, too," she said, then sealed her mouth to his.

He didn't move. Not until she repeated it against his lips, and urged him against her, and then he was filling her, stretching her, pushing her, heavy and fast. Her hands moved frantically over his back, his head, down to his waist. She clawed at his trousers, urging him to go faster.

He ran his mouth down her neck, burying his head at her throat, and she tipped her head back, caught in the rush of ecstasy as her hips rose again and again to meet his thrusts. She saw the lightning flash across the sky, felt him lift his chest away from her. She tried to pull him back, but he pushed his hand between them, stroking, stroking at her flesh. Leah cried out, wrapping her legs tightly around him, and her scream was quickly followed by his own cry as he found his release, his hands gripping her waist with his final thrust.

She held him, sheltering his head against her neck, her hand keeping the rain away from his eyes. Taking a deep breath, she let the air fill her lungs, let it push her closer toward him until there was no question that they were one, the rapid beating of his heart matching hers.

Sebastian lifted his head and looked down at her. Suddenly shy, Leah tried to glance away, but he cupped her cheek and directed her gaze back to his. Then he smiled, the most breathtaking, devastating crook of a smile that she'd ever seen.

Lightning seared the black sky, turning the entire world white. The roar of thunder soon followed. And he kissed her again.

Chapter 23

How I wish that he were yours, that I had met you first...

Leah sat on the floor in Sebastian's bedchamber, toweling her hair dry before the fire. She heard the soft thuds of his footsteps as he walked toward her. He sat behind her, his legs stretching out on either side of hers, and tugged the towel from her hands.

He eased her back against his chest, then wrapped his arms around her, his chin resting on top of her head as they watched the fire burn and let the heat soak into their skin.

Leah relaxed gradually, allowing his strength and warmth to comfort her. Each muscle loosened, from her calves to her shoulders, until she lay against him, boneless. Trusting.

He shifted, trailing the ends of her hair through his fingers. He spoke into her ear, his breath stirring the tension of awareness back into her body. "This is what I've wanted for so long," he murmured. "Just to hold you. To have you trust me."

Leah tilted her head back until she could meet his eyes, lifted her palm to his jaw. "But I did. It was myself I didn't trust."

A glimmer of humor shone in his eyes, and stubble scraped the flesh of her palm as he smiled. "You mean to say that I was too much for you to resist? Is being irresistible another one of my flaws?"

"Yes." Her own mouth curved, and she twisted until she knelt in the circle of his arms, locking her arms around his neck. "I knew you wouldn't allow me to do as I wanted, to stay locked away inside myself. I was afraid to touch you, afraid if I gave you any control, there would be nothing left of me."

His smile faded, his hands gentle, almost tentative as he bracketed her ribs. "And now?"

She sifted her hand through his hair, traced her finger over his forehead, across his brow, down his nose. She parted his mouth with her thumb, and when he sucked on it, biting down softly with his teeth, it wasn't fear that made her pulse race and the rush of blood pound in her ears. "I'm touching you now," she whispered, "and I have never felt more powerful." She leaned forward, brushing her mouth across his cheek, teasing the soft flesh of his earlobe with her lips and teeth. "You give me strength."

His hands fell away and he leaned back, bracing himself against the floor. "Tell me what I should do, Leah."

She ran her gaze down his chest, pausing at the skin visible above the edge of his dressing gown. She continued further, past the breadth of his ribs, the flatness of his stomach, the jut of his arousal. Lowering her hands, she knelt back and placed her palms on his ankles, then leisurely swept them up his calves, savoring the crisp texture of his dark hair against her flesh, the warmth of his skin against hers. "Let me give you pleasure," she said. Pausing, she reached up to her own dressing gown and drew it off her shoulders, baring her breasts. His eyes darkened, his chest rising sharply. "For now," she added.

Her fingers perched on his knees, then climbed upward, pressing into his flesh, her thumbs skimming the insides of his thighs.

He growled a curse as his hips jerked beneath her touch. Leah smiled and untied the belt of his robe. When he tried to lean forward and nuzzle at her neck, she indulged him, but only for a moment while she pushed the dressing gown off his shoulders. She didn't know which pleased her more: knowing that Sebastian was now fully naked before her, or the wondrously wicked things he was doing with his lips and tongue at the juncture between her neck and shoulder. Probably both.

She couldn't resist; she balanced herself against his shoulders as he trailed kisses along her collarbone, into the valley between her breasts.

"This is not me pleasuring you," she said.

"No?" His lips brushed across the swells of her breasts. "Then I fear I must beg for your forgiveness, for this is what pleases me."

The control which she'd sought for so long unraveled completely; it was impossible not to give to him, impossible not to take pleasure from his caresses. Selfish and selfless, both strong and vulnerable—there was no room for control when she was in Sebastian's arms, simply the understanding that she was his and he was hers. There was no loneliness here.

Leah sighed as Sebastian leaned forward to cup her buttocks, moaned as he bent his head to draw her nipple into his mouth—the sounds of her own pleasure almost as arousing as the hot, supple texture of his tongue. She rocked forward, teasing both of them as she pushed against his cock.

"You told me your fantasies, Sebastian," she murmured, then broke off into a mewling approval as one of the hands cupping her buttocks moved, a long finger inserting itself into her from behind. She arched back, lengthening his stroke, then slid forward again. Sebastian's mouth turned rough, biting her nipple before soothing it with the flat of his tongue. "However"—she panted around a particularly exquisite thrust of his finger—"I . . . I never had a chance to tell you mine."

Cool air streamed over her breast as he blew onto her skin, making her ache for the warmth of his mouth again. "Anything, my love."

"After the house party, when you returned to London and proposed, do you remember that carriage ride we took around the park when I agreed to marry you?"

"Of course."

Using one hand on his shoulder for balance, Leah slid the other down his chest. She reached between their bodies and folded her fingers around him. Sebastian closed his eyes, his jaw clenching. "I might not have wanted to desire you then, but I did. And I thought about this."

Holding him tight, she stroked up and down, fascinated by the play of passion across his expression, the way he seemed to be trying to steady his breath by inhaling and then exhaling slowly.

"Let me tell you my fantasy," she whispered in his ear.

Sebastian groaned at the firm grip of her hand around him. He turned his head, seeking her mouth, only to have her press a quick, hot kiss to his lips.

"In my fantasy," she said, her voice that of a temptress, "I imagined lifting up my skirts there on the seat beside you in the carriage." Her thumb slipped over the tip of his staff.

Sebastian arched into her hand. "Leah."

"I imagined you kneeling before me as I wrapped my

legs over your shoulders. And you kissed me ..." She sighed, her face flushed by her own desires, and Sebastian had never seen anything so arousing. "You kissed me down there."

Sebastian altered the tempo of his finger, slowing down, circling her clit until he barely touched her. She gave a little cry of despair, and he rewarded her by sinking back into her fully, thrusting hard and deep.

She released him and put her hands on his shoulders, pushing him back until he was no longer sitting, but lying against the rug. "What happened then?" he asked, then gritted his teeth as she moved over him, straddling his waist, positioning him at her entrance.

She bent down and kissed him, teasing him with the slow, seductive pressure of her lips and tongue. "Then, before I could come, you moved up from the floor of the carriage, brought my legs to your waist—"

She captured his gaze as she gripped him again, her eyes half-lidded and hot. Then she sank down, impaling herself on his cock. Only the greatest amount of self-restraint kept Sebastian from coming at that very moment. She was so tight and wet.

"—and then you fucked me."

She bit her lip and lowered her gaze, almost as if she were uncertain of saying the word. But he wouldn't let her be ashamed—not here, not with him. Holding her hands, he urged her to use him for balance as he lifted his hips, pushing more deeply inside, experimenting with a rhythm until he found one she seemed to like—a hard, steady pace that had her parting her lips and throwing her head back with abandon. Her breasts bobbed up and down, the hardened tips of her nipples teasing him, causing his body to tighten even further. The pleasure built almost to an unbearable crescendo. Sebastian released her hands and gripped her waist, his anchor as he sent them both spiraling closer to ecstasy.

He groaned when her muscles clenched around him. His fingers dug into her skin. "Did you like it when I fucked you, Leah?"

She opened her eyes and stared down at him. A slow, pleased smile pulled at her lips. "God, yes."

And then, without looking away, she leaned forward, braced her hands against his chest, and rode him hard and fast until Sebastian could no longer control himself, until pleasure washed over him, pulling him under and constricting every muscle, and he was pouring himself into her, his breath completely stolen away.

When at last he was able to open his eyes and breathe again, Leah held herself above him, her expression a combination of tenderness and smug satisfaction. "I did that to you," she murmured. "I made you lose control."

Sebastian lifted his head and kissed her. "Yes, you did," he said, then withdrew and shifted until she was beneath him on the floor, his hand flat over her belly. "But you didn't come with me."

Raising a brow, she covered his hand with hers, then dragged it up until it lay over her breast. "And do you intend to rectify that, my lord?"

"Immediately," he replied. But instead of caressing her, he dipped his head and kissed her. "Once I hear you say you love me again."

She smiled and wrapped her arms around his neck. "I love you."

"I didn't hear you."

"I love you."

"Hmm." He nipped at her bottom lip, lazily circled her nipple with his finger. "Still nothing."

"Is this your way of torturing me, Sebastian?"

"Perhaps."

"Very well. I love you. I love you. I love you."

"Once more," he said, "though honestly I doubt it will ever be enough."

"I love y—"

She shuddered as he flicked her nipple, then smoothed over her stomach to stroke her below.

He kissed her nose, her lips, her chin. "Hush, Leah. I love you, too."

She was quiet for only a moment. "Did I ever mention 'overbearing' as one of your flaws?"

He chuckled against her throat.

She moaned as he slipped another finger inside her, then asked, "What is it?"

He kissed her collarbone.

"Sebastian?"

A minute elapsed, maybe more.

"Oh." She took a deep breath. "You do overbearing very well."

"Leah?" he murmured against her thigh, then kissed her again.

"Yes?" she asked, her voice quavering on that single syllable.

"Do be quiet."

She gasped, and he smiled.

"As you wish, my lord."

Epilogue

I will send you one more letter when I confirm the time, and then we will be together.

London, April 1850

Leah set the teapot down and handed the cup to Lady Elliot, smiling. "I'm glad to hear Lord Elliot is feeling better."

"Oh yes." Lady Elliot waved her hand in the air. "He'll be fine. The viscount has the stamina of a man of twenty, if you take my meaning."

In the chair to her left, Adelaide choked a little on her tea. Beatrice patted her back as she coughed delicately into a handkerchief. She hadn't even needed to draw the square of fabric out; it had been laid across her lap, at the ready, as if anticipating another risqué comment from the viscountess.

Lady Elliot glanced at Leah, her brow raised. "Should I apologize?"

Mrs. Meyer gave a deep sigh and settled back against

the sofa. "Not every man has the sort of constitution as yours does, Verna. Talk about it often enough, and it will seem like you're gloating."

Leah leaned forward and stirred another spoonful of sugar into her own tea. "I wouldn't say Lord Elliot's the only one—"

"Leah!" her mother admonished, giving her a pointed look.

"—although perhaps we should turn the conversation, as my sister is unwed."

"Mr. Grimmons is still besotted." Adelaide folded the kerchief and tucked it away.

"Mother," Beatrice warned.

"I'm only saying, although I'm confident I've instructed you well enough to catch a husband during the Season, there is always a last resort. I'm certain Mr. Grimmons will be waiting for you when we return to the countryside."

Leah glanced at the empty chair to her right. Although Miss Pettigrew's father had allowed her to keep company with Leah once she married Sebastian, the young woman only came to take tea with them from time to time. She claimed that Leah's mother and Lady Elliot intimidated her, but Leah was more inclined to believe that Miss Pettigrew chose instead to visit her father at the bank in an effort to catch a glimpse of a certain clerk.

At the sound of a child's voice outside the drawing room, all of the women turned toward the door. Henry entered, tugging Sebastian along by the hand. Leah's heart turned over in her chest to see the two of them together, her husband and son. Henry's hair had begun to darken at the roots, and although his eyes were still as blue as Angela's, his smile was a younger, more innocent replica of Sebastian's.

"Grandmother, Grandmother, look at my crat."

Sebastian gave them all an apologetic shrug, a corner of his mouth curved upward. "He insisted he too wear a cravat today."

Henry broke free from Sebastian and ran toward Adelaide, who held out her arms.

"Henry," Leah said. "Don't forget your manners."

Sliding to a halt, Henry turned toward Lady Elliot and bowed. Then Mrs. Meyer. He smiled up at Beatrice, who gave him a wink.

"What a fine young gentleman," Lady Elliot declared.

Henry touched the blue dotted silk bow at his throat. "Did you see my crat?"

"Oh, yes," Mrs. Meyer said. "Well. You look just like your father now, don't you?"

Henry beamed, then turned into Adelaide's arms. "Did you see my crat, Grandmother?" he whispered.

Sebastian leaned down and gave Leah a kiss on her cheek. "Hullo, my love."

"You couldn't stay away for an hour or two, could you? A cravat? Truly, Sebastian, I'm beginning to think you might be quite infatuated with me."

"Oh, but I am," he whispered in her ear, sending a smile to Lady Elliot and Mrs. Meyer, who watched them closely.

"I suppose I forgive you. I missed you, too."

"You're not going to chastise me for interrupting your tea again?"

"Did I chastise you last time?"

"No, but that was only because Henry was able to distract your mother."

As soon as he spoke, Henry squealed, catching Leah's attention as well as Lady Elliot's and Mrs. Meyer's. "But Papa says I shouldn't have ice cream," he told Adelaide, then cast a sad look over his shoulder at Leah and Sebastian.

Adelaide sniffed and scooped him into her lap. "As well you shouldn't if that's what your papa says. But Grandmother will let you have some when you're with her."

"Oh, Sebastian," Leah whispered. "You just wait."

Soon the other women were rising, their tea unfinished. Apparently a decision was made that they should all go get ice cream.

"I can't believe ..." Leah began, then paused as Henry turned and ran to her, a grin splitting his face. She bent and hugged him, squeezing him tight. "Did Papa tell you to ask Grandmother for ice cream?"

Henry stepped back and looked up at Sebastian, then back at Leah. Grinning again, he nodded. Leah laughed. "Go on, then." She turned him around toward Adelaide. "Wait, Henry." He glanced over his shoulder. "I love you," she said.

"You too, Mama," he said, then rushed in between Adelaide and Beatrice to grab ahold of their hands. Leah swallowed, then waited for everyone else to leave the drawing room before she turned to Sebastian, her arms crossed over her chest.

"What is it?"

"Next time, don't wait so long."

"You want us to come in after half an hour?"

"Twenty minutes," she said. "No, ten."

Sebastian smiled and took hold of her arms, uncrossing them and placing them over his shoulders. He set his hands at her waist. "I'm beginning to think, Lady Wriothesly, that you are the one obsessed with me." He kissed her temple, then her cheek.

"And if I am?" she asked, lifting her mouth toward his.

"By all means, don't stop."

"I don't intend to."

"Good."

A moment passed, then: "Are you going to kiss me?" she asked.

"I was waiting to see if you would change it to five minutes."

"I have a better idea. Next time, we'll just send Henry and his nurse to have tea with the ladies at Mother's house. Perhaps they'll take him shopping. And we'll dismiss the servants for the day. We'll be alone."

"All by ourselves?"

Leah nodded.

Sebastian smiled, a wicked curve of his mouth that lifted the heat pooling in her stomach to flush across her skin. "Now that, my lady, deserves a kiss."

Read on for a preview of

Seducing the Duchess

an enthralling historical romance
by Ashley March.

Available now from Signet Eclipse.

She was exquisite, a sin to be indulged in and never repented.

The sound of her laughter, rich and full, a siren's song, caught at his soul. It lured him to the edge of his seat until his nose was nearly pressed against the carriage window.

She did not walk like a lady; she didn't walk like any other woman he had ever known. Every move was calculated to draw masculine eyes to the voluptuous lines of her body—the taunting sway of her hips, the subtle arch of her spine, the inviting tilt of her head. Even the moon desired to be her lover, its long fingers caressing her face and throat in admiring regard before she disappeared into the gambling den.

She was stunning. A beautiful harlot.

Six months he'd spent wooing her. Invitations to the theater, the opera ... giving his undivided attention in the hopes she would at last turn her affections toward him.

He'd tried to ignore the other men, knowing that soon he would be the one she graced with her smiles, the one she would return home with each night. He'd waited patiently, desperately. Even this night, he'd followed her across London, watching her flit from one social engagement to the next, on the arm of a different man each time . . .

But no longer.

Philip stared at the building's entrance, his heart speeding foolishly.

Straightening, he opened the door and stepped from the carriage.

No sooner had he passed through the foyer of the gambling den than he spotted her, perched on the lap of some rotund, fortunate bastard, her half-naked bosom exposed to his leering gaze. One gloved arm was looped around his neck, a purchase for balance as she leaned forward over the table, the spin of dice cast from her hands in a cheery clatter.

As Philip strolled toward her, he lifted his hands to his cravat, slowly, single-mindedly, untying the careful knot his valet had perfected earlier in the evening.

The cravat fell apart easily in his fingers, and he dragged it loose, the mangled cloth dangling from his fingertips.

"Good evening, gentlemen."

Immediately the gaiety at the small table ceased. Upon spying their new guest, a few of the men scraped their chairs backward, their eyes darting nervously between Philip and the woman.

For too long he'd allowed them to believe that her actions and the company she kept didn't matter to him. Now he was prepared to create a scandal in front of everyone for his message to be undeniably clear: despite her past lovers, she would soon belong to him alone.

The man whose lap she occupied met his eyes and then quickly glanced away, his tongue creeping forth to wet his lips. Philip couldn't blame his indecision; if she had been sitting upon his lap, he would have been loath to give her up as well.

Philip nodded to him. "You, there. What is your name?"

The man's eyes bulged out of their sockets. "Lord Denby, Your Grace. My name is D-Denby."

Philip nodded. "Very good. Denby, my dear fellow, I believe you have something which belongs to me."

A bead of sweat popped out on the man's forehead. "Y-Your Grace?"

The woman, who thus far had only watched the proceedings with an amused smile, narrowed her eyes at Philip and tightened her grip on Denby's neck. "He means *me*, Lord Denby."

"Oh." The man started, and with trembling fingers grasped her arm, frantically trying to push her away. His breath came in short gasps, and he looked at Philip with a plea in his eyes. "She won't come loose, Your Grace."

"Oh, Denby, you coward," she murmured. With a toss of her head, she detached herself from him and rose gracefully from his lap. She stared up at Philip for a long moment, her bright blue eyes daring, mocking.

When she attempted to brush past him, he caught her arm easily in his hand.

The entire room hushed. Philip could feel the heat of a hundred eyes scrutinizing his every movement.

Tomorrow morning this would be in the scandal sheets, upon everyone's lips. Even if he wished it, there was no going back now. He had made his decision.

Her chin had lifted when he halted her departure, and he smiled down at her, a quick flash of teeth. Her sharp indrawn breath gave him no small measure of satisfaction; she was not as immune to him as she would have him believe.

"Lord Denby," he said, his eyes still focused on her sweet, temptress face.

"Yes, Your Grace?"

Philip maneuvered her until she stood between them. "Be a good fellow and hold on to her for a moment, would you? Don't let her escape."

"Er, yes, Your Grace." Denby settled his thick, ring-laden fingers on her shoulders.

"What is the meaning of this?" she demanded, twisting in his grip, her eyes furious, darkening from sapphire to the dusky haze of twilight.

Philip ignored her struggles. He drew her arms together with one hand and draped his cravat over her wrists with the other. Then, quickly so she didn't have a chance to resist, he knotted the material and gave it a tug.

Perfect.

"Very good. You may release her now, Lord Denby."

"What are you doing, Philip? This is ridiculous. Untie me at once!"

It had been a very long time since she had said his name. Even though it fell like a curse from her lips, it was good to hear it all the same.

Philip grasped her upper arm again and looked around the room. Trollops and whores, rakes and scoundrels gaped at him, openmouthed. He nodded to them, ever aware of the sinuous heat seeping from her skin—a twisting, vagrant fire now burning past his gloves to the flesh of his palm.

The woman tried to jerk away, but Philip held her tightly. He would never let her go again. "Release me, you arrogant son of a—"

Philip clapped his hand over her mouth. With a shake of his head, he withdrew a linen kerchief from his pocket. "I had hoped this wouldn't be necessary, but you force my hand, dearest."

She tried to sink her teeth into the flesh of his palm, but fortunately he withdrew it in time. He was certain she'd meant to draw blood. While she sputtered more curses, he proceeded to wrap the cloth around her head, careful only to muffle and not gag her. He tied it at the back of her head, his fingers lingering on the silken tresses of her upswept hair. The sable locks gleamed beneath the dim, smoky lights, tempting his restraint, provoking memories of a time when his hands had tangled freely in her hair. When she had sought his touch, his embrace—

Philip wasn't fast enough to block her kick, her foot connecting painfully with his lower shin.

He crushed her against him, her back to his front, his hands clasped together beneath the delicious swell of her breasts. He tried to move her toward the door, but she hung like a dead weight in his arms. Only when he dragged her did she begin to writhe against him, her body pitching against his.

His audience had apparently recovered from their stupor, for their voices rose in a fevered crescendo as he neared the exit. But the noise was only an indistinct rumble in the background as he focused on her attempts at freedom.

Her elbow managed a sharp blow to his ribs. Philip grunted, then hoisted her over his shoulder and carried her out the door. Her gag was loose enough that her curses brutalized his ears, but Philip continued on with grim determination. She struck his back with her bound fists at every step, but he didn't stop until he stood in front of his carriage.

The groom opened the door.

"Here we are."

She shrieked as he dragged her down and shoved her headfirst through the entrance, his hands helping as they pushed against her bottom.

"Damn you, Philip!"

He climbed in after her, careful to avoid stepping on her skirts or any scattered appendages. Leaning down, he grabbed her by the elbows and assisted her to a seated position.

The door closed, the carriage shifting as the coachman and groom took their places. The sharp crack of the whip rent the air, and they were off.

Philip allowed a brief sigh of victory.

He'd done it. He had kidnapped his wife.